PR

THE INFERNIS DUOLOGY

and Oralia crackles with tension and undeniable chemistry, but it's their individual journeys—of healing, self-discovery, and transformation—that truly make this story unforgettable... *Ruin* is a book you won't want to put down once you start."

— Angie @thebiglittlelibrary

"*Ruin* is a wonderful debut for Gillian Eliza West and it left me panting for more. I am also terrified about what's coming next but Oralia and Ren had me in a choke hold by the end. I will be waiting anxiously for book two."

— Jenn @thebookrefuge

"*Ruin* is going to have fans of dark, immersive, sexy fantasy screaming. Incredibly well paced world-building that isn't overwhelming, paired with complex characters, and a sizzling, angst-filled, slow burn romance that pays off!"

— Whitney @whitneybrownreads

"Oralia and Ren are my new Feyre and Rhys. I am that level of in love with this world, story, and characters that Gillian has created. The world is interesting, but not overly complex. Her writing is lyrical and romantic, but not overly flowery. The characters are multifaceted and endearing, but not perfect. In short, Gillian has created a world that I didn't want to leave and cannot wait to return to. *Ruin* has easily risen to my top five (if not the top!) reads of the year."

— Jordan @abluenest

RUIN

RUIN

THE INFERNIS DUOLOGY
BOOK ONE

GILLIAN ELIZA WEST

Cover art by Story Wrappers
Map and Interior Design by Travis Hasenour
Editing by Lydia Shamah
Copyediting by Jen Bowles
Revision edits by Eleanor Boyall

For rights and permissions, please contact:
gillian@gillianelizawest.com

979-8-9901389-0-2 (Paperback)
979-8-9901389-1-9 (E-Book)

*To absent friends and the grief
that never lets us go.*

AETHERA

Vaelorian River

CYVON SEA

CHAPTER
ONE

Oralia

As much as I could, I tried to remember my mother.

There were times, in the moments between sleeping and waking, that I could almost see her gentle, smiling face. Yet it was intangible—like wisps of curling smoke. And as the daylight grew and the darkness waned, I found I could no more hold onto the image than I could hold onto vapor. The feel of her motherly affection evaporating in the morning sun.

"Hello, friend," I murmured while I wandered into the grounds, gazing high into the wide oak tree where a large black raven perched.

As always, the raven did not acknowledge my greeting, nor my presence. But he was often there. I wondered if perhaps he was a familiar or a guardian sent by the Great Mothers to watch over and protect me. It felt only natural to wonder, as he had arrived days after I'd been bitten and my life had taken on a nightmarish quality from which I could not wake.

Ribbons of gold light slithered around my shoulders, cascading over the rough brown bark of the wide trunk before me. My skin prickled, discomfort slinking through my veins, magic within me shying from the light. With a deep breath, I turned and lowered to my knees, head bowed and fingertips pressed to my brow, shielding my eyes from the blaze. Behind me, armor groaned as my guard also fell to a knee.

"I thought I might find you here," a deep voice rumbled, punctuated by the rustle of feathers.

With a swallow, I lowered my hand, gazing up into the shining face of the Golden King. His skin shined, especially here in the sunlight, a golden hue that hurt my eyes. But he was smiling for once, gilded hair waving around his face as he gestured toward the tree.

The tree my mother had coaxed to maturity with her power, the last mark of her magic upon this world.

"I hoped to spend the day honoring her here, Your Grace," I answered, the ache in my throat squeezing the words.

Throughout the centuries, I'd stolen bits and pieces of information about her. Peregrine Solis had been fiery and strong. She had loved to swim in the river that danced through the castle grounds and to listen to the whispers in the wind.

Today was her birthday...or so I'd been told.

King Typhon hummed, a shining hand sliding over his gold-spun beard. His bright white wings flared behind him as he turned away from the tree, gazing toward the castle. "You are needed in the orchards."

Lightning sliced through my chest. My hands clenched into fists, straining the white leather of my gloves. The anger always simmering beneath the surface flared at his innocent words.

"You had allowed me the day." The words were stilted as I reminded him of the promise he'd made a fortnight ago.

The king's lips curled into the semblance of a frown. "I remember no such promise."

A huff of frustration slipped from my lips, and I shook my head. Of course he did not. And truly, I understood that for a king, idle promises made to me were lost beneath the cacophony of truly important matters. There was a darkness that slithered from the kingdom of Infernis—the kingdom of the dead—onto our land, growing stronger each day, blighting crops and starving our people in its wake.

Yet he had promised. It was rare that I found the courage to make such a request. It was one of just a few I had made in my paltry two hundred and fifty years of existence.

"You have a duty to this kingdom," King Typhon snapped as he turned back to me, wings stretching as if to encompass the land around us.

I swallowed. My throat was thick with unsaid words. The temper I'd battled my whole life pushed against my ribs, banging upon the bones as if they were the bars of a prison. It was moments such as these that reminded me who I was to the Golden God, the Golden King—the king of Aethera. Or rather who I was not. Because this god was not my father. I'd learned that the first time he placed my mother's opal and emerald crown upon my head on my eighth birthday.

"Are you my father, my king?" I had asked, touching gloved fingers to the circlet of gold a bit too large for my head.

King Typhon had gestured to perch on the steps of the large dais and sat only a few feet away—which, for him, was almost like an embrace. Ever since I had been bitten by one of the monsters of Infernis, daemoni, that plagued our lands, he had forbidden any physical contact, lest my power should harm someone. My eighth birthday marked three years of isolation. Three years of harsh words and fearful glances. Three years of something in the king's eyes that spoke of horror. Three years of aching knees as I knelt all too often on the marble floor of the throne room while healers tried to banish the dark power festering inside of me.

"You are mine in every way but blood," the king had answered, but the warmth in his voice had not touched his eyes. No, a bitterness I knew all too well lived there instead.

The bitterness of gazing upon the product of his queen defiled. Not an heir, nor a daughter. Merely a reminder of the evil within this world. And yet the king had taken me in when she died in childbirth, her magic passing to me as my tiny lungs screamed for air. His revelation on my eighth birthday had soothed some aching part of my soul, even while it tore my heart apart.

He told me how my mother had been traveling back from the human settlements on the eastern edge of the kingdom when she was attacked by a god. A god whose soul had been corrupted by the dark, twisted by the land of Infernis and its king. That god had planted his seed inside her womb and though King Typhon eventually found his revenge, the cruelty had broken her. Broken him.

It had broken me too.

The knowledge of my origin festered deep within my heart, fanning flames that I could not seem to smother. Shadows pulsed in the corner of my vision, pooling out from my chest.

"Oralia," King Typhon called, his voice slicing through my ears. *"Control."*

Pain lanced across my arms as Typhon's golden light blinded me. I cried out, bowing forward, hands splayed across the lush green grass as shadows erupted from my chest. Typhon's magic burned away the darkness that my anguish revealed.

In the span of a heartbeat, the light vanished. A sizzling, burning agony was left in its wake. Air choked through my lungs as I gasped, black spots blooming across my vision. I shrank back from the gleam of gold that cascaded across the grass as the king knelt beside me, soft shushes slipping through his lips.

"If you do not find control, you will destroy us all."

I nodded, the sun reflected off his golden skin, painting my lids blood red. He despised this as much as I did—he had to. But there was never any comfort that followed such punishment, only the reminder of my duty and the danger I posed to his kingdom.

"Yes, my king." Tears splashed across the backs of my gloves, a tremor rolling through my spine as the pain slowly abated into a hollow throb.

King Typhon sighed heavily. I sat back onto my heels, wiping my face with the sleeve of my gown, careful to avoid the curling burns singed into my forearms from his power. My limbs were heavy, weighed down with my grief and chagrin at losing hold of the curse that roiled within my veins.

"I must go. Caston and his men will be arriving soon, and I must be there to greet them."

A small spark flared, cutting through the tar-like shame curling in my chest. Caston's visits were brief bursts of sunshine in my existence. From the age of fifteen, King Typhon's heir had lived mostly a soldier's life so that he might understand the sacrifice that the human soldiers and demigods made on behalf of all who lived within the kingdom.

"The orchards, Oralia. They must be tended or else the pestilence of Infernis might reach our crops as well." King Typhon's voice was firm, the kind that brooked no argument.

Duty above all else.

"Yes, Your Grace," I answered, dipping my chin and placing my fingertips on my brow.

With another flare of his wings, the king rose, running a hand down his face. "Tonight, after dinner, we will again discuss finding a solution to your curse."

Dread prickled down my spine as the king vanished in a gust of wind, pushing himself into the sky. The ghost of childhood agony throbbed through my limbs, the echo of his first attempts to rid my magic of its darkness. My knees ached at the thought of long nights spent kneeling on the cold marble floor of the throne room, healers' magic searing through my veins. The ashes that sifted through my fingers. The blood that was left behind.

For ruin followed me wherever I went.

CHAPTER
TWO

Oralia

O ralia..." Drystan murmured. "The orchards?"

I sighed, pushing heavily to my feet and smoothing down the front of my pale blue gown.

Drystan had been my guard since before I could walk—at that age, he'd carried me on his hip, golden cloak protectively wrapped around my shoulders while we wandered the orchards and fields of the castle grounds. But that had been before I was bitten. After, it had been too dangerous for me to be so much as assisted to my feet.

His skin was dark, with the same blueish undertones as the midnight sky, but his hair was a shock of bright white, threaded into thick strands gathered at the nape of his neck with a golden cord. It was his eyes I loved the most, the paternal love and care that shined from his gray irises with every look.

"Of course," I replied, voice cracking. "Let us not keep them waiting."

Drystan's armor sparkled in the sunlight. His shoulders were tensed around his ears. The stress of witnessing such an outburst and being unable to assist always hung heavy on his heart.

"I know this is not what you planned for today, but the apple trees have not blossomed. Ilyana grows worried."

With a nod, we set off through the winding path of white stones that wove through the castle grounds. The grasses were lush, a deep green that swayed in the early autumn breeze. Though there were no flowers now, in springtime it would be a sea of pinks, purples, and blues as far as the eye could see.

"I am sorry," I murmured.

Drystan shook his head, shifting the helmet tucked beneath his arm. "The king will find a solution, Oralia." The rest of his sentence hung between us.

He must.

"Perhaps he will seek out the advice of other old ones," Drystan continued, offering some shred of hope.

But the hope died as quickly as it came. King Typhon was a rare god—one who had existed before time was made, *timeless*. His father had created the world, assisted by the Great Mothers. They crafted the very earth beneath our feet, the wind blowing through our hair. Even the sun in the sky was crafted by his hands, inspired by his golden son.

Most of those timeless gods vanished over the millennia, or else found their end in the great wars wrought first by the giants who sprouted from great mountains, and then by the Under King of Infernis, the ruler of the land of the dead.

There were no other old ones left to turn to now. King Typhon was the last. Well...besides the Under King.

"Perhaps it is a matter of controlling my temper," I replied, thinking of all the times shadows had burst from my skin.

As a child, it had happened often, and though I had learned a semblance of control as the centuries passed, the curse was a wild creature locked within a cage. One merely needed to rattle the bars to feel its ire.

Drystan pursed his lips, gray eyes flicking over my face before turning back to the path ahead. "You have lost much, Oralia. It is understandable that you would be angry."

I shook my head. "I should not feel the loss so keenly. I did not know my mother."

He tilted his head from side to side, expression growing distant. "That is not the only loss I speak of."

There was no need for him to say the words. To describe the isolation I endured. How I had not been touched in over two hundred and forty-five years unless it was to feel skin crumble to ash beneath my palms. I had been denied the comfort and companionship of others, the hope of true connection.

Of ever finding a lover, someone to call my own.

Once I had felt the hope in my heart that perhaps it was possible, but that hope had turned to ashes, leaving only horror for the monster beneath my skin in its wake.

In silence, we approached the orchard with its wide leafy bows. I spotted Ilyana, their pale and willowy frame easy to find among the dense foliage. They stood beneath one of the apple trees, a hand splayed out on its rough bark as though they were comforting an old friend. Swallowing back my own selfish bitterness, I pulled a warm smile to my cheeks.

They turned at the sound of our approach. Their brown eyes were soft with affection as they bowed their head, placing three fingers on their rosy brow. I bowed my head in response.

"My lady, I am grateful for your assistance," Ilyana said.

I eyed the rows of trees. "I wonder what they are waiting for."

"Perhaps they are waiting for you, my lady," they replied.

Discomfort roiled within my chest. In all likelihood, they were waiting for me. I would have preferred to allow nature to take her course without my interference. Yet, I suspected that the longer I lived, the more reliant upon me these crops would become.

Magic sang across my skin when I stepped forward between the trees, my hum weaving into a melody I could never quite recall once the moment was over. The power was much like lying in a rushing river in the warmest months: powerful yet soothing.

As I wound my way through the orchard, the song echoed through the breeze, and the trees shuddered, sighing as leaves unfurled around me. Behind, I could sense Ilyana from where they followed beside Drystan, both murmuring appreciatively at the size and color of the sprouting apples. The magic was as easy to harness as it was to breathe.

By the time we had paced the entirety of the orchard, beads of sweat trailed over my temples. The powerful force of magic swirled around me like the sound of many fluted instruments on the wind, thrumming through my veins and tangling with the trees. Before my eyes, tiny pink blossoms appeared, spreading wide into star-like shapes before the leaves dropped and tiny round fruits took their place. My song swelled higher, lighter through the breeze as the fruit grew larger. Warmth skittered across my skin and circled my throat until they hung heavy and ripe on the branches.

Life in merely a matter of moments, sustenance for our kingdom and its people.

Yet as my magic stirred inside of me, blossoming the final few trees, darkness trickled through my veins. Only a few drops at first and then it was a great, yawning ocean of shadow. Fear burst through my consciousness, panic mixing with the power—an endless expanse of inky dark magic that skittered across my soul.

Not again, *please* not again.

"My lady..." Drystan cautioned, yet his voice was muffled as if my ears were filled with smoke.

The power was too strong, unyielding. A wave of black night rose from my chest, blocking out the sun, the warmth, the life of this world. Feathery tendrils of darkness stroked my wrists, the palms of my hands, spreading my fingers wide. One moment, the orchard was filled with my voice as I weaved that unconscious melody, and the next, it was silent except for the muffled scream of Ilyana.

"*Oralia!*" Drystan cried, breaking through my haze, heavy footfalls crashing through the grasses.

The wide apple tree that had stood before me, heavy with its burden of fruit, was gone. Instead, blackened bark, gnarled and gray, crumbled into ash at my feet. The corners of my eyes pricked at the sight that no amount of my song could remedy.

It was a remnant—a curse, the king called it—from the bite of the daemoni, a lingering gift from the realm of suffering.

Not for the first time, I wondered what it meant: that darkness and death lived inside of me as surely as light and prosperity did.

THREE

Oralia

M y heavy feet struggled as we climbed the gilded stairs to the castle.

The castle itself was beautiful. Golden leaves covered spiraling towers, interspersed with tall redwood trees that burst through the various rooftops. When the castle was built, it had been created around the forest. In any room, one could find at least one trunk or branch artfully incorporated into the floor plan.

In the morning light, the castle sparkled like diamonds.

In the sunset, it glowed deep orange like the embers of a fire.

But in the midday sun, it was a reflection of the celestial planet itself—so bright one must shield their eyes against the glare. It was said the light from the castle was visible even in the human settlements to the west of the grounds, the light pouring through the trees like rivers of gold stopped only by the thick mists that lay beyond.

"You must rest," Drystan said when we passed through the ornately wrought doors of the palace and into the cool marble entryway. He paused, searching my face before he continued. "No one is angry with you."

I did not have it in me to respond, knowing full well that someone would be angry with me. King Typhon had spoken of control, and within the hour, I had lost it once more. I blighted our crops the same as the Under King.

Destruction had found its way to our land, as King Typhon had foreseen.

Drystan and I turned left into a narrow, winding hallway. Bright afternoon light poured in from the various curved windows until the deep jade doors of the library loomed ahead. They slid open at our approach, the sentient magic of the castle responding to our intention.

I tried not to look above the gilded mantel as we passed it, but my eyes inevitably strayed to the impenetrable glass that hung above it. Surrounded by the protective magic of the kingdom were two great night-black wings, pinned as one might a butterfly.

Taller than a grown man, they appeared soft, not the feathers of the king's wings, but like silk. Similar in texture to what I'd seen in the books I read on various nighttime creatures that inhabited the kingdom and beyond. The soft orbs of sunlight placed as torches around the room caught on the wings that gave off a faint silvery sheen, like the twinkle of stars in the night sky.

They were gorgeous, though I would never breathe the words aloud.

Drystan cleared his throat. "It does not do to dwell on hardships long since past."

My brows furrowed. "What do you mean?"

"The loss of the... Under King's wings... Do you not contemplate the cruelty of it?"

"Cruelty? *Burning Suns,*" I cursed, attention dancing over the sharp uppermost point of the wing, black melting into silver. Perhaps it was not cruel enough for his crimes and had not been enough to stop him.

He had allowed one of his inner circle to defile her. The king of Infernis had also crafted a plot to kidnap and murder her. He resented the wealth and grandeur of our kingdom, resented King Typhon, and the love of his people and his queen. King Renwick sought to punish him for his happiness and prosperity.

Of course, he failed. My mother had been steps from the wards of the palace when Renwick attacked, and the king sensed her danger through their soul bond. She held Renwick off using that bond, which allowed her to access King Typhon's power, giving him enough time to arrive. The king killed Renwick and cut his wings from him with a golden blade dipped in the resin of a kratus tree. Kratus resin was the only substance in our world that could harm a god—a fact the king of Infernis now knew all too well.

However, the Under King was beyond death. For him, death was merely a pause on his journey toward havoc. Renwick always came back more terrifying than before.

Sighing, I turned away, navigating my way through the stacks to the alcove I'd long since called my own, with its large picture window and plush cushions. With a huff, I fell into the large wingback chair. I drew my knees into my chest and rested my chin on them while Drystan settled himself onto an ottoman nearby. Sometimes, I read in silence or else I read aloud for both of us. I had limited options for entertainment as I was barred from leaving the castle grounds.

The power I'd been cursed with knew no limit, like a black ocean as vast as the night sky. And like an ocean, I knew very little of what might be creeping beneath its surface. We had been lucky today that it had been the tree to meet its end, rather than Drystan or Ilyana.

Now I wanted nothing more than to sit with my forehead pressed against the thin glass of the window and stare out onto the rolling grounds, trying to calm the rising panic and quiet my racing heart. Through the window, I could just make out the tops of the now blossoming apple trees from this morning's work. The ashes of the tree I'd destroyed were a dark smudge against the idyllic picture. It was futile to try to see past it to the small creek that edged the perimeter of the grounds. In the distance, all I could catch were small spiraling streams of smoke from the human settlement, and beyond, the thick wall of mist that separated our kingdom from Infernis.

From this distance, I could not quite make out the mist, but I wanted to. Every time I caught sight of it, the darkness beneath my skin roiled and itched deep within my bones. I knew it must have to do with the curse, the darkness that was left behind by the daemoni and magic from Infernis. Absentmindedly, I ran one gloved finger beneath the cuff of my other glove, across the black crescent-shaped mark that lined the curve of my wrist.

The mark that, once left, had plunged me into this life of solitude. It was a mark that made King Typhon fearful, even sometimes outraged. There were times that I caught him staring at them, mouth twisted in a grimace as if he were deciding which part of me was stronger—the darkness or the light.

What did it mean to have the power of both life and death inside, battling for dominance?

I was not sure I would ever know.

CHAPTER
FOUR

Renwick

I could remember when time began.

The first rainfall.

The first autumn.

The first winter.

The first spring.

But I could not remember my mother's face.

Sometimes, in dreams, I thought I could see it. Thought I could hear her calling out to me, the stars dripping down her cheeks before they spread into the night sky. Sometimes, I thought I could see the curve of her lips while she chastised me and my half brother Typhon.

You will be the ruin of each other, she chided gently in these dreams.

But now, as I beheld real ruin in front of me, I wondered if that was true, or if we were to be the destruction of everything, not just each other.

For the last two and a half centuries, I had taken to spying on the kingdom, keeping an eye as best I could on Typhon and his soldiers.

Through that time I had found a new form that allowed me to slip through the cracks, unnoticed by those who watched for my return.

Carried on wings so like the ones he'd torn from me, with talons sharp enough to pierce, and feathers black as night. As a raven, hidden from Typhon, I perched high above the trees, watching, waiting.

The princess was settled beneath my tree when Typhon arrived. Their sharp words floated on the breeze, a burst of temper slicing through the sunlight. I thought perhaps my mind was playing tricks on me when I saw the shadows burst from her skin.

As quickly as it had come, the darkness vanished, burned away by Typhon's golden magic. I knew all too well the sear it would leave upon her skin, the aching pain it left behind. Then she had been shepherded off toward the orchards. I followed her magic like a beacon in the shining sun to see if what I'd witnessed was real.

But when she stepped between the apple trees, they *blossomed* in her wake. Her power was something beautiful to behold, a bright shining light in this bleak world, and I was sure now that I had misunderstood what I'd seen before. There was no darkness in this god. How could there be when such powerful glittering magic swirled around her?

The princess paused before a particularly beautiful tree, staring at it in contemplation. Darkness trickled down my spine, my power waking, stretching as if I had reached for it.

Magic called to magic, and mine rushed through what was left of my soul.

Familiar shadows slithered from her shoulders and wrists, gliding over her hands until two white gloves fell into the swaying grass. As if in a trance, her pale hand reached out, fingers outstretched, to press against the bark. My breath caught—an echo of surprise, if

I could still possess such a feeling—as the tree withered, falling to ashes at her feet. I could barely hear the cry of her guard and demigod behind her.

Ice spread in my chest, the ever-present frost deepening until my bones ached.

The power of life and death, in one god, and in his *hands.*

This changed everything.

If she had the power of darkness, then she would be a means to Typhon's ends. When I closed my eyes, that ancient battlefield swam behind my lids. The cries of the wounded. The tang of the mist on my tongue as it sprang from my fingertips.

I had to act, and soon, before he learned to harness her power.

The moment she re-entered the castle, blazing in the afternoon sunlight, I swept from the tree and into the sky, aiming toward the mists that separated our lands. It was a boundary I'd put in place millennia ago, similar to the wards that surrounded Aethera which kept out all those who would do them harm—and Oralia in. If one was to enter the mist without my favor or invitation, they would be doomed to wander until their bodies gave out. But as an extension of my magic, it also lingered in my kingdom as well, calling to me, alerting me like now to an intruder on our shores. One that had been intercepted.

My power shimmered. The longer I spent in Aethera, the more concentration it took to channel it. Every god possessed a conduit through which they used their magic. For Typhon, it was the sun. For my mother, it had been the sky. But I drew my power from the dark, just as it seemed the princess did.

Dipping low, I slid through the mist and shifted forms so my feet soundlessly hit the soft bracken of the forest floor. Uninvited humans and demigods were often found within the mist, wandering lost until they died of dehydration. Of course, I welcomed their souls into the fold. Often, I found them wandering the grounds of Infernis, panicked and wild, until I or another member of my court came along to take them back to their part of the kingdom.

The mist parted, swirling ribbons of fog curling around my wrists and ankles like the creature it was, welcoming its master home. An onyx boat waited at the lapping shoreline—a gift from Kahliya, one of my mother's sisters. The front bow of the ship curved out of the dark water, a lamp filled with glowing blue flame hung from the end, pointing toward the aft that lay flat against the shore.

"*Myhn ardren.*" The rough, rumbling voice held a bit of feminine edge. The old tongue spoken now only in Infernis slithered through the darkness at the front of the ship.

My king.

I nodded in greeting. "Vakarys."

Her skeletal hand pressed against where her heart would be if there had not been a gaping hole, barely visible through her black robes.

"Many souls passed this morning, Your Grace," she said while I stepped onto the boat.

"And Thorne?"

It was a useless question. Thorne was always there at the water's edge to greet the new souls that passed into Infernis and shepherd them into judgment with Horace.

"Thorne welcomed them with respect, as always."

Slowly, she dipped her long, black staff into the waters, pushing us from the shore. The light of the lamp cast her cheekbones into sharp relief. The sunken skin of her face clung to the bones.

Regardless of the wind that pushed my hair from my face, her long black hair did not stir, nor did her robes.

As we set off, the smooth water rumbled around us, splashing over the bow. In seconds, hundreds of bodies emerged from the water, clustered around the edges of the onyx ship. Some with full heads of hair, now silvery blue from the depths, others mere skeletons, and many variations between.

"Hello," I whispered, reaching a hand toward those beneath the waves.

They did not respond—they never did—and the boat churned on toward the shores.

Toward home.

"They are waiting for you, Ren," Dimitri announced the moment I stepped into the antechamber of the palace. The blue flame of the surrounding torches reflected in his onyx armor, glinting off the starburst sigil at his left shoulder.

The sign of my second in command.

"I suppose it is that time again," I murmured before sweeping past him.

"That it is," he mumbled with a frown.

We entered the throne room. The blue flames in the sconces roared to life. They illuminated the black marble floor that led, like a river of oil, to the raised dais where my throne sat, flanked by two arched windows. Through the old, warped glass, the city of souls was almost visible. Slowly, I climbed the steps, the heavy black cloak at my shoulders slithering on the stones the only sound in the room.

Dimitri melted into the shadows, his blue-black skin so dark he all but disappeared at my right-hand side while five of my men escorted three outsiders into the chamber. It was easy to spot the difference between them. My men were outfitted in the same black armor as Dimitri. The men they held captive were their opposites with golden armor that even here reflected the meager light of the sun.

I hardened the ice within my heart, the only armor I truly possessed. A cold, unamused smile pulled at the corners of my mouth.

"Ah, Hollis, has it truly been a year?" I mused, clapping my hands together.

The man in front grimaced faintly, his pale complexion growing rosy with the anger that lingered beneath the surface. Though these men still had their swords, they knew better than to touch them in my presence.

"It has, Under King," Hollis answered.

I detested the title bestowed upon me in my brother's kingdom. For one, it made no sense as our kingdoms resided beside each other. For another, it inferred that there was a king higher than me. Only one guess was needed to say who that king was.

Every year, Typhon sent his men into the mists, trying to find a way around the river that divided our kingdom and therefore a weak spot in our defenses. And each year we would find them, save them, and send them on their way.

"As much as I enjoy your annual visit, I must admit that I grow tired of this dance." Sighing, I took a step off the dais. "I think, perhaps, it may be time to change the steps."

Hollis's eyes widened. The scent of his fear was as palpable as the favor Typhon had bestowed upon him centuries ago.

"Tell me, did he grant you immortality?"

His throat clicked with a swallow. One bead of perspiration dripped from his temple beneath the gilded helmet. Hollis's mouth opened, then closed before Dimitri's voice rang out from the shadows.

"Answer him."

We were close enough now that I could scent the sunlight of his armor. My shadows recoiled from his presence. I tried to find a semblance of anger beneath my skin. Some spark of heat or indignance at this latest attempt upon my land and its people.

But there was only the hollow depth of nothingness, an expanse of cold darkness like the tunnels in which even now souls cried out for forgiveness.

"He did."

Dimitri's tongue clicked in annoyance.

"Your Grace," Hollis grunted.

With a tilt of my head, I examined his widening pupils and the twitching of the muscle in his jaw. "Do you know what the horrifying thing about immortality is, Hollis?"

No answer, only the sharpening scent of his anger in the air.

"It is that your body may be utterly destroyed and yet you will live. For you do not possess a god's skin nor a god's magic. Why, I could chop you into pieces, scattering the parts, and you would feel every moment until the parts were reunited." I leaned closer, my lips brushing his ear. "It could take centuries."

My attention flicked to the men behind him, their wide eyes, lips parted in horror. I wished they did something to me, those looks. Once they had. Once I would have felt a sickening lurch that would make my stomach clench and my chest ache.

I longed to feel such discomfort again.

"So, you will thank me that *this* is all I will do." A sharp *crack* echoed through the room as I thrust my hand forward.

Here was the only touch I could endure. The touch of violence, of retribution, of reckoning. I could no longer stomach anything else.

With a jerk, I drew my hand back, fingers wrapped around the pulsing mass of tissue in my palm. Hollis looked down, his face pale, gaping at his heart in my hand. The dripping of his blood against the floor matched the beat of ice through my veins.

"Tell your king I am done with these games. Next time, I will not be so merciful."

He staggered, one of his men reaching a hand to steady him. Even as we stood there, the stream of blood slowed, then stopped, the edges of the wound sealing.

"Ah, you see? You are already healing." I squeezed my hand into a fist, the tissue bulging through my fingers. "What a *gift*."

With a wave of my hand, the doors opened. Dimitri's power flew through the room, urging the men back. One of them threw Hollis's arm around his shoulders as they stumbled out.

The moment they were gone, I threw the still-warm heart to the floor. I tried to will any feeling at the sight of it. But it was a lost cause as it had been for the last two and a half centuries. Though that length of time was nothing to a timeless god, merely the blink of an eye.

My mind flicked back to the image of those ashes amid the fragrant apple blossoms. The look of horror on her face and the brief spark of feeling that had flared within me. The steady *drip, drip, drip* of the blood clinging to my hand like the ticking of a clock reminded me that Typhon had the princess in his grasp.

The young god, whose downfall was because of me.

How long until he learned how to twist her power to his will? Had he already begun? Soon he would have a legion at my door ready to finish what he started millennia ago, I could sense it.

"I must return," I breathed, eyeing the blood dripping to the floor with a sick fascination.

"Tomorrow is the ascension. I cannot guide them without you," Horace, my magistrate of souls, rumbled behind me.

From the moment a soul touched these shores, they were placed upon a path that would eventually lead them to ascension, to giving their small piece of magic back to the world to begin again. The kingdom was split into different parts that a soul might wander for a time to face whatever burden might rest upon them, whether it was wiping their memories clean by drinking from the Athal river, wandering in isolation in Isthil, or facing their fears within the caves of the Tylith Mountains. A soul might work toward ascension for a century, or two, or ten before they were ready to give up their magic and begin again.

And it was my responsibility as ruler to help shepherd them into that next stage—into the unknown that I alone was barred from.

"I will be there." Wiping my hand across my trousers, I lifted my head, exhaling deeply through my nose. Horace's head bowed respectfully, his deep brown skin shining faintly in the light. "But I must return to Aethera."

"Why?" Dimitri urged, his footsteps clicking against the smooth floor until he was right beside me.

"To watch," I answered, wiping my hand on my cloak.

Dimitri gave a small huff of annoyance, but I paid it no attention, already halfway to the heavy double doors.

"To watch for what, *exactly?*" he pushed.

"For a chance to save us all."

CHAPTER

FIVE

Oralia

Soft fingertips stroked my cheek, my temples, my lips. The touch was alien on my skin, wrong. *Dangerous.*

A woman's voice that I thought might have been my mother's called over the distance, through time and space. Her voice sounded panicked, frightened even. My eyes flew open, blinking wildly and taking in the sunset that set the sky ablaze. I jerked away from the soft magic that stroked my jaw, and my head bounced off the window of the library. Somewhere close, a tongue clicked in amusement.

"Jumpy, jumpy."

My muscles clenched as I froze. "Aelestor..."

Drystan stood a few paces back, his eyes bright in anger. A swirl of wind akin to a cyclone held him in place. I looked up at the god before me. His alabaster skin was flushed, and a wine bottle hung limply in one hand.

"You may as well get used to the feeling of my magic." He laughed bitterly. "One day, we will be wed, you know."

Aelestor sounded as excited about that prospect as I was.

Whispers of the negotiations between the king and the God of Storms had slithered through the castle. It was a point of contention within the court that I was not yet betrothed. Though love matches happened, they were rare and couples that performed the soul-bonding ceremony were rarer. More often than not, marriages were made within our kingdom to produce powerful heirs. Though I could not be touched, I knew King Typhon was devising ways for me to conceive without danger to Aelestor. There had been whispers of armor, vials, and shackles. They all made my stomach twist with fear.

I would rather my power turn on me than ever marry him, but I knew better than to say so aloud. He was too powerful and too favored by Typhon.

Drystan groaned, fighting against the storm that pinned him in place.

"Aelestor..." I started, clearing my throat and rising to my feet. "Release him."

He grinned at me in a daze, smoothing back his wild copper curls with a lazy hand. I knew of his conquests throughout the court. Gods and demigods alike had fallen into his bed over the millennia he'd walked this land. What they ever saw in him, I would never know.

There was a slight sway in his steps as he ambled closer. His gray tunic lined in elaborate gold beading tinkled with each movement. It was a sound so similar to a sprinkle of rain that one might mistake the two when he passed the castle halls.

"What are you willing to give for your guard's release?" he purred, glazed eyes tracking over my face.

Bile rose in my throat. A spike of adrenaline pulsed, and I

swallowed down the rising tide of magic swimming through my veins, begging to be released.

"We are expected at dinner. The king will not forgive our lateness."

Aelestor raised a coppery brow, leaning close enough that the stale wine on his breath ghosted over my cheeks. My heart thrummed in my ears, and I gritted my teeth, trembling against the heat creeping up my neck like a too-tight collar.

"What is it like, *my lady?*" He sneered the title. "To know that you are nothing but a reminder of all the king has lost?"

A feral grin slid across Aelestor's face as his words hit like a dagger to my heart. With a lazy lift of his hand, he stepped closer to brush a stray hair back from my cheek. I grimaced, instinctually shying away from his touch even as my power roared, wanting its revenge.

Yet before he could come close, a strange flash of dark flared behind him and a golden glove covered his wrist.

"She is not to be touched, Lord Thyella," Drystan rumbled.

Aelestor and I blinked at him, astonished that Drystan had broken free of the bonds Aelestor had cast. Given how intoxicated he was, perhaps it was not much of a feat.

"Come, Oralia," Drystan continued, stepping between us so I could rush past.

As we raced through the gilded halls of the palace, I wrung my shaking hands through my soft leather gloves. We did not say a word, there was no need. Aelestor would seek revenge, and I knew, deep down, the king would side with him.

The god was invaluable to the kingdom. Not only could he

summon storms, but he could also disperse them. Violent storms were rare, but they did occur, and he was always there to stop them before the damage became too great.

"Take a breath," Drystan murmured, his voice dropping low enough that I alone heard, despite the human maid who passed us and flashed me a tentative smile.

I tried to return it before doing as Drystan asked.

"Again," he said, even softer.

So, I breathed again. And again. Until my hands stilled and my shoulders relaxed and we stood in front of the double doors of the family dining room. I slid a hand down the bodice of my gown, the light blue fabric straining with each breath I took.

The doors opened slowly as if the castle was giving me one more moment to collect myself before facing those who waited inside. I sighed with relief when the first god I beheld was not Typhon, but Caston.

I cried out his name in delight. The instinct to throw myself into his arms was only a bare whisper in my mind, but the desire was there. It was enough to make me jerk in his direction, even after all this time. He rose at once from his place at the table with his wide smile and mop of unruly golden hair. His arms spread wide as if we could embrace, wrapped in armor and muscle: a true soldier.

"Oralia," he greeted, the dimple in his left cheek prominent with his joy.

The king rose from his seat as well, wings flaring and a muscle in his jaw working as he looked me over. With the two of them side by side, it was easier to spot the differences. Caston's complexion was lighter, more rose gold than yellow, though gold flecks dotted the skin across his cheekbones and forearms like freckles.

If Typhon was the blinding light of the sun, then Caston was the warmth—all kindness and sweetness.

"Why are you late?" Typhon snapped, his voice booming through the small space, golden cheeks darkening.

He had seen the orchard, it was clear on his face. Of course there would be no hiding it from him.

"Are you all right, Lia?" Caston asked at the same moment, eyes searching mine.

Taking a breath, I pulled on the cuff of my gloves and drew a soft smile to the surface of my face, dipping my head low.

"I apologize for my lateness, my king. Lord Thyella delayed me," I answered as quickly as possible.

Concern flickered over Caston's face at the name. There was a softness in him that was absent in his father, a compassion that led him to defend those he loved fiercely. I hated how often he was away. Perhaps with Caston around more, we might have found another way to control my power.

"*Burning Suns,*" Caston cursed, mouth tightening into an angry line. "What did he do?"

I did not answer. Instead, I rounded the large table, passing Caston's guard, Michalis, and one of Typhon's advisers, Mecrucio, keeping my head low until I reached the king. Slowly I dropped to my knees, hiding my wince as they hit the hard, cold stone floor. The rhythm of my heart pounded in my throat while I pressed three fingers to my brow, gaze fixed on the ground.

"My king," I murmured respectfully, bracing myself for his fury.

King Typhon had more on his plate than dealing with his unruly ward. The stress that hung heavy on his shoulders was easy to see. The welfare of his people was always his duty and I...

I threatened everything.

Silence lengthened in the room as I knelt, not daring to drop my hand or lift my gaze. My knees ached, an echo of my childhood there within the pain, but I did not shift even an inch.

"Rise, Oralia." His voice was quiet, tired.

We stood in front of our usual table places, waiting as was proper, for the king to sit first. I took my seat to the left of him at the head of the table while Caston took his right. Drystan settled beside me. His eyes were already fixed on the terrine of venison stew in front of him. Michalis' pale cheeks reddened as Caston's shoulder brushed his. We sat in silence for a few minutes, each of us focused on our meals until the king saw fit to begin the conversation.

"I see you made it to the orchards…" he started. There was a compliment and a warning hidden within the statement.

Dabbing my napkin at the corners of my mouth, I realized he wanted a response from me. "None of the trees had blossomed, Your Grace, and I—" My throat clicked with my dry swallow. "I will do better."

Typhon nodded, his sharp knife cleanly cutting through the roast on his plate. "As we discussed, I have some ideas on how we might best control your magic."

I exhaled in a gust. The relief that he would not yet punish me was so palpable that the lights in the room appeared to brighten. Even the threat of his new attempt at finding my control could not hamper it.

"I hear congratulations are in order," I murmured, smiling at Michalis and Caston.

The former's entire face flushed, sneaking a glance at Caston. "Thank you, my lady. It is good to be home to celebrate. I have to admit I have been dreaming of it for weeks."

Caston laughed, bringing Michalis' hand to his lips. "You have been dreaming of the cook's honey cakes, love."

Michalis shrugged, throwing him a wink. They stared at each other for a long moment, and there was so much love within that gaze it made my throat ache.

Typhon's adviser, Mecrucio, hummed, sweeping a hand through his thick brown curls. "Your return is excellently timed, Your Grace. The people will enjoy the festivities of a soul bond. I believe it will bolster the morale amidst the...difficulties wrought by the Under King."

Caston cleared his throat, turning toward me with a twinkle in his eye. "We could have used you today, Lia." My brows raised in surprise. "My men brought me through the human settlement right on the boundary line of our land beside the mist."

My stomach twisted, and I pushed away the plate piled with roast and potatoes upon it.

Caston's face lost its usual sparkle, eyes tightening with the memory. "Their crops are dying from the Under King's blight. People are starving."

My head jerked toward the king, who was eyeing his son as a general might observe his soldier.

"But... But..." My fists opened and closed in front of me as if I could hold the solution in my very hands.

But I could easily fix that. I could remedy their problem in merely an afternoon. However the words got stuck somewhere between my mind and my mouth with the threat of Typhon's anger looming across the table.

Drystan turned his attention to me, a warning with his eyes that I did not want to heed.

"I can help," I blurted out, fingers closing over the lip of the table to hold myself steady.

"What were your orders, Caston?" Typhon's voice was like ice flowing through my veins.

Caston bristled at the tone. "Oralia can help, Father. She is exactly the solution."

"You know she cannot leave the grounds," Mecrucio murmured, attempting as always to defuse any disagreements within the palace.

"If I went during the day..." I pushed, voice cracking. My words were like a bright flame that could burn me alive.

"That is a good idea, Father," Caston agreed louder. "The daemoni fear the sunlight."

It had always been Typhon's reasoning for why I never left the grounds—the threat of the demon creatures that lurked beyond the castle grounds, repelled by the light of the castle. But I knew better. He had witnessed my lapse in judgment, my loss of control, one too many times to allow me to leave.

"I am in control," I added. The lie tasted like the ash of the apple tree on my tongue.

With blinding speed, his golden fist landed on the table, a crack spiderwebbing across the gilded wood. "*ENOUGH!*"

My ears rang in the silence that followed. Typhon took a steadying breath before his golden gaze flicked to each of us in turn before settling upon me. "Enough. This is not up for discussion. It is not safe for you, or our people, for you to pass the wards."

Injustice clawed its way up my throat. I was not a child. I was fully grown, well into my prime.

"Mother would have wanted me to help."

Typhon took a deep breath, his gaze dropping to the table,

exhaustion heavy across his features. "Seeing as you killed your mother, Lia, I suppose we will never know."

His words hit me like a sharp stab to the chest. It was not the message that hurt the most, but the lips from which it fell. Before me sat a stranger, so different and yet the same king I had grown up knowing. And though his face fell, eyes widening with the words he'd said, I was bleeding out across the table.

Something had irrevocably broken between us. A single stone slipped from the wall I had built between my love for him and his innate cruelty.

Heat burned my cheeks. His face blurred before me into a muddled distortion. Grief and fear fed the inky blackness until I could practically see it curling around my wrists.

Seeing as you killed your mother.

The pain doubled, then tripled.

With a breath, shadows exploded from my chest. Blackness shrouded my eyes as the inexplicable vastness of my dark power found its way out. This had never happened before. I had never ever seen these kinds of shadows—striking out like arrows made of night. My cry of panic tangled with the screams of others in the room until rays of golden light pierced the darkness.

The fear turned to agony as the golden light encircled my wrists and arms, burning my skin.

Typhon's light destroyed the shadows in a flash. A sob bubbled in my throat as I blinked rapidly in the sudden brightness. I caught sight of the limp form of Michalis face down on his plate, blood trickling from his ears. Behind him, the body of a human servant was crumpled on the floor, blood dripping from her nose.

Harsh breaths tore through my lungs as I found Caston,

protectively covered by Mecrucio and Drystan. My guard's eyes were wide with fear as he looked at me. Now they all knew exactly what I was.

A monster, as I had always feared.

The king's golden eyes fixed on the dead, his building rage a tangible presence in the room.

Run, my dark power urged, shadows pulling me to my feet in an instant.

I raced to the door with my stomach churning, before Caston's first wail split the silence. Typhon's large hands were soothing on his back, combing through his hair. Comfort I knew nothing of. Comfort I would never feel.

Tripping over the hem of my skirts, I fell against the door at the far side of the room. The stairs beneath my feet drifted in and out of focus, as the image of their dead bodies swam before me.

Night air stung my cheeks as I stumbled out of a side door at the base of the stairs, the palace glowing at my back. The clamor of shouts echoed from above. Heavy footsteps hammered down the stairs. I clawed at the bodice of my gown, trying to take in the air I desperately needed. Black spots bloomed at the corners of my vision. The dark magic beneath my skin continued to hum, hungry for more. It stretched, purred, urging me on—closer toward the boundary line.

Another sob caught in my throat. But I pushed on. The instinct to create as much space between myself and the bodies in that room won out against the need to fall to pieces. More shouting rang out through the night with the clang of swords drawn from sheaths. And there was the roar of Typhon over the rest, commanding his soldiers to find me.

The moment I hit the perimeter of the castle grounds, the wards

King Typhon had placed to keep me in burst into my consciousness, driving me back. Sizzling embers of sunlight blazed across the surface of my skin and immediately those same deadly shadows reared up to meet it. Fear churned in my stomach, nausea coating my throat at the sight of them.

I pushed forward, shrieking as I struggled to rip through the wards. The shadows sliced and tore at the boundary without effect. And though I tried to focus on the task at hand, my mind would not let me forget:

I killed them.

I killed them.

I killed them.

CHAPTER

SIX

Renwick

The quiet night of Aethera was rent in two.

A figure stumbled from the side passage of the golden castle, hair wildly streaming behind her. The heavy taste of dark magic was in the air. Only moments before, my power had rumbled like a wave meeting the shore, reacting to *something*. There was a soft whimper in the darkness, swallowed by the shouts echoing from the golden castle. As the figure ran, the light of the moon caught on her strawberry-blonde waves.

The princess. She was heading straight to the boundary line where the wards were placed to keep me out and her in. I knew acutely the sizzle of golden pain she felt as she smashed against the unyielding magical barrier.

Soldiers poured from the small door she'd tumbled through, their gilded armor and weapons glinting in the moonlight. Already they were gaining on her, chains laced with kratus resin in their grip, prepared to imprison her and her magic.

Familiar shadows burst from her chest, attacking the wards as she shrieked, her panic clawing its way toward me like an insistent tapping upon the empty cavity of my chest. Air sped through my lungs at the sight. For the first time in over two hundred years, there was a spark of fear within my veins instead of bland indifference. She was trying to get out, and Typhon was going to stop her. Take her. Imprison her.

And then turn her power into a weapon.

My wings spread wide, pushing from my perch and gliding through the wards that held her captive so I could take my true form on the other side. Her hair was wild, curling around her face, cheeks ruddy and wet from the effort. Loud gasps of breath tore through her lungs. Shreds of fabric from her gown hung around her arms.

If she wanted out, then I would get her out.

We attacked from both sides. My shadows tangled with hers, like puzzle pieces sliding together as her darkness merged with mine. We had to do this quickly—the soldiers grew ever closer with their swords drawn. Pushing my magic outward, I forced her shadows to strengthen around my own, to do what we could not have on our own.

We tore a hole through the wards.

The princess gave a small cry of relief, shoulders sagging as she scrambled through the small tear before it sealed once more. Panicked gasps slipped through her lips when she stumbled, her knees hitting the wet bracken of the forest.

I stepped forward. She cried out in terror at the sight of me, falling onto her hands and skittering back, the skirts of her gown tearing against the sharp branches of the forest floor. And at that sight, the small spark of fear from a moment ago winked out with the ice rushing through my veins.

"You are safe. We must leave now."

There was a wildness in her eyes as she pushed quickly to her feet, fumbling within the tattered fabric of her skirts. A dagger glinted in the moonlight. The scent of kratus resin dripped off the blade—the only thing that could truly kill a god. But my magic slithered around her feet, holding her in place. Before the shadows could move to her arms, she jutted the dagger forward, missing my chest by mere inches.

My shadows curled around her wrist, twisting it with a jerk so the weapon fell to the bracken below. "Do not fight."

Another sob tore from her throat. The soldiers were upon us now, their armor glinting with the harsh rays of their king. With a growl, I sent more shadows outwards, forcing them back before they could cross the boundary of the wards.

This moment might be the only chance we had.

With a flick of my fingers, my power wrapped around her wrist expanded, sliding down her legs. Her eyes pierced mine, and I knew, lost somewhere in *the in-between*, those broken pieces of my soul were aching at the sight of those green eyes, so much like her father's. They reminded me of what would be lost if we lingered much longer here.

I could not fail again. Could not stand to lose any more than I already had.

Finally, she drew in a deep breath. Her voice was so soft it was barely audible. "Let me go."

Her fear was heavy in my nose. The perspiration at her temples and at her nape and the way her hands trembled beneath her bonds deepened the scent. Even her long strawberry-blonde locks shivered in the dark as she tried, but failed, to hide her fear.

She was more afraid of me than she was of facing the soldiers trying to fight their way through my power.

"Do you know who I am?" I asked softly.

She had to crane her neck to look up at me. Her gaze danced along my face before flicking to my shoulders where my wings should have been. Something shifted in her expression, her delicate brows pulling together and lips tensing.

"You are the Under King," she answered, voice breaking on the last syllable.

I could see the monster she beheld reflected in her eyes, and the ice around my heart hardened further.

"*Sleep,*" I commanded.

Within the span of one heartbeat, her lids closed and her body swayed toward the forest floor. The shadows rose to cradle her when I flicked my fingers and I began down the path through the darkness and toward the mist.

I had thought that perhaps she would recognize the familiar magic within me. That perhaps, she would see a rescuer. Yet she saw what they always did. Her fear was the same as the souls who came to Infernis and encountered the Under King of their legends, the God of the Dead, the bringer of destruction, the reckoning.

I had hoped that by saving her, not only would I save my people, but that perhaps, I would find some peace from the guilt that burrowed deep within my chest. I was not so foolish as to believe I would recover the lost and broken pieces of my soul, but perhaps something akin to that. Relief from the past. Yet as I tugged us quickly through the thick, curling mist, I knew that wish had been for nothing.

Peace and relief were gone from me as surely as everything I had ever loved.

CHAPTER
SEVEN

Oralia

onsciousness returned slowly.

There had been no fighting his command. *Sleep*, he'd said and my eyelids closed and my body went limp—my mind, just for a moment, quiet.

I had known him from the moment I saw him with his moon-pale skin, sharp cheekbones, and wavy black hair that curled around his collarbones. I would have called him beautiful if I had not known the depravity and violence that lurked beneath.

But it was not his midnight eyes or his towering height that told me who he was. It was the darkness that wept from every pore, the curling shadows that wrapped around my ankles, and the way the poison inside of me moaned with pleasure at his presence.

The few times that I'd imagined the Under King, it had been with the same wings that were set upon the mantel in the library. I'd assumed, like with every other appendage of a god or demigod, that they would have grown back.

But they had not.

Instead, in their place, a thick cloak spilled like liquid night over his shoulders and down to the forest floor. So black it absorbed the surrounding light.

Blinking, I tried to adjust to the glowing blue light that we approached. I was floating, borne across the ground on a shadowed wind, trailing a little behind the king of Infernis. The mist circled my bindings, soothing the ache in my wrists and arms from the burns left behind by Typhon's power. Much like feathery hands sliding over my cheeks, they wiped away the last of my tears. The sensation even of these phantom touches made me shiver, an echo of comfort I had never known. It was foolish to want to lean into them, to find some small comfort in the echo of a caress, but I did.

"Thank you," I murmured to the mist.

The Under King turned at the sound of my voice, his face a blank mask. With a movement of his fingers, his power shifted me so I was upright but floating across the ground. With a shake of my head, I attempted to remove a tendril of hair from my face, and then I paled, dread slicing through my belly. Somewhere along the way, I'd lost my mother's crown.

My eyes grew wide, searching the ground beneath me as if I would find it there in the small pebbles and rocks that lined the bank of the river where we now stood. But there was nothing there, and now, there was nothing left to connect me to her.

The Under King continued to watch me, contemplating the anguish on my face perhaps. His eyes were as dead as the sickening magic that lay within him.

I shied from his gaze as an ominous black boat approached through the fog. Its flat base faced the bank, the opposite end curving in an elegant arc—or would have been elegant if it had not appeared to be the replica of a spine. Or perhaps it *was* a spine from one of the giants that used to roam this world. Standing at the fore, beside the large lamp with a glittering blue orb, stood what I could only describe as a skeleton encased in blueish-gray skin.

The creature croaked a phrase in an unfamiliar language, the voice slightly higher than I expected. Their fathomless black eyes flicked to me in question.

"A passenger?" they asked in the common tongue.

The Under King hummed in confirmation, stepping onto the boat and drawing me with him.

My heart thrummed in my chest, and I fought back a scoff. *A passenger? More like a prisoner.* Was there any chance of escape, to fight back? My palms itched beneath the leather gloves. If I could get close enough, perhaps I could destroy him with a touch. Even as the thought rose to the surface of my mind, nausea roiled through me. Could I do that again? Could I witness the monstrous power that lay within me?

To destroy him? I would. I must.

"You favor your father, Princess," the skeletal creature observed in a gentle rasp, drawing an onyx rod from beside her and placing it into the water.

The word of thanks caught in my throat before I swallowed it down. For most, my strawberry-blonde hair was streaked with enough gold to satisfy those who looked for a connection between myself and King Typhon. The comparison that once would have brought me comfort now made my stomach twist. His words echoed through my head along with the carnage I had left behind.

Or perhaps it was the man who sired me that this creature

referred to. Both options twisted my lips into a grimace. The title rankled as well. I was not a princess. I had no claim to the throne.

I was no one.

Nothing.

The Under King's eyes pierced mine. His face was an unmoving mask as they read each minute detail of my expression. "I do not think the princess wishes to converse, Vakarys."

Vakarys nodded before turning her attention to the shore beyond.

The boat glided soundlessly through the water, the dark blue depths churning around us. A groan echoed from the wood, and I tilted my head to peer over the side of the boat at the rocks below.

I gasped.

They were not rocks... *Burning Suns.* They were people. Some with matted, wet hair and rotting skin, some completely bare to the bone. All were varying shades of blue, from palest gray to deep as night. They pressed as close to the boat as possible as if they were the ones who shepherded us across.

"Who...who are they?" I could not stop myself from asking.

I swallowed. The water lapped at their faces, sweeping back the small tendrils of hair and flesh that clung to them. The Under King did not respond, his expression vacant as he stared at the waves.

"Are they in pain?" I pressed louder.

Dark eyes flicked to me. His face was unreadable in the glow from the lamp, but he did not speak. The silence between us was only broken by the surrounding water and the soft creaking of either the boat or the bones as we glided through the thickening mist.

Ahead, the spires of an enormous castle melted into view. The black rock of the shore glittered in the muted moonlight. Sharp, jagged mountains loomed far to the east. And the dark power inside me shifted.

"No," he said. His tone was velvet smooth, gaze fixed on the skeletal creatures now retreating into the depths below. "They are not in pain."

Vakarys pressed the rod into the water until we turned and slid onto the shore. The Under King's boots dug into the small rocks, dispersing them as he walked and I, helplessly, floated behind him.

We wound down a dark graveled path. On either side were large expanses of loose soil and dead grass that swayed in the wind. The only breaks in the vast, dead earth were the tall, obsidian mountains that towered over us. It was difficult to see in the dark, but I thought there might have been caves carved within the cliffside. I wondered if humans or gods resided within.

A sadness clung to this place, a weary hopelessness that leached through my soul. Was this how mortals spent their eternity within this desolate kingdom? The afterlife was said to be an eternity of despair where deceased humans and demigods were conscripted into the Under King's army and forced to serve the monster of a god. Seeing this bleak place, I could believe it even more surely.

The curse within me groaned, now fully awake, and skittered beneath the surface of my skin, curling around my heart. The weight of the darkness hung within in my very soul. Trying to shut it out, I closed my eyes, but I stifled a cry when the vision of the bodies strewn across King Typhon's dining hall appeared behind my lids. I snapped my lids open, the horrors before me paling in comparison to what I had already witnessed tonight.

The Under King paused, his icy gaze contemplative before he walked a few paces farther and a large, gnarled tree came into view where the river curved. I wondered where we were headed as he stepped beneath the branches, pulling me along. Suddenly, his hand closed over my wrist in a vice-like grip.

The touch was a shock, a lightning strike zinging through my bones. All at once, my skin heated and cooled, tingling at the connection until his darkness flooded my senses. My magic purred, murmuring in a language I did not speak of satisfaction and strength.

With his magic surrounding us, I could not draw breath, could not see nor move. One moment, I was suffocating. The next, I was blinking in the faint light of the mist-covered moon and gasping for air. I found myself suddenly standing in a new place. His hand dropped, smoothing back his hair. Relief swirled through my heart even as a hollow pang echoed through my stomach as if I'd been left bereft.

That was the first time someone had touched me in over two hundred years.

I tried to survey my surroundings instead of giving in to the itching beneath my skin. The frantic need to be touched again warred with the revulsion that his hand had been the first. Out of the corner of my eye, he flexed his hand as if he, too, had felt that spark.

We were no longer beneath the tree. Instead, before us was an expanse of scorched earth, dotted with gnarled trees and patches of rough stone. My breath caught in my throat, lips parted in a silent cry as the Under King's magic drew me forward.

The castle loomed over us in blacks and grays, sharp, night-tipped tower turrets thrust into the sky. The entrance was surrounded by irregular stonework, but the rest of the castle was covered in onyx and gray slabs—the antithesis of Aethera's palace. I wondered at the material as we approached until bile filled my throat and I could see clearly what lay ahead. They were not stones... No, they were not stones at all.

This castle was made of bones.

CHAPTER
EIGHT

Renwick

I stopped before the steps that led up to my castle, noting the horror that filled her face as she gazed upon it. There was no way she could know the true origin of these bones. I doubted Typhon educated his charges with the stories of the beginning of time.

Are they in pain?

It was the same question that Zephyrus, her true father, had asked the first time he'd traveled the river. The question had caused a pang of hollow grief to wrap its bony fingers around my throat until I had not been sure if I could answer. One of the only emotions I felt besides the ice: my failure, my grief, my despair.

As I pulled back my shadows, her body dropped with a huff to the ground. On trembling knees, she righted herself, shaking back her mussed mane of hair while taking in our surroundings. A muscle ticked in her jaw.

I halted, noting the indecision on her face. "Do not try to run. If you do, the daemoni who reside along our borders will begin a hunt.

No doubt they can scent your weaknesses even now."

The dark creatures prowled the woods on the perimeter of the kingdom, repelled for the most part by my magic. The daemoni were varied in appearance and strength, but one alone could destroy her given the opportunity.

She was safe with me whether she believed it or not.

With three quick steps, she was up the staircase and swirling past me until I lengthened my strides to lead her into the castle. Silently, I observed her as her eyes widened with each figure that drifted past, some as faint as smoke swirling from a candle, some as solid as if they were alive.

Could she sense which were souls and which were not? Usually that was a power only those who lived within this kingdom possessed. Some of the gods who passed between Aethera and Infernis picked up the skill, however. Part of me wanted to ask, to try and speak with her, but every time I opened my mouth, she flinched and the words came out wrong.

The doors to the throne room slid open with a whisper. I did not stop to watch her take in the obsidian room with its blue flame torches, nor my gleaming throne built from ash and bone. Her reaction would be the same as all the rest, and I did not wish to read the horror on her face.

Dimitri stood closest to the dais, along with many of the others of my inner circle: Mecrucio, the God of Travelers, the sprinkling of freckles across his peach nose creasing with his assessment of the princess. Horace stood beside Mecrucio, ruby-flecked eyes boring into Oralia's soul. Farther back, toward the towering windows, stood Thorne, his wide shoulders imposing in the crowd, his booming laughter silent for once.

The rest of the crowd was comprised of demigods who had fled Typhon's rule, and souls who had proven themselves over the millennia. They all flanked the dais, turning as one at our approach and either bowing their head or lowering to a knee.

The princess stopped a few paces into the room. I did not encourage her to move any further. Instead, I approached Dimitri and Horace while they gracefully made their way back to their feet and Mecrucio stepped back into the shadows until the princess could not see his face.

"What is your plan, Your Grace?" Horace asked with a respectful dip of his chin, his attention darting to our guest and back again.

"I would like to find out what it was that forced her to flee, if possible," I answered quietly. "It will help us plan for any attack Typhon may wage in pursuit of her."

"*Stars*," Mecrucio cursed to the pair, low enough that I could barely hear it.

I ignored him and the small huff of agreement Dimitri made as I strode to the steps in front of the dais, my cloak curling around my ankles as I turned to her. Silence hung heavily in the room as I spread my hands wide as if to encompass my kingdom.

"Welcome to the kingdom of Infernis."

She stared at me for a long moment before her green eyes hardened, and she took a few faltering steps toward the dais.

"What is it you want from me?" Outrage tinged the words.

My hands lowered slowly. "I want nothing from you. I saved you."

Her eyes flashed, top lip curled with indignation. "Saved me?"

Ice rippled along my veins, but something else shifted beneath the surface at her spark of indignation. "I shouldn't be surprised that you see a villain standing before you, just like the rest."

No one saw past the lies Typhon told, not the souls who journeyed to these shores, not even the demigods who fled from his rule. Over time, perhaps, they learned that things were not as they seemed, but the look on her face was one I knew all too well.

She took an involuntary step back, her words rising in volume as shadows flared across her shoulders and wrists. "It is a murderer I see. A tyrant. *A monster.*"

Her mouth snapped shut, and she cringed away as if fearing my retribution.

But I had played the villain longer than she had existed—before the creation of time, even. Perhaps it was for the best that I had lost those pieces of my soul that would have crumbled at the look of revulsion upon her face. That would have made me wish to prove her wrong.

"What happened tonight to force you to flee the castle?"

Her gaze deadened, an impenetrable door closing within her mind. There was a flutter in her throat as her fingers flexed, then relaxed, but she did not reply. Moments passed, but only the shallow breaths of those in attendance filled the chamber.

And yet, she did not speak.

"What do you believe Typhon will do next?" I pressed.

Her fingers flexed again, shifting as if she wanted to draw her hands together but stopped herself. Slowly, the light in her eyes flickered, then died. She had given up or given in to something, but what I could not tell. The flames around us shuddered as my anger lashed out through the room, whipping through the hair and robes of all present, yet leaving them untouched.

Closing the distance between us, I breathed in the sunshine and apple scent of her. "Who will he send to retrieve you?"

The muscle in her jaw worked, and I wondered if she was biting her tongue. I wanted to see that spark of fire flare within her eyes again. To see if I might feel that shift beneath the ice as I had in the forest.

I tilted my head to the side. "Will you not speak, Princess? Are my questions beneath you?"

But she did not answer.

"How far do you think he will go to save you?"

One of her hands shot out, trembling, to lay across my cheek. I waited for the wave of itching discomfort to glide across my skin, to jerk away from the warmth of her palm. But...nothing came. There was no grief, no shame—only the warmth of her touch. That same, strange shift curled in my chest, like a distant bird beating its wings.

But then her eyes widened further, flicking from my face to where our skin touched and back again. All the fight, all the strength, left her as a single tear fell from her eye before others followed, splashing across her cheeks and dripping down the column of her throat. Her palm dropped from my cheek. Devastation splashed across her face.

And all the pieces fell into place as her bare hand dropped to her side, and I remained instead of ashes in my place.

"I am beyond death, Princess. Your power has no sway over me."

It was true. I was beyond death. I could die, *had* died, many times in the past. The most recent death was when I failed her own parents on the edges of the mist. And each death I suffered stole a small piece of my soul until all I knew was coldness, grief, and shame.

I took a breath and the words came out too harsh, drenched in all my failures. "How far will Typhon go to retrieve you?"

"To the ends of the..." Her voice cracked, eyes glassy before her lies spilled down her cheeks and over her closed lips.

Oralia

The lie burned so deeply that I could not finish it.

There was not any circumstance in which I believed Typhon would retrieve me from this place. Caston might, though he was bound by any order the king gave, and that was if they could even find their way through the impenetrable mist. I had been alive long enough to understand that when Typhon looked at me, all he saw was loss. I was the physical embodiment of his grief. That fact was why I had no title, why I had no power within his court, and why I had never fought him to leave the castle grounds until now. Because his grief was my shame.

Perhaps, with me gone, he would finally feel relief.

If the Under King found out how worthless I was, he would more than likely destroy me. Rumors of his taste for violence had spread through Typhon's castle for years. I had thought if I could kill him, it might save our kingdom from his dark magic and earn my place back at Typhon's table.

But when I touched him there had been...*nothing*. Somehow, he alone appeared immune to my power, to the darkest magic I possessed but could not control. That monstrous ability had been my one advantage. On realizing even my darkness had deserted me, all my walls crumbled to the ground.

The heat of his skin continued to burn against my fingertips. It had been otherworldly to feel another beneath my hand and not have them turn to ash. The roughness from the stubble of his beard had rasped against my palm and yet the skin of his cheek was so soft, so warm—a contrast to the coldness within his eyes. And though I had reached out to kill him, I suddenly did not feel so alone.

He stared at me now, dark eyes searching mine. There was no softness, no compassion, but there was understanding. The Under King could see right through me. And then he turned his head, catching the eye of someone in the crowd before turning back to me.

"This is Sidero." Someone stepped from the small grouping behind him, olive skin glimmering faintly in the light, features gentle. "They will show you to your chambers and assist with anything you might need. Perhaps, with time, we may come to an understanding."

Panic twisted through my chest.

The soul bowed their head, long black braid bobbing against their wide chest, before gliding across the floor to stand beside me. They offered me their arm.

"Shall we, Princess?" Sidero asked, voice as gentle as their countenance.

The Under King and I stared at one another for a long moment. The tension of so much history and hatred was tangible between us, where the words I had not spoken and the vengeance he wanted against Typhon lived.

Despite my failure to kill the Under King, I abstained from taking Sidero's elbow, all too aware of the danger that lay between my bare hands. My gloves lay only a small distance away on the floor where I'd dropped them, but a part of me recoiled at the thought of picking them up ever again.

I had expected all souls to be incorporeal, like the ghosts in the human fairytales I'd read. Though I'd seen a few as we had made our way through the castle, I'd also noticed the figures who were as solid as me, clad in clothes and jewelry. I was not sure how I knew these figures were not gods or humans. It was a feeling when I gazed upon them—a slight prickle of my skin, a shivering within my intuition.

Sidero, solid as any living being, guided me from the throne room. I did not look back at the Under King. How horrible to know that he had seen the anguish I'd been unable to hide.

The doors closed behind us with a bone-rattling crash, spurring my feet to move faster.

"It is all right, Your Highness," Sidero said comfortingly.

"Please...do not call me that."

The soul blinked, their stride slowing to study me. "Do you prefer the title of princess?"

I was not sure how to answer them. The truth was, I loathed it as much as I loathed the nickname, *Lia*. Most often I was referred to as *my lady* within the castle as a sign of respect. Though all within King Typhon's inner circle were aware I had no title of my own.

We turned a sharp corner and climbed a wide set of dark stone stairs. Shafts of dim moonlight poured in from the high windows above. It was a surprise that we were climbing. I had assumed I would be taken to the dungeons. As we traveled through another winding hallway, lit with strange blue flames and dappled moonlight through the windows, I cleared my throat.

"Call me Oralia, please."

Sidero hesitated. Running an olive hand over the side of their head, shaved short in contrast to their long braid on the other, they nodded and stopped in front of a large double door.

"Oralia, then," they said with a kind smile, before turning the knob and gesturing to step inside and up another small set of stairs.

I could not stifle my soft gasp of surprise. The room was considerably smaller than my chambers at home, but part of me felt thankful for the lack of space. The high ceilings and vast expanse of my rooms in Aethera were empty and isolating. I'd always longed to be cocooned in smaller spaces like the family library, as though the furniture could provide me the comfort of another living being I craved.

Regardless of its small size, it was grand. The floor was made of sumptuous white marble with gray veins running through the stone like a complex river system. Three large, arching windows on the curved wall farthest from the door indicated I was in one of the towers at the back of the castle. Beneath one window, there was a large bench with a cushion built in, big enough for two people to sit comfortably facing one another.

To the left of the door was a medium-sized hearth with a fire—blue, like every other flame I'd seen so far—roaring inside. In front of it were two plush wingback chairs and a small couch made of dark green velvet that shimmered slightly in the light. Beside the fireplace was a towering bookshelf brimming with old texts. Across the room stood a sturdy dark wardrobe decorated with ornate carvings of leaves, wind, and stars delicately inlaid across the soft-looking wood.

I spied the bed. The frame was made of the same elaborately carved wood as the wardrobe. The bedclothes were the same dark green velvet as the couch and bench cushion. The pillows looked so plush that it took everything in my tired body not to run over and jump onto it.

"This was to be your mother's room," Sidero said unobtrusively, drawing together the thick, drapes over the windows.

Their words stopped me before I could lift a hand to caress the soft fabric of the couch.

How could I have forgotten that the Under King had planned to kidnap and murder my mother? It might have taken almost three hundred years...but he had finally achieved his goal, with her daughter instead. My blood ran cold. I was not sure what my face looked like, but Sidero turned from the last window, their brown eyes wide as they crossed the room.

"Oralia?" they asked softly. "What is it?"

No matter the kindness of this soul, I could not bring myself to speak. I had already revealed too much by asking them to call me by my name.

"I am sure you are tired. Perhaps it is time to prepare for bed," they continued, trying to lead me toward some sort of conversation.

But I was drowning beneath waves of guilt, dragged farther down by the darkness pulsing within my veins.

Sidero guided me toward a small door that led to the bathing chamber and, with a hand on my arm that made me jerk away, invited me in. They paused, deep-set eyes assessing for a moment before lighting a few lamps.

The marble flooring continued in here as well. There was a dark gray countertop against one wall with a large mirror above it. A large soaking tub, big enough for four, was already filled with steaming, fragrant water.

Sidero moved closer, gesturing to my clothes that were torn and dirty from not only my run through the forest but the altercation with the Under King. Leaves and twigs tangled in my hair and poked my scalp. But I shook my head at their silent offer, pulling at the fastenings before they could assist, letting the fabric fall to the floor as I wrapped my arms around my chest and stepped gingerly into the water.

I jumped and jerked my arm from their fingertips as they traced the burns left behind by Typhon. Their mouth was a tight line and there was a calculating look in their gaze. Each touch was a shock and left my chest tight and aching like a burning wound. I had craved this connection for so long, but I also feared it.

"May I assist you with washing your hair, or would you prefer to do it yourself?" they asked in a gentle voice.

"Myself, please," I choked.

It could have been minutes or hours later when I was tucked beneath the thick bedclothes of the four-poster. Sidero gave me a comforting smile before making their way toward the door. Despite the anxiety of what would come next and the dark magic within me that seemed even more present than before, my lids grew heavy and sleep pulled me under.

Sidero paused at the door, a small shaft of blueish light spilling into the room when they turned around to face me.

"May I give you some advice?" When I did not answer they pressed on. "Listen to your instincts, not the words of King Typhon that live in your mind. Those will always be poison."

Without another word, they closed the door behind themselves, plunging me into darkness.

CHAPTER

TEN

Renwick

I stood, rooted to the spot, as she left with Sidero through the double doors of the throne room. She had shied away from their offered arm. I could not help but wonder what that meant as I turned to face my inner circle. A flash of white caught my eye.

Bending down, I plucked the white leather gloves from the floor. The leather was worn and soft like a second skin. They had been used so thoroughly that I could tell she favored her left hand over her right from the way the fingertips were worn down and discolored. The cuffs were frayed, small threads broken free as though she had made a habit of picking at them.

How long had she worn these gloves? How long had she itched to remove them?

"What do you see when you look at her, Horace?" I asked, turning the gloves over.

Horace heaved a sigh, and though I did not look at him, I knew he had folded his arms across his chest and dipped his chin in contemplation. It was the same stance he took when in judgment with the souls.

"I see a god who is broken," he intoned, choosing his words wisely. "I see someone who is haunted by the actions of others, actions she believes are her own. And despite it all, I see someone who cares and feels deeply."

"And her fear?" I clarified, turning to look at him.

His ruby-flecked eyes did not waver as they stared into mine. "I see the fear. But it is the fear that gives her the strength to continue on. Her power, however, rages within her, desperate for a way out. It lives beside her fierce loyalty, her compassion, and her capacity to love. She is strong, Ren, stronger than she believes."

"Deep feeling and strength," I intoned, revolted by the dead quality of my voice.

She feared me more than Typhon, more than her power even. That was clear by the look on her face when she pressed her bare hand to my cheek. The princess was willing to face her inner darkness if it meant destroying me. Horace did not respond, merely raising a brow in question.

Beside him, Dimitri shifted, placing a hand over the pommel of his sword. "I saw a god who ran out of choices long before she ever set foot across the boundary line of Aethera."

Humming my agreement, I carefully tucked her gloves away for safekeeping, should she ever request them.

I see a tyrant. A monster.

The words echoed in my mind as if she had pulled them directly from my blackened heart. Before me had stood the personification of my failure, and yet I had treated her as if she was one of Typhon's soldiers.

"What do you plan to do with her, Your Grace?" Mecrucio asked.

Sighing, I ran a hand down my face. Before tonight, if I had ever gotten the chance to remove her from Aethera, I was certain we would have helped each other. Perhaps I would have sent her through the veil to the human realm to start again with new gods and new lands. But now, with her powers being what they were, such a solution was impossible—Typhon would no doubt track her down and drag her back if I did so.

"She has the magic of both life and death within her."

Dimitri's face colored with shock. "Life and death? Creation *and* destruction?"

Nodding, I ran a hand across my face again, a weariness that rarely touched me sliding over my shoulders to join the weight of my cloak.

"I am almost certain," I said before reliving the afternoon's events with my inner circle.

Dimitri's hand gripped tightly around the pommel of his sword, jaw tensing with each word while I described the apple tree that had turned to ash beneath her fingertips. Horace's eyes flicked back and forth, obviously considering what he had seen within the soul of the god when she had stood before him.

"Then what will you do with her?" Horace asked when I fell silent.

Slowly, I turned toward the door, my footsteps echoing in the quiet hall.

"I will teach her how to control her power with the hope that in doing so, she might decide not to destroy us all."

The light was steadily growing through the windows of the library, spilling across the slate-gray floors and the thick green and silver rug beneath my feet. The warmth of the fire beat against the side of my face and arm, but it was never warm enough.

No, these days—these centuries—I was always too cold.

But I kept my back to the window, unable to watch the muted light fill the sky that was never fully clear of the mist that hung about the kingdom, giving the drab and dreary world an ominous quality. But from the moment my father created this place, at first as a way to enslave human souls for his means, it had always been that way.

We must give them a purpose, son. This is the haven for those burdened by time.

A prison, more like, and I its reluctant warden.

Instead, my focus was set on the circlet of gold in my hands. I ran my thumb across one of the emerald leaves inlaid within the delicate crown. The last time I had seen that flash of gold in the light had been almost three centuries ago. Tonight, it had fallen as I'd compelled the princess into sleep and I had not been able to resist sliding it into the inner lining of my tunic.

"Your Grace." Sidero's voice cut through my contemplations.

Hanging my head, I sighed before straightening, neck cracking. "Yes."

They circled the chair until they were beside me, their hands clasped in front of their simple gray robes. Disquiet rolled off them in waves.

Sidero had been a member of my court for close to a thousand years. In life, they'd been a warrior, talented on the battlefield, and yet, a reluctant executioner. Their existence haunted them even while they lived, and in death, it haunted them still. Horace had sent

Sidero to the caves for the first century to atone for their crimes. It had not taken long for them to find their way out again.

Souls always found the exit when the tumult within their hearts calmed.

Over time, I learned to rely on Sidero as surely as I did on the other members of my inner circle. They were intuitive, observant, and whisper quiet. The perfect spy.

"What is it?"

"Oralia is sleeping," they answered, taking the seat across from me when I offered it with a wave of my hand, "but fitfully."

"Oralia?"

Sid nodded, their back straight with tension. "When I addressed her as *Your Highness*, then *princess,* I thought she might be sick. She asked me instead to call her by her given name."

Cold dread trickled down the back of my neck, but Sidero pushed forward, unable to see the effect their words wrought upon me.

"She is haunted, Your Grace. I know that look. I have seen it in my mirror."

Blowing out a breath, I shifted forward until my elbows rested on my thighs. Peregrine's crown dangled off my index finger as my brows drew together.

"There is another thing, Your Grace..." They trailed off. The discomfort in the room grew so thick I looked up at them, recognizing a fury on their face I had seen in their memories of the battlefield.

"She has burns on her arms."

With two fingertips, Sidero illustrated the winding path of the burns, a pattern I was all too familiar with. Typhon's light had wrapped around her flesh—scorching it. And though I had witnessed the crime myself from my place high within the trees, ice rippled through my veins. My pulse pounded within my ears for the briefest of moments before quieting once more.

I blinked, giving my head an experimental shake.

"Do they need healing?" It was a foolish question, gods healed on their own unless the wound was dealt with kratus resin.

Sidero's lips curled down as they considered, hands clasping easily in front of them before they shook their head. "She needs time, Your Grace. His mark is all over her, and I do not mean merely on her body. It is there upon her soul. And..." They paused, eyeing me warily.

"What?" I hedged, opening my palm in encouragement to speak freely.

With a sigh, they pushed to their feet, gray robes swirling around their ankles. "I believe you are the only one who can help her heal it."

CHAPTER

ELEVEN

Oralia

After only a few hours, I woke up with a start, sitting straight up in bed.

The rhythm of my heart beat wildly in my ears as I took in the room. The blue embers of the fire had burned out in the night and a soft gray glow emanated from behind the thick drapes. Shoving the heavy bedclothes off, I padded to the window and pulled back the fabric with a sigh before settling heavily on the plush emerald cushion.

Dawn was breaking over the horizon. Drawing my knees up to my chest, I slid the chemise Sidero had offered me last night over my feet to protect them from the chill. With my forehead pressed to the window, I searched for some semblance of calm.

A thin mist hung in the sky, softening the light coming in from the east. For a moment, I thought it must be the lack of true sunlight that sucked all the color from the grounds, before realizing the swaying grasses I observed from the window were truly a muted brown. They almost completely encircled a mottled blue lake that was perhaps too wide to comfortably swim across.

There in the field, figures drifted through waving grasses and rolling mist. Some wandered without purpose, while others stood motionless, staring at the calm water of the lake. On the occasions that I'd thought of Infernis, I'd always assumed that the souls were kept in cells that doubled as torture chambers.

I did not know, nor could I understand, how this kingdom worked and what it meant to be an eternal soul.

A light tap on the door shook me from my thoughts, and I drew my knees closer to my chest.

"It is Sidero, my lady."

With a deep breath, I pulled my forehead from the window, smoothing the fabric over my legs. "Come in."

Sidero eased into the room, a soft smile playing around their lips. Last night, I had not noticed the soft gray robes they wore curling around their sandaled feet, much like the mist the Under King had pulled me through. In their hand, they balanced a large tray laden with fruits, various kinds of cheese, meats, and a steaming pot of what I hoped was tea.

"How did you sleep?" they asked, sliding the tray onto a small table beside the window bench and then clasping their hands in front of them.

With a sigh, I rested the back of my head against the glass.

"I slept for a few hours," I said, my attention straying back to the low mist.

Sidero nodded, waiting another moment to see if I would say any more before they crossed to the large wardrobe. From within, they drew out a thick black robe with silver leaves embroidered along the sleeves and collar and offered it to me.

Smiling at them gratefully, I pushed to my feet, sliding my arms through the thick fabric before drawing it closed around myself.

"Are you ready for the ascension?" they asked, careful not to touch my skin as they passed me the heavy mug.

I blinked, my head tilting to the side. "Ascension?"

Sidero frowned, gliding toward the window to touch their fingertips to the glass. "Watch."

A small *"Oh"* escaped through my lips as, far in the distance, bright lights shot into the sky, piercing the thick mist that hung low. They were stars catapulting through the air, one after another, leaving streaks of darkness in their wake.

Rushing back to the bench, I placed my hands against the glass, trying to follow their progress. "What was that?"

"That is the ascension," Sidero said, a smile clear in their voice that fell when I turned with furrowed brows. "You truly do not know?"

I shook my head.

Sidero sighed, shaking their head and stepping closer to me. "When a soul's journey toward healing has come to an end, they ascend. His Grace sends their energy back into the world to begin again."

Fear prickled on the back of my neck. Did they have any choice in this? How did one decide that a soul's time had *come to an end?*

"Today sixteen souls ascended," Sidero said, their eyes trailing over my face.

I swiped a hand over it to hide whatever judgment might be lingering there. It was clear that, to them, this was not a horrifying occasion, but I could not help but wonder if the souls who ascended felt differently. Did they give their consent to relinquish their magic back to the world or was it taken from them?

"Oralia... May I ask..." Sidero's eyes lingered on the black cres-cent-shaped scars I'd revealed by rubbing my face. "Those scars, are they from a daemoni?"

Biting the inside of my cheek, I weighed the cost of revealing the truth. If I said no, I would have to think of another story to tell, and I did not think that well on my feet.

I replied slowly, instead, weighing each word. "Yes, I was bitten when I was very young."

They blinked. "And you survived?"

I made a small noise of confirmation, tugging the sleeves of my dressing gown over the scars.

"That is...impressive. Most do not."

My teeth dug into my lower lip, trying to remember all I knew of the creatures. "They do not?"

Sidero shook their head, their black braid falling over their shoul-der. "Daemoni teeth carry venom. Most die within minutes of being bitten, even gods, though it takes longer...hours or days perhaps." When I opened my mouth, they hastened to add, "You must be very strong to have survived."

I tensed, tracing my finger over one of the leaves embroidered into the cuff of the dressing gown, trying not to look too interested in fear they would realize I knew almost nothing about the creatures. The feeling of the fabric was so odd beneath my hands, though. The delicate thread of the gown, the cool glass of the window, the rough wood beneath the cushion, each sensation was something new.

"I do not know about strong," I mumbled, thinking I would con-sider myself out of control instead. A wildfire in danger of destroying everything in its path.

The memory was as clear as if it had only been the night before.

Typhon carrying me through the forest, pointing out the various plants and trees as we walked, speaking of the human settlement to the west and what lay within the mist to the east. The portals to the human realm and other worlds we could not imagine. Preparing me for a life as his heir.

I'd squirmed out of his grasp eventually, wanting to run free through the forest. I could remember that thought—wanting to feel the grass beneath my toes, the branches against my fingertips. Then the snarling, barreling movement through the wide ferns, and the riotous sound of paws against the ground that shook me to my very core. The black eyes of the three-headed, dog-like daemoni as it sprang, two of its mouths closing over both my wrists.

Pain and blood followed. Acid coursed in my veins, lightning ripped through my bones. My screams echoed for miles as King Typhon carried me through the forest, back to the castle. I was lost in nightmares of dark caves and twilight skies. A cool cloth brushed against my forehead, and a kind female I did not recognize with midnight eyes sat at my bedside, her gentle voice whispering, *Wake up, Oralia.*

My wrists were bandaged for weeks, and the wounds had taken months to heal. But only a few days after the first of the bandages were removed, I grabbed one of my nursemaids in fear during a storm and watched them die before my eyes. They shriveled into ash.

I had become a murderer before I'd even known how to read. More died before we truly understood, and they covered my hands in gloves never to be removed. But I never forgot the look of revulsion on Typhon's face. He never held me again, never comforted me when I cried. His gaze was a constant reminder that I would always be a monster.

"It changed you," Sidero guessed.

I nodded.

I did not look at them. I did not want to see the expression of disgust on their face—the same revulsion Typhon had shown.

Sidero sighed, but the sigh did not sound heavy. "Come. I'll get you dressed and ready for the day. Perhaps I could show you some of the kingdom if you wish. Below us is Pyralis, which is easy enough for us to get to. Others, however..." They trailed off for a moment, thick brows drawing together. "Others, like Isthil, I do not believe are safe to show you. Their magic is too volatile."

I thought about all I had seen this morning, the ascension and the waving grasses and wandering souls, before making a small noise of agreement.

"The fields then..." I said, gesturing to the window. "I think I'd like to see the fields."

CHAPTER

TWELVE

Oralia

Though it had been early autumn in Aethera, Infernis was in the midst of winter.

Sidero offered me an embroidered gown of deep purple silk before braiding my hair around the crown of my head and sliding a thick black cloak around my shoulders. We stepped out into the hazy light. The mist curled around our feet as we walked down the steps and onto the blackened earth.

"Did you have many assistants or guards when you were at home?" Sidero asked, hands clasped behind their back, scanning the horizon before us. In some ways, they looked like Drystan with his constant awareness of our surroundings, always on the lookout for potential threats.

Pursing my lips, I gave an apathetic sort of shrug to hide my discomfort. "No, not many. I spent most of my time on my own or else in the company of a single guard."

Sidero led us on a path curving around the side of the castle. The path before us blurred before my eyes. I shook my head, trying to clear my vision.

To the left of the castle, northwest of where we walked, lay what looked to be a towering maze. But instead of bright green hedges like the ones that dotted the palace at home, this one was made of huge, gnarled brown branches as if a single tree had created the shape.

Their brown eyes flicked to me and then back to the way ahead. "That sounds lonely."

"It is... lonely. Though Drystan, my guard, has never been fearful of me. Nor Caston, King Typhon's heir, whenever he is at home."

My breath hitched. Would Caston be fearful of me now? The sound of his wailing was fresh in my ears. The image of Drystan's terrified expression burned into the back of my lids.

"Are they kind to you?" Sidero asked, breaking me from my spinning thoughts. Their eyes flicked to my arms and then ahead once more.

At their question, my panic ebbed slightly, a soft smile tugging at my cheeks. Though I had only been gone one night, I missed them both terribly.

"More than words can say. Caston is truly...*good*. I do not see him often, busy as he is with his battalion and learning what it means to be a prince. But he has always seen the best in others, even when they do not see it in themselves."

Sidero hummed their understanding.

I sighed as the mottled grayish-brown field I'd seen from my window came into view. The grasses in the field were high, almost to my waist, swaying lightly in a phantom wind. The mist hung a bit lower and thicker here, forcing a shiver down my spine. Farther off, I could just make out a blackened, rocky field, strange figures flickering in and out of view.

"And Drystan?" Sidero prompted.

I did not answer. It felt like too much to reveal that Drystan was more of a father to me than anyone else had ever been.

"What is this place?" I asked instead.

Sidero sighed, and the sound was ancient with its weariness. "This is the Field of Pyralis. It is where the souls who must grieve for what they lost in their life are sent."

I paused before the high grasses, wishing I could run my hand over the soft, feathery tips. A spark of anguish tugged deep within my chest the closer we came. One soul slowly moved past, her body as solid as mine and Sidero's. Her thick black hair was drawn over one shoulder. Tears streaming down her ocher cheeks caught the muted light through the mist.

"The magic imbued into the grasses pulls grief to the surface," Sidero explained. "No one can hide from it here."

The soul was wringing her hands together, mumbling softly to herself before her breath hitched and a shuddering gasp tore from her chest. I rocked on my toes, my heart pulling painfully as I witnessed her heartbreak. That feeling was all too familiar to me, and her grief called to my own.

"Should we help her?" I asked, gesturing to the soul.

Sidero frowned, shaking their head so their braid bobbed against their chest. "No, we cannot help. It is not our place."

My eyes widened. A noise of disgust flew up my throat. "So we must sit by and observe as she loses herself to this pain?"

"Yes, that is the way of things, Oralia." Their voice was soft, almost chiding.

The soul let out another retching sob, knuckles bleached against her robes as she doubled over, falling to her knees until the top of her head was barely visible above the reeds. I rocked forward onto the tips of my toes. How many times had I wished for someone to intervene, to be there with me in that hollow, empty chamber of my grief?

I scoffed at Sidero. "Just because it is the way of things does not mean it is right."

Before they could answer, I set off through the grasses toward the soul. I was unsure of what sort of comfort I could provide, but I could at the very least be a witness to her pain.

The soul was swaying in the breeze, head shaking from side to side as I stopped beside her. Sidero called my name, but their voice was lost in the mist.

I shushed her in soft tones, awkwardness curling around me as I second-guessed my rash choice to barrel through the high grasses. But at my voice, she gazed up, eyes widening, before wrapping her arms around my waist, pressing her face to my chest.

A jolt of panic raced down my spine before dying away at her tight embrace. Slowly, I raised my arms to tentatively wrap around her shoulders, feeling a little awkward at first from the touch.

"It is all right," I whispered, before rocking us both beneath the heavy weight of her grief.

The mist curled around us as she continued to weep. I rubbed soothing circles into her back and murmured words of comfort, trying to emulate all I had wished for when I felt as she did now.

"It is all right," I repeated, the words spilling like water, my own hope fusing into them. Time passed as she cried. Our tears mingled at our feet into the dry grasses below until she drew away, her thick black lashes sparkling in the muted light.

"Thank you, my lady," she rasped as if we had shared centuries of our grief within this field.

Before I could stop her, she grabbed my hand, pressing her lips to the back of it. I tried to wrench my hand away, but she held fast. A soft whimper of horror echoed in the space between us. As her skin touched mine, she stiffened. Dark magic uncoiled from where it rested inside my heart.

I stared open-mouthed in terror as her eyes turned hazy. A heartbeat passed, then another, before a wide, joyful smile pulled up the corners of her thin lips.

"Autumn," she whispered with wonder. "I'd almost forgotten."

She blinked, a few stray tears falling over her round cheeks before she pressed another kiss to the back of my hand.

"Thank you, *thank you.*"

The wind shifted around us. A tall, regal man I thought I'd seen in the throne room last night appeared within the circle of mist. Though I could sense he was a god, he wore robes similar to the souls around him, except the thick gray fabric was embroidered with tiny feathers around the collar and cuffs.

"Lana," he greeted in a deep, comforting rumble. "Are you ready?"

The soul, Lana, gazed up at him. I helped her to her feet, and though I made to let go, she refused, gripping my hand tightly. My throat ached at the contact.

"What is your name, my lady?" she asked. The peace settling on her features was such a stark contrast to when I'd first seen her. She was almost unrecognizable.

I dipped my head. "Oralia."

She smiled, squeezing my hand once. "Thank you for that gift." Finally, she turned to the god. "I am ready, Horace."

The god's ruby-flecked eyes flickered to me, then back, before extending a roughened palm. Lana released my hand and grasped his. They vanished, leaving behind only the thick mist and waving grasses.

"Come, my lady. We should go," Sidero said softly, placing a hand on my arm to lead me from the field.

But I was rooted to the spot, unable to comprehend what I had witnessed. She had not screamed in pain, nor had she shriveled to ash. Of course, just like Sidero, she was already dead, but she'd looked...joyful. There had been a wonder and elation in her expression that I could not understand.

Autumn, she'd said. *I'd almost forgotten.*

She had called it a gift, grateful for my touch.

"Where did they go? Who was that?" I looked over my shoulder at the spot they had vanished from.

Sidero looked toward the castle, then back at me.

"That was Horace. He is the one who leads the souls to where they must reside. That soul has finished with their time in Pyralis and is moving onto the next place."

"Next?"

I allowed them to tug me from the field and lead me back the way we came. There was a tension around their mouth, a stiffness to their shoulders as they set a brisk pace.

"Souls are complex, as we were in life. When new souls arrive, Horace weighs their hearts in a sense. He is able to look within them and see what makes them who they are. Their joys, their sorrow, their pain, their crimes, and good deeds. All of it. Then he sends most to where they can best heal from their mortal life. To recover, I suppose."

I nodded, but then Sidero stopped in a swirl of gray, turning to me.

"That soul should have been in Pyralis for perhaps half a century," they said quickly, the tension that had ebbed as they'd spoken returning.

Icy dread trickled through my chest. "And...how long were they there instead?"

Sidero sighed, their eyes flicking between the field and the castle. "A month."

CHAPTER
THIRTEEN

Renwick

A muscle ticked in my temple.

I stood before one of the large windows in the library, cataloging Sidero's and *her* progress across the grounds, making their way back from Pyralis. Anger should have been coursing through me as if it were a living thing, but there was nothing. I did not know why I even bothered to reach for those feelings anymore, only that she brought memories of them to the surface.

Today, I wanted to speak to her, to apologize for how we started and try to find some common ground. But unfortunately, that would have to wait.

The air shifted as the door swung open, the smell of the mist and apples swirling into the room. The scent of her only stoked my rage higher. With a grind of my heel, I turned to face them, noting the cautious way Sidero appraised me as they entered beside the princess who was striding into the room with some approximation of ease that did nothing to hide the apprehension in her eyes.

"Leave us," I said to Sidero, who stilled in panic before looking toward her with a protective air. "That is an order from your king."

Sidero bowed their head once, then retreated with a whisper of fabric and the shutting of the door.

"What did you do?"

Her face blanched, all the rosy color from her cheeks draining into the soft curve of her lips.

"I—I do not know what you mean," she answered.

"Let us see... You strolled into Pyralis and destroyed a soul's natural path toward peace."

Her eyes flickered with emotion, but she was holding herself back, even as her shadows flickered across her frame.

She took a deep breath, the magic receding, and though her voice was quiet, it hinted at the power roiling beneath her skin. "That soul was hurting, they were grieving—"

"That is what they are supposed to do," I interrupted, pointing toward the window. "That is what that place is for. They are there to grieve, to face their suffering, to learn from it, and grow strong enough to move forward with it."

She shook her head, turning away from me and pulling the black ribbon around her throat free. With trembling fingers, she snatched the thick fabric of her cloak from her shoulders. "I could not merely stand by and—"

"You believe that to be within your right?" I gave a hollow laugh. "Who do you think you are?"

Purple fabric swirled as she spun to face me, green eyes alight with fury, familiar shadows coiled tight around her arms. She gripped the back of the chair, her fingers flexing against it, punctuating every word. "Someone who cannot sit idly by and watch another suffer."

My chest gave a hollow throb, and I resisted the urge to rub my hand against it.

Her implication rang in the silence, along with the strange feeling echoing through my veins. In two long strides, I was in front of her, the chair the only barrier between us. I stared down into her face. Full lips drawn tight, nostrils flaring. Was my scent driving her fury to new heights? Hers was sweet, bright with sunshine and her ire— almost intoxicating.

"Ah, yes." I circled the chair until I stood before her. Slowly, I reached with two fingers to gesture to the spot on her arm where her burns lay. "At least, according to you, I do not pretend to be anything other than a monster."

There was something about the way the light of the blue flame played across her brow. I could have sworn she shuddered before I dropped my hand. But then she reared back and a slap rang across my face. A shimmer of pain blossomed over my cheek like a caress before immediately fading away.

The silence in the room grew as the slap echoed across the stone walls and old texts. I had not been struck in such a way—not for over a millennia. The princess was shaking, chest heaving with breaths that swirled across my face and moved back the loose tendrils of my hair that had escaped from the ribbon I'd tied it back with. And then, once more, her face dropped, the scent of her fear acrid in the air.

"I— *Burning Suns*," she gasped, falling to her knees, fingers splayed wide on the floor. "I apologize, Your Grace."

Her head hung submissively low, and my stomach turned. It was as if Typhon was here with us in this room, his hand at her neck.

I could hear my mother's cautious voice in my head from millennia before. *A fire roars until it consumes everything, including itself.*

With a deep breath to prepare myself, I reached for her. It took me two tries before I wrapped my hands around her upper arms and encouraged her to rise. An ache within my chest echoed at the contact, my power thrumming in my veins, and then sighing when she shrank from me, her eyes squeezing shut.

Perhaps she was like me—unable to bear another's touch. So, I resisted the urge to try again. To stoke the flames of her anger further, to see if the shell of my soul might shudder once more.

But she kept her head low, avoiding my gaze, her hands worrying the cuffs of her gown.

"What did you do to make that soul move on?" My voice revealed no hint of the strange change that was already fading beneath my skin.

Her chest trembled with her breath. "I do not know..."

It sounded like the truth, especially when she pressed her fingertips to her eyelids and a soft sigh slipped through her lips.

"What do you mean you do not know?"

"I comforted her and she..." Her voice faltered, her face losing the last of the color that had danced across her cheeks. "She ascended," she finished lamely.

The words were flat as they slithered through the air. The use of the term *"ascended"* was wrong. Lana had not ascended, merely moved to the next step on her path toward ascension. Even then, each soul could choose whether to remain or to send their magic back to the earth to begin again.

"I will find out what you did. You would do better to tell me now so we can try to—"

"And you would do better to care for your people," she interrupted, a flush rushing back into her cheeks.

The suggestion that I did not care for my people froze the blood in my veins, even as satisfaction roared at the small spark within her.

"And you do?" I asked in the dead voice I hated, wanting that spark within her to catch fire, to melt this ice within my soul. "You have been here for less than a day, and you think you understand this kingdom and its people? Their needs?" I stepped closer until her ragged breaths ghosted against my lips. "Tell me, Princess, should I wade into the fields of Pyralis and cry with each soul there? Should I venture into the caves of Tylith to fight the shadows of their pasts for them?"

She stared at me, wide-eyed. Her lips parted as if she wanted to speak but could not find the words. And I wanted to crawl into her very skin to destroy us both from the inside out.

"Or shall I drown myself in the lake of Mirvath and weep until it overflows with my tears? How do you suggest I continue to protect my people from your king if I do so?"

Her lips parted to reply, but instead, I thrust the small roll of parchment that Thorne had intercepted this morning forward. "How shall I ensure that all are protected and watched over if I am weeping and screaming and beating my brow? It is not strength to do such things; it is weakness."

She did not respond, but she did not look away either. With a trembling hand, she took the parchment from me, unrolling it to read the words I now had memorized:

Come home, Lia, and all will be forgiven.

"He is not certain you are here of your own free will," I muttered, withdrawing my own letter from the Golden King full of promises of my people's destruction if she was not returned unharmed. "He is only certain that you are here and that you cannot return."

"So take me back," she argued, even as her fist trembled around the page.

I raised my brows. "And what will happen the moment you are back within his clutches, hm? Do you truly believe you will be welcomed home with open arms? That *all will be forgiven?*"

Blood drained from her cheeks. Her bottom lip trembled while her eyes danced over the page once more. She took one step back, then another. My lips parted to speak, to somehow break through the frost, to soften our exchange and offer to teach her how to control her power.

But from the set of her mouth, it was clear there would be no arguing with her. The true horror was pacing the boundary of the kingdom, trying to find his way through the mist, and yet she was terrified of me. But no matter her fear, I would not allow her to be sacrificed for the sake of Typhon's power and goals.

"If you must believe it is a monster who shelters you... a monster who will not return you to him, regardless of his threats, then so be it."

I stepped closer, fighting the urge to reach out with my magic—to show her that we were kindred in our power. That she did not need to fear me as she did him. I tried to find the words to offer my knowledge, to provide her the tools to protect herself.

Slowly, so slowly, she placed her hand on my chest and moved me away before drawing up her cloak and folding it over her arm.

"I have had enough of monsters for an eternity."

CHAPTER
FOURTEEN

Renwick

Muscles burned as I ducked, rolling over on my back to spring to my feet, dead grass clinging to the sweat on my bare back. The heavy axe in my hand sailed through the air, but before it could meet its target a clang of steel rang through the mist.

"You are distracted," Dimitri chided. He thrust his sword forward to unseat my weapon, providing himself space to defend.

I did not respond, swinging the axe once around my wrist before slicing it in an arc. But Dimitri was already there, stopping it from hitting its mark across his chest.

"Is it her?" he asked, his expression alight with confusion. "Is she the one who has you so absorbed?"

Pivoting, I drew up the handle of my weapon in time to block his strike. Though we were settled far away from the castle in the flat plains between the maze and tunnels, my shadows spiderwebbed outward to protect my back.

"It is not *she* who distracts me," I answered. "It is what she does."

Dimitri's bushy white brows rose with surprise. With a jerk, he withdrew the blade from the handle of my axe, flipping it once before sheathing it back in its scabbard. "And what is that?"

Biting the inside of my cheek, I wiped the blade on the side of my trousers. "Defies the natural order of things."

Dimitri's booming laugh echoed off the nearby caves, reverberating back until it sounded like ten gods howling at my statement. He leaned forward, hands on his knees, taking deep gasps of air before wiping the back of his hand over his eyes.

"Perhaps, Your Grace, that is exactly what you need," he rumbled after he composed himself, moving to the place where he'd thrown aside his cloak and helmet. His white hair shone in the weak sun, braided close to his skull for comfort when donning his helmet.

"What I need is for her not to meddle in things that do not concern her. She forced a soul forward today, Dimitri."

And she brought about some...change within me. I thought it had abated but I was almost certain it was still there, simmering, growing beneath the surface. As if the magic swimming within her soul was calling to me. After she left, I'd thought for hours about how I could not seem to resist getting close to her. How I'd had to ball my hands into fists to stop myself from touching her.

He stopped laughing then, pausing in the act of refastening his cloak. "How could she have done such a thing?"

It was a question I had been asking myself for hours.

"I do not know, and neither, it seems, does she."

Dimitri gave a frustrated grunt as he finished fastening on his cloak. "She is powerful."

I did not respond, pulling my tunic over my head before tucking it into my trousers and refastening my weapons. The sweat beading on my brow stopped me from donning my cloak and instead, I threw it over my shoulder.

"You do not think so?" Dimitri hedged, watching me closely. "Can you not sense it?"

Cracking my neck, I turned, scanning the entrance to the tunnels. A cold wind blew from deep within the bowels of the cavern, swirling around my face, phantom screams curling through the air to echo in my mind.

"I sense it." I paused, adjusting my baldric. "As much as I sense her anger and fear."

"Then perhaps you are both well matched. Perhaps she will bring that old fire out in you as well."

I did not respond. Instead, I turned away from him, making my way toward the tunnels and ignoring the part of me that agreed with him.

She was not my enemy, regardless of whether she believed it. I had to make her see that—force her to understand—but every time I opened my mouth, the words came out all wrong.

"Will you still try to teach her?" Dimitri called, already faint.

Rolling my neck, I threw the cloak over my shoulders and fastened it quickly. I tried to find comfort in the way its heaviness mimicked the old weight of my wings.

"Or will you kill each other in righteous consternation before you have the chance to find common ground?" he added louder.

The shadow of the smile in his voice sent my feet faster into the dark caves ahead.

"Please." The voice was half-strangled, garbled by the thick fountain of blood spilling through his lips as my axe struck home. Cold sweat prickled on my forehead and down the back of my neck.

The cry for mercy twisted the hollow parts of me. I squeezed my eyes shut as if that might block out the sound. In moments like this, deep within the tunnels, the ghost of my father's hand was heavy on my shoulder, his cold breath tickling my ear.

You must punish those who do wrong. It is an eye for an eye, my son. How else will they find ascension if they do not pay for their crimes with their blood?

With a jerk, I pulled my axe from the soul's sternum. He slumped over his metal chair, chin resting heavily against his chest, not even a breath escaping. It would take a few minutes for him to reanimate— for the wounds to heal and the blood to replenish.

I spent the time with my back pressed against the cool stone wall, damp from the moisture leaking in through the cracks. The skin on the back of my hands itched with drying blood. With a deep sigh, I slid down to the floor, pressing the tips of my fingers to the space between my brows.

The drip of blood slowly faded, replaced by the rhythmic sound of breath. It was a relief and a penance to know that I could not do any lasting damage.

My mind flicked to the fight this afternoon. She had moved a soul forward half a century before it was destined to. In the span of two minutes, she achieved what it took Horace centuries to accomplish. I had *felt* the moment the soul had changed. Even from my place inside the castle, it had been palpable—the taste of lightness in the air, a shimmering joy.

And she also knew the dangers of Typhon. It had been clear in her eyes when she asked to be returned. Something twisted inside my chest, and suddenly, I could not stand that she did not know the truth about her real father.

"You appear troubled, sovereign," Gren rasped.

He was fully healed, seated straight in the chair as if waiting to be served dinner, hands lightly clasped in his lap. A tangle of thick reddish-gold hair curled around his ears. The smattering of freckles across his nose was a strange childlike juxtaposition to the rottenness of his soul.

"When am I not troubled?"

This time Gren laughed good-naturedly. It was a sound that froze my blood. How could he laugh so easily and experience such pain?

"I would not know, Your Grace. Sometimes..." He trailed off, gaze sliding away from mine, head tipping from one side to the other in contemplation.

"Speak freely, Gren," I murmured.

"Sometimes, I think this place is more a punishment for you than for us."

Heavily, I pushed myself to my feet, nodding in agreement. He was right, and he did not need to tell me how he knew. It was in the cry of anguish I released as my axe found its home. For centuries, he'd watch me as I retched after. How, before I had lost those last pieces of my soul, there had been times that he would wake with my hand pressed over his heart, silently begging for forgiveness.

"What is the one thing you miss most, Gren?" I asked after a long stretch of silence.

He stared at me, mouth agape in surprise. "The... The sky, Your Grace."

I nodded, rolling the axe over my wrist before catching it again. A small spark flared behind his eyes. There was a light there I had never seen before, a glimmer that looked like hope.

"And what does it feel like to suffer day after day, century after century, millennia after millennia, and know you might never see the sky again?"

Gren took a deep, rumbling breath, his lids drooping shut. Something slunk into the room, curling like a cat between our ankles. I thought it might be the beginning of his remorse.

"It feels like justice, sovereign. *Justice.*"

CHAPTER
FIFTEEN

Oralia

I t was quiet in my chamber. The only sound was the crackling blue flames in the hearth and the slide of parchment between my fingers.

The tray of food Sidero brought me for dinner sat mostly untouched on the small table in front of the fire. The roasted meats and vegetables taunted me, but I could not find the appetite. Instead, I continued to stare at the familiar handwriting, the plea, and the threat that tangled in the words.

Come home, Lia, and all will be forgiven.

But there would be punishment, and though I knew it would be lessened if I returned, I could not find it in myself to go. It was not the thought of punishment that had my feet rooted to this land. Even if the Under King let me go, I was afraid of what I would face if I returned home, and the destruction I might bring with me with my power so unchecked.

How could I look Caston in the face after what I had taken from him? Knowing I had ripped from him the person that he loved most on this earth? I knew only a small slice of what it meant to lose someone who you felt so strongly for.

My own cowardice made my head swim. So, instead, I thought of the soul from this afternoon.

Autumn, I'd almost forgotten.

There was a part of me that was elated at seeing what my touch had given her. The peaceful, almost joyful expression on her face. But then I remembered the Under King's words, his insistence that I had disrupted that soul's natural path, and my elation shriveled into ash.

Once again, I destroyed everything I touched.

Then there was the way I had spoken to him—had struck him. I could not understand it. In Aethera, if I had spoken that way to the king, my shadows flaring around me, his power would have silenced me in an instant. Yet this king had merely stared at me, and, for all the coldness in his expression, I'd thought for a moment something shifted behind his eyes.

A soft knock echoed on the door, and I jumped, crumpling the paper in my hand. I smoothed down the front of my skirts and crossed to the door.

"Yes?" I asked, placing my hand against the knob.

"May I come in?"

I froze, my sweaty palm slipping against the metal before I dropped my hand to my side, swallowing the biting words tripping off the tip of my tongue. A low sigh slipped through the door.

"I promise, I am not here to accuse you of anything more," he continued, correctly reading my silence.

Steeling myself, I took a deep breath, opened the door, and immediately turned away. I crossed to the couch I'd been sitting on before his arrival before turning to face him, surprised to find him hesitating in the doorway.

Slowly, he made his way inside, hands clasped behind his back. He approached one of the wingback chairs and placed a hand atop it. My skin itched as we stared at each other, and I reached for the cuffs of my now non-existent gloves before my hands fell uselessly at my sides.

His dark blue eyes tracked the movement, and I tensed, waiting for some sort of comment, but none came. His hair was down, soft and shiny. It tucked around his ears and curled down to his collarbones.

The Under King stepped around the chair, carrying a small leather book in his hand. "I have something for you."

The tone of his voice was so gentle I would not have known it was him if I had not seen his mouth move—soft and yet still with that edge of ice. For a moment, he was not the wrathful king of Infernis who had plotted to murder my mother, nor my kidnapper, but merely a god floundering beneath awkwardness and tension.

When there were only a few feet between us, he extended the book toward me. The leather was soft, as was the binding. As I took it, our fingertips brushed. Fire zinged up my arm, and heat coiled in my heart so fiercely I had to stifle a whimper. The book flopped open—a few of the pages became visible, revealing slanted yet neat handwriting.

"This... It was your..." He cleared his throat. "Your father's journal."

Dread trickled down my spine, blotting out the heat. It was clear from the way he said *father* that he did not mean Typhon. For all the ice in my veins, however, my cheeks flushed with ire.

I took a deep breath, forcing the words out slowly instead of in a rush. "What makes you think I'd like to read the thoughts of the man who raped my mother?"

The Under King took a sudden step back. But his eyes were glassy, as though he was feeling some deep emotion that skittered away as quickly as it had come, like leaves on the wind.

It looked a lot like fleeting grief.

"That is what you think?" His voice was cold, edged in steel.

"It is not what I think... It is what I know." I threw the journal onto the small table in front of the fire. The room blurred as I swallowed back the angry tears. I would not cry in front of this god again, no matter what weapons he wielded at me.

"No," he said, face smoothing into that expressionless mask. "It is what you have been told by a god who lies more often than he tells the truth."

A small laugh huffed its way past my lips. I turned away, trying to escape the circle of his presence that drew me in. Even now, despite wanting nothing more than to throw him bodily from the room, my dark power purred in response to his proximity, tempting me to come closer.

"King Typhon—" I started, but he cut across me.

"He is not your father." The Under King punctuated each word, a dangerous violence dripping from each syllable.

"*I know!*" I cried in frustration, my hands rising before falling with a slap against my skirts.

Silence rippled through the room as we stared at each other, my chest heaving. There it was again, a strange shift behind his eyes, the briefest moment where the muscles of his face relaxed before hardening once more.

"I have known since he first placed my mother's crown upon my head that he was not my father," I said in a cold, quiet voice. "Just as I have known that the man who sired me did so through an act of violence."

She had been accosted on a journey home by one of his own men, and that rogue god had planted a seed within her womb that would one day become me.

The Under King grabbed the journal from where I'd thrown it and crossed the space between us slowly, giving me time to retreat. When I did not, he grabbed one of my hands with a small tremble in his fingertips. I tried to pull away, but he tightened his grip and at the contact, the magic deep within me pulsed. Darkness curled itself around my heart with satisfaction while heat flared through my cheeks. *Burning Suns,* his touch had such power.

Firmly, he pressed the journal into my palm, dipping his head until we were eye to eye.

"You may be surprised what you learn if you allow yourself to look past the lies of a man who has locked you inside a gilded cage for the last two hundred and fifty years out of fear."

His soft tone baffled me as much as his words did, though I did not answer. I merely stared at him in bewilderment. With his other hand, he curled my fingers around the book before releasing me. The brief contact was too much, too overwhelming. Heat thrummed through my limbs. I had to take a breath, to stifle the way my body responded to his touch.

"I will wait for you to come to me once you have read the truth."

The banging of the door echoed once more into silence. I stood staring at the journal in my hand. Part of me wanted to look, wanted to explore the words on the page and understand what truths they might offer me...

But a louder part reminded me that this god was my enemy. He was the reckoning, the god of death. The Under King blighted the crops of the human realm in order to build his armies. He murdered and conspired, and no matter his soft words or pleas, I could not trust him.

I considered throwing the journal into the fire, but I could not bring myself to do it. There was something akin to betrayal in my heart at the thought. So, I crossed to the large bookshelf across the room and slid it between two larger tomes.

I will wait for you to come to me...

With a scoff, I turned toward the bed and undressed quickly.

I doubted that day would ever come.

CHAPTER

SIXTEEN

Oralia

*O*ralia...

I sat straight up in bed, blinking in the darkness. A cold sweat clung to my forehead, the back of my neck, and my palms. My stomach lurched.

Oralia... A soft, familiar voice floated through the door. I jumped, sharp pain lancing through my neck as I turned my head.

Oralia... the voice repeated, more insistent. With a small amount of hesitation, I drew back the covers, shivering when my bare feet hit the cold marble floor.

Oralia... The fourth time, I was moving, not caring that my chemise was too thin or that I wore no shoes. I knew that voice. I'd heard it in my dreams so many times before. Knew the sweetness of it, the care and love that infused the syllables of my name. I did not bother to shut the door or grab one of the torches from the wall. My feet carried me soundlessly through the halls until I reached the landing at the top of the wide curving staircase.

Oralia! She was more insistent now, panicked. The thin fabric fluttered around my ankles as I flew down the stairs, through the antechamber, and out the double doors into the night. The air was biting, immediately clawing at my cheeks. Jagged rocks and tough dead grasses dug into the soles of my feet, forcing me to stumble. But I pushed on as the panic in her voice increased.

My mind was blank, singularly focused on getting to her—to my mother, who somehow miraculously lived. The mist curled around my wrists and ankles as if trying to stop me. Shaking it off, I ducked beneath a gnarled branch.

It was so dark that I could barely see. The torches from the castle were enough illumination to lay out a meager path. I did not question how I knew where to go, only that I trusted my mother would guide me. My chest ached with the thumping of my heart, and I swallowed back the scream that wanted to tear itself from my throat.

Mother! I wanted to cry out. *I'm here!*

I stopped and looked around. To my right was Pyralis. I could tell by the swaying grasses and glittering water of the lake. To my left was the maze, ominous in its stillness. Dread curled near the pit of my stomach. I did not know where to go next or how to find her.

Oralia! she screamed.

I pivoted, running toward the sound in the maze. I had to get there. I had to find her. If only I could—

My feet skidded on the dead grass, arms flying out to steady myself.

A figure was crawling from the darkness ahead. Though perhaps crawling was not the right word. Whatever it was, it was tall with a strange angular gait that appeared not to be of this world. Fear froze my feet to the spot as it made its way through the mist. The only thing truly visible in the gloom were its bright red irises.

Oralia! my mother called, but it was a scream of pain.

I wanted to race off toward her cries once more, but the creature turned its head toward me. I was frozen by fear. My knees buckled.

There, barely illuminated by the faint light of the moon, stood a daemoni, so different from the one that had bitten me as a child. Its black body was humanoid in nature with a torso, shoulders, and hips. But the limbs were long and segmented, almost insect-like. Its arms, longer than its legs, jutted out and forward to rest on the grass before it. The thing stood at least ten feet tall. A faint rasping noise rumbled from its chest.

Yet it was the face that frightened me most of all. Its head was bone white and perfectly round. The eyes were large ovals that took over half its face with bright red irises. The mouth was wide and gaping, stretching from one side of its face to the other. Two rows of bright, daggered teeth glinted menacingly in the dark as it opened its maw and my mother's voice came out.

"Oralia!"

I took a step back, then another, but its bloody eyes were trained on me.

Foolishly, I put my hands up as it rushed me, fruitlessly attempting to pull my power to the surface. A scream tore through my lips at the same moment that the beast gave out an ear-shattering shriek. The sound was nails dragging over porcelain, bones breaking, death.

The daemoni's front legs reared. The sharp tip of its arm was going to crash down upon me. Before I could so much as scream again, there was a rippling of darkness, the silver-tipped blade of an axe arced through the air, connecting with the belly of the daemoni. The monster gave another soul-rattling shriek, falling to the side before its sharp limb could crash down upon me.

"*Run*," the Under King commanded. His hair was wild around his face, and his blade gleamed in the weak light.

I did not need to be told again. I twisted, pushing myself as fast as I could. The roaring cry of the daemoni was barely audible over my ragged breaths and the frantic beating of my heart as I crashed through the grasses of Pyralis. Pain lanced through my side, but I kept moving, veering around the wandering souls who wept softly in the dim light.

I burst from the field into an expanse of flat, black earth, a vibration rattling my teeth as if I had jumped over a boundary line. The daemoni's screeching clung to me like a nightmare. I thought I might also have heard the snarl of a god, the rumbling echo of an axe once again hitting its mark. The hollow ache in my chest intensified, and suddenly, I found there was no more air left to breathe. My feet slowed as the gravel grew larger and sharper. I tried to pick my way through as carefully as I could.

An imposing figure stood before me, his gold-flecked skin glittering in the sun that did not shine here.

"Papa," I cried, the name I had used for him from my childhood slipping through my lips, reaching out my arms. "*Help.*"

But King Typhon merely stared with a look of revulsion on his face, arms tucked behind his back beneath his wings. He turned on one grinding heel and vanished. I whimpered, hands clutching my empty chest. The world grew hazy as I tried to blink away the sudden wetness in my eyes. My knees buckled, pain slicing through my skin as they hit the sharp stones below.

Then a boy stood in his place, barely on the brink of manhood. Straw-yellow hair waved around his face. His eyes were wide as he stumbled back. Piece by piece, his body broke into hunks of cinder and ashes that were carried away by the wind.

I stretched out my hand as I screamed out for someone, anyone to help me, to comfort, to hold, to reassure me that I was not the monster that lived inside my soul.

Hands circled my waist as I tried to fight them. I did not know these arms or recognize the scent of ash and sandalwood that washed over my face.

A deep voice soothed me with a quiet hush. "I have you."

I pushed at the chest that drew closer as I felt an arm slide beneath my knees. My fingernails clawed at the black tunic while I sobbed.

"I have you," the voice said again.

Slowly, my panic receded. I wrapped my arms over the wide shoulders of the figure, drawing myself closer until my cheek brushed against rough stubble. Tears scalded my eyes, and I pressed my face against the exposed skin of his throat where the fabric was torn away by my frantic hands.

"Shh," he crooned.

My body went limp, and the last thing I heard before darkness swirled up to take me was that same dark voice whispering:

"You are not alone."

Soft light glowed against my lids, and I groaned, reaching for a pillow to pull over my face. My head throbbed, eyes swollen and sore. With a sigh, I slowly blinked through the dryness and shoved myself into a seated position. I could not remember how I had gotten back to my chambers, could not remember anything except for the crushing feeling of loneliness, the sight of Typhon turning away from me.

"You may be the luckiest god I have ever met." A cold voice sliced through the silence, his words accented by the thud of glass hitting wood.

Suddenly, I was very much awake, gaping at the Under King where he sat on the bench below the window. His head rested back against the glass as if he belonged there.

"Get out," I rasped, pointing toward the door.

He raised a smooth black brow at me before lazily drawing the glass back to his mouth and taking a deep drink of the amber liquid inside. "Why would you go into the grounds in the middle of the night?"

I stiffened, clenching the sheets before pushing them off and making my way to my feet. The last thing I wanted was to fight with him while sitting in bed.

His gaze trailed over me from my mussed hair to my torn chemise and down to my bare feet then up again. The look was not one of desire. It was calculation—like he was a predator sizing up his prey.

"I heard something," I said.

A hollow laugh rumbled through his chest, like the coming of a storm. He placed his glass on the small side table and rubbed his palms together. His black hair was loose, tumbling over his face to curl around his shoulders. Smears of dirt and a thick, dark substance covered his cheekbones and forehead. The tunic he wore was ripped around his shoulders as if someone had clawed at him.

"Were you never taught of the ways of daemoni?" he asked with a shake of his head as though he already knew the answer.

I stared at him in disbelief. "Why would I be educated in the creatures you created other than to be taught that they are dangerous and lurk at our borders?"

Though that was not entirely the truth. I had spent years in the library of the palace researching the monsters, only to find little to no information about them. Only that Ren had created them searching for more power, and that they infested every corner of the world.

His nostrils flared, and a muscle in his jaw feathered. It was the most emotion I'd seen in him since arriving here.

"That thing would have killed you. You were reckless," he said as if I had not spoken.

And then all too quickly, the frost returned, all the tension leaving his face. Even his hands relaxed at his side. I shivered at the change.

"I suppose it was a good thing that Typhon locked you in your golden cage," he mused without emotion. "You would not have survived to prime if he had not."

I gritted my teeth as he rose from the bench and stalked closer. My shoulders trembled.

"Powerless, weak, incapable of defending yourself."

My lips parted, exhaustion and rage circling my ribs, dark tendrils pooling at the tips of my fingers.

"Tell me why," he commanded. "Why would you be so thoughtless?"

A cord snapped inside of me, and I lost the tenuous hold I had on control.

"It was my mother," I answered, the words catching in my throat. "My mother. Calling for me, screaming for me."

He was right in front of me as the words left my lips. I slammed my hands into his chest, pushing him back. Last night had opened some old wound deep within my soul, a hurt I mistakenly thought had knitted closed with time.

"So spare me your hurtful words," I spat through my teeth,

slapping my palms once more to his chest. My head swam with the exertion. My shoulders slumped as my knees failed, hitting the hard floor with a *thump*, the next words barely audible. "I already have all the hurt that I can bear."

CHAPTER
SEVENTEEN

Renwick

For a long moment, I merely stared at the god heaped upon the ground in a ball of anger and shame. The posture looked so familiar that for a moment my hand spasmed at my side as if it had a mind of its own.

She had cried into my skin last night, her body shaking with her silent sobs. I did not know what made me bundle her into my arms. Perhaps it had been the fragile way she'd looked, reaching out for ghosts of those who were not there, pleading with them. The way she clutched at her chest as if she could tear out her own heart.

That was the thing about Isthil, the clearing she stumbled into, it had been created for souls who needed to be alone. I'd never known what would happen if a living soul passed beyond the borders, but it had treated her like any other. She had been crying out as I approached, her hands grasping at air, breath choked in her lungs.

Papa, please, she'd begged. Broken and lonely and afraid, pleading for someone to comfort her in her moment of terror.

She'd fought me when I'd lifted her, of course, tearing at my tunic before pressing herself as close as she could like her next breath depended on it. As if I were the oxygen she so desperately needed. I'd soothed her in uncertain words, the connection of our skin pulsing within my chest, forgotten emotions of anguish forcing me to cling to her just as tightly. I had touched her more in the last few days than I had touched anyone in the last two and a half centuries. But the moment I'd compelled her to sleep and slipped her between the sheets of the bed, ice crept back through the dark.

My hand twitched again toward her mass of strawberry-blonde waves, but I clenched it into a fist.

"Some daemoni, like the one you saw last night, use their prey's deepest fears and desires as a lure," I said, trying to find my footing once more. "They feed upon souls, consuming their small bit of magic. Once it had finished with you, it would have turned to those nearby in Pyralis."

Her gaze was resolutely fixed on the ground, and I wondered if she was even listening.

"It crossed the wards because you answered its call, but you were not strong enough to destroy it. Not yet, but I—"

"Leave," she cut me off.

My hands clenched into fists. I had done it all wrong again. I had wanted to tell her that though she felt powerless and out of control, she did not have to be so. I wanted to tell her that I could teach her, train her. That with me, she could be unstoppable.

With me?

The thought drew me up short, a daydream of us side by side, our power protecting this kingdom, her warmth bringing light into this world—into my world. I shook my head. Why would she ever want that?

I left as she commanded. When the door clicked shut behind me, I pressed my back against it, rubbing a hand over my forehead and grimacing as black blood flaked beneath my fingertips.

"Ren," Dimitri called, appearing around the corner of the hallway with his helmet under his arm.

I pushed off the door, feet like stone as I met him halfway down the corridor. He appeared as tired as I felt, with purplish bags under his eyes and a tightness around his mouth that told me he'd been clenching his jaw.

"Horace gave us clearance to speak with the soul from yesterday," he said without preamble.

Nodding, I rolled my shoulders back. Good. This was good. If I could speak to the soul, I could better understand what powers the princess possessed. "Where is the soul now?"

Dimitri's gaze was assessing, the way a general would a soldier. He reached out and brushed a bit of the blood from my forehead. I slapped his wrist away. A prickle of nausea crawled across my skin, shame squirming through my soul.

"Stop it."

He dipped his head in apology. For over a thousand years, we had exchanged simple touches as gestures of friendship, and sometimes, he found himself lost in those old days. Forgetting that the man who stood before him now might as well be a stranger.

"What happened? You are covered in daemoni blood."

I shrugged and turned to walk down the hall to my chambers.

"This is about Oralia, is it not?" He fell into step easily beside me. "I can smell her on you."

Without breaking my stride, I looked at him and lifted a questioning brow.

"What?" He shrugged. "I can."

I scoffed, shaking my head. "A daemoni called out to her last night, luring her toward the tunnels."

"*Great Mothers*," Dimitri cursed under his breath. "Is she all right?"

I nodded, more than a little frustrated with his lack of annoyance that she put the entire kingdom at risk.

"You are angry." He hefted his helmet up a little higher, gripping the curved edge of the black steel. His voice softened. "She did not know, Ren. You cannot fault her for that."

I did not answer. Of course she did not know. Last night, she could have been destroyed by a daemoni, and when I'd seen her there, standing before it all I could think was: *not her*.

Pushing open the door of my chambers, I pulled off my tunic and threw the tattered piece of fabric into the roaring hearth of the small sitting room. I tugged at the latch of my baldric where it hung around my waist. My sword and axe clattered to the floor as I passed through the doors of my bedroom.

"Sidero told me she was bitten by a daemoni when she was younger." Dimitri raised his voice. "It was you that unleashed it upon them, Ren. I remember."

My hands stilled before the doors of my wardrobe. Images flashed into my mind of that night. Her screams, the scent of blood.

Slowly, I opened the wardrobe and chose the first tunic my fingers fell upon. Without answering, I drew it over my head and pulled my hair from the collar. Then I grabbed a pair of trousers, shucking mine off unceremoniously along with my boots before pulling the clean pair on.

"Do you think she gained power from the bite? Is that where that power originates?"

I looked at Dimitri after splashing some water on my face. He was standing on the threshold of my bedroom, his hand resting characteristically on the pommel of his sword.

At first, it had been a surprise to even learn that she'd survived it. I'd been sneaking into Aethera in my other form to observe Typhon and his plans before I had caught sight of her again.

For all my spying on the Golden King, however, I'd never once heard that she had power beyond the ability to make things grow. Even then, I did not quite understand it. Typhon kept her secrets well protected.

"Anything living she touches dies," Dimitri said, repeating my words from that night, his voice heavy with implication. "Turns to ash right in front of her."

Frost coated my tongue.

Quickly, I tucked my tunic into my trousers before pulling on my boots and grabbing a new cloak. The old one had been ripped from me by the daemoni and no doubt lay beside the corpse near the entrance of the tunnels, waiting to be burned.

"Can you not imagine how difficult her life has been?" he pressed.

I grabbed up the baldric, fastening it and the weapons around my chest before throwing the heavy cloak around my shoulders. But Dimitri would not let me pass. His feet were planted wide, taking up as much space as possible. There was a hard look in his eye—the look of a man who could squeeze water from stone.

"Do you not think you should show her at least an ounce of understanding? Of mercy? The only comfort she's known has been in the kindness of her guard and pseudo-brother who was almost never present. Her whole life she has been neglected—treated as tainted. She is the one thing that Typhon fears aside from you."

Placing a hand on his shoulder, I dug my heel into the back of his leg, right above his knee. He faltered, tipping to the side and allowing me just enough space to pass. But before I could get to the door, his voice rang out through the silence.

"Because of you."

CHAPTER
EIGHTEEN

Renwick

Silence fell the moment we stepped into Rathyra.

The small, town-like dwelling created by my father count-less millennia ago was not as nice as I would have liked, though the souls that resided here did not appear to mind. Or, at the very least, they never complained.

The city was a series of small gray buildings, interconnected like a spider web. Since souls did not need to eat or sleep, the buildings were mainly used to gather, tell stories, or rest. Occasionally, they liked to create, whether it was to paint, sew, or even hone metal. I tried to ensure, through Horace and Thorne, that they always had what they needed.

But I was not naïve enough to believe it was a pleasant existence. No matter how I tried to change it, nothing ever took hold. It was drab, without feeling or color, and often as quiet as the grave when I passed through. Though perhaps that had more to do with me than with Infernis itself.

As one, the souls spilled out from doorways and large courtyards and dropped to a knee, pressing their hands firmly to their hearts, their eyes downcast. I could smell their fear and tried to ignore the way they skittered back if I came too close. Instead, I tilted my chin up, casting my gaze forward. These were beings who had already suffered so much, and yet they trembled in the face of their king. Each soul in Rathyra had been through unending trials to heal their hearts and minds. They resided here, continuing to heal, before they were ready for their ascension.

Dimitri walked silently beside me, displeasure rolling off him in waves. I'd said nothing to him in response to his monologue, and I could tell his silence was merely an intermission in what would undoubtedly be a very long night.

We arrived at the small courtyard where Horace waited. Beside him stood a female soul with hands clasped in front of her, black hair braided over her shoulder with the hood of her robes pushed back from her forehead. But it was not her hair or the clothes I focused on, nor the way she stood comfortably beside Horace as if he were an old friend.

No, the soul was *glowing*. Peace radiated from her in waves, illuminating her from the inside out. When she caught sight of me, she swept to one knee, pressing a fervent hand over her heart as she bowed her head.

"Hello, Lana."

Her eyes flicked up to me in surprise. But of course I knew this soul. I knew all the souls who came into our land, though I chose not to directly interact with them until the ascension to make their existence as peaceful as possible. This one I had seen when she'd stepped off the boat and fallen, weeping, into Thorne's arms.

"It is an honor to be in your presence once more, Your Grace," she said rising to her feet. "I am so very grateful to you and your queen."

I took a surprised step back. Dimitri huffed a laugh that he tried unsuccessfully to turn into a cough. The right corner of Horace's mouth twitched.

My jaw tightened. "She is not my queen."

Lana blinked at me, brows furrowing before nodding. "I apologize for the assumption, Your Grace. I meant nothing by it. As she is the princess of Aethera, I assumed..."

Sighing, I nodded, reminding myself that this soul would have no idea of the turmoil that existed between me and the princess. Of course she had recognized her name, even if she had not known her face.

With a tight smile, I gestured to a stone bench nearby. The courtyard was small and simple with a large circular patch of black earth in the middle that I assumed at one point had been meant for something to grow. But nothing ever grew here. It only withered and faded away.

She took the seat gracefully, pulling her robes around her to allow me room to sit as well, though I merely perched on the edge farthest from her.

"Would you mind telling me what happened yesterday?"

The curves of her lips softened, eyes turning to glass. "I was in Pyralis, Your Grace, where Lord Horace left me to face the grief of losing my life." She thought for a moment, hand running over her braid. "The king refused an annulment to my marriage as my husband requested...so he and his mistress took my life." Another pause, her straight black brows pulling together, head tipping to the side. "I was overcome with the pain of it—of losing my husband and my life in one fell swoop—when she appeared."

Lana's face took on that glowing quality once more, a soft smile tugging at the corners of her mouth.

"She comforted me, told me that what I felt would not destroy me, no matter how much I feared it. It was... It was what I needed, Your Grace. Someone there to help me shoulder the burden. Then, when I pulled back to thank her, I took her hand and..."

Her voice trailed off as did her gaze, staring at the small ring of dead earth at the center of the courtyard. Her hands opened, then closed, before she rubbed her palms together as though searching for that feeling again. I thought I could understand searching for such a thing. After I left the princess, I'd fought the urge to press my fingers to my chest to find that stirring inside my soul.

"Even as I lived, I'd forgotten the things I loved. My life revolved around him, his happiness, his needs. I had forgotten myself long before I came here."

"What happened when you touched her hands?" I prompted.

She took a deep breath before her face broke into a wide smile, and she turned back to me, tears clinging to her lashes. "I saw autumn, Your Grace. The orange and gold leaves. I could smell the change in the season, and it reminded me of who I was. And though I had lost so much, I was still me, and I was free."

Stars, that the princess had this power. When I looked at the woman beside me, I saw more than the typical soul. There was a confidence, a contentment inside of her that none of the others possessed. I did not understand how the princess could have done this. Neither, it seemed, did she.

"I owe Lady Oralia a great deal of gratitude, Your Grace," Lana continued after a moment, "and to you for allowing her to help me."

She took my hand then, giving it another squeeze before pressing her lips to the back of it.

Discomfort roiled in my gut, and I fought the urge to draw my hand back. I had not allowed the princess to do anything—quite the contrary. I had accused her of disrupting the natural path of a soul. But as I looked at this soul and at Horace, who was a few feet away and gave a tiny shrug of his shoulders, I could not see any sign of damage—not at all.

She had changed everything.

CHAPTER
NINETEEN

Oralia

I was not sure how long I sat there, but it was long enough that my knees ached and my body shivered from the cold marble as my gasps died. Instead, I sat limply and stared ahead without focus. Flashing images moved through my vision like lightning across the sky.

King Typhon turning from me.

Shadows exploding from my heart.

Bodies limp across a gilded table.

Fallen against a golden floor.

Blood.

And the quiet darkness rippling within me, begging for release.

How long until I lost control again? Even now, there was an itching beneath my skin, embers glowing and begging for the flames to be fanned.

"My lady," Sidero murmured, kneeling beside me on the floor. "Are you well?"

Mutely, I nodded, pushing myself to my feet. I ignored the hand Sidero offered, and they quickly withdrew it. I was relieved they did not press the matter. Instead, they headed into the bathing chamber to fill the tub.

My mind wandered back to that cursed place as I followed them. Shame heated my cheeks for all the mistakes I'd made as I stripped off my sodden chemise and stepped into the tub.

I did not often wonder what life would be like if I had not been bitten—if I had been allowed to grow with only the power of my mother singing through my veins. But I wondered now. I imagined that other life full of comfort, perhaps of friendship. Maybe even love. And the thought was bitter.

With my knees pulled tight to my chest, I wrapped my hands around my elbows, pressing my nails into my skin until my fingers shook. I had no memory of life before the bites, only that night and after. And since that night, I had felt nothing but abhorrence for what I had become.

And it was easy enough to see that reflected within the world around me.

Outside, the full light of day broke over the kingdom. Through the bathing chamber window, the mist grew thinner in the light, though the land remained a drab, gray expanse. Even from here, the souls wandering Pyralis were visible.

Once the water cooled, I pulled myself from the tub, wrapping the dressing gown tightly around myself. Sidero quietly ambled back into the bathing chamber to lean against the doorframe.

"Lana, the soul you helped, is quite well."

I jerked, fingers slipping on the tie before I tucked my arms around myself.

"I did not wreck everything?" I asked, my voice catching on the last word.

Slowly, Sidero shook their head, a kind smile pulling up one corner of their lips. "Not at all." They gestured to the bedchamber, and I followed, taking up my usual spot against the window. "She is settling in nicely at Rathyra. I believe the king is going to see her if he is not already there now."

Discomfort squirmed through me at the mention of the Under King. His face blazed into the forefront of my mind. Midnight blue eyes chipped with ice as he gestured with a pale hand. But then there was the swing of his axe, the desperate way his voice had rumbled through the darkness.

Run.

He saved me, though I suspected it was only to keep me alive until my death served his purpose. He must have also retrieved me from whatever sun-forsaken place I'd stumbled into, though I could not quite remember. I could only recall the suffocating feeling of emptiness in my chest, and the look on King Typhon's face. The pleading.

You are not alone, someone had said—I was sure of it.

Had it been the Under King? No. Impossible.

I cleared my throat after a beat too long. "I am glad to hear it. The Under King inferred I may have done some sort of damage..."

Sidero sighed in a way that communicated millennia of frustration before settling onto a nearby chair.

"His Grace is fiercely protective of those who reside within his kingdom." Their voice was careful, weighing each word.

I gave a small huff in response, crossing my arms over my chest. At this, Sidero gave the tiniest of grins. "You are more alike than you know. At least, from the little I have gotten to know of you."

Bristling at the comparison, I turned my attention to the window instead.

"You are both protective of others. You are both passionate."

My shoulders rounded in protectively toward my chest. I did not see that within myself—could not recognize the passion they were referring to. The way I had yelled at him, my voice reaching a pitch I was unsure I'd ever found before, could not be called *passion*. My anger had lashed out like a whip. I felt the sting of my palm against his face. No, that had not been passion. It had been recklessness.

The Under King had not lashed out in response. What did that say of him?

"I do not think the Under King feels at all, except for anger perhaps."

Sidero pursed their lips, shifting their braid over their shoulder and lowering to sit across from me on the bench.

"He has lost much in the last few centuries... I have known the king for close to a thousand years, and yet sometimes, I feel it is a stranger who stares back at me—hollow and cold. It is a look I only used to see when he emerged from the tunnels, but now he bears it unendingly."

My brows pulled together. I refused to feel the slice of borrowed pain that rippled through my chest. "The tunnels?"

Sidero shifted, unwinding their braid slowly to give themselves some time.

"Those who did evil in life—murderers and the like—are sent to the tunnels when they arrive. As king of this realm, Renwick was taught that he must help to orchestrate punishments to ensure they understood their crimes through suffering."

Nausea roiled in the pit of my stomach. "Why?"

"That is a question best left to the king," they answered, closing the discussion with the tense set of their jaw.

I did not press the issue, merely nodded and managed a smile as they excused themselves. I dressed in one of the gowns from the large wardrobe. This one was a deep indigo with tiny leaf embellishments across the collar. The sleeves hung elegantly off my shoulders before splitting at my elbows to keep my hands free.

For a long time, I stared into the blue flames of the hearth, trying to will the voice of King Typhon echoing inside my head to quiet. Instead, I shifted my thoughts to the Under King, who even now might be torturing countless souls within the tunnels. But somehow, thoughts of Typhon broke through.

I tried to reconcile his cold fury from the night I left with the one who cared deeply for his kingdom. But I could not make the two meet—vital pieces were missing between.

All I could see were the sharp planes of his face aglow in the light of the orbs that hung above the dining table, one large finger circling the rim of his glass like a hunter circling its prey. I thought I had seen exhaustion in his face, but now in my memory, he looked cold, his eyes like ice and words like fire.

Seeing as you killed your mother, Lia, I suppose we will never know.

Come home, Lia, and all will be forgiven.

CHAPTER
TWENTY

Renwick

Tell me what he is planning," I commanded, pressing the blade of my axe into his soft flesh.

Sunlight shimmered from his armor. His rasping cries echoed off the roughhewn walls of the tunnels. The Aetheran soldier had been found within the mist, clutching another message addressed to me.

I will find a way through and finish what I started. Return her unharmed.

"You have no i-idea what h-he is capable of." The soldier gave a painful hiccup as my axe sliced lightly through the taut skin of his shoulder where his arms were bound above his head.

As always inside the tunnels, I wrapped the cold pieces of my broken soul around me, sheltering me from the sight that in centuries past would have made my heart ache. This man was helping Typhon in his quest to retrieve the princess, to put her back in chains.

A hollow chuckle slipped through my lips. "I am more than aware what he is capable of. Tell me what he plans to do."

With a jerk against the metal of his restraints, he leaned back on his knees, the whites of his eyes bloodshot.

"I—" He gulped a deep lungful of air. "He has called in his armies from the farther territories. But he is h-holding off the attack until he knows for certain she will not return on her own."

I nodded, twisting the smooth wooden handle in my palm. "And the princess?"

The guard blinked dazedly at me.

"Oralia." Her name was fire on my tongue.

"I do not know," he answered quickly, his face paling at his incompetence. "H-he says only that she is crucial to the kingdom. A *weapon to be wielded.*"

It had been eight days since I'd last seen Oralia. Eight days of her words rattling in my mind. What she had said about her father, Zephyrus, violating Peregrine was unfathomable to me. But I could tell from her face that she believed the lies Typhon told her, and that realization had stoked my rage. The way she had crumbled at my harsh and thoughtless words was another blight of shame upon my soul. I had not been able to face her since. And all this time while I had been licking my wounds, Typhon had been planning his attack.

I was a fool.

The soft weeping of the human cut through my fury. "*Please.*" Tears tracked through the dirt on his cheeks, clean streaks of light brown skin peeking through the grime. "Y-you have no idea what I have done. The things he has made me do."

Even without Horace's powers, the crimes that weighed on his soul from his time in Aethera spoke as if they were present in this room. The shadows of his misdeeds curled around him until the weight was crushing him from the inside out.

"I know…" I knelt beside him, placing my axe on the ground.

Unintelligible words caught on the guilt dragging its way through his throat before he swallowed loudly. "Is it true that in death we atone for our wrongs?"

I nodded, a muscle jumping in my jaw. I was surprised that he knew. Most in Aethera believed the afterlife was one of endless servitude. A hollow pang echoed through my chest, so deep I pressed a hand to my heart. This was not empty grief… It was an echo of his agony and wish for forgiveness. And I could no longer see the soldier beneath me as an enemy. No, he was merely another pawn within Typhon's grasp, desperate for escape.

"It is true." I leaned closer, brushing the limp hair from his face before I could stop myself, fingertips tingling as if singed by the heat from his skin. "What is your name?"

Tears welled and he swallowed loudly. "J-Jesper… Jesper Grayson."

Taking a deep breath, I nodded, wrapping my hand around the hilt of the axe. Hope sparked within the silvery blue of his irises.

"Close your eyes, Jesper."

He nodded, and a sigh of relief slipped through his lips as he obeyed. The tension of mere moments ago melted from his shoulders, and he appeared softer, younger. He was merely a boy on the cusp of manhood with so much promise already destroyed by a god's greed.

I swung my axe and sent him painlessly into death.

"Jesper Grayson, your soul is set free from this mortal casing. Cast off your sorrow, for now is the time of reckoning. Infernis awaits you." For longer than I could say, I sat encased within the silence of his passing. My hand pressed over the boy's quiet heart. The weight of so many millennia crashed against my shoulders.

Through my magic, I sensed his soul begin its journey through the mist and toward the shore where Thorne would be waiting, welcoming him with open arms. Jesper would never see these tunnels again. All would see in his soul that he had already suffered enough.

I pushed myself to my feet and flicked my wrist. My shadows swallowed it whole as I turned to make my way into the thin morning mist.

Two figures skirted the space between Pyralis and the dead grasses of the castle ahead. The muscles of my chest clenched painfully, and yet I was unable to look away.

Stars, what was she doing to me?

Her hair was gathered in an intricate bun atop her head. A few tendrils of sunset waves escaped to frame the side of her face. The sapphire-blue gown draped off her shoulders, exposing the long line of her neck, and gathered around her waist. Whatever Sidero was telling her caused the princess some sort of discomfort. Her hands were laced in front of the full skirt of the gown, twisting together as the muscles around her mouth twitched and behind her...

Behind her, the dead grass moved as if caught in a windstorm. The yellowed and brittle blades lengthened, deepening in color until they were a rich, healthy green. Tiny, white, star-like flowers sprouted in her wake.

Infernis *bloomed*.

I crunched through the dead grass until I reached the softer blades. The sweet scent of blossoms and grass swirled to greet me. As I approached them, I heard the barest whisper of a soft song she was humming to herself, as if to comfort Sidero as they told her the tale of how they had died.

Reaching out, I closed my hand over her arm. She gasped, turning on the spot and wrenching it out of my grip. But angry words died on her lips as her gaze fell onto the lush flower-dotted grass at our feet.

"I... *Burning Suns*, I am so sorry," she cried, tripping over the words in her haste. "I am so sorry... I did not— I can..."

She dropped to her knees, hands outstretched. It took me a moment to understand what she meant to do, how she meant to kill the life she had just brought into this kingdom. Before her fingertips could touch the grass, I fell to my knees as well, grabbing her by the wrists and pulling them to my chest. A sweet floral smell wafted around her and ghosted across my face.

"No," I pleaded, squeezing her hands, her skin a flame against mine. Warmth slithered up my arms to settle in my chest. "Do not."

Creation, here within Infernis. Creation that did not wither and die mere seconds after sprouting. It was something I'd always wanted, always imagined, and she had brought it here. Her pulse fluttered in her neck as I slowly drew us both to our feet and then quickly dropped her hands, stepping away to give her space.

"Will you come with me?" I tried to soften my tone, to push a semblance of warmth through the cracks.

Behind her, Sidero stared at me as if I had grown two heads.

Oralia nodded mutely, clutching at the skirt of her gown before smoothing it. The patch of green grass was not overly large, but it was a small oasis in an endless desert, a single star in an unending obsidian sky.

It was beautiful.

Her breath was uneven as she followed me. No doubt my attempt at calming her had failed as everything I tried to do failed with her. But I did not want to look back—could not look back. Some small, foolish part of me feared if I looked, she would disappear.

Eventually, we passed the maze and entered through one of the tiny winding walkways into Rathyra. The souls darted from the doorways, eyes widening as they caught sight of her behind me. Unlike the oppressive silence that usually greeted me here, whispers curled around us. As one, they dropped to their knees, their hands pressed over their hearts, their eyes not respectfully lowered, but fixed upon her. Though I could sense their trepidation, there was also a new curiosity there.

I looked back at her. But she was not watching me, she was observing the way the souls appeared not only to bow for me, but for her. Their eyes flicked between us, but it was to her they returned. She made their features soften, a reverent wonder slackening their lips and widening their eyes.

We moved through the curving walkways and small alcoves, the whispering growing more distinct, a word repeated over and over: *lathira.* I stiffened, gaze flicking to her, again and again, to see if she understood. Though she heard it, her delicate brows pulled together in confusion. She quickened her pace until she was only slightly behind me, her hand moving for a moment before dropping it back to her side.

Had she meant to touch me?

"Where are we? Are these your barracks?" she asked, voice soft.

I slowed until we were side by side. At this, the surrounding souls murmured louder, their faces brightening with an emotion I could not quite understand.

"Barracks?" The quarters for my soldiers were far to the east, closer to the mist.

A flush stained her cheeks and her hands clenched in the skirts of her gown. "For...your soldiers."

I blinked, remembering that Typhon perpetuated a myth that I drafted every soul who entered Infernis into my army. "This is Rathyra, the City of Souls. Though some choose to protect the kingdom, mostly those who were warriors in life, they are not required to."

She pursed her lips as she examined my face, no doubt looking for any hint of a lie. But then her attention flicked over the crowd, across the looms, instruments, and various other implements nestled within the rooms we passed. She made a small noise in the back of her throat while her eyes drifted over the gray walls, the black rocks beneath our feet, and the drab buildings where the souls gathered and worked.

A confession slipped through my lips. "I know... It is not as I would have it either."

After a brief moment of silence, she turned her head, dark green eyes catching on my neck and jaw. "Did you kill him?"

"Who?" My hand flew to my throat, rubbing away the blood splattered there.

"The soldier Sidero said was found within the mists. The one you brought to the tunnels." Though her voice was soft, judgment dripped from each word.

Guilt curled in my chest at the image of the boy slumped against his chains. "I did."

She faced me fully, tension clinging to the corners of her mouth. "*Why?* Why kill them?" When I did not respond, she pushed on, red on her cheeks blossoming like a flower opening in the light of the sun. "Why must you lead with violence, with cruelty? Why do you torture the souls?"

"Because that is the way it is done," I replied and grimaced when I heard my father's voice leave my lips.

Loose tendrils of her hair swirled around her face as she shook her head and stepped closer. A slither of *something* writhed through my chest, responding to the shadows flaring from her chest and wrapping around her shoulders in her anger.

"Just because it is the way it has always been done does not mean that is how it should be. A wound heals and scars less with care, not through fresh blood."

Her words were sinking into my soul like fresh rain on the ground, forcing a shiver down my spine. Was there another way? When I had asked Gren, the soul I so often visited within the tunnels, what he missed most, remorse had taken root within his tainted soul. Even now, he was on his way toward the next step in his ascension.

We stared at each other, tension thick between us like the mist around our shoulders before she gestured for me to lead on. My skin pricked with her disappointment, the soft frown pulling at her lips sparking shame within the broken spaces of my chest. But I nodded, striding into the same small courtyard where I'd spoken with Horace and Lana, Oralia at my side.

I guided her to the small blackened pit of earth in the center. My palm burned as I placed a hand on her lower back to guide her forward. Before I could speak, a delighted cry came from a nearby group of souls, and I dropped my hand.

"Lady Oralia!" Lana pushed to her feet from where she knelt beside another familiar but dazed-looking soul. She ran toward us and dropped to her knees to kiss the hem of Oralia's gown. The princess's face flushed at the reverent gesture.

"Lana, you look well," she said in a warm tone, pulling the soul to her feet.

"And you, my lady," she replied with a dip of her head. "Please excuse my boldness. I was so overjoyed to see you."

At this, the princess took the soul's hands in hers, pressing a small kiss to the back of them, the way Lana had done with me. The instinctual gesture was shocking for one who had spent the majority of their existence without touch. Even more shocking was the idle wonder of what her lips would feel like against my skin. A small tendril of heat curled through my chest before dying away.

I fought the urge to press my fingertips to my heart as if I might pierce my flesh to capture the sensation.

"I am grateful to see you and so glad to know I did not hurt you," the princess answered.

Guilt clawed its way through my stomach. I was the reason she had been so worried, the reason she looked over this soul for injury.

Lana blinked at her in surprise before her attention shifted over the princess's shoulder to me in silent reprimand. I had the decency at least to drop my gaze to the ground and shove my hands into the pockets of my trousers.

"I am very well, my lady," the soul replied with another bow.

The crowd behind her murmured again, *lathira* slithering through the space. I bit the inside of my cheek, cutting off my frown before it could reach my face. The princess's shoulders stiffened with confusion.

"I apologize again for my rudeness. I was teaching Josette how to loom when you arrived."

From behind her, the soul knelt, hair like white spun gold, her eyes glassy and mouth slack. A thin bolt of material was clutched in her shaking fist. Josette had been in Rathyra longer than Lana, and yet for her, it might as well have been the first day. Souls like Josette took centuries, sometimes millennia to come back to themselves.

"Thank you for guiding her," I murmured.

Lana's brows furrowed, but she bowed her head, placing a hand over her heart. "It is an honor to help those who have drunk from the Athal, *myhn ardren*."

The princess turned to me as Lana moved back to the crowd, expression wide and searching. "What is the Athal?"

"It is a river that runs between the Tylith Mountains and Isthil. Those who drink from the river are wiped clean of their memories."

Questions were clear in her eyes, but she dipped her chin. "That sounds like a mercy."

"It is not one we take lightly." I gestured to the small patch of dirt we had been standing beside. "Could you... Would you try?" I cleared my throat, trying again for some kindness—to extend another branch of trust.

"Would you try to use your power here, my lady?"

CHAPTER
TWENTY-ONE

Oralia

I stared at the Under King, surprise forcing my lips apart.

Perhaps it was the request he was making or the earnest way he appeared to care so deeply for his people regardless of their obvious fear of him. His eyes had widened at my accusations of torture before ultimately softening in surrender, and some of the ice in his expression chipped away. Or perhaps it was the way he'd said "my lady" after only addressing me as "princess" for the entire time I'd been here.

This was not the wrathful king I thought I knew.

But I did not call attention to it, just as I did not question him about the word floating through the crowd of souls. Instead, I nodded and turned to the circle of blackened earth.

"I do not know what will happen," I warned, not daring to touch my fingers to the soil. "I do not believe I can make life out of nothing. Was there something here once?"

He shrugged as he rested a hand over the strap of his baldric. "I do not believe so... When I inherited Infernis from my father, there was nothing here."

I nodded. It would not hurt to try. Perhaps there was something here once, but I struggled to wrap my mind around the idea of so many eons that even he could not remember perfectly.

The old melody I could never quite recall floated up through my chest and out of my soul while I focused on the patch of earth ringed in dark gray rocks. My lips moved around the unfamiliar language.

In my peripheral vision, the Under King stiffened, his jaw tensing. But I had no attention to spare for why he was gazing at me like a god witnessing the sunrise for the first time. I focused on the patch of earth. Slowly, a small sapling with soft green oval leaves pushed through the soil, which had turned a deep brown. My magic sang through my veins. I clenched my hands against the itching in my palms, the dark power aching to strike until it was a fire beneath my skin.

The sapling grew taller, the leaves lengthening and softening to a light sage. The stem thickened; branches multiplied. Tiny, round blossoms dripped from the bark until the tree towered over us.

The tree grew, and the itching intensified beneath my skin, darkness bubbling through my veins—desperate for escape. The light and dark were battling inside of me, tearing me in two. My arms jerked. The song faltered while I fought the urge to place my hand against the trunk. A soft rumble of power thundered as if the curse within my body would bleed from my ears, my eyes, my nose.

And then two calloused hands covered mine. His touch was soft despite their rough exterior. It was soothing like a balm over an aching wound, or water over a raging fire. I did not need to look at him to recognize his soft black shadows threading through our fingers, wrapping around me to soothe the aching, broken parts of my soul.

He alone could understand the destruction roiling inside of me. But I did not meet his astonished gaze. Nor did I look at the souls murmuring excitedly behind our backs. Instead, I poured my magic into the tree growing in front of us. The trunk widened, deepening in color, gnarled roots tangled in the dirt before sliding deep beneath the earth. Finally, my song ended, and I stumbled back a step, panting.

"An olive tree..." he observed, one of his thumbs running across my knuckles.

My belly swooped, and I drew my hands away. When I looked up, it was to find him staring at me with a strange wonder in his eyes. His shoulders shook as he took a deep breath before he dropped his hand and ran it through his hair.

"Seems fitting..." I answered with a soft chuckle.

The Under King's dark eyes shone in the weak light that spilled in from atop the walls of the courtyard. One of his hands pressed over his heart in an identical gesture to the souls as he dipped his head.

"Thank you, Oralia."

My name sounded both foreign and reverent on his tongue.

By the time I was back in my chambers, I was reeling.

I might have said *you are welcome.* Perhaps I had said something else. The surprise of my name falling from his lips had been exponentially greater than him calling me *my lady.* Yet both were overshadowed by the sensation of his thumb brushing against my knuckles that forced an ache deep within my heart.

The Under King guided me back through Rathyra, through the humming crowd of souls all expressing their gratitude for the new life within their home. They inched significantly closer to their king than they had on our arrival. I could have sworn on more than one occasion I'd felt the heat of his palm against my lower back, guiding me through the jostling crowd, but whenever I looked over, his hand was always at his side.

I tried to understand why my stomach swooped at the contact, why I struggled to catch my breath. And, most importantly, why my cheeks flushed as I thought of the way he'd looked at me and the soothing feeling of his hands over mine. That dark power had wanted to destroy the magic I'd wrought, but his touch had quelled the urge.

It is not him, I told myself repeatedly. *It is only the touch.*

Sidero had been waiting, and we had said nothing as we made our way back up to my rooms while the Under King strode off to a different part of the castle. I settled into what was steadily becoming my favorite spot—the cushioned bench nestled into one of the windows—and gazed down on the new patch of bright green grass between the castle and Pyralis.

"Oralia," Sidero murmured, holding out a cool, damp cloth, "is everything all right?"

"Thank you," I breathed, taking it to dab at the overheated skin of my neck.

Slowly, they sat on the other side of the bench, searching my face before the corner of their mouth tugged into a small smile.

Oh, yes, I had not answered them.

"I am fine. Merely overwhelmed," I replied, gesturing to the patch of grass beneath the window.

Sidero nodded, smoothing their robes over their knees and appearing content to allow me to flounder in silence.

I sat with my head pressed against the window, watching as the small diffused light of the sun dipped below the horizon. I could not help but wonder if everything I had been taught was a lie. The image of the souls in Rathyra floated unbidden into my mind: the fear on their faces as they looked at their king. That fear was familiar. I had felt it myself when I'd first looked upon him, but now? Perhaps it was merely a trick, a way to lull me into a false sense of security. But the way his face had looked as he'd commented on the state of the city... The elation in his eyes as I'd made something grow...

The god who had knelt beside the olive tree was not the same god I had been taught to fear.

I pulled my gaze from the window. "Sidero..."

They looked up too, their eyes also having been trained on the patch of grass. "Yes, my lady?"

"Is the king someone to be feared?"

Sidero's brows pulled together for a moment, searching my face. Their heavy hands smoothed over their robes once more as they thought. "He is a god to be feared, but not for the reasons you may think."

I blinked at them, brows furrowing.

"He has lost so much and therefore has little to lose. His people, his kingdom, are the only things he has left. He would do anything to protect them. That makes him dangerous to those who would threaten them."

My swallow was loud in my dry throat. I thought of the conflict

I had brought to his borders. The countless gilded soldiers who had attempted their way through the mist. The message continued to circle through my mind:

Come home, Lia, and all will be forgiven.

I was sure my opportunity to come home willingly was long gone. And part of me wondered if Typhon would try to retrieve me if he could break through the mist. Even now, I felt the ticking of a clock, counting down the seconds until I was back in his grasp, back in that golden castle. And if Ren was a danger to those who threatened his kingdom, then that made him a danger to me.

A gentle smile played around the corner of Sidero's mouth as though they could hear the words I could not say aloud. "Your power comes from this realm, Oralia. You are a part of this kingdom even if you deny its call."

We stared at each other, the rest of the thought hanging unsaid between us.

He would do anything to protect you.

I looked back out the window at the misty grounds below, searching for a change in topic. Heat licked at my neck, snaking up my cheeks at the thought of the Under King protecting me—at the memory of his rumbling growl that night with the daemoni and his command to run.

"What does lathira mean?" I asked.

Sidero's mouth tensed as they thought. Their words were slow, careful as their hands tangled together in front of them. "It is an old word harkening back to one of the very first languages of this world."

Silence followed, their eyes growing distant and brows drawing together.

I leaned forward. "Yes, but what does it mean?"

They bit the inside of their cheek, taking a deep breath before sighing and fixing me with an unwavering stare.

"It means 'queen.'"

I was not sure how long I stood in front of the bookshelf, staring at the thin journal that I had pressed between two large leather-bound tomes. Long enough that the light had darkened in the sky and the fire had roared to life in the hearth.

The truth.

What was the truth? Because the god I had been taught to fear and hate was not the god I saw within the city of souls. That god had been soft-spoken and looked upon his kingdom with so much dissatisfaction at its gray walls and dead grasses. Whose eyes had been filled with gratitude for Lana and concern for the soul they'd spoken of briefly.

"Oralia?" Sidero asked.

The clatter of a tray on wood told me they had brought in my supper, but I did not look away from the bookshelf.

"What would you do, if you were me?" I murmured, tracing the spine of the leather journal before drawing it from the shelf.

Light footsteps echoed through the room before they stood beside me, looking over my shoulder. "I would read, my lady. Free yourself from the prison of the lies you have been told."

Without responding, I opened to the last page with writing on it—though there were a good number of blank pages after. The neat, slanting writing on the page forced a shiver down my spine as if the writer's ghost was in the room.

My father.

> *Though I laughed when she first gave me this journal, Peregrine said it would allow me to "focus my mind on the present moment," and I always do as my queen commands. I have to admit writing has helped me to do just that (yes, you were right as always), and so I continue.*
>
> *I worry, however, that what I write here may one day be our destruction—Peregrine's and mine. But it is a risk I must take to rid myself of the fears that haunt me.*
>
> *Write, my queen, my love, commands, so I must continue.*
>
> *I must be strong and brave, as she is. Must center my mind and my magic if we are to make our way out of this place alive—so that one day we can see our little girl grow without fear of the reckoning that comes with truth.*
>
> *Tomorrow, we run.*

CHAPTER
TWENTY-TWO

Renwick

Hours after leaving Rathyra, I sat in the library, pressing a glass to my forehead as I stared into the roaring flames of the hearth. Though my pulse had quieted, my mind spun with the idea of life within Infernis. The scent of the olive tree lingered in my senses. The memory of the souls' faces alight with joy was breaking what was left of my heart in two with gratitude.

That gratitude echoed within me alongside the memory of the warmth that had splintered through my veins. The urge I had to touch her—desperate for her heat against my palm, to feel her heartbeat on my skin after centuries of cold.

The library was silent, save for the crackling fire. Darkness churned within me, as though my magic had taken on a life of its own. This was a darker power than merely my magic. Grief had its claws deep in me, pushing against my bones and reaching for something I did not know.

A door slid open, and I heard quiet footsteps muffled by the thick rug. They drew closer, and I held my breath, waiting for the judgment Sidero would no doubt cast. Yet when none came, I sighed.

"What is it?"

"Is it true... That they loved each other?"

I started, turning in my chair to find Oralia standing only a few feet away with Zeph's leather-bound journal clutched tight to her chest. The bun she had worn hours ago was out now, her mane of hair waving around her face as though she'd been running her hands through it. Deep smudges of purple curled beneath her eyes, the corners of them tight with tension as she looked upon me with trepidation.

She rocked back onto her heels, her cheeks flushing with embarrassment. "I... Never mind. Sorry to have disturbed you."

Stars, I was an idiot. Jumping to my feet, I grabbed ahold of her wrist before she could take a step. A small gasp whistled through her lips, a blush creeping across her cheeks. Heat, there was that heat beneath my palm, snaking up my arm to curl within my heart.

I swallowed. "You merely surprised me... I was not expecting you."

Slowly, she turned back to me. Her wrist slid through my grasp and, with it, a small tremor of power at the connection of our skin. She flexed her hand once before placing it back on the journal across her chest while she searched my face.

"You told me to come to you...once I read the truth."

Relief flooded through me even as her mouth twisted around the last words. Her eyes were bloodshot and crystalline tears clung to her lashes. Gesturing for her to take the chair opposite mine, I sat. She drew her skirts around herself, placing the journal reverently on her lap like a priceless artifact. The dark crescent-shaped marks that circled her wrists appeared as she did so, glimmering in the blue light of the fire as she moved.

"They are from the daemoni that bit me," she explained softly, following my line of sight.

My mouth pressed into a hard line as I cataloged the scars that marred her pale skin. The one sign that her power was not only that of Aethera. A self-conscious look crossed her face before she tried to cover the marks as best she could with her hands.

I did not know what to say. So instead, I cleared my throat and took a long sip from the glass in my hand.

"Yes, they loved each other very much." Before I could stop myself, more spilled out. "More than I have ever seen anyone love since before time was made."

The corner of her mouth curled up. It was the first time I'd seen even a whisper of her smile. *Stars,* it was the first time we had been in a room for more than a minute without being at each other's throats. Angling her body toward mine, she spread her hands against the leather cover of the journal in her lap.

"Tell me something about them," she requested in a voice so quiet I wondered if she feared I might refuse her.

I placed my glass down on the small table between our chairs, fighting the ice that had hardened my heart. "What would you like to know?"

At that, her face broke into a wide, radiant smile. Though I had seen the sun only a few days before, it felt much like when I had witnessed it rise for the first time. There was wonder, awe, and *elation* stirring within me. But as soon as the feelings came, grief sank its sharp claws into them, dragging them back down beneath the surface.

Her smile, too, faltered. She blinked a few times before taking a slow breath and replying:

"*Everything.*"

CHAPTER
TWENTY-THREE

Oralia

I was surprised by how warmly the Under King spoke of my mother and father. The way his mouth softened around their names, the corners of his eyes crinkling. The rare, small chuckle he'd let loose at a memory of them.

His quiet laugh disarmed me most of all. I had not known he possessed the ability, and from the surprised look on his face, neither, it seemed, did he. The sound was soft and resonant, but it filled the room, enveloping me the way the darkness of night might.

There was also the way he spoke with his hands. The stories so vital that he needed to illustrate his meaning with gestures. As if it was important to him that I not miss a single detail.

The truth had not come quickly. Though I'd read that last passage with surprise, it had taken going back to the beginning to truly believe. To read the small anecdotes of each day, the little hurts my true father had experienced while being secretly in love with my mother, and the notes she would write in his journal, tucked into the corner of a page:

One day we will be in paradise because I will be with you.

She had left him countless little notes like that among his entries, and it was easy to read the elation in his words after she had done so. His writing would get a little more hurried, a little messier—though it was nothing in comparison to when he was angry. The words were barely legible then, the letters short and spiky rather than his usual neat calligraphy.

To read how my mother had been treated by King Typhon had stolen my breath. The court was practiced in paying no attention to cruelty. I was all too aware of that myself. And though I knew he had many lovers now, I'd always been told that when my mother was alive, he had been faithful to her.

How childish I had been to believe.

Each line I read filled in the gaping space between the king I thought I knew and the one I had seen that night in the dining hall of Aethera. Each brick laid was another weight upon my heart until the grief I felt was so heavy I might have fallen through the floor.

When I entered the library, I had been wary, wondering if perhaps it had been a deceit—some sort of fabrication to turn me against King Typhon. But when I asked if they loved each other and the Under King had finally answered, the honesty that radiated from his very being was enough for me.

More than I'd ever seen anyone love since time was made.

However, the longer we spoke the more the crushing weight of guilt settled over me. The Under King spoke in his quiet, measured voice of their excitement when they discovered I had been conceived.

"They planned to leave this world through the portal to the

human realm," he explained. "This was before anyone save myself and Zephyrus knew she was pregnant, and they knew they had a small window of time to make it out before Typhon caught wind."

He stared off into the fire, the blue light reflected on his face, throwing his sharp cheekbones into relief until the sight of his wistful smile became unbearable. I looked at my hands as they knotted together in my lap.

"She died in childbirth." My voice was soft, colored with that long-lived shame.

He gave some soft noise of disgust, but I did not look up at him in fear that he might blame me for the loss of his friend as Typhon blamed me for the loss of his wife.

"No."

I looked up. "What do you mean, 'no?'"

The king's attention was fixed on me, something like pity ghosting across the corners of his eyes. He shifted, one hand spreading wide before squeezing into a fist.

"She did not die in childbirth."

My heart gave an uncomfortable lurch. I shook my head. "Yes, she did. She died as I was born. She bled out and I received her magic."

Silence followed my statement, the soft crackling of the fire popping loudly in my ears. The Under King merely continued to stare.

"What?" I asked as my skin started to crawl with the first signs of my power.

He leaned forward, resting his elbows on his knees and leveling his gaze. "I do not know the full story, I was not there. I had been barred from the kingdom long before." There was a small pause, his chest rising with a breath before he sighed. "I do know that she lived past your birth, locked within her rooms in the palace. You were taken from her the moment your lungs were cleared. Passed to a wet nurse. But Peregrine lived minutes...even hours after."

Horror coated my throat, and I shook my head. "No."

The king's mouth opened, a choked note falling from his lips before he closed it again. The blue light of the fire danced over his sharp cheekbones, deepening the lines around his eyes until I could almost convince myself that grief lived there.

"Typhon killed her. How I am not certain, but it was enough that she was gone. It was staged so that she appeared to have bled out during birth. A rumor was spread that her magic turned inward and killed her."

Suddenly, the light was too bright within the room, and I squeezed my eyes shut to block it out. When the silence lengthened, I slowly opened them again. The king was frozen in his seat, dark eyes fixed on the roaring flames. The same horror I felt was splashed across his face.

"I tried to get them out before you were born," he breathed, voice lifeless. "When Peregrine was first beginning to show, she and Zephyrus knew their time within Aethera had ended. I offered to bring them here, to put them under my protection—I had their room made ready—but Zephyrus was adamant that they would go to the human realm. They did not want to bring conflict to these shores."

The journal said as much. Zephyrus...my father, wrote of his plans, cataloging the knowledge he had of the human world from those he knew within the kingdom. There were different gods there within that realm, ones they would have to contend with or else appease, but they had done their best to prepare.

"I used my shadows to transport them out of the kingdom and get them as far into the woods as I could without detection, but shadow walking is tricky enough with two people, let alone three. We had to be careful and..." He trailed off, eyes closing in defeat.

"He caught you," I whispered.

The king nodded, head hung in defeat, shoulders rounded in protectively upon himself. Compassion burned within my chest, the guilt we shared hung heavy between us in the room.

He took a shuddering breath, pressing the tips of his long fingers to his eyelids as if he could shove back the memories roiling to the surface.

"Right on the edge of the mists. Typhon shot a kratus arrow through my wings." His throat made a clicking noise as he swallowed, but he did not open his eyes nor drop his hands.

"He shot another straight through Zeph's heart. The last thing I remembered was Typhon telling Peregrine that she—and you—belonged to him. Then he cut off my wings. I tried to fight it, tried to stay conscious, but then he..." He cleared his throat. "He killed me."

My brows pulled together, eyes stinging. The knowledge that Typhon had killed Zephyrus tore some fresh wound inside my soul right in the middle of all the love I possessed for the god who raised me. And then I froze, understanding what he had said.

"I thought you said you could not die. That you were *'beyond death?'*" I quoted.

"Oh, I die," he answered with a haunting chuckle, "but the death does not take root. My heart may stop and my body grow still, but I will always return." The Under King looked at me then, and his gaze was somehow...ancient. "It is not a gift, this power. It is a curse. To know that there will never be a release from this life—from this world. I will go on even when those I love die. And with each death, I lose a piece of myself—of my soul." He gave a soft shake of his head.

I thought I knew what guilt was until I saw it written on his face. The shame he carried, buried beneath the ice. It was easy to see why he allowed himself to be so distant.

"That night..." He took a shuddering breath. "When my magic resurrected me, I woke beside Zeph's body, and Peregrine was gone. Never again did I feel anything but...cold. Unable to stomach an ounce of warmth, the slightest touch of another. I am damned to an eternity of ice and shame."

Despite his broad shoulders, the Under King looked so small curled in on himself. It felt as though I was looking into a mirror of my own agony. Slowly, tentatively, I reached out, brushing the back of his wrist with my fingertips. His skin was warm beneath my touch, a contrast to the coldness he spoke of. And though he stiffened at first, he soon relaxed, pressing into my hand. I could not help but wonder at the way the connection made my heart beat wildly in my chest.

Here I was touching another and they were not crumbling to ash.

"I failed them," he breathed.

I knew there was more in those words than just his failure. They were an apology for the life I could have been living.

Shaking my head, I tried to focus.

"You did not fail them. You were willing to sacrifice yourself to ensure they lived happy, safe lives. That I would live a happy, safe life. I cannot blame you for any of this."

How strange to sit here comforting the god I had always thought of as my enemy. To have my entire existence turned on its head in a matter of hours. Perhaps I'd always known deep down Typhon was not the hero he always claimed to be. He was too ruthless, too fiery in his anger and yet so cold at the same time. I'd seen the result of his cruelty and calculation over the centuries and been at the mercy of it so many times myself. Even if I always found a justification for it.

Was that why this was so easy to believe? Why, once I had enough evidence, it was easy to stroke my thumb once along the Under King's wrist as I tried to provide the tiniest bit of comfort that he might allow.

He cleared his throat and slid a palm over his hair. But then his eyes fell to my wrists before moving up to my face. "There is darkness inside of you... Darkness you fear."

I stiffened, my hands balling into fists.

"I know what you can do," he continued. "It calls out to you here, does it not?"

Biting the inside of my cheek, I nodded, drawing my arms protectively around my torso. He rose from the chair, wide shoulders blocking out the light of the fire.

"I know the darkness you feel," he murmured in the same, soft voice, but now it had an edge to it, the words steeped in promise. "Allow me to teach you its song, not to shy away from your power."

A heavy weight dropped into the pit of my stomach.

The word power dripped from his lips, swirling through my ears, and slithered down my spine, attempting to take root in my heart. But I fought the temptation to give in, to say *yes, yes, yes, make me unstoppable.* Part of me wanted to learn how to control my power, more than part. But the fear was too strong.

"No," I answered, pain sparking at the bite of my nails into my palms.

He blinked at me, giving the tiniest shake of his head. "Why not?"

I took a deep breath and held it, thinking of all the reasons I wanted to say yes. The power that ran through my veins, curled through my soul, and lived in my fingertips. It purred at the idea of getting out, of gaining strength. The idea of having control over it and therefore the ability to protect myself was tantalizing.

And then...the bodies on the floor, the horrible shame of the lives I had taken, and the ashes of the apple tree at my feet, stirred by the gentle autumn breeze. The power within me was too wild, too vast to control. It would consume me.

Blowing out my breath in a gust I shook my head. "I do not want it. I never asked for...*this*." I gestured with an open palm. "You...you cannot know what I have done."

He rocked back on his heels, and a muscle of his jaw worked.

"You are afraid of power because all your life you have been taught to be small. I can change that. I can help you."

"You mean, *I can change you*," I snapped, jolting to my feet.

Ice trickled back through his features, frost curling around his voice. "That is not what I said. Our power is similar. I know of its depths and its call. If I can control it, then so can you."

I laughed without humor. Perhaps it was his softness of the last few hours that had unnerved me but I could not stop myself from trying to prick his irritation. Part of me wanted him to be my enemy.

Because if he was not my enemy then that meant the people I loved were.

"I refuse to give in to such a monstrous power. I refuse to become a slave to the dark the way you are. You might be all right with it, with the bodies that lie piled at your feet, but I am not."

Faster than lightning, he crossed the space between us, towering over me. I turned to make my way toward the door but a tight grip on my hip stopped me. The embers within my chest ignited. My heartbeat pulsed in my ears.

"I am not the one who is a slave to my power." His lips were only inches from my ear and his breath swirled the hair beside my temple, forcing a shiver down my spine. "You have lived your whole life cowering in the presence of those who fear you for what you are capable of. Silencing yourself and your magic to make small men feel tall."

Another hollow laugh bubbled up my throat. Shadows flared around my shoulders before winking out. "You know nothing of my life. You keep to the barbaric old ways—torture because *it is what is done*. Forcing the souls to suffer."

"Ah, yes, there it is," he crooned, delight sparkling in his tone. His hand spasmed against the fabric of my gown. "There is that fire Typhon tried to snuff out."

I gasped at the heat of his chest against my back as he took a step forward. His sigh slid through my hair, snaking around my neck. My pulse fluttered, a hot desire curling through my belly so forcefully I had to stifle a moan. It was not him, I told myself, just the act of being touched. I was starved for it, regardless of who offered it. I could not lean into his touch, must not press myself against his chest, turn within his hold.

"Get your hand off me," I commanded.

But his hands tightened, thumbs pressing into the sensitive skin above my hipbones. A soft cold laugh escaped through his lips. "Do not command like a queen if you are unwilling to act like one."

I twisted, broke his hold, and stormed toward the door. When I reached it, I turned, staring back at where he stood. There was a stiffness in his shoulders as he balled his hands into fists, a coldness seeping into the room with each breath he took. But there was something else there in his eyes. I could not quite understand what it looked like…

Perhaps like *regret*.

CHAPTER
TWENTY-FOUR

Oralia

So much had changed in a week.

Despite the argument we had that night in the library, the Under King arrived the next morning to ask if I might continue the work of bringing life back to the grasses around Pyralis.

"Perhaps it will help to ease their suffering," he'd said earnestly. "To see something beautiful."

I agreed wholeheartedly, and thus, we started the routine each morning of going out into the grounds to bring life into Infernis. Sometimes, we spoke on the way. He would tell me stories of my parents while I would listen hungrily to any bit of information I could gather.

Zephyrus had been the God of the Wind, bringer of good rain and cooling breezes.

Peregrine had been the God of Harvest, of food, and crops.

We settled into a tentative understanding, though we often argued. Sometimes, our tempers boiled over until we stood toe to toe, arguing in a newly grown patch of grass and asphodel flowers. And though the disagreements started in many ways, they always came back to the same: I did not want him to teach me the ways of my dark magic.

"Your power consumes you because you fear it," he pressed with his hands spreading wide to illustrate the shadows flaring from my skin in anger. "That is always the way."

We were taking our usual morning walk through the grounds, focusing on the ground closest to Rathyra. The scent of the new life was thick around us, especially as he turned to face me, his heavy cloak swirling through the blossoms.

"You do not know what it has done. What I have done," I answered, a snarl sharpening my words.

He stepped closer, his mouth drawing into the barest of frowns. "You keep saying that. If I do not know, then tell me. Make me understand." His voice was cold, but there was a pleading note to it. But how could I speak of the crimes I had committed? The horrifying mistakes I'd made?

The words caught in my throat until I was choking on them. The argument I gave him day after day had become brittle. I wanted to learn my power. I wanted to control it. The desire to defend myself grew stronger with each subtle threat Typhon threw into the mist—the messengers found wandering, the letters passed. Yet every time I wanted to agree, every time I opened my mouth to say yes, the fire of Typhon's power licked my skin, forcing it back. I smelled the death in the hall, mixing with the roast meat and vegetables on the table.

I had killed those people without even trying, and my power had purred like a cat waking from a long nap. The most horrifying part of it had been the peace that had followed, that brief respite from the itching beneath my skin.

"Typhon will not stop," the king continued, moving until only a few inches remained between us, and I had to crane my neck to look into his face. "He will push and push until he has his hands on you, and then he will snuff the light from your eyes. He wants you, Oralia, because you have the power he needs to conquer these lands."

Shaking my head, I turned toward the castle. This was not a conversation I was ready to have. I wanted to blot out the noise, to hide from the sword hanging over my head. But his fingers wrapped around my wrist, the connection zinging through me as my power hummed in delight. Though his grip was firm, it was not punishing, merely holding me in place while I stared toward the black spires of the castle. I was afraid of what would happen if I looked at him, afraid of the heartbeat that pulsed in my chest for more than anger.

"I know you do not want to hear it, but you must."

I shook my head and shut my eyes against the wind that gusted around the palace. "You are wrong. I have no such power."

His thumb brushed once against the scar on the inside of my wrist, and I shivered.

"Your magic is from this land, and this kingdom responds to you. Look at all you have already done here. If I was gone—"

In a swirl of skirts, I turned, jerking my arm from his grasp. "Do not say such things."

His dark brows ticked up and loose strands of his hair fluttered across his face, catching in his lashes. "Do you understand what is at stake? This is not simply about a god retrieving what he believes belongs to him or a king rescuing a kidnapped princess. Barely a fortnight ago, the soldier I caught in the mists told me Typhon called you *'a weapon to be wielded.'*"

I shook my head, not in negation, but to focus. My blood roared in my ears. My lungs burned for oxygen. Before the king could say another word, I turned, hiking up my skirts and running through the grasses.

"Oralia!"

Crashing through the scorched earth in front of the castle, I took the steps two at a time, pushing the heavy doors open with shaking hands. Seeking the staircase for my chambers, I turned the sharp corner and hit a wide chest. Hands clamped around my upper arms, steadying me.

"Oralia?"

I gave a quiet shriek of surprise, blinking wildly. Aelestor, the God of Storms, stood before me, fiery hair wild around his face. Deep purple shadows were etched beneath his gray eyes. Somehow, I struggled to understand what I was seeing with him here in Infernis instead of in Aethera, without the sneer on his face as he discussed our betrothal. Then an expression of relief passed over him.

"*Burning Suns,* Oralia. You need to come back. I am here to bring you back."

He was speaking quickly, stumbling over his words. One of his hands wrapped around my arm, the other pressing between my shoulder blades. Before I could reply, he pulled me the way I came, my feet tripping over my gown as I struggled to keep pace.

"How did you get through the mist?" I asked, trying to tug myself from his grasp, which only tightened with each jerk.

There was a wild, panicked air around him. In all my time knowing Aelestor, he had been confident, always attempting to charm and sway anyone around him, even if I most often saw the cruel bitter side of him, but this...this was different.

"I can travel between the two kingdoms," he said simply, as though that was an explanation. "But we must hurry, we have to get you back. There is much at stake."

His words echoed the king's of only moments ago.

"Aelestor, what does Typhon plan on doing with me?" I stumbled on the lip of an uneven stone. But he paid me no mind, pushing open the obsidian doors and all but dragging me through.

A sigh heaved through his chest as his hand tightened on my arm. "You have been inside Infernis, Oralia."

My teeth clenched together, jaw clicking in frustration. I grasped my skirts to stop myself from falling down the steps we raced over. The mist curled around my cheeks, through my hair like many weak hands trying to stop our progress.

"So have you, what does that matter?" I countered, trying to understand his reluctance to answer the question. "What does he plan to do with me?"

Aelestor pursed his lips, though I could only see his profile as his attention fixed to the long way in front of us toward the river. "I do not know."

The clipped response told me more than he ever could. Aelestor knew what Typhon had planned for me, and from the way his eyes tightened and jaw worked, it frightened him.

You have the power he needs, the Under King said. Panic clawed its way up my throat. Typhon wanted to bring me back to use my power to claim some sort of upper hand over Infernis. Did he finally know how to control my power? Would he use me to destroy this kingdom and take it for his own? How much longer until he used my power to conquer other kingdoms beyond Infernis? The veil to the human realm lay within the mist—just how far did his ambition go?

"No," I ground through my teeth, digging my heels into the dry earth.

Aelestor's eyes widened as if he did not recognize me. His head whipped back and forth between us and the band of water that lay far in the distance.

"I will not become his weapon. I refuse to be the cause of so much suffering."

A growl ripped from his chest. Twisting my wrist, I attempted to tug out of his grasp. My shadows flared around me, and I desperately tried to reach for them, to push them toward Aelestor, but they were as insubstantial as the mist. His free hand slipped to the inside of his cloak, drawing free a shining, kratus resin-dipped dagger. But even as he threatened me, I could see the truth of my words hit him.

Typhon would use me to conquer this land and others like it.

"Please, Oralia. You do not understand. I have to bring you home."

Lightning sliced through my heart, my breaths turning into rapid pants. With a shake of my head, I pushed against his chest with my free hand, trying to create distance between us. Sweat dewed on my brow as I groaned, twisting within his hold.

"If I go with you, I condemn Infernis and its people to something worse than death. I cannot, Aelestor. I *will not*."

His hand trembled around the dagger. Aelestor had bullied me endlessly in Aethera. The threat of our betrothal constantly hung over our heads like a guillotine. But for all his contempt, for all his subtle threats, I never truly thought he would hurt me.

I did not believe it now, either.

"What has he done to make you go through with this?" I asked, even as he tightened his grip around my arm and dragged me farther.

My feet tripped across the ground. I scrambled to grab his hand, brushing his fabric-covered skin. Aelestor was wearing gloves. That realization froze my feet, and I lost precious ground. In fact, his entire body was sheathed in thick fabric save for his face. Typhon had ensured he was protected from my touch, rightly assuming I would resist.

"You would not understand," Aelestor growled.

My power. I had to reach for my power again. It was the only way to stop this. Panic roared within my veins as the muted blue river swam closer into view. This was the time for shadows to burst from my chest. This was the time for the darkness to stretch, to purr, to claw its way through me. And though I could feel it within, it was retreating from my grasp as if my fearful reaching forced it to pull back.

I could not call it to the surface...because I had no control over it.

But I could not allow him to take me back. Image after image flitted through my mind: Sidero's gentle comfort, the curious souls in Rathyra, and those who wandered Pyralis. Yet I could not help but come back to the Under King and the way he begged to teach me to be strong, his dissatisfaction with the despair within his kingdom, and his joy when I made things grow.

There was no way I would be the cause of his destruction. I eyed the dagger poised at my side. It was a long enough journey through the mists and the forest that if I positioned myself correctly upon its blade, I would not survive before he was able to get help. If the resin pierced my heart, I could be dead within an hour or two. That was assuming Typhon's men were not waiting for me on the other side.

It was a risk I had to take.

With a deep breath, I rushed forward, catching Aelestor off guard. The blade in his hand shifted, but I pressed myself roughly upon it, gasping as searing pain tore through my side.

"*Oralia!*" Aelestor cried.

The blade slid from between my ribs, but before he could release me, shadows curled around us. A sigh of relief slipped through my lips as my power finally responded.

"Touch her again and you die." The Under King's glacial voice slipped through the mist, appearing in a swirl of darkness behind Aelestor.

They were not my shadows at all.

With a jerk, Aelestor catapulted away from me, landing with a crash that rattled through my bones. His eyes were wide in fear, mouth opening and closing with silent babbling.

"This is how you repay me?" The king loomed over him. Shadows rippled off his shoulders and wound their way around Aelestor's wrists. "After everything I have done for you?"

The king's dark hair was wild, curling around his cold face as Aelestor babbled again.

"You do not understand!" he wailed, his hands slamming together in the shackles of the king's power. "You must listen to me!"

Mist swirled, and the surrounding landscape lurched sickeningly. I stumbled forward. I needed him to stop, to listen.

"Ren."

The king paused. His lips were drawn into a tight line that softened at the sight of me calling for him. I was cold, all the way down to my bones. But I had to make him understand, had to explain. My arms outstretched, reaching for him.

"*Please,*" I gasped before darkness filled my vision and I knew no more.

CHAPTER
TWENTY-FIVE

Renwick

I caught Oralia right before she fell.

The aroma of blood thickened in the air, blotting out her sunshine and flower scent that I had not known I craved until it was gone. Cradling her close, I slid my arm beneath her knees, drawing her up to my chest. Her head lolled, her usually rosy cheeks gaunt in the weak light through the mist. When I lifted her, the wound on her side gaped, and a low snarl slipped through my lips.

"Ren," Aelestor whimpered.

A whisper of shadows curled around us as Dimitri appeared, sword already drawn. Within the space of a heartbeat, he had it pinned to Aelestor's throat. For all the spying Aelestor had done for me in the past few centuries, the trust between us had always been brittle. Now, it was all but broken.

There was a riot inside my mind I could not quell, burning away the frost and ice. I wanted to lash out, to kill. No, not merely kill—*destroy*. I swallowed the feeling, using my power to suppress the cold fury that roared within me. There would be a moment for rage, for revenge, but this was not it.

"I have no time for your pleading. Dimitri, keep him here until I return."

Turning my back on them, I called forth the shadows. With a deep breath, I shadow-walked, focusing on my destination. Oralia's chambers slowly swam into focus as the darkness ebbed away.

"Ren," she whispered, rustling in my arms and blinking blearily up at me. I hummed my acknowledgment, trying not to jostle her as I moved toward the bed. "I want you to teach me."

The steady drip of blood onto the floor was a clock ticking down. Even with the crush of guilt and anger that clamored inside of me, a small piece of satisfaction twisted at her words.

Yes, I wanted to say. *Yes, let me teach you to be strong.*

When she opened her mouth again, I nodded. "I heard you."

Gently, I laid her down across the bed. The door clicked. A quiet breath rushed from Sidero as they came barreling into the room. Oralia winced, twisting her torso to look up at me. Placing a gentle hand on her shoulder, I encouraged her to lie back.

"Are you not pleased?" she wheezed, cheeks growing paler by the minute.

I shook my head, pressing my hands over the wound at her side. Cold dread circled my gut as blood slipped between my fingers and seeped into the white linens beneath her.

"At the moment, I am more concerned about you than gloating."

Sidero was already back from the bathing chamber, supplies in hand. "Shall I call Thorne?"

Thorne was one of my inner circle, and though he spent most of his time shepherding and training the souls who wished to protect the kingdom, he was also one of our most gifted healers.

I was half tempted to say yes, but I shook my head. "I do not believe he will be necessary unless we cannot clean the resin from the wound."

A small whimper of pain drew my focus back to Oralia. Tears beaded in her eyes as she looked at my face, unaware of the conversation happening above her.

"Why? Why are you concerned for me?"

The way she asked made me want to scream. It made me want to raze Aethera to the ground along with anyone who ever made her think she was not worthy.

"You are injured." I pressed more firmly upon the wound, punctuating the point while Sidero circled the bed to lay out their supplies.

Oralia's teeth chattered as she searched my face. Her wild mane of strawberry waves spread across the pillows, some locks falling over her eyes. I could not stop myself from brushing them from her cheeks with one of my bloodied hands. At the touch of my fingertips, her eyelids fluttered, relaxing into my hand.

Some of the tension seeped from my shoulders.

"Your Grace," Sidero murmured beside me. "Allow me."

I nodded. My palm slipped from her wound. But Oralia's eyes flew open and her hands shot out, wrapping around my tunic.

"Stay," she cried. A fresh wave of panic coursed through her as she tightened her grip, even while the rest of her body grew slack. "*Please.*"

Slowly, I wrapped my hands around hers, nodding once before working to release her grip so Sidero could get to work.

"Promise me," she pleaded, grasping again for my hand.

The light behind her eyes flickered. Fresh blood spilled onto the linens of her bed. The rise and fall of her chest stuttered, and though I knew the wound was not fatal, it made my stomach churn. Squeezing her palm, I ran my thumb across the black curve of her scar before nodding again.

"I promise," I answered, right as her body went limp and her lids closed.

I sat at her bedside for a quarter of an hour while Sidero worked, cleansing the wound of the kratus resin that impeded her natural ability to heal. I was unable to pay attention to anything but the movement of her breath and the softness of her mouth as she relaxed into sleep.

Sidero said nothing as they worked, content to allow me to stew in my anger and fear until they were ready to change her bed linens.

"Lift her, please," they requested.

With a nod, I moved forward, cradling Oralia so Sid could strip the blood-soaked sheets from the bed. I kept her in my arms as they laid out new ones, unable to stop staring at her face.

The scent of wildflowers clung to her, mixing with blood. More of those soft white flowers had sprung up this morning with her gentle hum, changing her scent ever so slightly. I looked forward to our daily walks more than anything else in this cursed existence.

"Ren?" Sidero's voice called, cutting through my thoughts.

My brows flew up. They so rarely called me Ren, though I'd asked them to on too many occasions to count. Sidero was a soldier through and through, preferring to call gods according to their station, even when there was no need for that here.

A small smile quirked up the corner of their lips. "You can put her down now."

I paused, glancing down at her. "Oh. Of course."

Carefully, I placed Oralia back onto the bed, brushing away a few strands of hair that fell into her face before straightening up again.

"I..." Clearing my throat, I ran a hand through my hair. "I will leave you to the rest of it while I deal with Aelestor, but I will return before she wakes."

Sidero gave me a small bow and I moved toward the door. But I stumbled at the whisper of *her* voice from the bed.

"Ren."

CHAPTER
TWENTY-SIX

Renwick

Through the shadows, I reached the river just in time.

Aelestor was pinned to the ground beneath Dimitri's boot. Easy enough to see that he had tried to run amid a gale of wind and rain as cover. The water of the river crashed angrily against the black rocky shore as if it were another member of my court. Lightning cracked overhead, thunder rumbling through the sky, but it might as well have been a springtime day in Aethera for all the attention Dimitri paid it. Mecrucio was on his other side, broadsword trained on the God of Storms. His usually amused face was twisted in rage, his kind eyes alight with fire.

Welcoming the bitterness that curled through my heart in Oralia's absence, I allowed it to strengthen my walls. "I see you are getting better and better at making friends, Aelestor."

His face was wild, snarling, and his red hair writhed like snakes in a pit.

"Call off your dogs," he screeched when Dimitri's boot pushed further into his solar plexus.

I strode forward until I was right beside the three, hands loosely in my trouser pockets and cloak swirling in the wind. Lightning struck, but my shadows spooled up to meet it, absorbing the light and energy before dispersing it across the sky.

"I see no dogs, my lord. However, I am happy to call Erybus if you'd like to say hello."

At the mention of the three-headed daemoni, his face paled, and the churning storm waned. I raised a brow at him. Slowly, the skies quieted, the clouds parted for the thick mist, and the rain tapered into a drizzle. As I knelt beside Aelestor on the bank of the river, all gathered focused on my bloody hands.

"Sire..." Mecrucio started.

I shook my head, willing him to be quiet as I snatched up a fistful of Aelestor's hair, drawing his head back until his neck strained with the pressure. I leaned close. My shadows curled around my shoulders, slithering down my arms to wind across his chest.

"Tell me what happened."

"I do not know—"

I clapped a hand over his mouth, watching with satisfaction as Oralia's blood smeared across his face. "Do you really wish to try my generosity, Lord Thyella? You will start from the beginning."

As I drew my hand away, his storm-gray eyes widened in panic.

"I..." His throat clicked with a rough swallow. "Typhon learned of my visits here. He—He said if I did not retrieve Oralia then he would ensure I never made it back to...to Rathyra."

Dimitri huffed a hollow laugh. "So, you thought the best course of action would be to stab her?"

Aelestor's face paled further as he shook his head furiously. "I had merely drawn the blade to intimidate her. I-I did not mean to harm her. We struggled, and it...it was an accident. I swear it. Please, Ren."

Above us, Mecrucio cleared his throat loudly.

"Your Grace," Aelestor amended.

Releasing his hair, I sat back on my heels, considering.

"Fix it," I instructed, pushing to my feet.

Aelestor's mouth opened and closed in panic, his eyes darting from my face to the shadows that pinned him to the ground.

"Fix it?" he argued, some of his arrogance rising despite his fear. "I cannot—"

With a flick of my fingers, my shadows pulled him from the ground, pushing him toward the water's edge. He hovered for a moment before they dragged him farther out until the toes of his boots cast small ripples in the water. His sharp cry of fear echoed across the river.

"Would you prefer death?" I asked with a raised brow. "Would you prefer to shepherd my boat with the others?"

Aelestor shook his head, sweat trickling down his cheeks and into the high ruff of his collar. "N-no."

I took a step toward the shore, clasping my bloodied hands in front of me. "Am I your king?"

When he did not immediately respond, his focus trained on the churning waves below, my shadows disappeared. He fell with a cry, but they caught him as his feet breached the water. The surface bubbled around his boots, the skeletal forms of those who had tried to cross the river without Vakarys rising to the surface.

"*Yes, you are my king,*" he screeched.

A bitter smile pulled at my cheeks. I nodded, drawing him back to the bank. With a groan, he dropped to the rocks, fingers splayed wide and hair tangled around his face.

"Then you will fix this, however you must, to ensure that your time here does not endanger Oralia further and that you may reenter the kingdom for your own means when the time comes."

He blinked up at me, his bottom lip trembling. "But...but what if I am not allowed back?"

I shrugged, already moving toward the castle. The ache in my chest tugged toward the room where I knew she would soon be waking.

"Then we will know you have failed," I said over my shoulder before pausing. "I meant it, you know... If you touch her again, I will give you a fate worse than death and perhaps she will have the honor."

Stepping away, I gestured to Dimitri and Mecrucio.

"Enjoy your trip back to Aethera, Lord Thyella."

Oralia was still asleep when I made my way into her chambers after changing into dry clothes.

Sidero had just begun to set the bandages. The scent of lilac and mint hung in the air from the water they had used to clean her wound. Dropping my baldric beside the hearth, I strode over and placed a hand on Sidero's shoulder.

"I can do it, you go rest," I said softly, lest I woke her.

They raised a brow at me but did not respond. Nodding once, they smoothed a stray lock of hair from her face before stepping away.

"You care about her," I observed.

Their face softened. "Yes, Your Grace. She makes it easy to do so once you allow her the chance."

I nodded, unsure of what else to say to such a statement.

With a sigh, I set to bandaging the wound. It had needed time to breathe after the thorough cleaning of kratus resin and time to be observed to ensure we had gotten it all. The deep sleep she was in now was normal for a god who had been wounded as she had—her body needed time to heal.

Sidero's quiet footsteps rounded the bed once more, and they laid a black dressing gown, embroidered with gold leaves at the collar and cuffs, at the foot of her bed. "There is food beside the fire for when she wakes."

I nodded, not looking up from where I smoothed the last bandage across her side. The blade had slipped between her fifth and sixth ribs, dangerously close to her lungs.

"Sidero..." They stopped beside the open door, and I looked up. "Thank you."

Surprise flickered over their face before they placed a hand over their heart, bowing their head. "It is an honor, Your Grace." And then the door shut closed with a *click* behind them.

Moving back to Oralia, I checked the bandages, ensuring they were not too tight or too loose, before sighing and gathering up the rest of the supplies to place on her bedside.

"A king and a healer..."

I turned, eyes wide as she slowly blinked up at me, a soft smile tugging at the corner of her lips. There was a tightness spreading through my throat as she took a slow breath, wincing with the movement.

"I have many talents," I intoned.

She raised a brow at me. "Oh, of that I have no doubt."

A chuckle escaped my lips, the feeling foreign in my hollow chest. Though her complexion was pale, it was nothing compared to what it had been. For the first time, I noticed the constellation of freckles dotting her cheeks. The sight twisted something deep within me.

"Are you hungry?"

She nodded.

Unable to fight the instinct, I scooped her into my arms as gently as I could, glad when she only slightly winced.

"You do not need to carry me," she mumbled, even as her arms wrapped around my neck, head pressing to my chest.

"But then how would I show off how godly and capable I am?" The jest slipped from my lips, an echo of a piece of me that had long ago been lost.

Pulling back, she stared up at me, dark eyes wide in surprise before she burst into peals of laughter. The sound twinkled around the room, reminding me of the way the stars had glimmered in the sky as my mother had made the constellations.

It was beautiful.

She was beautiful.

CHAPTER
TWENTY-SEVEN

Oralia

"W"hen does the reprimanding start?" I asked, fighting another grimace as Ren carefully set me down on the couch in front of the fire.

He stood frozen, and I wondered if he was trying to decide where to sit or perhaps what I meant. Eventually, he reached for the covered bowl on the table and handed it to me.

"For pushing myself upon Aelestor's blade," I clarified as I took the bowl. "For making a mess of things."

His eyes darkened, mouth tensing.

"Why would you do that?" There was something there on the edge of his words that sounded a bit like heartbreak.

I weighed the bowl in my hands, inhaling the rich scent of the stew inside. Biting my lip, I sighed through my nose. When I looked up, his eyes were wide, his lips parted slightly, and he was standing in the same place he'd been when I'd first spoken.

Burning Suns, was this the same god who had dragged me through the mist?

"Why, Oralia?" he repeated.

My name on his lips was so rare I shivered, unable to stop the explanation as it poured from me. I stared at the bowl rather than him as I spoke. "You said Typhon needed my power, that I was *a weapon to be wielded.* If I were to return, he would use me to conquer Infernis... I-I could not let that happen."

Slowly, he lowered himself beside me onto the couch, hands clenching into fists. The heat from his body slithered across my skin, and my stomach clenched. I fought the urge to draw closer.

"If you returned to him and he found a way to destroy me, you might become ruler here. Yours would be the only magic left that could maintain these lands," Ren murmured.

"I would be a puppet on a deadly string," I countered. "I would rather die than see that happen."

We stared at each other, and within that look, I knew he finally understood why I pushed myself upon the blade. And I thought, perhaps, that might have been respect beneath the midnight depths of his irises. But as the silence lengthened, the look deepened until my cheeks flushed and my stomach fluttered. His attention drifted over the planes of my cheekbones and the curve of my jaw until it settled on my mouth.

His hand twitched against his thigh. "Tomorrow."

I swallowed, blinking. "What?"

He cleared his throat before shifting away from me. "The reprimanding will begin tomorrow. Eat, you must replenish your strength."

I did not fight him as he guided the bowl to my lips. It smelled too good. When I gulped down the thick, hot broth, I shivered—the cold I'd felt only a moment ago returned. He rose with a soft sigh and moved away from the couch. I assumed that would be the end of our conversation until a heavy weight draped over my shoulders and a hand wrapped around the now half-empty bowl.

"Easy, not too fast," he scolded lightly.

Sighing, I allowed him to take the bowl from me while I slid my hands through the sleeves of the dressing gown. There was a twinge in my chest at the gesture, causing my eyes to prick before I swallowed it back.

"Will you teach me?" I asked, blinking them away. I tried not to dwell too long on the fact that he chose to sit beside me instead of the chair beside the couch.

While he thought, he handed me back the bowl. Our fingertips brushed as I took it. Heat danced across my fingertips, winding its way up my arm until it blossomed across my cheeks. Each touch felt like a revelation, like a flower opening in the midday sun—significant and soul-altering.

"If that is what you wish," he answered with a slight bow of his head. "Perhaps in the morning. You should feel almost normal by then."

I frowned. "Do you think so?"

He nodded, brushing a lock of hair from his face before resting his arm against the edge of the couch, his fingertips only an inch from my shoulder. "I do. Now that the resin is out of your system and you are eating, your body will recover quickly."

While he spoke, his hand on the couch flexed with his words. Now and then his fingertips would catch on my hair. Each moment of contact sent another spike of warmth down my spine, anticipation curling in my belly.

"How long did it take when you lost your wings?" I breathed, distracted.

Ren froze, hand splayed wide. I counted the seconds as they passed. He stared at me with a blank expression, then took a slow breath as his fingertips closed over a lock of my hair.

"A while..." The reply was so soft I was unsure if I'd heard him correctly.

I remembered his wings displayed above the mantel in the library back home. The way they'd glittered faintly in the firelight and how I never seemed to be able to enter the room without staring at them.

"They are beautiful, your wings."

The light of the fire danced across his features, the cold blue flames deepening the hollows of his cheekbones. His eyes slid from my face to the floor.

"It has been so long. I admit I have almost forgotten what they look like."

A hollow ache blossomed inside me as despair bled into his eyes. I placed the bowl back on the table. A soft gasp of pain whistled through my teeth with the movement. He jerked, hand darting out to support the bowl as it made the final few inches back to the tray. There was some sort of reproach in his eyes at my hasty movement, but I covered his hand with mine when he made to place it back on his thigh.

"They're beautiful, Ren," I repeated, my heart fluttering wildly in my chest as I spoke his name. "Night black and wild, terrifying and awe-inspiring—just like you."

CHAPTER
TWENTY-EIGHT

Renwick

It was silent as we walked in the dim morning light bleeding across the castle walls.

Oralia's attention was focused on the ornate bones that sculpted the side of the castle. Disdain clung to the corners of her lips, her silent questions heavy in the air.

"They gave them willingly."

She jumped, gaze darting between the castle and me.

"They built this castle in the first years after time began," I continued. "Back when giants roamed these lands and there was no Aethera or Infernis. Humans were rare, only coming through the rift by accident or chance."

Her eyebrows raised before they drew together, a soft wrinkle forming between her brows. "Then whose bones are these?"

I sighed, taking one last look at the towering wall before we approached the enormous shadow beneath it. "They are the bones of some of the very first gods. Gods who were driven mad by the creation of time, who could not stand to be in a world where things died. They asked my father to be sacrificed to the one thing they feared, to use their bones to build the castle where the king of death would rule."

"That is horrifying."

I stopped us, brushing her elbow when we reached the deep shadow of the castle, and I could not fail to notice the blush that immediately stained her cheeks before she drew it back. Throughout our time together, I had come to understand that though she was unused to such touches, she did not appear to abhor them as I did.

"Is it? In that act, they conquered the thing they feared most. Their magic helped to create these lands to guide the souls who reside here now."

She thought for a moment, attention darting behind me—no doubt eyeing the bones set within the mortar. I tried not to watch the way her teeth bit into her lower lip and the way that lip moved as she softly sucked on it in contemplation.

I had to say something or else I would be in danger of saying too much. "It is not horror. It is courage."

She nodded, her teeth releasing her lip as a small smile drew up the corners of her mouth. "I suppose you are right."

A hollow pang echoed in my chest at her smile, the corners of my lips twitching in response before they settled. I extended my hand. "We will go to the base of the Tylith Mountains. On foot, it takes three-quarters of an hour, or mere seconds if I walk you through the shadows."

She gazed at my hand with trepidation, so I wiggled my fingers at her. It felt strange to tease like this as if I was finding some part of myself I had lost. Oralia appeared to make a choice, and though

I knew she might, it still surprised me when she took my hand. A flicker of heat wound its way through my palm and up my arm when our fingers interlaced.

We stood like that, my mind at once deafening and silent. Her palm pressed against mine. The power that clung to her soul, that swam through her veins, called out to me. I wanted to swim in it—no, not swim, I wanted to *drown* in it. To bury myself within her and never come up for air.

"Ren?" she asked breathlessly.

Desire roared deep within at my name on her lips, wanting to tear its way up and out of my chest. The feeling of it was heady and foreign after centuries. *Stars,* my name on her lips made the ice in my heart crack into pieces.

She cleared her throat, eyebrows rising.

Right.

I blinked, reaching for the shadows, focusing my intention on the dark shade of the yew tree that stood at the base of the mountains. With a tug, I stepped forward, taking her with me.

The moment the shadows retracted, I dropped her hand, flexing my fingers from the scalding heat of her skin before striding out beneath the wide branches. The ground here was flat, laid with dark obsidian stones that hummed with the same power that lay within our veins. This was the perfect place for her to call forward what she feared, beside the mountains where countless souls did the same and came out triumphant.

I turned back to face her. The mist—thicker here than near the palace—curled around her neck and wrists like a caress. She eyed me warily, her attention flickering now and then to the gargantuan peaks beside us.

The mountains were hewn from the same stones beneath our feet with jagged edges and steep drops, the wide mouths of caves dotted the mountainside hundreds of feet above. A few small openings appeared at the base nearby when a soul moved forward toward their ascension. Horace had informed me there were no souls destined to do so today, and we would not be interrupted.

"What do you fear the most about the power within you?" I asked, raising my voice against the wind that swept across the mountains.

Her eyes widened a fraction, and that damned lip was caught between her teeth again. How had I never noticed that before?

"Losing myself to it," she answered with measured words. "Becoming consumed by it."

Nodding, I clasped my hands behind my back.

"I will not lie to you and say that is not a possibility. The more a god fights their power, the more volatile it becomes." At this, panic bled across her face. "But it is unlikely if we approach with caution and deference. Your other power is the same, though it comes to you much more naturally."

Her lips pursed lightly. "I do not think so."

"You do not? I could feel it the day you grew the olive tree, the temptation to let the magic sweep you away. To become nothing but the light and earth and life. It is why your other power calls to you in such moments, why your palms itch to destroy as you create. That darker magic you fear is trying to protect you as it always has."

Her mouth popped open in surprise before a look of consternation took its place. "No, you are wrong."

I strode closer. "Your blush tells me otherwise. There is no such thing as goodness, Oralia. Just as there is no such thing as evil. Magic just is."

TWENTY-NINE

Oralia

I did not want to believe him.

Burning suns, I did not want to even as the truth skittered over my skin and circled its way around my heart. Because, deep down, I knew it was true. Especially from the way his eyes, clear with the truth of his words, looked over me with compassion.

"No..." I repeated, wanting to fight it, to fight him. "This power inside of me... It is wrong. It is not trying to protect me; it is trying to destroy me. And it tries to destroy everything around me with it."

"Your power tries to destroy that which would hurt you." Ren shook his head, stepping even closer until only a few tendrils of mist were between us. "Close your eyes."

I stared at him and he raised a black brow. The stray waves of his hair loose from the tie at his nape swirled in the wind, every so often catching in his long eyelashes. When I did not follow his direction, his hand rose, two fingertips sliding down my forehead, encouraging my lids to close. My stomach clenched at the contact, and I suppressed the urge to hold onto him. He let his fingertips rest across my brows, his thumb and ring finger against my cheekbones, and I thought there might have been the whisper of a caress before his voice rumbled low in my ear.

"Reach for it," he breathed. My shoulders stiffened. "I am right here, I promise. Reach out and, for the first time, greet this part of yourself that has been an enemy for so long."

I wanted to trust him, to reach out, but that gnawing fear had me by the throat. There was no way I was calling to this power. No way I would welcome it inside of me. Not when it had been the source of so much agony. Yet even as I denied it, the magic heard his words, swirling within my veins, uncurling within the pit of my soul.

I squeezed my eyes tight against the dark. It was not merely death. It was the vastness of oblivion. This was the deep reaches of power that transformed the universe, the same power that created the cycle of life and decay, of the seasons, of the world as we knew it.

My body shook, hands clenched into fists at my sides as if I could fight this power, even as it hummed within my chest.

"It is your fear you feel. The fear amplifies, the fear multiplies, and it is the fear you are a slave to," Ren murmured.

In response, the power lessened, retreating to a dark cavern within my mind, saying in its own quiet way, *That's enough for today.*

My shoulders slumped, and I let go of the breath I'd been clenching between my teeth. Ren's hand was cupping the back of my neck, his other bracing my shoulder. When I opened my eyes, he was right there, dark eyes echoing a desire I thought perhaps I recognized deep within myself.

His breath ghosted across my cheeks. "It is a start."

Slowly, gently, his thumb brushed against the column of my neck, and a longing blossomed deep within my belly. I knew now that I wanted this god—perhaps for longer than I wanted to admit—and as much as the thought terrified me, I did not resist his gaze.

"It was nothing," I answered, biting the inside of my cheek.

The corner of his mouth pulled up the barest amount—the closest thing to a smile I'd seen. I tried not to watch it. Tried not to run my tongue against my bottom lip. Tried not to notice the way his gaze tracked the movement.

"It was more control than you have ever shown before, Oralia. It was the beginning."

His attention dipped once more to my mouth, the hand on my shoulder sliding down slowly—so slowly, to curve around my elbow. The longing intensified, skating up my chest and dipping down between my thighs. The beating of my heart was a kettledrum to the want dancing in my core. That a touch could feel like this, could elicit this response... I never wanted it to end.

"You are more powerful than you know," he whispered, his head tilting ever so slightly to the side.

A growl rended the air, slicing through the space between us. Ren jerked, eyes snapping wide before he threw me protectively behind himself.

Something slunk low to the ground through the mist that had thickened as we worked. The wide haunches were barely visible from where it prowled. Its too-large head swung left and right. The snuffling grew louder as it scented the air. Dread clawed its way through my stomach, eating away the heat that had been there only a moment before. It was a daemoni, I was sure of it, and my power snarled in response.

Ren clicked his tongue twice, snapping his fingers and whistling low. The creature halted before giving a loud, echoing bark and bounding forward. I screamed as three dog-like heads erupted from the mist. Its wide jaws frothed as it headed right toward Ren.

I knew this daemoni, I had seen it a thousand times in my dreams—*nightmares*. Never could I have forgotten the silver markings upon its head, the way they glimmered against its night-black coat. But most of all, I remembered the feeling of its teeth against my flesh, the burning, acidic pain of its venom in my veins.

Horror tore through me. The daemoni bounded forward, ever closer, but my horror turned to shock as it stopped at Ren's feet and flopped onto its back. Three heads gazing up at him expectantly, three tongues lolling out of three mouths.

Ren's shoulders stiffened. I did not know what my face looked like, but whatever it was closed the shutters behind his eyes.

"He belongs to you…" I rasped, my voice fading with the last word.

Taking a deep breath, he held up his hands, fingers spread wide. "Listen to me, Oralia, *please*."

I shook my head, sharp pain slicing through my heart. "You are the reason I have this power. The reason I spent so much of my life alone, treated like a pariah in my home, by my own people. The reason I have taken so many lives." My voice was rising in volume. Tendrils of darkness spread out around us. "And you knew? This whole time?"

His face darkened. "Yes, I knew…and I watched over Aethera ever since."

Hazy memories floated back to me, the pain, the fear, the solitude. "The raven… You are the raven."

I swore I could see right down into his shredded soul as he nodded once. "I am."

Hot tears pricked my eyes, and I wondered if they would be tinted black with my power that was beginning to escape. The raven that had come after... The magical creature I had been sure was sent by the Great Mothers to watch over me.

"You say there is no such thing as good and evil and yet..." I gestured in a way that encompassed his entire being.

He did not answer, and it was his impassive, blank face that hurt more than anything else. Hurt more even than the knowledge that he had been the one to bring about my downfall. I thought I had wanted this god...

"Why?" I begged.

But he did not respond, not even as the tears slid down my cheeks. There was only ice in his expression. And what I hated most of all was that I was not surprised that he would not speak.

One of his large hands closed over my wrist and shadows swallowed us in a blink. His magic was so similar to my own it made me shiver despite myself. Power caressed my face and hands before the towering wall of bones suddenly blossomed into my vision.

Ren dropped his hand as though my skin burned him, and the last thing I heard before he vanished once again into the shadows, leaving me alone, was merely:

"Perhaps I am the monster you believe me to be."

CHAPTER
THIRTY

Renwick

I landed in the tunnels. Oralia's stricken face, the betrayal and the hurt etched across her features flashed behind my lids with each blink.

You say there is no such thing as good and evil and yet...

And yet here I was, evil incarnate.

My feet began the well-worn path down, down, down. Passing the many caves where the screams grew so loud the earth shook and dirt crumbled. With each scream, the agony in my soul burned deeper. Because she was right. I was the reason she lived such a horrid existence. Perhaps, without me, she would have been the pampered princess I had long ago assumed her to be.

I entered Gren's familiar cell. His red-gold hair glinted in the blue light of the torch that hung against the far wall. The sight made my stomach twist.

"My..." Gren gasped through the blood choking him. "*Myhn ardren.* You honor me."

I stood staring at him, cursing the gaping hole within my chest. Gren could be her brother in another life, their coloring was so similar. I wondered about that other life, the life where she had never been bitten—never been shunned by the Golden King who killed for his own means and called it justice.

I slid the axe into my hand, the familiar weight feeling more like a shackle.

Perhaps she would have been coddled.

I twisted the axe, drawing it up.

Perhaps she would have been loved.

I held it above my head, the blade shining in the firelight.

Perhaps she would have been a princess.

But then she would not be what she was now and that would have been the true tragedy. For her to not possess the kindness she did, the compassion—the need to protect the helpless. It was her darkness that made her light shine brighter, the power of death that fueled her power of life.

Just because it is the way it has always been done does not mean that is how it should be.

The axe clattered from my hands onto the dirt floor below.

"Horace," I rasped, staring into Gren's wide green eyes.

With a whisper of power, Horace appeared in the room.

"Take Gren to Rathyra. Take them all out and place each soul where they are best suited."

Once it was done, I would destroy these tunnels. I would burn them to the ground along with all the whispers of my father damning me to the existence of a monster.

Yes, Oralia could have been a princess, but now...

Perhaps now she would become a queen.

I did not stop to speak to Dimitri who waited beside the front doors of the castle when I strode by.

"Ren," he started before his jaw snapped shut.

I took the stairs two at a time, rounding the corridor until the familiar door loomed in front of me. My chest ached with the unfamiliar pounding of my heart as I reached for the knob and swung open the door, hoping against hope that she was alone in her chambers.

All the familiar furnishings were picked for Peregrine and Zephyrus. Did she like them? Did she feel at home here? I shook the thought from my head. It was dark, save for the roaring flame in the hearth, and it took me a moment to find her.

Oralia sat at the window, sunset waves cascading down her shoulders with her knees pulled to her chest. The black dressing gown was drawn tight across her body, but the thin, white fabric of her nightdress peeked out from where the fabric of the gown had fallen to the side. *Stars*, she looked so...small. Fragile. So different from the roaring personification of power I'd witnessed earlier. Now, all her anger had been eaten away by time, leaving merely a shell behind.

Oralia said nothing when I strode through the door, but she looked me over, her dark green eyes noting each breath I took. Sidero, thank the stars, was nowhere to be found. I closed the distance between us, sinking to my knees in front of her. As I did, she unfolded her legs until her shins were only inches from my chest, the tips of her bare feet brushing the cold marble floor.

I steeled myself for her rejection, for her recriminations, but none came. Gently, I pulled the book from her grasp and placed it beside her on the thick damask cushion. With a soft tug, I drew her arms down, gazing up into her face. I refused to acknowledge the confused expression there, how her cheeks lacked the usual blush at my touch. Then with a deep breath for courage, I tugged back the sleeve of her dressing gown.

There, against the ivory skin of her flesh, lay the black crescent-shaped scars that were the mark of her power—the sign of her darkness. I had done this to her. Embers burned inside my chest, flaring painfully after the centuries of ice. The burning intensified, moving up through my neck and lingering in the corners of my eyes. Slowly, so slowly, to give her time to draw back, I leaned forward and pressed my lips to the scar that curled around the back of her hand.

Her soft gasp broke the silence in the room. I turned her wrist until her palm was face up. My thumb slid down as I drew her hand to me and pressed another lingering kiss to the thin skin of her inner wrist and the raised skin of her healed wound.

She was sweet, so sweet against my lips. The desire to rise and capture her mouth almost overtook me. I wanted to taste more, to lick the sunlight on her skin, the warmth that resided between her legs. But I fought the urge, resisted it with all my being. Instead, I reached for her other hand.

"Erybus was not intended for you, but for Typhon," I breathed, my voice low as I drew up the sleeve of her other arm. "I did not know you were there in the forest until it was too late." I pressed my mouth to the scar that curved the back of this hand. "Guilt has been my constant companion for longer than you know." Even slower, I turned her hand over, tracing the black crescent against her skin before letting both my thumbs slide down her palm.

"Why?" Her voice curled across my cheek as surely as the tendrils of her hair.

"Because I felt responsible." I kissed the heel of her hand. "Because I was the cause of your pain." I kissed the center of her palm. "Because I brought about your ruin."

I whispered the last words against her skin, sealing the damnation with a kiss. Leaning back on my heels, I slowly slid my hands from hers, bracing myself for her anger, for the return of the distrust that had only recently left her eyes when she looked at me. The words were already scalding my throat. Words I so rarely said but felt every single day of my existence.

"I am so sorry, Oralia."

But instead of rage, I only saw sorrow. Her trembling fingertips grazed my jaw before she pressed her palm to my cheek. Tears clung like stars to her lashes, but her mouth was soft as it formed words I'd never thought I would hear.

"I forgive you, Ren."

CHAPTER

THIRTY-ONE

Oralia

At my words, Ren closed his eyes.

"I forgive you," I repeated.

He shook his head even as his hand circled once more around my wrist. He leaned into my touch as if he was as starved for contact as I was. This was not a king before me, nor a wrathful, timeless god, merely a man who laid himself at the feet of one he had wronged and resigned himself to his fate.

"You should not," he rasped.

The fading light spilling in from the windows cast his face into relief, illuminating the shame that marred his features.

"That is not for you to decide," I answered, my hand tensing against his cheek, the stubble on his face tickling my palm.

A small chuckle escaped his lips. His other hand closed over my forearm, pushing the fabric of my sleeves farther up my elbow. I barely suppressed a shiver as his soft lips caressed the marks that no one else had ever dared to even acknowledge. At his touch, heat circled its way across my heart and dipped lower toward my navel. My body was alight with the sensation.

"You are right," he said, his thumb sliding against the skin above my wrist.

Ren opened his eyes, the midnight blue of them searing. There was a heaviness in his gaze, as if he carried all the power of the universe within himself, ready at any moment to tear the world in two. Hot breath danced across my palm. I let my thumb brush once against his cheek, so close to his mouth that the curve of his bottom lip ghosted against the tip.

"Dine with us tonight," he whispered.

I blinked at him. Sidero had told me more than once of the dinners he took with his inner circle whenever he was not preoccupied with the tasks of the realm. Since I'd been in the kingdom, Ren had not hosted a single one.

Finally, I nodded. "If that is what you wish."

He turned his head, his lips moving against the heel of my hand. My stomach clenched, the sensation rippling through my body until I whimpered. I needed his touch like I needed oxygen. I needed to drown in his ash and sandalwood scent, needed him to consume me. Ren's eyes closed, and his lashes brushed against the tip of my finger, soft like the mist outside the window.

"It is not all I wish for."

I swallowed, heat pooling deep within my core. The ache I felt today blossomed anew as the tip of his tongue slid against my thumb. And though it scared me, I knew I had never wanted in such a way. The want quickly approached a need I was fearful to fulfill.

I swallowed, trying to collect my thoughts, pressing my thighs together.

He tracked the movement, a dark smile curling up his cheek as it traveled to my scar. The kiss lingered. The wet slide of his lips against my skin was hot as he angled my palm upward so my fingertips rested against his throat. His mouth moved above my wrist as he rose onto his knees until my shins pressed against his chest. Tension, so close to combustion, tightened through my middle.

Slowly, his hand slid up my arm, tangling into the hair falling across my shoulder before he pushed it back to expose the curve of my neck. I shivered as his fingers wrapped around my nape, his thumb brushing against the hollow of my throat.

"Ren," I breathed across his lips, my fingertips shakily rising to run across the stubble at his jaw.

His eyes closed, and once again, he leaned into the touch. And then he shook his head, pressing his mouth once to my palm before rising to his feet. My brows furrowed, and I fought the urge to hold on to him, to drag him back.

"I will see you tonight," he murmured, before vanishing in a swirl of shadow.

The dinner was nothing like what I had imagined.

I had envisioned something similar to the dinners I had attended with Typhon. A grand table with him at the end in a chair slightly taller than the rest, while he lorded over us all. Those meals had always been stiff with ceremony.

This was nothing like that.

I dressed in a deep wine-colored gown, ignoring Sidero's smirk when they'd come to fetch me. The gown differed slightly from others I'd worn, the neckline cutting across the tops of my arms to expose the entirety of my shoulders and dipping down between my breasts. The sleeves were long, the tips of the fabric falling halfway down the skirt and exposing my forearms and wrists that burned with the echo of his lips against my skin.

"Is this a bit..." I had struggled for the word as I combed my hair one final time, encouraging it to wave down my back. "Much?"

Sidero had blinked at me as if they did not know what I meant—the effect slightly marred by the tiny grin present on their face—before turning and leading me out of my chambers.

Now, standing in the small room where Ren and his inner circle dined, I could not give a single thought to my clothes. The room was brightly lit with the blue orbs of flame I'd grown accustomed to in Infernis. A large black chandelier hung from the center of the room, though for all its size it was simple in construction—nothing like the ornate filigree I'd grown up with in Aethera. That same simplicity was echoed in the sconces on the walls, even in the place settings at the table.

The large, *round* table.

"Here, there is no place of honor," Sidero murmured. "Here, everyone gathers as equals."

There were already a handful of people present, most already seated around the large, black wood table. I skittered to a stop, gasping at the sight of the brown-haired god I knew from Aethera, Mecrucio, seated farthest from the door, his back to a large, curved window. We gazed at each other for a long moment, his light blue eyes gleaming in the lamps overhead as they looked me over before he nodded once, raising a glass to me as if in welcome.

"Sidero..." I breathed when Mecrucio turned to the thick-set man with waving auburn hair standing over him.

"Yes, my lady?" they answered, eyes fixed upon the pair as the standing man laughed riotously, slapping Mecrucio on the back and drinking deeply, some of the wine dribbling into his dark red beard.

"That god... That is—" I cleared my throat. "I know him, from Aethera."

Sidero hummed, nodding. "Mecrucio has been one of Ren's inner circle for close to a thousand years now and plays his part as one of His Grace's spies within Aethera."

When I turned, a bland expression covered their face, as if this information was nothing of importance. "And you are not worried he will in turn spy for Typhon?"

With a frown, they shook their head. "No, Mecrucio has proven his loyalty countless times over the millennia, and Typhon has taken much from him over that time. Like many of our court, the God of Travelers sought Ren out when he had no other hope after his father died, looking for a purpose."

A purpose...like spying on Typhon for the greater good of Infernis. I wondered then if Mecrucio ever spoke of me, of my isolation, or if it was beneath his notice.

"Beside him is Thorne," Sidero said when the silence stretched. "He is a healer who helps to oversee those who protect the king-dom but also welcomes new souls into Infernis before taking them to Horace for judgment."

As we moved closer, a tall, lithe figure rose from the table, the movement much like that of a snake. From behind, I had only been able to see her waterfall of shiny blue-black hair, but my mouth almost dropped open at the gorgeous planes of her face.

"Morana." Sidero bowed their head respectfully, placing a hand across their heart. "It is an honor to see you again."

Morana bowed her head in the same respectful gesture, but her eyes never left mine. Her skin was a rich obsidian, so dark it was difficult to tell where it ended and her gown began.

In many ways, she looked like the power that I so deeply feared.

"I have heard of your coming," she said, her voice a lyrical caress. On a phantom wind, she glided until she stood so close that the shards of white in her ice-blue irises were visible. Her fingertips skimmed my cheek. They were freezing, though exceedingly gentle. "He has been waiting for you for a long, long time."

I frowned, brows drawing together. Her thumb brushed the space between them softly until I relaxed my forehead.

"Who?" I asked. She could not mean Ren.

She gave me a warm smile. It was a smile that spoke of secrets and darkness and everything in between.

"If you do not know, then you are not ready yet," she whispered, her long fingers sliding through my hair.

Morana leaned forward and pressed a soft kiss against my cheek. The dark power within me pulsed like lightning, roaring to life.

"Do not fear it, Oralia, daughter of Zephyrus," she breathed into my ear. "The darkness nourishes, the darkness strengthens, and the darkness protects."

THIRTY-TWO

Oralia

Without another word, Morana glided away from us.

Sidero chuckled beside me. I turned to see them rubbing a hand over their eyes, their other arm crossed over their chest.

"What... What was that?" I rasped as quietly as I could.

They shook their head before grabbing my arm and steering me toward the side of the table farthest away from her. "Morana is a mysterious god. No one, save herself and perhaps His Grace, knows the extent of her powers. But it is easiest to say that she is the God of Night. It is said that the night whispers to her of the future from time to time." Sidero shook their head. "Regardless, it makes for strange dinner conversation."

I huffed an agreement, trying my hardest not to think of who it was that had been waiting for me for such a *long, long* time. Thankfully, the double doors glided open, and Ren strode through, his night-black cloak billowing behind him. He'd cleaned up and changed into his usual black tunic and trousers. But this time, there were no weapons to be seen. His inky hair was pulled back from his face with a thin cord, though a few tendrils escaped, curving around the hard line of his jaw.

My breath caught. It was as if a new awareness had awoken within me—or perhaps had been waking within me and was now fully conscious. He strode into the room with all the confidence of a ruler, but it was clear he possessed what Typhon lacked.

The love of his people.

The moment Ren entered, everyone jumped to their feet. It was not a movement born of ritual or expectation. In Aethera all rose because they must. Because it was what one did in the presence of a king. Here, all rose because they respected the god who ruled over them. There was a light of fierce loyalty in their eyes—a fervor that came with following someone to the ends of the world, no matter where the path might lead.

I wondered if he could see it, and wondered what kind of god he had been to have cultivated such fervor before he lost everything.

Ren made his way slowly around the room, taking time to greet each member. No one moved to touch him or embrace him, even to offer a hand. But all nodded or bowed with reverence. Then his eyes caught mine.

Slowly, he extricated himself, saying something to the large god, Thorne, I could not hear. But, as he walked toward me, his attention slowly slid down to my neck, to the exposed slope of my collarbones, down to the dark red skirts of the gown almost black in the candlelight, and back up again.

"My lady," he hummed, stopping before me.

The title, so commonly used on me for the entirety of my life, made my blood sing. Ren pulled my hand into his, but instead of the typical kiss I'd seen so often in Aethera, he flipped my palm up and pressed his lips to the center. A flush crept up my cheeks as his eyes roved across my face before I placed my free hand over my heart and curtsied low.

"Your Grace."

Using the hand he held, he drew me back to my feet. "I believe that is the first time we have ever properly greeted one another."

"I would be happy to slap you again if that makes you more comfortable," I answered in my sweetest tone.

Stepping closer, he leaned down until his mouth was at my ear. I could have sworn the ghost of his hand slid against my hip, holding me in place.

"You know, I think you would like that a bit too much," he whispered, his lips brushing the shell of my ear.

I shivered, but before I could respond he drew back, rare heat dancing on his face. "Are you hungry?"

For a moment, I wondered if that was truly what he was asking. His eyes darkened when I licked my lips and took a deep breath. They tracked the movement, dropping to my heaving chest before moving back to my mouth.

"Starving."

The air crackled with power as we looked at one another. Booming laughter cut through the room, reminding me that there were others around us. I blinked, shaking my head experimentally.

Sidero, now slightly farther away, was speaking with a tanned soul with close-cropped brown hair and soft hazel eyes. Their body was turned toward me, and though they conversed casually, it was clear they were watching us. On the other side of Ren's shoulder Horace and Dimitri—who I supposed had entered with Ren—were speaking quietly together with Mecrucio, their attention flicking to us and away again.

Ren also appeared to become aware of everyone else in the room. He straightened and offered me his arm. Without another word, he guided me toward the table, and everyone else followed suit.

He drew out my chair for me before taking the one next to it. I sighed, crossing my legs beneath the table in an effort to abate the ever-present ache. Part of me hoped that I would be seated else-where—perhaps in another room—so that I could calm my trai-torous body. But as he adjusted his seat, I was wholly aware of him beside me. My nerves sang with every breath he took, every graceful movement of his hands as he acknowledged those around us.

"My lady," Mecrucio called to me from across the table. "How did you fare today training with His Grace?"

It was impossible not to smile in response. Mecrucio's grin was wide, mischievous, and full of secrets. I assumed with how loud our quarrels were on the subject, it was no surprise that those around the king knew of our training.

Beside me, Ren's hand slid down his thigh, fingers spread wide enough that the heat of his hand caressed mine. I swallowed loudly.

"She is powerful, much more powerful than you or I," Ren answered when I hesitated another beat too long as his hand slid back up his leg.

Mecrucio's smile widened as he looked between us and grabbed up his goblet. I mirrored his action, taking a large swig of the warm, spiced wine.

"Perhaps before long, you will be able to put His Grace on the flat of his back. Great Mothers know he needs it."

I choked, a blush heating my cheeks, quickly placing the goblet on the table and drawing my napkin to my lips. Around us, the table laughed at Mecrucio's words.

A warm hand patted against my back, and I stilled.

"Are you well?" Ren murmured quietly enough that no one around us could hear, his sweet breath ghosting across my cheek.

"Yes, thank you," I answered, taking one deep breath after another.

One rogue knuckle drew a line down the column of my neck, and my breath hitched in my throat. But before I could truly quantify the feeling, before I could beg him to do it again, it was gone, leaving a raging fire in its wake.

It was going to be a long night.

If there was ever a time that a god might combust, I thought this would be it.

Dinner was an enjoyable, yet mildly overwhelming affair. Conversation was loud, with Thorne's booming laugh echoing throughout the room like thunder rolling across the sky. Ren spoke mainly to the individuals nearest him, though it appeared he mainly preferred to observe.

Dimitri sat on his other side. It was the first time I'd seen him without his helmet. A feeling akin to homesickness circled my ribs. He was the spitting image of Drystan, from the wide set of his eyes to the generous curve of his mouth. But it was also his mannerisms, the way he held his knife and fork, the longing way he cut into his venison and closed his eyes as he chewed.

I wanted to ask if Dimitri had a brother, but every time I opened my mouth, Ren's eyes would slide to mine, and my mind would go blank. Every so often, he would shift, his long thigh pressing against my knee, and the ache would begin again until I was sure I would expire on the spot.

Sidero sat on my other side, occasionally filling in the blanks on different souls or gods in attendance at the table, or else drawing me into conversation with the soul, Lucas, they had been speaking with before we sat down. The souls did not eat, though Lucas had sighed appreciatively when the roast had been carved, wistfully describing the meals he missed from his life.

Even with that distraction, I was painfully aware of Ren beside me, each movement of his arm as it brushed against my own, and the scent of ash and sandalwood that I could smell even through the rich spices of the meal before us.

I did not know if Ren was as affected as I was. Though his hand did occasionally grip his knife tightly, and his throat bobbed when our legs brushed one another. Yet, besides his occasional gaze, he did not show that he felt the same crushing need steadily taking over his body as I did.

Dinner eventually came to a close, and it was with relief that the occupants of the table took their leave. The moment Thorne grabbed Ren's attention, I rose quickly, needing to place as much space as I could between us. Because the truth was, I did not know what it meant, this ache—this longing. Of course, I knew it was attraction, but why? I had told him earlier that I was starving, and I was in more ways one. But was I so starved for attention, for touch, that I would have taken it from anyone? Or was this desire for him alone?

There had only been one other time in my life, over a century and a half ago, that I remembered feeling a brief wanting. Where I had wondered what it would be to press my lips to another, to be held in their embrace. And that had ended with screams choking from my lungs and ashes carried off on the breeze. After that, I knew it would never be a possibility, that my life would consist of only fantasies.

But now?

"Are you well, my lady?" Sidero asked, rising to follow me from the table and out into the hall.

I looked behind me, grateful to see that Ren had not noticed I'd left. "Yes, of course, thank you. I… I need to be alone. I think I will take some time in the library."

Sidero nodded once and gave me a small smile.

"I am glad you came, Oralia," they said softly, placing a hand comfortingly on my shoulder before gliding away.

I sighed, moving in the opposite direction. The library was close to the dining room, and I knew it would be empty given that most of the castle's occupants were in their chambers or in the dining room. With a soft exhale, I pushed through the doors and took a deep breath, relishing the scent of the parchment and leather.

Hastening down one of the narrow aisles of books, I collapsed onto a small bench beneath a large window. I did not quite know why I'd come here rather than my rooms. But the quiet helped me think, to try to scrub away the feeling of his lips against my palm, to cool the burning desire deep within me.

I slid my hands over my face, pushing my hair across one shoulder and off my neck. The fabric of my gown shifted against my thighs, maddening me, and I could not stop myself from drawing a hand down the bodice and through the slit in the skirts that would allow one access to a weapon if needed.

But right before my fingertips touched the skin of my thigh, I jumped. The door banged open and then shut with a snap, a whisper of magic clicking the lock. From where I was seated, I had a clear view of the sitting area in front of the large hearth. My breath caught as Ren barreled into view, throwing himself into the chair and dropping his head into his hands.

He sat like that for a long moment, breathing deeply, before he leaned back, his head tipped up toward the ceiling and his eyes unblinking as they stared into the high rafters. His groan was loud, almost pained before his hands unfastened his trousers.

My heartbeat spiked as he drew out his cock. Though I knew anatomy and was no stranger to a male's appendage—many of Typhon's soldiers enjoyed streaking through the grounds of Aethera when they were deep in their cups—I had never seen anything like this.

The dark magic within me fluttered in response to the sight, thrumming across my veins, sparking against my skin.

Ren's chin tilted down as his thumb swiped across the head, circling once before twisting his hand. He groaned as he worked himself, his hips thrusting up to meet each pump of his palm.

Heat built through my core until my thighs were slick and my heart pounded in my chest. I knew I should look away—knew I should try to leave before he noticed me, but... *Burning Suns*, I could not move. Could not do anything but watch as he worked himself, as his teeth bit into his lower lip and his eyelids fluttered in pleasure.

My hand moved on their own accord between the layers of my skirt until they found the apex of my thighs. But then I froze.

"*Oralia.*"

CHAPTER
THIRTY-THREE

Renwick

I could not stop the moan that rumbled through my chest at the first stroke.

All I could see was her. The curve of her cheekbones. The swell of her breasts. The fiery look in her eyes when she yelled at me. The way her sharp mind pierced through my control, my resolve. The way her mouth had curved around my name, how her thighs pressed together as I'd kissed her soft skin. I had almost taken her tonight, covered her lips with mine, and breathed her heat into my lungs before I had remembered myself and who I was to her.

But this heat... I had not felt it in so long. My body had been all but a corpse for almost three centuries until she had caught fire within my veins. Now my heartbeat echoed in my ears, and my cock pulsed with the crashing need of her. A need I could not quite control.

"*Oralia.*" Her name escaped my lips before I could stop it, my eyelids fluttering, my hand moving faster, twisting at the head of my cock.

A soft gasp fluttered through the stacks, and I froze, eyes snapping open in shock. I breathed deeper, realizing the scent I had thought to be clinging to my clothes was newer than that, darker even.

She was here, in this room.

I looked toward the sound of the noise, a groan escaping my lips when I spotted her. Oralia, seated on a far bench, barely visible between the shelves. She leaned back against the window, teeth biting into her lower lip.

Embarrassment flared to life deep within my chest as I realized she had caught me. But as I breathed deeper, the scent of her arousal crashed over me like the tide. This had been the same scent I'd been breathing in throughout dinner—even earlier than that, perhaps. This whole time she had been as affected as I was. But now she was frozen in her small alcove, eyes glued to mine. As the silence lengthened, I noticed one of her hands had slipped between the folds of her skirt.

Stars, I thought I might come right there and then.

We stared at each other, both completely still for a heartbeat before I gave my cock another long, experimental stroke. Her eyelids fluttered, cheeks flushing deeper as she tracked the movement. I stroked myself again, and she whimpered, her arm flexing with the working of her hand between her thighs.

Was she matching my rhythm? Was she imagining it was my hand between her thighs as I was imagining it was her hand on my cock? Would she be frightened if I asked her to come closer? If I begged her to lie at my feet and pull apart her skirts? It would be enough, I would promise her, just to see her dripping before me, laid out as if on an altar.

I shuddered, my pleasure cresting. Her eyes widened, lips parting as I groaned louder, my eyes never leaving hers. I needed to see it—needed to know she felt it too. It was more than need, it was *desperation.*

"Come for me," I rasped.

She let out the tiniest of moans, eyes squeezing shut as her body shook, as she fell back against the window, her thighs parting wider so the fabric of her gown dipped between them. Around her, her shadows burst forth, tumbling books to the floor and wrapping us both in a cocoon of darkness. But I could see the barest sliver of her thigh where the skirts parted, glimmering with her need. It was enough to send me over the edge, my head tipping back as I came with her name on my lips, my hand growing slick with it.

When my body quieted, I took a deep breath. I did not know what I would say, only that I wanted her to come closer. I wanted to taste the wetness between her legs, to turn that quiet moan into a roar.

But when I opened my eyes once more, she was gone.

I took a deep, steadying breath staring at the door to her chambers the next morning.

All night I had paced my rooms, forcing myself to give her space, not to allow myself to come barreling into her chambers and slide my hands into her thick hair. Not to dip my head to lick the column of her throat, to taste once more the delicious combination of creation and destruction on her skin.

My need for her was difficult to understand. In the past, I'd had lovers, but I had never felt this kind of longing. And after Typhon had delivered the killing blow two and a half centuries ago, I had thought I'd lost that part of me with the resurrection. Longing, want, *need*, seemed as far away as peace and hope.

Yet now, the ghost of it was here, haunting my every breath, and I did not want to let it go.

I rapped on the door twice with my knuckles and steeled myself for her scent, for the way her cheeks would flush. Would I bring up the night before? Or would I act as though it were any other morning and invite her to continue her work on the grounds? My breath slowed. My pulse thrummed. I would let her lead.

The space of a heartbeat passed before the door swung open. Sidero's expression was guarded, uncomfortable.

"Your Grace," they said respectfully, a hand over their heart.

"Good morning, Sidero," I answered as politely as I could given the way my stomach seemed to be somewhere near my knees.

But before I could continue, they cut across me. "Oralia is not feeling well, Your Grace. She instructed me to convey her apologies." The words were stilted, rehearsed.

She did not wish to see me. Shame prickled hot like a collar around my throat.

Of course, I understood. I was a monster, a god of destruction. Why would she want to see me? Last night we had both been lost in the tension that had built between us. Now, in the dim light of morning, she had seen reason.

The spark of light that had only recently flared inside of me dimmed, then extinguished, and the frost spread painfully across my hollow heart.

"Ren?" Sidero asked, their heavy brows pulling together in concern.

"I—" Clearing my throat, I tried again, but no words came out.

With a grind of my heel on the floor, I turned, ignoring the sad look on Sidero's face and the words they tried to speak in comfort. My hands shook at my sides as my eyes pricked in the strangest way.

The doors of the castle burst open with a push of my shadows. Though my feet carried me toward the tunnels to begin their destruction, my gaze drifted over the waves of deep green grasses. The sweet scent of wildflowers maddened me, curling around my cloak and through my hair. But right before the darkness of the tunnels swallowed me whole, I caught sight of her strawberry waves cascading over a gray cloak, standing beside a lithe frame dressed in night itself.

Morana.

Was she seeking Morana to replace me as her teacher? My chest tightened until I could not draw breath. My hand rose up to slide over the leather covering my heart. The God of Night's fingertips pressed to the scars on Oralia's wrist. I knew Morana's powers almost as well as my own, she could instruct Oralia just as well in the ways of her darkness.

Yet I had wanted to be the one to help her find her strength. I needed to be the one to witness her finally realize how powerful she was. To watch what would happen when she realized the world would bend a knee to her will.

I wanted to be the first to kneel.

CHAPTER
THIRTY-FOUR

Oralia

My heart would not stop its wild race through my chest. I had struggled with it all night, never once finding my rest. Every time I closed my eyes, Ren's face was there behind my lids, head tipped back, mouth slack with pleasure. In the quiet moments right before dawn, I could have sworn I'd heard the echo of his moan sliding into my name.

The way he seemed to want me was *terrifying*. It had been glorious at first, like the rushing of a river the way he'd commanded me to come, the way my body had responded to him so readily. It had been ecstasy to watch him fall apart with my name on his lips, and I had wanted nothing more than to drop to my knees at his feet and drink down his release like the elixir of life itself. I wanted to lose myself within him and never find my way out again.

And then my power had exploded around me, enough to displace the books from the shelves and shake the very foundations of the palace. The realization had snapped the world back into focus. Fear burned away any other desire as I ran from the library. And I had sensed his presence later when he had lingered at my door on the way to his chambers.

Yet I knew above all else that I could not trust myself, not again.

My face burned with shame thinking of the message I'd left Sidero with as I pushed open the doors of the castle. The cold mist curled around my cheeks, and I shivered with the lingering presence of his magic in the fog.

But my priority was defending myself. I could not lose track of the situation at hand. Typhon would get to me one way or another, and I had to be prepared when he did.

From what Sidero said of Morana, she seemed the perfect substitute for Ren's instruction. Though now as I set out across the grounds searching for her—Sidero had instructed that was all I needed to do and she would find me—it felt like a betrayal to do so. My eyes flicked to the tunnels and back again, looking for the whisper of a black cloak, the curling of a dark shadow.

"Oralia." The feminine voice was a purr.

I spun. Morana stood with a smile on her face beside the tall grasses of Pyralis, dragging a hand over the wispy ends of the reeds.

"You were searching... But I do not believe it was for me."

My throat clicked with a swallow as I shook my head. "No, I mean, yes. I was looking for you."

She raised a smooth brow and glided closer, one of her graceful hands sliding over my shoulder and down my arm, her thumb sliding over the black scar. "Why do you fight it?"

I bit the inside of my cheek. My power rumbled, the darkness pushing out the light until it was slithering across my skin.

"I am afraid of what happens when I let it out. I have destroyed so much. I need to learn control."

A sad expression crossed her face as she lifted a hand to brush my hair from my neck in a maternal gesture that made my throat thicken with grief. "That was not what I was asking, sweet corvus, but I can see you are not ready for those questions yet."

Though the breeze wound around us, pulling up my hair and rustling my cloak, hers did not react. It was as if she were outside this reality, unaffected by matters as simple as wind or rain.

"Will you help me?" I asked, pushing away a hot slice of shame through my heart.

Ren should be teaching me. I knew that. Ren, who I wanted to witness my strength, my triumphs, to keep me safe in the dark. But I could not let myself grow closer to him, for both of our sake. He was a king, a powerful, timeless god, and I...

I was one who destroyed everything I touched, who sifted the ashes of those I loved through my fingers.

Morana's icy eyes searched mine for a long moment, reading the play of emotion inside me easily. Her thumb brushed gently beneath my eye, wiping away the wetness there.

"Of course I will teach you," she answered gently. "Of course."

Perhaps asking Morana to train me was not the best idea.

Not for her lack of knowledge or skills as a teacher, but for the ruthless way she instructed. For all her warmth and maternal kindness, I had been right in thinking she was very much like the darkness I feared. Ren's power felt like an extension of my own, comforting and safe, whereas Morana's felt ancient and unpredictable.

It had been a week of lessons with Morana and a week without even a glimpse of Ren. Sidero told me he was keeping to the tunnels, destroying all that lay there. That news made me ache for him all the deeper—to know he had listened to me that afternoon in Rathyra when I'd spoken of taking a different path other than merely violence and punishment.

With each day that passed, the hollow feeling in my chest intensified and guilt took permanent residence in my throat. I could not swallow the lump that settled there, choking me with the decision I'd made to run from him.

And yet, even though I did not trust myself not to hurt him, I still needed him in a way that left me breathless and dizzy. But I wondered what destruction we might create together, how our union might somehow rip apart the world—or perhaps just me. Now, I was not only afraid of myself, but what I would do the next time I saw him. And I was angry that he'd stayed away—that he had not fought harder for me. A small part of me wondered if he regretted what happened in the library.

"Focus, Oralia," Morana chided as we stood beside the waving grasses beside Pyralis.

I apologized in a soft voice with a dip of my head. Regardless of how brutal of a teacher Morana was, I harbored a respect for her that bordered on worship. In the time we had spent together, I learned that she was one of the rare gods from before time. *Timeless.*

She stepped closer, her freezing hands cupping my jaw. A sliver of ice prickled in the back of my neck at her touch as my power responded to her ancient magic.

"Reach for it," she instructed, her words floating on the breeze while she took a step back. "Fear does not have to be your enemy here."

Closing my eyes, I took a deep breath and reached for the power. In moments like this, the image of a hand reaching into a birdcage came to mind. My power hopped around, unused to being called for, as frightened of me as I was of it. Only in the last few days had I been able to coax it out.

So, I called to it. Dark power unfurled within my chest like the passing of silk across my soul, making me shiver.

Morana continued to speak in a low voice, but it was a language I did not understand. She explained when we first began that it was one of the old languages of the kingdom, a language the power might respond to—recognize even.

But as the magic curled, stretched, and reached, my mind strayed back to the voice I wished was speaking to me. Fingers I wished were touching my cheek. Breath I wanted sliding over my face. A moan that continued to replay in my dreams.

A crashing of boots in the grass rippled through my ears. A low growl. The scent of ash and sandalwood. Then two rough hands closed over me.

CHAPTER
THIRTY-FIVE

Renwick

A week.

A week where I could not sleep, could not eat. A week of clenching my teeth and forcing myself not to stop at her door, of unsaid words and imagined conversations. Of fisting my cock and pretending it was not Oralia I thought of as I sought my release. A week of watching her train every morning with Morana from my viewpoint in the tunnels.

I was standing in the deepest levels of the tunnels, now empty of the souls who had languished here. They had all been taken to the next part of their journey, and I resolved that not another drop of blood would be spilled in my lands. Oralia had made me see the error of my twisted ways, even as she learned how to embrace her own darkness.

The thought brought me up short. The idea that right now she could be exerting control over the shadows, that her eyes could be filled with a dark light. A contrast to the golden glow she exuded when she brought life into Infernis… But it was not only that, was it? A small voice in the back of my mind whispered that perhaps she was learning that she did not need me at all—did not want me the way she had thought she had.

Without another thought, I was jumping through the shadows to the mouth of the tunnel. My heartbeat pounded in my ears, unfamiliar and loud. There they were, standing in the large, grassy field she had grown. It spread across most of the land between the maze, Pyralis, and Isthil, dotted with the tiny, star-like flowers she called *asphodel*. The souls had taken to watching us, and even now, they were gathered around the entrance of Rathyra to observe her power.

Oralia's back was to me, but I could sense the darkness around her, practically see it manifest into the same shadows that never left my side. Her sapphire-blue dress was maddening, clinging to her waist and dipping low to expose the line of her back. Her hands were spread wide, shoulders rolled back and head tipped to the sky. The shadows unspooling from her chest were darker than before, wilder, curling around her body like serpents. There was a depth there I had not seen before, and it shocked me how her power might have grown within this short time.

Morana was speaking to her low enough that I could not hear, but her ancient eyes locked on mine as I crashed through the grasses. When I reached them, my hands moved on their own, closing over the soft skin of Oralia's shoulders, lightning zinging through my palms at the connection. I turned her, and for a moment I could only stare at the inky blackness within her eyes.

"Your Grace!" Morana cried, uncharacteristic in her show of emotion.

"Leave us," I commanded, not even sparing the God of Night a glance as she retreated toward Isthil.

The black slowly retracted into Oralia's pupils, leaving in its wake the deep green I craved. As it did, however, anger marred her features, twisting her mouth as she jerked away from my hold.

"What are you doing?" I snapped, fingers clenching into fists.

"What does it look like?" she replied.

Her arms spread wide like she could embrace the entire field we stood in as she took a few steps farther away from me, the last of her shadows melting into the mist. But I moved closer, refusing the space she tried to create.

"It looks like you are out of control," I bit back, unable to say aloud what I wanted to.

It looks like you are night incarnate, the stars in the sky, the power in my veins. Do you still want me? Do you ache for me the way I ache for you? Has this week been torture for you as it has been for me?

Her cheeks flushed, and I swore I could feel the heat from where I stood. "I am in control."

Pain curled through the words, an aching wound pulsing beneath her heart.

I shook my head, a low, unamused laugh slipping through my lips. Somehow, I was closer to her than I had been only a second ago, and I liked the way she had to force her chin up to see me. Liked the fire that flashed in her eyes, a contrast to the ice that burned through my veins. That look sparked some hope in me that perhaps I had not been the only one dying in the last week.

"Morana is not the right teacher for you."

She exhaled sharply, her arms slapping against her gown. "You said that you wanted me to learn my power."

Indignation pulsed within me that she'd conveniently left out the most important part. "I told you I wanted to teach you your power."

"Why?" she countered, shaking her head. "Why does it matter who trains me? You get what you want out of it!"

A soft growl rumbled in my chest, and I pressed a hand over my heart, vibration humming through my palm. "What is it you think I want out of it?"

She did not answer for a moment, but her eyes moved back and forth across my face hungrily, lips parting as she sipped in air. Her chest rose and fell with the movement, stray locks of hair swirling in the mist where they had wrestled free of her bun.

"I do not know!" she answered in a huff, throwing her hands up in the air. Her lower lip trembled, attention flicking everywhere but me, and her voice lost a small bit of its fire. "I do not know what you want."

I took a step forward, reaching through the space between us to wrap my hand around her wrist. "I want you to be strong."

Satisfaction purred within me when she did not move away.

"Then what does it matter if Morana trains me? If you want me to learn to control my power, then you have gotten what you wanted."

Stars, how wrong she was. Had she no inkling of what I wanted from her? The moment I realized what she could do, I wanted nothing more than for her to come to her full potential. Yes, I knew it would keep her safe and bring about Typhon's downfall, but it was about more than that now. So much more.

"It is not merely the training. It is not just your power. You are more than your magic," I rasped.

She stared at me. Her eyes were wide in confusion or shock—I could not tell. "No, I am not..."

I nodded, braving another step closer. "Yes, you are, Oralia. You are more than a god who can bring life, more than the darkness that can take it away again. Do you not see? How can you not see it?"

She shook her head, eyes squeezing shut as if she could block out my voice.

"I brought about your ruin," I choked, the grief clawing its way up my throat. My thumb traced the line of her scar. "And you took that ruin and turned it into life. But you are running from it now." That was not the truth; she was not running from her power, if anything she seemed now to be moving toward it, to reaching out with both hands. I took a deep breath, pushing away the ice that threatened to claim my heart once more, resisting her warmth. "You are running from me."

A tear escaped down her cheek. Her inhale was sharp, painful, but when she opened her eyes, the refusal to believe was clear. There was some hurt there I did not understand, simmering beneath the surface of her skin.

"I do not know what you want from me," she repeated, voice catching on the last two words.

"Then ask me, Oralia, ask me what I want," I whispered, the hollow pain in my heart sharpening to a point as I tugged her closer.

It drove me mad that she could not see how important she was. That she could not see that I had been in agony for the last week, wanting nothing more than to worship her, to show her how much I wanted her. I thought again of how I wanted to raze Aethera to the ground, to punish all who ever thought that she was less than the brightest star in the sky.

"What do you want, Ren?" The words were more of a rasp as splotches of red dotted her high cheekbones.

I grasped her face, my fingers pressing into the delicate skin of her throat.

"You."

Tilting her head back, I crushed my mouth to hers, swallowing her gasp as I drew my other arm around her waist, pulling her to the tips of her toes. This feeling. *Stars.* It was more than the way she had burrowed her way beneath my skin. More than the way she had carved out a place for herself in my chest. She had dug her way into my very soul, filling the space where the broken pieces had lain.

CHAPTER
THIRTY-SIX

Oralia

As his lips covered mine, I awoke for what felt like the very first time.

My body flared into life, singing with the sensation of his soft mouth moving in confusing patterns against my own. This was sunlight and shadow. It was sweetness and bitterness. Darkness and daylight and everything in between. Ren pulled me closer, drawing me up until I was flush against his chest, but it was not close enough. I grabbed ahold of his tunic, fearful that he might pull away.

"Why do you run from me?" he pleaded against my lips, his fingers sliding across my cheeks.

My mouth opened, but before I could answer, his tongue delved inside, claiming it for himself. I whimpered, arms winding around his neck, and though the words were there, they lodged within my throat.

"I..." I gasped as his mouth moved down my jaw.

I had been terrified of what it would mean to want him, to

need him. And, further, what sort of destruction we might wreak together.

But now, as my hands clutched his wide shoulders and his mouth claimed mine once more, I could not help but wonder why I would have wanted to stop this. Never, in the two and a half centuries I'd been alive, had I ever truly contemplated a kiss. Not with my power and all its dangers. But this?

This was magic. *Power.* It was the great yawning expanse of the universe rolled into a singular moment between our lips.

Ren did not allow me even a moment to wonder if I was doing it right. Not with the way he moaned or the hardness that pressed against my belly. His hand slid across my temples, pulling through my hair until he'd drawn out all the pins from the bun I wore, and it fell down my back.

He nipped at my bottom lip, soothing it with his tongue a moment later. His arm around my waist tightened as his fingers splayed across my hip. The pressure sent a warmth zinging through my chest, healing that long-broken part of me that continued to throb with raw edges.

"This last week has been agony," Ren murmured.

Tears bled into the corner of my eyes, and I clutched him deeper. My power reached out to meet his, tangling within his darkness. Agony was the perfect word to describe it. Even now, it was agony. And yet, the warmth grew, blossoming once more into that deep ache centered in my core until I was dripping between my thighs.

We broke apart, but before I could protest, his mouth was moving across the line of my jaw, down toward my throat, kissing and nipping at the space below my ear.

"Ren," I moaned, clutching at his biceps.

"*Stars*," he cursed, grinding himself into me.

He murmured in that ancient language against my skin between kisses, biting at the space where my neck met my shoulder. My head tilted to the side to allow him better access, my body moving against him to plead *more, more, more.* Yet he pulled back, his midnight eyes aflame. Ren's lips were kiss-stung, his hair blowing free in the mists that curled around us, and there was something in his expression I could not quantify as we tried to catch our breath.

"Tell me," he whispered. I blinked at him, unsure how to say it even as I clutched at his cloak. Ren leaned closer until his lips were merely a breath away from mine. "Tell me what you want."

I shook my head, embarrassment flooding through my veins because I did not know how to ask for it. How did I put into words that I wanted this to never end and feared he would not want the same?

A small smile curled at the corner of his mouth. His eyes were half lidded. But when I tried to close the distance between us once more, he pulled back. "No. With your words, Oralia."

I gulped a deep lungful of air, my knees weakening at the way my name passed across his lips. It was that, more than anything else, that spurred me to action, and had my mouth moving with the words that I knew he needed me to say. I had been the one to run, so I must be the one to speak.

"Kiss me."

"Yes," he groaned, drawing his magic around us until it was as dark as midnight.

My back hit the curved wall of the palace, deep within the shadows where no prying eyes could see, but he gave me no quarter before his lips covered mine. I took his bottom lip between my teeth, the way he had done, and a surge of heat tore through my very soul when a moan broke through his chest. The sound of his pleasure made me bolder, licking and sucking at his mouth. My hands slid through his hair, trying to commit every piece of him to memory.

His hands drew up my arms, rounding over my shoulders to slide against my back, bracketing me against the wall. The ache between my thighs was now burning so intensely I thought I might combust if it was not relieved. Ren pressed against me, allowing me to feel the weight of his arousal against my hips before he leaned back, his eyes bright in the shadows.

Slowly, so slowly, he lowered to his knees, his attention never leaving mine. And he was like one of the human pilgrims when they first set eyes upon their chosen god, like a man seeing the sun for the first time. I let out a small whimper, and his brows furrowed in response, palms sliding down the silken fabric of my bodice.

"I have wanted this all week. To supplicate at your feet, begging you to shine your light upon me."

My whimper this time was more of a moan as I leaned against the wall of the palace, against the bones of the gods who had given themselves to their greatest fear. He slid my skirt apart, drawing one knee over his shoulder. I gasped, hot embarrassment flooding my cheeks. But hungry gaze rested on the glimmering wetness of my inner thigh, though the fabric of my gown covered the rest of me.

"I kneel only for you," he whispered, pressing a kiss to the inside of my knee, his hand sliding up the outside of my thigh. "Tell me... Tell me you want this too."

The words caught in my throat as he kissed higher, licking at the wetness on my skin. His moan was soft but rumbled through his chest as he tasted my need for him. Slowly, he looked up, midnight eyes soft and hard all at the same time.

Unbidden, the sensation of ash sifted through my fingers. The bright light of the afternoon sun glinting off the golden castle blinded me. The scream that had burned my throat, the horror I'd wrought. I could not bear the same fate befalling him.

And I found I could not speak, could not find the courage to say the words to Ren. Fear had its grip on my throat until I could barely sip in the air I needed. Like frost across the ground, his wall built back into place in his mind. And though I knew it was to protect himself, the sight of his familiar, cold expression sliced through my chest.

Gently, he lowered my leg back to the ground, sliding the fabric of my skirts back together.

"When you are ready to say the words, I will be waiting."

And then, in a heartbeat, he disappeared into the shadows.

THIRTY-SEVEN

Oralia

I stood, panting, against the wall of the palace.

Burning Suns. Why had I not said anything? Why had I let fear grip my throat and squeeze? He had been right there, right where I so desperately needed him, and yet I could not say the words.

Pressing my fingers to my lids, I took a breath, willing the image seared within my mind back into the depths.

Could I say them now? If he were to reappear before me, would I be able to speak it aloud? I honestly was not sure. A small part of me knew the fear within me was not completely rational. My power could not touch him. I *had* touched him more times than I could count through my time here in Infernis. And yet, with each day that I grew stronger, I could not help but fear that I would reach out for him only to find ashes between my fingers.

Slowly, I pushed myself from the wall and made my way in a daze around the side of the palace and up the stairs. I found myself back in my chambers, fingers against my bruised lips to remind myself it had not been a dream.

You took that ruin and turned it into life.

It was true. I had tried as hard as I could to accept the hand I had been dealt, to find peace and contentment in an existence that was filled with grief and shame. No one ever appeared to notice that I was wilting inside the cage I'd be born into, that I was slowly crumbling into ash before their very eyes. Not even I had truly noticed.

"My lady?" Sidero murmured.

I jumped, so startled I gasped and my hand flew to my throat. "Sidero!"

They blinked in surprise. "I did announce myself. You left the door ajar... Are you well?"

I shook my head, nails biting into my palms. "Has... Has King Renwick ever had a consort?"

When they did not immediately respond to the unexpected question, despair circled my stomach. Of course, he would have had a consort. He was *timeless*. It was not inconceivable that he'd had many consorts in his existence. Whereas, before I came to Infernis, I could have counted the times I was touched in kindness on one hand.

I looked at Sidero, and there was an expression on their face I could not understand.

"His Grace has had lovers in the past," they said carefully. Discomfort squirmed in my chest. "But they were never lasting nor meaningful, and it has been quite some time since he has taken one."

I nodded, biting the inside of my cheek. It made sense that he would not have taken a lover after his last resurrection. Not when he could barely stomach the touch of another. Though...he had touched me—reached for me even before we had come to an understanding. His hand had been warm on my back as we walked through Rathyra. His thumb had stroked my knuckles when I'd wanted to destroy the olive tree, his mouth had traced my scars.

A blush fanned across my cheeks, and I looked down at my fingers knotting and unknotting in my lap. I had thought his coldness to be merely who he was at first, and then a part of his curse as the God of Death, but I had watched him fight the ice that lived inside him as often as I had seen him use it as a shield.

This last week has been agony, he'd said.

"Is it wrong?" I asked in a soft voice, attention trained on the scars peeking through the daggered sleeves of my gown.

"Is what wrong?" Sidero asked, concern etched in their voice.

"To want him so."

A soft hand brushed back the loose hair from my shoulder before resting softly upon it, their thumb brushing once against the silk of the gown. "To deny such a thing merely because you think you must would be wrong. Do you not remember what Morana said to you when you first met?"

I pursed my lips, trying to recall. "She said he had been waiting for me a long, long time."

During the last few days of working with Morana, she had taught me more about her powers and the precognition she possessed. Hers were not arbitrary premonitions. It was the knowledge of the night she held within her mind. Knowledge that could move mountains and tear down thrones.

Sidero let out another impatient sigh. "*Stars,* you both are infuriating. Can you not imagine who he might be?"

My brows furrowed. Sidero leaned closer, pressing a large finger to my forehead to smooth them. "Why do you fight what your soul already knows? Why must you run from destiny?"

Slowly, as though waking from a dream, I pushed to my feet.

"Where is he?" I was already moving toward the door.

"I am not sure, but perhaps in his chambers," Sidero answered, not bothering to hide the smile in their voice.

My footsteps clicked against the onyx floor, breath loud in my ears. I said the words in my head, repeating them until they slid effortlessly with every breath—until I was at his door and turning the knob, not even bothering to knock.

Ren was there, standing at the hearth with his arm propped against the dark mantel. As always, he was dressed in his night-black clothes, damp hair curling around his shoulders. He wore no cloak, no baldric, only his tunic. The sleeves were pushed up his muscular forearms. His eyes flicked up, surprise coloring his features. I was breathless as the door slammed behind me, crossing the room to stand only a few inches away.

"I want you, Ren."

CHAPTER
THIRTY-EIGHT

Renwick

I gaped at her for a long moment.

But then I took a slow, deep breath, allowing her scent to wash over me. Had it truly only been a few hours ago that I'd felt her mouth against mine? That I'd run my hands over her face, sensing just the barest taste of her need? It felt like a human lifetime had passed in those hours.

Her sapphire skirts were a pool of darkness around her. Her chest heaved, but there was none of the anxiety or uncertainty that I'd witnessed earlier today. None of the fear that had forced her to run from me a week ago.

Carefully, I touched her lower lip as my fingertips caressing her cheek. She leaned into the touch, mouth parted before she pressed a kiss to the tip.

"Why did you run?" I asked, sliding my hand through her hair until my thumb stroked her cheekbone. "That night in the library."

Oralia took a deep breath, and for a moment, I was scared she would retreat within herself once more. But then her eyes opened, and she licked her lips.

"I...I have never spoken of it aloud, not since that day," she breathed, eyes flickering with faraway memories.

Nodding, I softened my touch, tucking her hair behind her ear, content to wait until she was ready to speak.

"When I was first bitten, Typhon brought healers from around the kingdom and farther, even. Some from the northern plains, where the snows are so deep one cannot wade through them. And... nothing worked, but I was scarred by the attempts to rid the curse from my veins." She touched two fingers to her chest.

"For almost a century, I touched no one. I was careful, and Typhon's decrees did the rest. But with time, the fear softened, and childhood memories blurred as my strength grew and I approached prime."

Though I was a timeless god and I could not truly understand the experience of a god reaching prime—when their magic fully manifested and their body found its final form—I nodded all the same because I had witnessed it enough throughout the centuries. It was often a dangerous time for young gods where recklessness won against logic, pushing the boundaries of their magic and control.

"I met a human who worked on the grounds of the palace, tending to the crops and plants I grew." Her copper brows furrowed, mouth tensing. "Over time, we grew comfortable together. Simple greetings turned into conversations, which turned into him walking with me through the gardens. And my lonely life was suddenly...much more bearable."

I hummed my understanding. For a god so isolated, such companionship must have felt like a gift. Tenderly, I stroked her forehead, trying to soften the lines between her brows. When her throat clicked, and she did not continue, I pressed a soft kiss to her temple.

"You do not have to—"

"I was reckless," she breathed. "I had not seen my power fully manifest in years save for the moments the shadows flared and Typhon used his light to contain them. As time passed with my new companion, our feelings grew for one another. Though I understood rationally that we could never truly *be*..." She shook her head, a tiny shrug shaking her shoulders. "I do not know if it was me he cared for, or if I was merely a god he idolized with that strange fervor humans have. But one afternoon when we were settled beneath one of the apple trees, he leaned forward to press his lips to mine."

A soft click echoed through the room with her swallow. *You do not know what I have done*, she had said. I pressed a palm over her heart, fingers spread wide, and her soft hand covered the back of my own, scars shining in the blue light of the fire.

"Only the barest bit of his chest brushed my fingertip, but it was enough. I think that small touch drew out the process into something akin to torture. His eyes widened, he gasped in pain, and he crumbled to ash in my hands. That is when I was given the gloves that I never took off again." Her gaze, which had floated to somewhere around my throat, slid back to my face. "And that is why I ran. I could not bear for you to suffer the same..."

"I understand," I answered when her voice died out, crouching so we were eye to eye, both hands sliding to cup her face. "And I do not blame you."

And I did not. Truly, I understood. I had witnessed enough horrors in this existence to understand how such a moment would change her and make her believe she was a monster. *Great Mothers*, I could understand that all too well.

Relief splashed across her face, a soft sigh sliding through her lips as she melted into my touch. She turned her head, brushing her mouth against my palm.

"I will not run again," she vowed. "If...if you want this too."

My mouth brushed hers lightly, and her eyes closed. The small whimper she gave almost broke my control.

"You have consumed me, Oralia," I whispered in answer, pressing a kiss to the corner of her eye, sliding my lips over the thin skin of her lid until her lashes tickled my mouth. I brushed the space between her brows. "I cannot sleep." I moved to the other lid. "Cannot eat." Down to her other cheekbone. "You have crawled beneath my skin." My lips lingered at the corner of her mouth. "You have taken root in my very soul."

Then my mouth covered hers, forcing her lips apart. She let out a breathy whimper, hands clutching my arms, lips opening for me. I dragged my hand up her waist, my thumb brushing the underside of her breast. She shivered, pressing herself into my touch with a desperation that made me all the hungrier. Emboldened, my hand slid higher to stroke the hardened peak through the silken fabric of her gown.

"Please," she whimpered, eyes dark and lips already swollen.

"Tell me what you need, how far you want this to go," I breathed.

I kissed the side of her jaw, then the space below her ear that had made her tremble before. Oralia clutched my tunic until her nails dug into my shoulder. Her chest rose with a deep breath and she pressed herself tighter against me until I could not resist biting down on the delicate skin of her neck. Her moan was louder than any I'd heard so far. My cock throbbed in response, and my resolve cracked at the edges.

No, she needed to say it. Needed to understand what she was

asking for. After a lifetime of her choices being taken away, she must make this choice. And after she distanced herself from me that night in the library, I also needed her to be sure of what she wanted.

"Please, Ren," she started, swallowing loudly when I brushed her breast again. "I need you to take away this ache inside of me."

I drew away to look at her, the way her cheeks flushed in the firelight, the heaving of her chest. Slowly, I pushed her back until her legs hit the nearby couch and guided her onto it. I gripped the ornate wood of the back until I bracketed her in.

"How would you like me to do that, *eshara?*" The old term of endearment I'd never used before flowed from my lips before I could stop it. *My darling. My life force. My pulse.*

One hand slid from the back of the couch to her throat, sliding across the top of her breasts until I drew down between them over the stiff fabric of her bodice.

"With my hand?" I whispered, leaning down to press a kiss to one of her collarbones. "With my mouth?"

My traveling fingers grasped at her skirts, pulling them up until the smooth line of her calves was exposed.

"What—What do you want?" she asked in such a trembling voice it made me feel hollow.

It made me want to protect her, to take care of her.

"What do I want?"

She nodded, her eyes flicking from my mouth to the hand currently rucking up her skirt. The pale skin of her knees was broken only by the freckles that dotted her skin. My thumb rested against the outside of her thigh, and I drew small, reassuring circles there to calm her.

"It is not a want, Oralia. It is a need," I murmured, slowly dropping to the ground as if I were merely a human man before an altar. "I need you more than the air in my lungs, more than the magic in my veins. I need your light and your darkness. I need *you.*"

I pressed a kiss to her other knee but did not move her skirts higher. With each gasp, her breasts swelled beneath her dress, tormenting me. Her pupils were so dilated I could only see a bare glimmer of green surrounding them, an echo of that dark power roiling beneath her skin. I groaned as her teeth found her lower lip, sucking on it ever so slightly, my cock twitching with each pull.

Her mouth popped open, anxiety creeping into the corners of her mouth. "I have never... I have not..."

I shushed her, cupping her face. Pain burned within my chest at the look of uncertainty on her face, at the shame coloring her features. That she would be embarrassed by never being touched by another, worshipped by another, made me want to roar in anger. The realization that she had so rarely been touched in kindness that even these gentle caresses were new made the pain burn brighter still.

"I know you have not," I reassured her in a soft voice. "If you do not like it, we will stop."

Some of the anxiety in her face melted away as I pressed a lingering kiss to the top of her thigh. The burning feeling in my chest gave way to a wondrous, gentle warmth as her hand tentatively stroked my hair.

"Allow me to worship you."

Another breathy whimper escaped through her lips. Her fingers became bolder as her nails ran across my scalp, making me shiver.

"*Yes.*"

With a sigh of relief, I grabbed her hips, tugging her gently until she was right on the edge of the couch before looking up to ensure that she was comfortable. I drew up her skirts and curled my fingers into the edges of the lace covering her, tugging them down over her boots and tucking them into my trouser pocket before my palms skimmed over her knees, which were firmly pressed together.

"Open for me."

There was the barest moment of resistance before she relaxed, allowing me to pull her knees wide. I bit back a groan. The inside of her thighs glimmered in the firelight with the evidence of her need. With a glance up at her reddened cheeks, I licked my lips.

"You are perfect."

Slow enough not to startle her, I leaned forward, pressing a kiss to the inside of her thigh. I'd had only the briefest of tastes earlier when I kissed this very spot in the shade of the castle. The sweet, earthy taste of her on my tongue had maddened me. This time, I lapped at it, moving higher and pushing her legs apart to accommodate my shoulders. I was so hard I could not stop from stroking myself once through my trousers to relieve a bit of the ache.

Her hands gripped the fabric of her skirts until her knuckles bleached white and her fists trembled. Pressing one hand against her heart, I tried to ground her, slowly licking once up her center with the flat of my tongue.

Oralia arched almost completely off the couch, forcing me to push her back down with one hand on her hip to keep her in place. I lapped at her again, moaning at the divine taste on my tongue. It was sunshine and autumn and the cosmos all wrapped up into one. It was the beginning and ending of time, a great cataclysm of the stars to create the night sky. Her moans grew louder as her fingers dug into the fabric and her hips arched up to meet each movement of my tongue.

"Hold still, *eshara*. I need you to hold still for me."

Then I latched my mouth over her clit, sucking hard. She cried out, her hands flying to my hair, nails digging against my scalp. Her body trembled, back bowing, but her hips stayed as I'd asked. Withdrawing my hand from her torso, I slid one finger up the center of her while I swirled her clit.

"*Ren*," she moaned, her voice so low I barely recognized it.

Slowly, I pressed a finger inside. *Stars*, she was tight. A gush of desire drenched my hand, her walls clamping down on me.

"Just like that," I breathed against her heat. "Come for me."

I curled the finger inside of her, giving her clit one long suck. She exploded around me, shadows and sunlight dancing in the space around us as she came. Her shadows tangled with mine, the feeling more intimate than any physical act. Sunset waves spilled across the back of the couch, her head thrown back, eyes squeezed shut, her mouth forming my name over and over.

Ren. Ren. Ren.

It was the most beautiful thing I'd ever seen.

I kissed her clit again softly, drawing her back down with the soft pumping of my finger until her body calmed. Slowly, I withdrew my hand and sucked my fingers into my mouth. A quiet moan of delight escaped my lips at the exquisite taste of her orgasm on my skin.

Pushing onto my knees, I leaned forward, slotting my lips over hers. Our tongues tangled together as I swallowed her moan and invited her to taste her own pleasure. Her hands threaded through my hair, nipping at my bottom lip. I could not resist pushing myself between her thighs, rubbing my aching, fabric-covered cock against her wet center.

Finally, we broke apart. I cupped her cheek and let my thumb brush her bottom lip.

"All right?" I asked, searching her face for any sign of regret.

She nodded, a smile breaking over her face the way dawn broke over the sky. Her cheeks flushed as she shifted, pushing herself closer to me.

"*More*," she demanded.

CHAPTER
THIRTY-NINE

Oralia

Ren's lips were swollen, glistening faintly in the light from the hearth as we stared at one another. All at once, I felt whole and bereft, satisfied and full of need.

I did not know what compelled me to ask for more, other than my need to feel him beneath my fingertips. I wanted to witness his careful control crumble and see him undone. At that thought, my power curled around me, swooping low into my belly before dancing out to tangle with his. I could not see it anymore, but I could feel the way our magic intertwined, the understanding that came with it.

Ren was not afraid of my darkness.

"More?" he asked with a slight raise of his brow.

His hand was so gentle on my face, his thumb pulling down my bottom lip, exposing my teeth. I flicked my tongue out to taste his skin. The soft groan that rumbled from his chest emboldened me further. I drew my hands from his hair, over the wide curve of his shoulders, before settling on his chest. The rigid planes of his muscles beneath my palms stirred the heat between my thighs. My finger-nails dragged against the fabric of his tunic as his cock twitched in his trousers.

I nodded in answer to his question, trying to figure out how to ask him for what I wanted. It seemed to be the only way he would give it to me: I had to use my words.

"I want to touch you."

A small smirk twisted the corner of his mouth even as his eyes darkened further, his thumb now resting against my teeth.

"Anything," he groaned. "Anything you want, I will give it to you."

Shaking my head, I slid my hands lower until they rested over his taut stomach. I leaned forward, and he allowed me to press a kiss to his cheek before I whispered in his ear, "Teach me, Ren."

His eyes were blazing as I drew back, and he let out a shaky exhale. Then, he looked down at my hands, his own moving to the cushions on either side of my thighs.

"Take it out," he murmured in a dark, commanding tone that reminded me that it was a king who knelt before me.

Fumbling with the fastenings of his trousers, I could not help but feel a bit inept. Yet he did not appear impatient while I worked. Instead, he merely watched my face, his eyes raking over each freckle, each curve as though he were trying to memorize them. Finally, when I had his trousers open, I willed my hands to stop shaking as I carefully reached inside.

His skin was smooth against my palm, warm and heavy. I gripped him but froze when a hiss whistled through his teeth.

"Gently, *eshara*."

Softening my grip, I pulled him carefully from the confines of the black fabric. Though I had seen it from a distance, that was nothing compared to being this close. It was thick and long, with a deep vein running up the underside of it that I traced with one finger. The tip was deep red and shining with his obvious need.

"Was that the first time you'd seen a cock?" he asked in a rasp, flexing his hips as I drew my fingertips along the base.

"No," I answered, unable to tear my gaze away, but he froze. "Typhon's men are prone to losing their clothes when they have had too much wine. Plus, I have read many books on the matter."

He let out a soft chuckle, and I could have sworn he brushed a kiss against my forehead, murmuring "books" under his breath.

"Wrap your hand around it," he instructed.

It was wide enough that my fingertips barely touched my thumb. Remembering what I had seen him do in the library, I twisted my wrist toward the tip, letting some of the fluid wet my palm. I did not bother to hide my grin at the deep groan that rumbled through his chest. When I repeated the motion, he thrust up into my hand.

With each moan he gave, each time his eyelids fluttered, the soft way he gasped, a spark of pleasure rippled through me. That I could be the one to do this to him, to make him feel this way made me understand better now what it meant to be powerful.

He placed his hand over mine.

"Slower," he said, guiding my hand into a rhythm he liked. "Yes, just like that. Perfect."

Wetness slid across my thighs at his praise, and I thought perhaps I might have made a noise from the way his eyes suddenly fixed upon mine, a feral grin spreading across his cheeks.

"*Stars.*" He thrust into my hand faster, jaw slackening, eyes dancing over my face, my breasts, to the bunched-up fabric of my skirts, my legs. I wanted to know what it felt like for there to be no space between us. Wanted to know what it might be like to have him inside of me.

Would it be as earth-shattering as his mouth upon my skin?

"So perfect," he groaned, one hand sliding to my waist, thumb brushing the underside of my breast in time with the rhythm of my fist.

With another rumbling moan his other hand covered mine. He rose higher to his knees, staring up at me as we worked him together to completion. Our power tangled once more around us, as if his shadows were reaching out for mine, drawing them closer. Ren's jaw clenched, his eyes squeezing shut for a moment before they snapped open, meeting mine as he came across our hands and the floor.

We breathed together in the room's silence, staring at each other until he leaned forward and pressed a kiss to my collarbone.

"Are you well?" he asked, using his clean hand to lower my skirts around my legs before tucking himself back in to his trousers.

I nodded while he stood and looked toward the rest of his rooms.

"Stay right here, all right?" His voice was soft, reassuring, and I nodded again before he headed into his bedroom.

In the space of only a few heartbeats, he was back with two towels, dropping one to the floor beneath my feet. He sat beside me on the couch. Gently, he took my hands in his, wiping them slowly. I stared up at him, wondering at the tender expression on his face that I'd never seen before and the way it seemed to flicker like frost might across warm glass.

He placed the cloths to the side and drew my hands up, pressing a soft kiss to each of my wrists, directly over the black crescent-shaped scars.

Insecurity pulsed through me as he ran his thumbs across my

palms. What was I supposed to do now? What would happen next? Would he... Would he hold me? Would I be able to stop the thunder beginning in my heart?

Slowly, he pressed a soft kiss to my palm, which made the aching begin again. I twisted, knees drawing beneath me as I reached for him with my other. He reached for me at the same time, fingers tugging at my hip to draw me across his lap.

A knock sounded loud on the door.

"Your Grace," a low voice rumbled.

Heat bled through my cheeks and I jerked away. A growl vibrated through his chest before he tugged me forward again.

"Your Grace, it is urgent," the voice pressed on, another knock echoing through the chamber.

I put my hand against his chest, and he dipped his chin, forehead pressing against mine.

"Stay," he murmured against my lips.

With a shake of my head, I extricated myself from his hold, rising to my feet on unsteady legs. He followed me like a predator, dark eyes intent upon my face.

"Ora—"

"*Ren*," Mecrucio's voice, muffled by the door, cut my name from his lips. "We must speak with you at once."

I took one step back, then another. "You are needed."

Ren followed. "I *need* you."

A blush crept up my throat and I swallowed loudly. "Tomorrow." After a moment, he nodded, running a hand through his hair. I fumbled at the door, ignoring the way his hand reached out to me again. "I. Um. Thank you."

Thank you? Burning Suns.

Without a backward glance, I threw open the door, slipped between the gods who wore twin expressions of shock on their faces, and dashed down the hall.

CHAPTER
FORTY

Renwick

She should have stayed.

There had been a moment where I'd almost stopped her and wrapped an arm around her waist to haul her back. I should have. There was no way I wanted her alone in her chambers, drawing herself into some anxious frenzy when there was no need. I sighed heavily, running my hand through my hair again before leveling Horace and Mecrucio with a stony gaze, all the warmth of the evening bleeding from my chest.

"Your Grace, I apologize," Horace said, placing a hand over his heart and bowing his head.

Behind him stood Mecrucio, the surprised look on his face slowly curling into delight. His hair was wild, disheveled like he'd been in a windstorm, and the light gray tunic he wore was rumpled, collar flipped inside out. The baldric strapped around his chest was the only thing that appeared firmly in place—even his dark blue cloak was slightly off-center.

"We have news that pertains to Aelestor," Horace explained when Mecrucio merely continued to gawk. "I think it best you hear it now."

With another sigh, I stepped back, motioning them both into the room. Horace came first, his footsteps faltering before he continued. His ruby eyes flicked over the couch before he decided instead to stand beside the mantel. I appreciated his discretion, especially when Mecrucio bounced into the room.

"It absolutely reeks in here."

In silence, I surreptitiously kicked the towel beneath the couch before throwing myself onto it, trying not to think about Oralia's scent and the way it clung to the dark fabric or the lace that now burned a hole in my pocket.

Mecrucio froze before he sat in the opposite wingback chair, his eyes wide. "Ren, did you—"

I clenched my jaw, leaning forward to rest my elbows on my thighs. "Finish that sentence and we will see how long it takes to regrow your left ear," I growled.

He did not so much as flinch. Instead, he smiled amusedly before drawing his hands up in surrender. Horace merely stared at us as if we were children, arms crossed over his wide chest, the barest glimmer of amusement in his eyes.

"Tell me what you know," I commanded.

Immediately, Mecrucio's demeanor shifted, leaning forward until his elbows rested on his knees, a serious expression transforming his face. This, I knew, was how he presented himself in Aethera. It was how he survived as a spy in a golden kingdom that would destroy him if they knew of the secrets he passed to me.

"Aelestor has done as you asked," he said, rubbing his palms together absentmindedly. "He told Typhon there was no sign of Oralia in the kingdom that he could find. Typhon was frustrated, but he appeared to believe that at least Aelestor could not find her."

"Will he be allowed back?" I asked.

Mecrucio shrugged.

"As far as I know, Aelestor will be sent to continue to look for her, though he has not yet tried. There was...however..." Mecrucio shifted uncomfortably in his seat, his eyes flicking between Horace and me. "The subject of Oralia's use to Aethera was discussed."

I bit the inside of my cheek, all the warmth of my time with Oralia consumed with bitter frost. "Did he speak of her powers?"

Mecrucio's face turned uncharacteristically dark and a muscle jumped in his cheek.

"He did not, but he alluded to her power of life somehow being able to fight the *dark magic* within the kingdom."

I exhaled with a shake of my head.

"So no one knows of her other power except for a select few? Does his court not wonder why she was so isolated? Why she was always so...alone?"

Mecrucio shrugged, tapping a foot against the ground. "His court cares for nothing but power. They jostle to stand as close as they can to the golden king, hoping to feel his warmth." He rolled his eyes. "They follow without question or care for the consequences, as it has always been."

As it has always been.

I could remember how they had disregarded Peregrine's suffering as she wasted away on her yew throne. The way they whispered behind their hands of Typhon's many lovers, paraded through the court like celestial birds on display. Pretended they didn't notice the bruises she covered with high-necked gowns and long flowing hair.

It took much force to bruise a god.

"What is his next move?" I asked.

It was Mecrucio's turn to sigh, running a hand through his hair. His focus wandered to the roaring fire. His mouth pulled into a small frown. "He would not say, but he eyed each and every one of us as if weighing our importance to Oralia. It was...terrifying."

Horace made a soft noise in the back of his throat and a gentle look was exchanged between the two gods.

I swallowed back my rage. "Is there no chance of convincing Typhon she is elsewhere?"

Mecrucio shrugged. "Caston, his heir, suggested they search as far as Iapetos, but Typhon dismissed it almost at once. The prince has only left Aethera to search for Oralia before returning to the castle for news. It is said that he will not return to his station on the Western Reaches until she returns."

I nodded. There was no way she'd gone to Iapetos. The island was treacherous to reach, guarded by a great ocean and winged beasts that might swallow one whole. No one who dared enter Iapetos ever came back alive. It was rumored that it was where all the old gods who had been lost to time resided. Well, the ones that had not given themselves up to time itself. I never wanted to go there. I did not want to know if those who shaped this world were alive and thriving while they'd left the rest of us behind.

I looked at Horace, one of the few timeless gods who had remained behind with me. His face was stricken with the same hopelessness I felt at the mention of the island.

"He will not stop," Mecrucio said. "Not until he has her."

A wave of protective fury washed over me at the thought of

Typhon with his claws in her. I could see it so clearly: her fingers wrapped around an innocent throat, her face blank with the pain and grief that would consume her. He would use her as a weapon, and she would kill for him again and again.

That could not—would not—happen.

"Then he must be stopped. He cannot have her."

She is mine, I wanted to roar. A new image of her replaced the first: blazing and triumphant by my side, her hand thrust high in the air wrapped around Typhon's golden crown.

She deserved vengeance—justice—as much as I did.

Horace shifted, drawing his arm from where it rested on the mantel. "There is another matter that we must discuss. Josette has been asking for Aelestor. She is remembering."

I stared at him in shock, watching the concern play on his face. Josette had been with us for centuries, her mind wiped clean from almost the moment she stepped onto our shores. Though each soul was an individual, and therefore their journey was singular, they all followed a similar path. Souls who had suffered as Josette had and drank from the Athal to remove their memories did not normally remember their lives, nor did they ask for those they should not remember. I tried to curb the temper rising inside of me that I had not been informed sooner.

"Since when?"

His hands clenched into fists before he exhaled slowly, the tension draining with his breath. "A day or so, perhaps more. She asked for him this morning."

Leaning forward, I rested my elbows on my thighs. "How is that possible?"

Horace looked uncomfortable, shifting his weight before

tightening his arms across his chest. "I am sorry, Your Grace, but I am not sure."

Suddenly, the night crashed heavily across my shoulders.

"Can we help her?"

The helplessness on Horace's face mirrored my own. "I am not sure. If Aelestor is able to make it back to Rathyra, I believe we should allow him a chance to help her remember."

Pursing my lips, I considered the human soul who had wandered Isthil for half a century and Pyralis for even longer after that. It was rare that a soul was granted a drink from the Athal, unheard of that even after they drank, they did not slip into a blissful forgetfulness. But she had been the exception. Yes, she no longer remembered her human life, yet for Josette all the pain, the trauma, lingered even after she had drunk.

That she now remembered Aelestor was shocking.

Eventually, I nodded my agreement. "I do not want him anywhere near Oralia."

They both blinked at me.

"Do you understand?" I pushed, standing to my feet.

Mecrucio stood as well, both gods placing their hands over their hearts and bowing their heads.

"Yes, Your Grace," they answered together.

I nodded, gesturing toward the door, weariness overtaking me. "Good, now get out."

Before the door could swing shut, however, a scream rended the air. A scream that sounded far too much like Oralia.

CHAPTER
FORTY-ONE

Oralia

On stumbling feet, I made my way back to my rooms.

The heat of Ren's mouth burned across my skin like a siren call, tempting me to turn around and return. I stepped into the darkness of my room, surprised that a fire was not lit. With arms outstretched, I felt my way toward the hearth, and at my touch, blue flames roared in the grate.

Air shifted, my power prickling on the back of my neck like several soft taps. A warning.

"Sidero?" I called out, turning from the fire.

A golden hand closed over my throat, another covering my mouth. I shrieked, the sound strangled by metal as I stared up into a gilded mask, horrifying with its serene expression and its slits for eyes.

I clawed at the hands, but the Aetheran soldier backed me into the hearth, smacking my head against the mantel as I twisted in their grasp.

"Do not fight," a deep voice said, muffled by gold.

The scent of sunlight and heat dripped from the armor, revealing Typhon's favor upon this soldier. There was another lingering beneath—the mist clinging to him.

His fingers squeezed harder against my throat, and I thrashed. He would try to render me unconscious and then drag me out. I had to find my power despite the fear thrumming through me at the thought of those shadows I both loathed and revered.

Swirls of darkness curled around my shoulders. I focused, forcing them forward. Though I could not see the soldier's eyes, he stiffened in fear. My shadows struck, spooling around his hands and forcing them away. The soldier fell, and I dodged around him, running toward the door.

But a hand caught my ankle, pulling me to the floor. My head hit the ground with a sickening crack. Stars danced in my eyes, the world lurching before righting itself as the grip on my leg tightened. A scream tore through my lungs, fingers digging into the mortar between the stones as I made to drag myself forward out of his grasp. His body, heavy with armor, fell upon mine, holding me in place.

I shrieked again, my hands slipping uselessly off his wrists and the helmet buckled to the gilded bevor around his throat. Similar to Aelestor, he was completely covered from head to toe, rendering my touch a useless defense. I reached for my shadows again but found only panic in their place as his fingers latched around my throat once more.

Breath rushed from my lungs with the heavy weight of his body atop me. Black spots burst in the corners of my eyes. I slapped uselessly against the mask, fingernails clawing for any seam I could find to rip it off.

Shadows, lighter than mine, circled his torso before he was wrenched off me, flying backward and landing with a crash on the floor. Pain shimmered across my skin before winking away as quickly as it came.

Crouching protectively over me, Ren was powerful and resplendent with shadows curling around his shoulders. His dark eyes fixed on the soldier stirring on the ground.

"Typhon should know better than to try to take what is mine," Ren growled.

In two long strides, he was on the soldier, claw-like fingers wrenching the golden mask off and throwing it with a clatter. The demigod's face was pale with fear, eyes wide and mouth slack. Sweat soaked the straw-colored hair stuck to his forehead.

"Who let you through?"

Slowly, I pushed myself to stand, a skittering ache throbbing through my limbs from the impact to the floor. The door opened, and heavy footsteps echoed through the room.

"No one," the soldier growled, trying to wrench himself free from Ren's grip, but shadows merely locked tighter around his limbs, holding him in place. A satisfied smile suddenly bloomed on the demigod's face. "I found a way."

My heartbeat stuttered in my chest before it picked up speed. If he found a way through the mist then that meant that others could. *Typhon* could.

"*Stars*," Mecrucio cursed.

"Tell us where," Ren commanded, his hands clamping around the gilded breastplate.

As easily as if he had been a child, Ren pulled the soldier up from the floor until only his toes brushed across the stones.

"I will not tell you anything, Under King. You will have to kill me," the soldier spat.

There was a glint of silver before Ren's axe rested beneath the exposed skin of his neck.

"He is telling the truth," Mecrucio said. "Typhon and Hollis have trained him well. He will not break."

Ren turned to me, and I knew why he had refused to acknowledge me before. I had seen the way his mask slid into place, more terrifying and heartbreaking than the gilded one now twisted on the floor. To look at me was to acknowledge the danger that lay between us.

"It is your right to make the killing blow," Ren said with unflinching coldness.

In his hands, the demigod jerked. I merely stared at Ren, surprised that he was giving me the choice. The soldier had to die. He could not be returned to Aethera with his knowledge of the way through the mist. But could I kill him now, without the fire of self-preservation to spur me on?

"Ren…" Horace warned, stepping to my side.

"He meant to take her." Fury dripped from Ren's lips, his face slipping for a moment into the rage that bubbled beneath his chest before frost covered his countenance once more. "He meant to take her and put her back into chains."

Ren's voice cracked on the last word.

"Of course, you would know much of chains, would you not, *Under King?*" The demigod sneered. My feet moved beneath me. "Others will find a way through just as I have, and soon, you will have an entire gilded army at your shores ready to tear this kingdom to the ground piece by piece, and you along with it."

My bare hand slapped over the demigod's mouth. His eyes widened in shock before he stiffened, his skin withering into a deep gray. Black veins spiderwebbed around the corners of his eyes and forehead. The pieces of his armor clattered to the ground until only his breastplate remained in Ren's hand.

The demigod crumbled into ash.

Renwick

There was no regret in her eyes.

Her breaths were heavy in her chest, her hand out-stretched in the act of silencing the demigod. And then slowly, it fell back to her side.

The remains of the soldier between us disappeared in a swirl of white mist—Horace's power—and the door clicked shut, announcing their retreat. I knew we would talk later to plan for what this new threat meant, but now was not the time.

Panic coursed through my veins. Her screams echoed in my ears, even now as she stood before me—whole and unbroken.

"I thought I'd lost you," I breathed.

"I thought he would take me from you," she replied in a voice infused with the fear that coated my tongue. "I tried—" A small hiccup escaped through her lips, the first sign of shock.

Closing the space between us, I slid my hand into her hair, tilting her head up and pressing my forehead to hers.

"I tried to stop him," she rasped. "My— My shadows. They helped me get away, but then—" Air whistled through her lungs.

My thumb brushed her jaw, shushing her as her hands wound around my waist. "You defended yourself long enough for help to arrive. You refused to go without a fight, Oralia."

Tears welled in the corners of her eyes, her breath stuttering in quick gasps. I brushed my mouth against her cheeks, catching the tears before they could fall.

"It was not enough."

"It was more than enough," I answered. "And with time, you will have no need of rescuers. You will be the one your enemies fear."

She rose on her toes before crashing her mouth against mine, fists balling into the back of my tunic. I tasted the sweetness of relief on her tongue as her shock slowly faded.

"I am ready," she said, her voice steadier when we pulled apart.

Brushing the hair off her face, I raised my brows. "Ready?"

She nodded, and her eyes hardened into emeralds. "I am ready to become the thing I fear most."

A smile tugged at the corner of my lips. "And what is that, *eshara?*"

"Powerful."

Pride sped up my heart and flushed my cheeks.

"I am ready, Ren. Let us begin—*now.*"

I spooled the shadows around us, forcing our bodies to move through space without stepping. Oralia gasped, looking over my shoulder at the tall obsidian mountain that now loomed over us and the yew tree we stood beneath.

Keeping hold of one of her hands, I pulled us from beneath the tree, ducking under one of the heavy branches and moving onto the black stones at the base of the Tylith Mountains.

When I found the spot I wanted, I turned back to her, ignoring the way my chest constricted at the sight of her discomfort.

"I want you to try to call the shadows to you," I said.

"They ran when I called before," she explained, the night's panic bleeding back into her eyes.

The mist deepened around us, curling over her shoulders and neck like a lover trying to comfort her. I stepped closer but did not touch her. "Close your eyes."

Her lids closed at once, and she took a deep breath. The air changed, darkening as it might before a rainstorm.

"Morana taught you to reach for the darkness, to greet it. Now you will learn to control it."

Oralia's mouth tightened. "It does not seem like it wants to be controlled."

I raised a brow. "Does it not? It wants to be controlled by me. It will also want to be controlled by you. It is waiting to see if you are ready for it." I stepped a little closer, my lips brushing her ear. "If you are worthy of it."

She shivered when I drew back. The small furrow returned between her brows, her hands flexing at her sides as if she were reaching for something just out of her grasp.

"It will come when you call. Soothe when you are hurt. Fight when you are in danger. Protect when you are in need. But you must ask—you must speak your heart to it."

Darkness curled at the tips of her fingers, winding its way between them like tiny snakes in tall grass. Beneath her, the dark obsidian stones rippled in response. A great groaning echoed off the mountain. Even the yew tree appeared to shudder.

"Yes," I encouraged. "You control it. It does not control you."

Her shoulders trembled against the shadows that twined around her wrists and arms. Her eyes moved beneath her lids, lips grimacing and teeth grinding together.

"It is testing you. Do not let it win."

Suddenly, her back bowed, arms splayed wide as the inky shadows poured not only from her chest, but from every pore, wrapping themselves around her like a great cocoon. It was too much, too soon. She had let the fear get the best of her, allowing the power to overtake her. I cursed, reaching through the freezing shadows to wrap my hands around her waist.

"*ORALIA!*" I cried. "Fight this. *Fight. It.*"

But her screams tore the air apart, and we descended into darkness.

CHAPTER
FORTY-THREE

Oralia

I was so cold.

Cold, like the freezing river on the boundary of Aethera's palace in winter. Cold, like the marble floor of Typhon's throne room where I'd knelt for hours as a child. Cold, like the very first smile I had seen on Ren's face when he had been merely the Under King to me.

Perhaps this was death. It was not as unpleasant as I'd feared it would be. Nowhere near as unpleasant as the kratus blade had been. The darkness, for all its frigidity, was gentle. It was kind. It whispered with sweet caresses, *Give over to me, let me in.*

I wanted to. I had told Ren I was ready, but fear held me back. The fear of what would happen if I accepted this part of me. The destruction I might cause if my power fell into the wrong hands. I thought of the kingdoms that would crumble to ash beneath my fingertips. I had believed I was broken for so long.

The darkness whispered, *Let me in.*

Yes, I wanted to reply. *Make me strong.* But I could not find my voice. It was lost in the vast expanse of the night sky, though not a single star shined.

The power tightened around me, like strong arms around my waist. It felt so loving. Like nothing I'd ever felt before—to be loved. To be cherished. I could imagine it was someone else, someone who wanted me to return, who did not want me to give my magic back to this world to begin again in someone new.

Open your eyes, the darkness commanded.

They are open, I answered.

And yet you do not see.

What was there to see? The blackness of night, the endless expanse of the universe welcoming me home? The seed of distrust in myself that Typhon had planted centuries ago? The empty space at my side where no ally had ever stood, no one to defend me from his tyranny?

No one.

I did, the darkness replied.

Pain lanced through my heart, or what was left of it.

It could have been minutes, days, centuries, millennia since I'd first reached for my dark magic at the base of the mountains while Ren watched with his black cloak swirling around him. The power had crawled up to meet me, tentative as a field mouse, but I'd grown frightened and tried to push it away. But it had latched on. Refused to let go, digging its claws into me.

I could sense frustration within the power now as if it did not agree with my assessment.

Did you not cling to me? I asked.

No response, merely another shimmer of annoyance.

Did I instead cling to you?

It hummed in answer. *And in doing so, you strangled your magic as you have always done,* it breathed. *We are done with weakness, Oralia, daughter of Peregrine. We are done with bending the knee to those who would asphyxiate your strength.*

I saw again that first night I'd spent kneeling in front of Typhon's throne. It had been only a few days after I woke from the daemoni attack. A storm had raged outside my window, and in fear, I'd clung to my nursemaid, my hand brushing her bare shoulder. She had died in my arms, crumbling to ash as I scrambled away from her body.

Typhon had burst into my room when I'd screamed. That had been the first night I'd ever seen him afraid. By the fabric of my nightgown, he'd dragged me to the throne room and forced me to tell him what had happened.

What does a timeless god fear? the darkness asked. *That which can destroy him. That which is most powerful. That which possesses all the vast magic of the universe.*

I'd been forced to kneel as healers worked over me for the rest of the night, shivering in my thin nightgown against the polished marble floor, screaming in agony. By the next morning, the court was informed that I had been cursed by the king of Infernis and must not be touched until Typhon's magic worked to cure me. Though no cure ever came.

And I was never touched again.

I am sorry, the darkness said.

It is not your fault, I answered.

Let me in, it begged.

My entire being sighed. I would let it in. I would become strong not only for me, but for Ren, so that we might stand together against Typhon.

Within the span of a heartbeat, the cold disappeared, and a tingling warmth spread from my chest to the tips of my fingers, to the roots of my hair, to the soles of my feet. Behind my lids—for I realized now they truly were closed—there was a great expanse of a starry sky with grass beneath our feet. A tall, moon-pale woman stood before me, silver wings sparkling, stretching out behind her as though she might take flight. The lush black locks of her hair swirled around her in the phantom breeze of this place. She looked at me with familiar midnight-blue eyes.

She was singing. The same song I knew from growing the trees and the grass and the apples in the orchard. It was a song of forgiveness, a song of strength, a song of peace. Because no matter what had been done to me—to us—power always prevailed.

I questioned the power of tyrants, the beautiful woman whispered through the song. *And when they shut me up I became the thing that could bring them to heel.*

She reached for me, her fingertips caressing my cheeks before letting them fall.

You must wake up now, she said.

But I am afraid, I answered.

Her smile was affectionate, and I knew then that we had been talking for years—she and I. It was a conversation that had gone on forever, perhaps since the beginning of time.

No, you are not, she replied. *Not anymore.*

A different hand, one I could not see, touched my face, brushing back my hair, while a powerful arm squeezed around my waist, shaking me. The woman smiled again, her familiar eyes glistening with tears, and I could not tell if they were filled with grief or joy.

He can grow quite impatient, can he not? she asked with an arch of her smooth brow and tender affection in her voice. *Though I hate to see him now so cold.*

The woman placed her hand over the phantom one on my cheek, running her thumb against the empty air. There was so much longing in that one small gesture, and I realized then that it was both grief and joy mixed in her tears that fell into stars. With a wave of her hand, a large, red pomegranate appeared resting against her palm. She broke it open, the seeds glittering in the starlight.

I stared at the fruit, at the representation of life and death within her hands as she pressed half into my own.

Sometimes destruction must come before creation, she whispered. *Ruin is the end of one chapter and reckoning the beginning of another. Ashes feed the soil, allowing new life to grow. Bones break and then mend, to begin again stronger than before. And so shall you both.*

She brushed her lips against the space between my brows before disappearing into the night.

I wanted to reach for her, to tell her to stop, to wait, to tell me her name. But I already knew it, did I not? I had known her for almost my entire life.

Asteria.

Ren's mother.

Those phantom arms were shaking me again, and I could have sworn lips pressed against my cheek before a rough, deep voice called out through the dark.

"Come back to me, *eshara*, please."

I blinked. His midnight gaze was wide with panic and fear. Reaching with a heavy hand, I touched the space between his brows.

"You have your mother's eyes," I rasped before the darkness of unconsciousness swallowed me whole.

CHAPTER
FORTY-FOUR

Renwick

Gently, I cradled her limp form in my arms, her words circling my head like blood in a drain.

You have your mother's eyes.

Oralia lost consciousness. This was nothing like the rigid, twitching state she'd been in only minutes ago. When she'd screamed, a bubble of darkness exploded around us and, at first, it had been like standing amid a freezing hurricane. I'd slowly lowered her to the ground, trying to maintain my center of gravity so we did not go flying. But, after a few minutes, the winds calmed and the breeze that remained was gentle and warm. As I held her, I thought I felt soft, affectionate fingertips moving over my own face and hands.

She had stopped seizing then, though her body remained tense, eyes moving wildly behind her lids. Her lips quivered once or twice as though speaking softly.

I took a deep, shaking breath, pushing her hair from her face. I slid my fingertips down the curve of her cheek, tracing her full lips.

Trying to convince myself she was here, she was breathing. The dark bubble of night had dissipated, letting in the weak moonlight and mist that surrounded us. At my touch, she smiled softly, leaning into my hand before drawing closer to my chest.

"It is okay," I soothed. "You are safe."

I pressed a kiss to her temple, then another, but when I drew back, her fingers wrapped around the front of my tunic. Oralia's breath ghosted across my face, pupils dilating, hands flexing against my chest. We stared at each other, relief and joy, heartbreak and grief, all mixing into a volatile cocktail of sensations.

"I did it, Ren," she breathed. A smile broke across her face like the dawn.

Without hesitation, I pressed my mouth to hers, and the taste of her lips was that of starlight and honey. A rumble of pleasure vibrated through my chest. Her hands flew to my hair. For a moment, I thought it was to push me away, but instead, she drew me closer. With a sigh, she opened for me. Our mouths moved in a dizzying mix of lips and teeth and tongue until I groaned.

My hand slid from her face, down her throat, gliding over her silk-covered breast. Her nipple pebbled beneath my touch as I plucked, before soothing it with soft strokes. She moaned. The sound was more delicious than the sweetest wine as I did it again and again until she was quivering in my arms.

"*Ren*," she murmured in prayer against my mouth.

My cock throbbed from the sound of my name on her lips, and I knew she could feel it against her hip—the way I could not stop myself from grinding against her. I kissed the corner of her mouth, the line of her jaw, sucked against her pulse point until I'd marked her as surely as she had marked what remained of my soul.

With a shift of her hips, she tried to make space. Turning toward me and climbing onto my lap, she had a confidence I had not seen in her before, drawing her skirts up so her hot center was pressed against my fabric-covered cock.

"*Oralia*," I sighed. Delicate hands gripped my shoulders, nails digging into the fabric of my cloak.

I wrapped an arm around her waist, savoring the heat that bled from her chest into mine. Her cheeks were flushed, hair a riot of sunset waves around her face. She gave an experimental roll of her hips. Lips parting, she moved again and her lids fluttered at the sensation.

"That's it," I praised.

Biting the inside of my cheek, I groaned at the exquisite press of her against me. It was dizzying to feel so much after so long. I thrust up, kissing her throat before reaching a hand to cup her breast. I twisted the tight bud between my fingers and she moaned, grinding herself down on me.

"It is not enough," she whimpered, rocking harder against me.

Her brows furrowed as I tugged lightly on her nipple. With her bottom lip caught between her teeth, she rolled her hips once more. I drew her up, letting the tip of my fabric-covered cock hit her clit, sliding over it again and again.

"Then take what you need," I growled, biting the space where her neck met her shoulder.

"More," she panted. "Your mouth... I need your mouth on me."

I pulled back from her, and a tiny whimper of frustration left her lips. I lay down on the grass beneath her. She raised an eyebrow as I pushed up the material of her skirts until she was exposed.

Grabbing her waist, I pulled her higher. "Come here."

Her teeth bit into her lower lip, and she shimmied her way up my torso until her knees were on either side of my shoulders. I dug my fingers into her hips a little harder through the gathered material of her skirts, maneuvering us until her knees settled on either side of my face. I drew the fabric covering her to the side until I was staring up into her dripping core.

"Use me, *eshara*," I commanded, pulling her down so I could drag my tongue through her glistening need. "Make yourself come."

Tentatively, she rocked her hips against my mouth. I could just make out the furrow of her brows, the set of her mouth as she did it again before uncertainty turned to pleasure. *Stars*, if I could truly die, I would want it to be like this: wringing each sound of ecstasy from her lips.

Slowly, she found a rhythm she liked while I continued to lick and suck, my tongue dipping into her entrance before sliding back up to suck on her clit. Her fingers found my hair, tugging to keep her balance. The sounds falling from her mouth made my cock ache as her thighs tensed around my face. Her moans grew louder until they were echoing off the side of the obsidian mountain.

Oralia cried out, my name on the air as she came. I lapped at the gush of sunshine and starlight, groaning when my cock throbbed and she shuddered. As soon as her body stilled, she climbed off me, scooting down until she could lay her head on my chest, my arms cradling her.

I kissed her forehead, running a hand soothingly down her spine again and again. We lay there, listening to each other breathe. She felt so small in my arms, yet despite her delicacy, she did not feel weak. If anything, she was more powerful than ever. I could taste the darkness around her as much as the sunlight. A ripple of power echoed throughout her entire being.

I took a few slow, deep breaths, trying to calm myself and convince my cock not to twitch against her.

"What happened?"

Her hand tightened in my tunic, but I could tell she was not afraid, merely remembering. With a heavy sigh, she drew back, eyes searching my face, fingers sliding up to trace the line between my brows.

"I am done with weakness," she whispered. "I am done bending a knee to those who would make me so."

There was some strange echo in her words. My blood roared in approval of it—of the light in her eyes that shined with conviction. I threaded my hand through her hair, tilting her head up to me.

"This is the beginning," she whispered, leaning up until the words brushed against my lips.

Stars, it was. Oralia did not need me to teach her. She already had everything she needed inside of her. All I could do was help her find it. And more than anything, I wanted to stand at her back, watching the world fall to its knees before her. Wanted to be the one to scatter the ashes, to sow the soil, to help her break this world so it might come back stronger.

No, she did not need me. Not in the way she thought she did.

But I knew as I looked at her, I needed her. Needed her in a way I'd never needed anyone before in my entire existence.

CHAPTER
FORTY-FIVE

Oralia

We lay at the base of the obsidian mountain until the sky began to brighten with the dawn, breathing in each other's scent and listening to the beating of our hearts grow quiet.

It was strange. I felt light. The heavy weight on my chest had been lifted, even if it was only for right now. The dark power within me was there, I knew, but it was not as present as before. Almost as if in accepting it, I had calmed it to merely a quiet purr, the way my other power resided within me.

When Ren was satisfied that I was strong enough to travel, he cradled me close, stepping beneath the shadows of the yew tree, through the darkness to the large oak tree he often used to shadow-walk. The light was at its brightest, fighting with the curling mist that appeared to ebb and flow like a tide. From the tree, the souls wandering Pyralis were just visible and, farther off, I could see the bustling small city of Rathyra, with its many souls going about their existence.

Carefully, Ren set me on my feet. He kept a supportive hand on my lower back while we walked from beneath the low-hanging branches along the path back to the castle. In the distance, I spied Dimitri standing at the entrance to Rathyra, his hand on the pommel of his sword and, for once, his helmet tucked under the crook of his arm.

The similarities between my guard, Drystan, and Dimitri struck me again, even down to the way Dimitri was casually leaning against one of the gray walls. It made some small piece of my heart ache at the sight. I missed my guard, who was truly more than merely a guard. Drystan was the closest thing I'd ever truly had to a father, with all his gentle chiding, care, and concern.

Drystan had tried countless times to help me find compassion for the god now striding beside me. With perfect clarity, his words from all those times we stood before the mantel in the library within Aethera's palace floated back to me.

The loss of the Under King's wings. Do you not contemplate the cruelty of it?

"Ren?" I murmured, cutting through the companionable silence we had found.

He hummed. My stomach fluttered when his thumb stroked lightly against my spine and he leaned in closer. I looked away for fear I might say something foolish, instead fixing my gaze on his second in command. Farther, in the distance, a cloaked figure was making its way toward him.

"Does Dimitri have a brother?"

Ren's thumb paused for a moment before continuing its stroking, but I was not paying attention, not really. I was watching the figure approach Dimitri, the latter's mouth pressing into a thin line of distrust.

"Yes," he answered softly.

A sharp pain lanced through my chest as the figure dropped his hood, a riot of bright red waves like a flame upon the mists.

"Aelestor," I gasped, turning on Ren. "Why would he be allowed back here?"

The God of Storms said something to Dimitri, who shook his head before gesturing toward Rathyra and guiding him inside.

"Aelestor is allowed back into Rathyra not for his benefit, but for a soul's." Ren's tone was soft, and he reached out to stroke a knuckle across my cheek. "Josette, the woman you saw with Lana, has been with us for almost four hundred years. She was Aelestor's human lover—his bride, though Typhon never allowed the union." I reeled at the thought that he had ever taken a human lover.

"Though Aelestor does not know it, my brother desired her for himself and tried to tempt her into his harem."

My stomach roiled. I knew of Typhon's harem of women—a mix of demigods and humans who paraded around the court like birds of paradise in their fine silks and upturned noses. There had been only one or two who had shown me any sort of kindness, but they had vanished long before we could have any semblance of a relationship.

"She denied him and was..." Ren's throat clicked with a swallow, refusing or unable to continue. "When she arrived here on the shores of Infernis, she begged to drink from the Athal in hopes it might bring her relief from the memories of her death."

His face twisted for a brief moment before smoothing once more. But it was easy to see that he truly cared about his people, truly cared for the souls who came here to heal. Though they feared him, he would have done anything for them—even if that meant playing the monster everyone thought he was. After a heavy sigh, he pulled me against him, wrapping his arms around my shoulders.

"Did she forget?" I asked when the silence had stretched between us for too long.

His forehead pressed against my hair, and his sigh saturated the strands. "Yes...and no. Usually, a soul drinks from the river, and they are wiped clean before we take them to Isthil where they adjust to this new existence. She forgot the cause, but not the pain. Her grief consumed her so completely that Horace took her to Pyralis after only fifty years in Isthil until Aelestor came to bargain."

He allowed me to pull back so I could look up at him. Ren's face was full of tension, his shoulders stiff, but I could see the light in his eyes—the fierce way he wanted me to understand.

"She remembered him?"

A sad look crossed his face as he shook his head. "He came offering a deal, offering to be one of my spies, to enact chaos upon the kingdom on my behalf. He used his power to create great storms and then, as if he had not made them, forced them to dissipate."

Though I was shocked, I was not altogether surprised.

"This was around the time that you were born," Ren continued. "I was barred from the palace grounds for my betrayal in trying to smuggle out your mother and father. In exchange for being my spy, I would allow him to see Josette. I agreed, though Horace or Thorne have always been present to ensure she never showed signs of distress." He paused for a moment, searching my face. "He watched her from afar in Pyralis for two centuries before she eventually moved to Rathyra, and there, he struck up a friendship with her. It has only been in recent days that she has begun to remember him."

I nodded. I thought I understood a little better why Aelestor was allowed back in the kingdom. Ren's people would always be the priority. That was the mark of a true king.

"He is allowed back because of the task he accomplished for me." His thumb brushed my chin, turning my head back to his. "To reenter Infernis, he was to convince Typhon he had not found you."

FORTY-SIX

Renwick

Shock crossed her face at the words.

"But...Typhon knows I am here," she whispered as though he could be listening.

I nodded. "Aelestor convinced him I was keeping you locked away as a prisoner. Typhon sent him back to continue to search for you, a benefit Aelestor is no doubt enjoying. Though we now know Typhon was relying on more than just Aelestor."

Her mouth tensed in thought, and she looked back toward Rathyra. "Should I go back?"

My brows furrowed in confusion, and she looked once more toward my face without truly seeing me.

"To Aethera. If Typhon knows I am here and he...he will continue to send soldiers and threats through this mist. Should I not return to spare Infernis?"

Her screams from the attempt to retrieve her last night bounced against my skull. If she had been human, or if the soldier had been a god, she would have been black and blue from the attack and yet here she was, offering herself up in sacrifice.

"Do you want to go back?" I asked carefully.

Her expression darkened, mouth thinning into a grimace. The centuries of isolation skittered across her irises like dead leaves. "If it will protect this kingdom, I would."

Slowly, I slid my hand up her arm, tangling in her curls and forcing her gaze up to mine. "Oralia, that is not what I asked. If you were to go back, he would change you into something unrecognizable. He would use you as a means to conquer, to destroy. You would have to be strong enough to withstand it, to defy him—to *destroy* him."

Her face paled and she shook her head. "I am not ready."

I pressed a soft kiss between her brows, trying to smooth them. She was right. She was not ready, but that did not mean she would never be. "Then Aelestor will not take you."

At the mention of Aelestor, contemplation came back into her gaze. "Does he... Does he love Josette?"

I nodded.

Her eyes flickered back and forth between mine, and it was clear she was thinking of something other than leaving the kingdom.

"Do you think..." She hesitated, insecurity coloring her tone.

"What is it?" I asked, dropping my head so we were more eye to eye. Yet she did not answer. "Tell me."

She shifted her weight before sighing. "Do you think I could help Josette? Perhaps my touch would help her remember...if that is what she wishes."

Her touch had healed Lana and helped her to remember who she was before all the trauma in her life and who she would be now that it was over. It was not inconceivable that it would be the same for Josette.

"I do not see why not," I said softly. "It is worth a try."

A smile broke upon her face, burning away some of her tension. She rose to her tiptoes, pressing a soft, lingering kiss to my cheek before drawing back, a blush creeping up her neck. She looked chastened as if she'd acted on instinct and was now unsure as to my reaction.

So, I closed the distance between us, my mouth brushing the corner of hers once, twice, three times. She sighed happily, her hands sliding over my shoulders.

"When would you like to see her?" I asked, pulling away.

"If we do not do it now, I am afraid I will lose my nerve," Oralia replied, face tightening with anxiety. "Perhaps, through this, Aelestor and I may find some common ground."

I nodded, but before she could go striding off, I grasped her hand, intertwining our fingers. As I guided her toward the city of souls, that unfamiliar warmth unfurled in my chest each time her palm squeezed mine. Every brush of my thumb against the soft skin of her wrist was a spark in my veins—the way lightning must feel when it strikes across the sky.

"Your people will see..." she breathed as Rathyra came into view, pulling her hand from my grasp.

That all-too-familiar ice prickled through my chest, eating away the warmth. What would it matter if my people saw us striding through the city hand in hand when they already whispered *myhn lathira* each time they saw her? I was almost positive a few had caught sight of our first kiss as well.

"And?" I asked, turning her to face me fully. A soft vee formed between her brows, her mouth flattening into a thin line. The morning light filtering through the mist caressed the curve of her cheekbone, highlighting the tension in her eyes. Gently, I touched a knuckle beneath her chin. "Do you not wish to be seen with me?"

"No, I do," she answered, her voice fading slightly, eyes trailing down to my chest as if she could not bear to look at me.

"You believe it is I who does not wish to be seen with you?" My tone was hollow, barely a question.

The answer was clear in the way her blush stained her cheeks and her teeth bit into her lower lip.

"Allow me to make myself very clear." I ran my thumb across her bottom lip, tugging it from her teeth. "It is an honor to be seen with you, Oralia, and it has nothing to do with your power. Look at all you have done in your short time here to heal from your past. The strength you have found within yourself." I leaned closer, my lips brushing hers. "It is I who is not worthy to be by your side."

I kissed her lightly, letting my tongue slide across the seam of her lips. She opened for me, sighing as I dipped into her mouth, tasting the relief there. As we pulled away, I drew up our interlocked hands to press a kiss to the scar on her wrist.

"Are you ready?"

She nodded, a little of the nervous tension crawling back into her shoulders, but she fell into step beside me. Silence rolled through Rathyra at my presence, but still, souls spilled from doorways to line the narrow labyrinth of streets. Though they always knelt at my arrival, their eyes were shining as they passed over me, small smiles curling at the corners of their mouths. There was something different about them, a change in the air I could not quite quantify. Oralia's thumb brushed mine once, tears welling in her eyes as she gazed between my people and me. I realized then what the difference was.

The scent of fear was no longer thick in the air. They did not look at me with uncertainty, their mouths did not twist in disgust. They gazed upon me as they did upon her—with reverence...

Gratitude.

My throat was thick, and I struggled to swallow back the rising tide of bittersweet unworthiness. Taking a deep breath, I nodded to a few who outright beamed at me, surprised when they did not cower but pressed their hands firmer to their hearts, their heads dropping in a respectful bow.

This had been her doing. They had seen me as a monster, heard the stories Typhon weaved, spinning his crimes into a cloak that he laid upon my shoulders. Never once had I thought to fight it. I never believed there would be any point. But she had shown them the truth merely through her presence. She had built the bridge between my people and me.

Throughout the city, I could hear the whispers.

Anh ardren regus lathira.

Anh ardren regus lathira.

Anh ardren regus lathira.

The king and queen.

CHAPTER
FORTY-SEVEN

Oralia

The slate walls of Rathyra rose around us as we made our way into the city. Souls spilled out of doorways, drawing back their gray cowls from their faces with bright eyes. Strange how entering a city inhabited by souls so vibrant felt like walking into a colorless world.

There was a pulling in my chest, a desperate need to let my song seep into each corner of this place, to fill it with color and light. More, there was so much more that needed to be done. Here I could be more than a prisoner content to grow flowers and bolster the crops. I could bring beauty to the souls who awaited their ascension, perhaps even give them a small bit of hope.

With each step through the city, tension crawled its way up my legs, curling through the pit in my stomach and creeping up my shoulders. What if I was wrong? What if I could not provide Josette with any comfort? Perhaps my touch was only for those who had not drunk from the Athal. And what would Aelestor—

"Breathe, *eshara*," Ren hummed softly, the vibration running down his arm and into mine, jolting my frantic inner monologue to a halt. The dawn was creeping up his chest. The laces of his tunic were undone to show a sliver of his pale skin, the muted light of the mist making him look as if he was made of stone. But there was a warmth in his eyes as he gazed down on me, and it lit a flame within my blood.

Any response I might have made was caught in my throat as we turned the corner into a tiny courtyard, almost half the size of the one in which I'd met Lana. Aelestor's copper curls were wild around his face where he knelt in front of the tiny soul, his hands clenched into tight fists, knuckles bleached white. He was on his feet in another heartbeat, protectively covering Josette, his hand falling to his empty scabbard.

"You *promised*," Aelestor spat, gray eyes fixed upon Ren.

Ren's hand tightened in mine as he stepped forward, subtly placing himself in front of me, voice as smooth as steel. "I did no such thing. It is not my secret to keep. Josette is under my protection."

Aelestor's nostrils flared, eyes narrowing to slits, but it was a soft voice that slithered through the tension like a petal upon a river.

"*Myhn ardren,*" Josette greeted, stepping out from the God of Storm's shadow to place a delicate hand to her breast. Spun white-gold hair fell around her cheeks as she bowed her head. "*Eht natum myselna.*"

Ren's mouth softened at the soul's words, the old language a tangible being within the courtyard. "It is you who honor us, Josette. I hope you will forgive the intrusion."

Lightning crackled overhead, and I jumped alongside the soul at the sound. But Ren did not flinch, not even as thunder rolled in its wake.

"Leave," Aelestor growled, fear roiling behind his eyes, and I wondered if he was afraid Ren might try to separate him from Josette.

"You banish me from my own kingdom?" Ren asked, eyebrows ticking up. "Or do you forget upon whose land you stand?"

Shadows slunk over his shoulders, curling around our intertwined hands. A shiver of cold trickled down my spine. The darkness within my veins pulsed like a separate heartbeat. I thought I could understand a bit of the panic in Aelestor's eyes at the sight of those shadows, at the promise they carried. Before us was a desperate god, hanging on to a single branch within a rushing river of grief.

"I can help her. My power—"

"Makes the grass grow and the apples shine," Aelestor spat. Blood flushed his cheeks. His eyes were glassy before he squeezed them shut. He gave the softest shake of his head, hands spreading wide before clenching again.

Josette frowned, a trembling hand extending toward him before falling. But he did not see the movement, focused as he was upon us. I reached out to her, my palm up in offering. The stark black scars upon my wrists glittered faintly in the next streak of lightning across the rain-darkened sky.

"It is not your permission I am seeking."

"You are powerless here," Aelestor rasped.

The words once would have been a series of slaps to my face. But now, I merely smiled sadly at the god.

"We could have been friends, you know," I began, stepping closer. "Two gods thrust into an impossible circumstance, thrown together into a betrothal neither of us wanted. And yet, at every turn, you chose to turn your pain outward, as if you desired nothing but to see your agony reflected upon my face." I was close enough now to count the dark freckles scattered across the flush of rage on his cheeks. The whipping of his breath was a storm wind on my face. "Now, I understand where the weapons came from that you used to tear me down. But I will say it again: it is not your permission I am seeking."

His gloved hand shot up, but it was stopped mid-flight toward my throat by a spindle of shadow that wrapped tight around his wrist. His eyes grew wide, flicking behind me and back again. I took a deep breath, focusing on this new power that felt so unwieldy. This magic was much like trying to cup water in my hands.

"What...what are you?" Aelestor's hand flexed within its restraint, testing the limits of my power.

"Able to do more than make the grass grow," I replied, voice cold in an imitation of Ren before turning to face the soul at his side. "Hello, Josette."

A soft smile tugged at her lips, and she dipped her head much in the way she had with Ren. "*Myhn lathira.*"

I pursed my lips at the title but covered it by returning her smile and gesturing to the bench behind her. "May I sit with you?"

The bench was curved, small flecks of stone crumbling off the edges as we sat and faced each other. This close, it was easier to read the glassy, vacant look in her eyes—the dazed and dazzled way she looked upon this world. And yet, there was the agony too in the tension that curled in her eyes and the tight tremor of her bottom lip.

"I am sorry," Josette whispered, voice rough with disuse. "Sorry for my...friend."

Aelestor's knees buckled at the sound of her voice. He staggered, reaching out to the wall behind for support. Her attention flicked to him for only a moment as if he were only vaguely within her universe.

"What do you remember of your life?" I wiped my palms against my skirts, swallowing back the creeping worry.

She blinked once, some of the vacancy vanishing with a small shake of her head. "Only that there was pain, some sort of— I wake each morning with a scream. I fear the underside of my bed as if monsters may appear. I look upon the sun in horror."

We stared at each other for a long moment, anguish heavy in the air between us.

"It is the not knowing," she continued in a broken rasp, "that haunts me."

I took a deep breath, looking over my shoulder at Ren who leaned against one of the walls of the courtyard, thumb tucked into the strap of his baldric. Dark strands of his hair swirled around his cheeks. Aelestor's winds had not abated, even if the rain and thunder had. Perhaps I was looking for some sort of doubt within his expression—a way to excuse myself from the task I'd set.

But Ren merely nodded once, his words as soft as the air on my face. "Go on."

So, I turned back to the soul, offering her my hands, palm up. "I offer you my power in the hopes it may bring those memories back to you...if you want them."

Josette's throat worked with a dry swallow. "It will hurt to remember, I think."

My fingers flexed in the space between us. "I think it will. But does it not hurt to forget?"

She nodded, and there was a soft whimper from Aelestor as if he were holding back a scream. But she only nodded once more with her eyes fixed on mine.

"Perhaps..." I paused, catching myself before my own grief bled into the words. "Perhaps in the knowing, we find our path to healing. But it is your choice, Josette. I will not force you."

It was silent for a long time as she deliberated. Her light blue eyes flicked from my face to Ren's and Aelestor's, never lingering long enough to show any lasting affection. Her lips fluttered with unsaid words, hands twisting within the cowl of her robes before she slowly placed them over mine.

Shadow and darkness uncoiled from my chest at her touch, but it was nothing like my final night in Aethera. This darkness curled between us like a long-lost friend, sliding between our palms. Josette's shoulders jerked, her head bowing forward, hands tightening over mine. And there, within the tether between us, I could taste the horror she spoke of and see the monster beneath her bed.

Gilded terror, golden screams, and soft feathers of agony.

Shame covered us both like a shroud from head to foot until I, too, bowed forward with the weight. Our tears mixed together on the stone beneath us, some falling onto the dry patch of dirt beneath our feet. My song slipped through my lips. The earth beneath us deepened to a rich brown as Josette gasped and she pressed her forehead against mine. Aelestor let out a growl.

"If you touch her, you will die." Ren's voice swam through the melody.

But we were too lost within the magic, riding upon the current of agony, holding each other's heads above the waves.

"I am with you," I breathed, squeezing her hands.

She gave the barest of nods, her fingers returning the pressure. "I know."

It might have been minutes later when Josette pulled away, cheeks pink and eyes bright with unshed tears. She licked her lips, recognition sparking in her features as she truly looked upon me for the first time. The magnolia blossoms behind her swayed in the wind.

"You are so like your mother." Her fingertips touched my cheek. "But you have your father's eyes." A sob caught in my throat, and I forced it back as her attention slid to Ren. Her lips parted, brows furrowing.

"He will be punished," Ren said before whatever question she had could cross her lips. "This I promise you."

A fierce look of satisfaction hardened the soft planes of her face, which melted away almost instantly as Aelestor stepped into view. The air rushed from her lungs as she reached a hand out to grip my arm and shakily rose to her feet.

"You..."

Aelestor's eyes were wide. His whole body trembled as soft rain misted around us. The blood drained from his face as she took a step forward. Her hand slipped from my shoulder.

"You were here...this whole time. You never gave up." The words were so heavy they appeared to curl Aelestor's shoulders as they landed until he was kneeling before her, head bowed. Her thin fingers slid through his curls. The soft rumble of thunder swallowed the first note of his weeping. And then he was gripping her robes, face pressed tightly to her belly as she stroked his hair. Her sparkling tears mixed with the rain that dampened his copper curls.

Slowly, Josette lowered to her knees. Aelestor's hands traveled up her waist to cup her cheeks. Centuries of grief were etched upon his face. I wondered if it was a good thing, what I had done, or if it had only brought more heartache. But then he leaned forward, pressing his lips to hers, the words delicate between them.

"Never, little bird. I will *never* give up on you."

And I thought, for once, I might have finally done something right.

Oralia

We turned to leave the pair in the courtyard to reunite in peace. As we left, Aelestor's gaze caught mine, and some flicker of understanding passed between us. I hoped that perhaps the rift between us would soon be healed.

"What happened after Josette died?" I asked while we made our way back through the winding pathways.

My hand was caught between both of his as he gazed down at my palm, playing with my fingers as if by exploring them he might find the root of my power.

"Typhon framed a demigod for the crime," Ren answered, his face hardening into a stone mask, "and allowed Aelestor to exact his revenge."

My stomach lurched, disgust roiling up my throat. I wondered who it was, the nameless demigod who fell upon Aelestor's rage to pay for a crime he did not commit.

"I do not think it helped Aelestor," he continued. "He said once that the kill had not been satisfying, the demigod's screams too frightened, too confused. I think, deep down, he has always known he did not kill her true murderer. It is part of why he turned to me."

Nodding, I took a deep breath. I wondered what it would be like if Typhon were not on the throne—if someone with goodness in their heart ruled Aethera. My brother, Caston, flickered into my mind.

Ren nodded to a few of the souls as we passed, their expressions fervent as they pressed their hands to their hearts. *Myhn ardren*, they continued to say, followed by *myhn lathira.*

I could only assume that *ardren* meant *king* in the old language the way *lathira* meant *queen*. Not for the first time, I wondered why he did not correct them, but I wanted to be worthy of their reverence, their awe. Perhaps there was a glimmer of opportunity for me to become someone who might be worthy of it. Who might be strong enough to provide these souls with what they needed. Who might be worthy to stand side by side with him and not hide within his shadow.

We did not speak again, though Ren would occasionally draw my hand to his lips, pressing kisses across my palm that stoked the fire in my core. *Burning Suns*, how I wanted him—to be his partner, his lover, his queen.

We passed my chambers on our slow walk, Ren not even sparing the door a passing look but instead continuing up the winding hallway, nodding at a few of the guards that were now stationed within the alcoves. I chanced a glance at him and found his eyes were dark and full of some unspoken promise. Our power tangled and untangled within the space between us. When we approached his door, he opened it before stepping back. He was giving me a choice: I was not required to enter.

The moment I stepped through the threshold, Ren grabbed me,

pressing my back against the rough stone wall. The taste of him was dizzying on my tongue. The frenzied way he nipped at my lips forced my mouth open so he could claim me.

"*Oralia*," he groaned, his mouth making a path down my jaw and against my throat, biting and sucking at my skin. I gripped his shoulders, pressing my hips firmly against his already hard cock.

It was overwhelming the way he wanted me. Scrambling for the buckle of his baldric, I unfastened it quickly so his weapons fell to the floor with a crash.

"Let me look at you," he begged, his hands sliding around my waist.

I nodded, running my hands through his hair as he pressed open-mouthed kisses across my collarbones, over the swells of my breasts. Each pass of his lips was an ember in the fire of need raging between us until I was burning as a star might.

"Use your words, *eshara*," he breathed, his hands not straying from my hips.

How easy now to nod, for my lips to part, and the answer to spill out.

"Yes."

His groan rumbled through my chest. Licking the line between my breasts, he cupped them through the silk of my gown, thumbs running across the hardened peaks. Heat rocketed through me at his touch, and I crossed my ankles in response, cheeks reddening in embarrassment at the wetness already sliding between my thighs.

Ren drew back with a hungry gaze. "Turn around." Without hesitation, I obeyed, a small whimper escaping through my lips. His hands fell to the fastenings of my gown. "Place your hands on the wall."

I did as he asked, staring unseeingly at the dark stones and the way my hands gripped them as though they could keep me afloat in a sea of desire. He pulled at the ties with confident movements until the gown gaped open in the back, falling around the tops of my arms.

His lips followed the line of my spine, licking at the curve of my back, gripping my hips through the fabric. My head lolled to the side, and I panted out the staccato rhythm of my heart.

One of his large fingers dipped into the gown, sliding across the sensitive skin of my belly and up to cup one of my breasts. I gasped, pushing myself into his hands as he rolled my nipple. His kisses moved higher until he was biting and sucking at my shoulder, his erection pressed firmly against my behind.

"Arms down."

Ren guided my gown, hands sliding to my ankles to slip my shoes off my feet before he rose. The ache in my core grew unbearable as the sound of his boots clicked on the floor when he rose and took a step back.

"Turn around, Oralia," he rasped.

Shivering, I turned. Ren's eyes were wide, darting over each part of me as if he could not decide where best to linger. Starving, that was what he was, starving as I had been. Slowly, he tugged at the fastenings of his trousers, lips parting as he pulled his cock out, thick and weeping in his hand. Those midnight eyes roved over my face, my breasts, my hips, and the pink of his tongue swiped against his bottom lip. I moved to cover myself, but before I could do more than lift my arms, his free hand grabbed one of them.

"No," he growled. "You are glorious. Watch what you do to me."

He stroked himself once, hips pumping into his hand as he pulled my arm away. Ren leaned closer. His free hand pressed against the wall beside my face. With every movement of his hand, his knuckles brushed my stomach, leaving a trail of goosebumps in its wake. I whimpered. Slick heat pooled in my core and slid down my thighs. A need so desperate I was unsure if it would ever be quenched, like a brand upon my soul.

My mouth opened, then closed as he continued to stroke himself.

"I want you," I breathed. But that was not the right word. No, it was *need*, desperation, not merely want.

His black brows rose. The hand on the wall slid until he was cupping my face. I shook my head, a hiss of frustration on my lips. I thought of the first time I'd seen him touch himself in the library, how I had wanted to kneel at his feet and drink down his pleasure.

"I want to taste you, Ren."

Ren's hand stilled on his cock, his eyes widening. "You...you would want that?" His thumb brushed my bottom lip even as an uncertain look passed over his features.

Sparks fluttered in my belly, mixing with anticipation. I hummed, nodding before my gaze dipped down to his hand and back up again. Power curled deep within my veins, shadows sliding out to tangle with his. "I think... I think I might need it, Ren. More than anything."

His lids fluttered for a moment, as though the words alone brought him pleasure. There was a small tilt of his head that spoke of the danger and darkness within him, a predator lurking within the shadows.

Dangerous, yes, but not to me. Not anymore. Perhaps not ever.

"I am yours. Take what you need."

Immediately, I dropped to my knees, my hands covering his until we were both working his cock.

Sitting back on my heels, I dropped my hands onto my lap and tipped my mouth open, my head back, hoping I was obvious in my request. Ren's free hand brushed the hair from my face affectionately while he continued to work himself. He placed the tip of his cock onto my tongue, his other hand curling into the back of my hair.

I did not close my mouth. Instead, I looked up at him through my lashes while he slid against my tongue. Fire shone behind his eyes as they gazed down at me, an expression of want and awe mixed into his features.

Ren gripped the back of my hair tighter, drawing me up to my knees, and my hands curled around his upper thighs.

"Suck, *eshara*," he instructed.

My lips closed over the tip, sucking softly. The taste of him was addictive—salty and sweet like the dewy nighttime breeze mixed with the heaviness of the cosmos. His eyes fluttered shut, teeth biting into his bottom lip. I slowly drew more of him inside my mouth.

"Cover your teeth with your lips."

I did as he instructed, pulling back to circle the tip with my tongue before tentatively drawing down once more. He moaned as he continued to stroke the length of him I could not fit into my mouth. His free hand in my hair guided me.

"Yes," he hissed. "Harder."

Wanting to hear him make that noise again, I sucked harder. The ache between my thighs became a riotous pulse in time with my heart as he growled. I was sure I was dripping between my legs, making a mess of the floor.

He swore loudly, both hands suddenly gripping my head and drawing me away. I sat, kneeling beneath him on the floor, lips parted and watching as he panted heavily above me before he tucked himself back into his trousers. We stared at each other, and all I wanted was...

"More."

CHAPTER
FORTY-NINE

Renwick

Stars, if I was not careful, merely her asking for more was going to make me come.

Those bright, big eyes as she used her mouth had almost been my undoing. Especially now when she was blinking up at me beneath her lashes, breasts heaving with uneven breaths, and that word hung between us in the air. *More.* Before anything else could be said, I hauled her to her feet and into my arms, mouth crashing against hers as we stumbled further into my rooms.

Kicking open the door to my bedchamber, I carefully maneuvered us inside and laid her on the bed. Her hair splayed out across the deep blue sheets, pale skin shimmering with a sheen of sweat. I drank her in. The roundness of her breasts, the small, rosy nipples that pebbled at my gaze. Licking my lips, I lingered over the slope of her waist, the flare of her hips, the down of hair between her thighs, and the way her long, shapely legs moved as she pushed herself to a seat.

"You look at me as if I am the brightest star in the sky," she whispered, a small blush creeping into her cheeks.

I touched the rosiness of her face, my thumb resting on her lower lip. "You are not just a star, *eshara*... You are the whole damned universe."

A small smile pulled at the corners of her mouth. Slowly, I unhooked the fastening of my cloak, letting it fall to the floor. The smile faded, uncertainty replacing it as I pulled my tunic from where it was tucked into my trousers, drawing it over my head and throwing it off to the side. Her teeth bit into her lower lip, and I reached forward to tug it gently away.

"Would you rather we did not?" I asked, leaning down until we were eye to eye.

Insecurity flashed along her features as she drew her knees to her chest. I did not stop her. Instead, I knelt down, covering her ankle with my hand.

"I want to," she whispered. "I want you."

My thumb brushed against her shin. "Are you frightened?"

She exhaled loudly, gaze moving from me to the dark blue bed hangings, to the black wood frame, and back again. "Yes...but not of that."

My eyes narrowed in confusion. "Tell me."

Allow me to soothe your worries. Let me take care of you, I wanted to say.

Oralia looked down at her forearms, at the scars that marred her skin. She shook her head, sunset waves falling forward like a shroud. But I refused to let her hide from me, brushing it back over her shoulder to see a tear sparkling against her cheek.

That she could feel *so* much... To have endured what she had and yet allow herself to feel? It was awe-inspiring.

"Oralia, tell me," I pleaded.

She groaned, pressing her forehead to her arms, so she was once again blocked from view. I gripped her ankle a little tighter, thinking of the story she had told me before, the horror of her past.

"I am afraid to feel so much," she breathed, throat clicking with a swallow. The bleach white of her knuckles tensed where she held fast to her elbows. "Afraid that it may take me away like a tide, like the power I am learning to befriend. I am afraid that there might be nothing of myself left behind and..."

Silence stretched between us as her gaze penetrated mine, cataloging each subtle expression on my face. Her tongue ran across her teeth, tension tightening the corners of her eyes as her chest pressed against the restraint of her knees with a deep inhale.

"And?" I pressed gently, brushing my thumb along the curve of her ankle.

"And I do not care."

A heavy weight settled into my chest so deep I could not find air. The green of her eyes flared. A flush crept through her cheeks, hot beneath the tips of my fingers that reached out of their own accord to bask in her warmth.

"But it is not you who will be swept away," I rasped, tilting her chin higher as I leaned down. "For I am already gone."

My mouth covered hers, swallowing the quiet note of surprise before it could escape her lips. She was soft, so soft beneath my palms, pliant in my arms. As that desperate need surged inside her, dark wisps of shadow unfurled from around her shoulders to slide over mine. Our magic danced together in the space between us, urging us closer. Her hands unclasped from her knees, sliding up my chest to trace the line of my collarbones as I memorized the feel of her hair through my fingers.

"I am yours," I murmured, wrapping my arms around her waist.

"And I am yours," she answered against my lips.

Her fingers slid through my hair and down my neck to explore the ridge of my shoulders. They lingered on the twin scars on either side of my spine. The scars were deep, twisted, and ugly from where Typhon had ripped off my wings—a constant reminder of my failure. The wings had never grown back and never would, though I'd hoped that if I was ever reunited with them, they could be reattached if I dared to open the old wounds.

"I am sorry," she whispered, pressing a kiss to my cheek.

"Do not be," I replied, stroking her hair.

Covering her mouth with mine, I relished the feel of her warm palms as they slid over my chest before wandering down my torso. I needed her more than I needed my power. But I would not rush this, would not rush her.

Her hands fell to the waistband of my trousers, popping open the buttons and pulling apart the placket. With slightly trembling fingers, she wrapped her delicate hand around my cock, stroking once.

"*Stars*," I groaned, grabbing her wrist.

Stepping away, I shucked my trousers and boots before closing my hands over her waist, drawing her up higher onto the bed. Her cheeks were flushed, her arousal sweet and thick in the air making my cock pulse in near agony. Slowly, I pressed one knee onto the bed, then the other.

"I kneel before your altar, ready for worship." My words rasped through my throat, attention flicking from her closed legs to her face and back again.

Her thighs fell open to allow me to slide between them. Small, gasping pants fell from her lips as I slid my hands up her thighs before pushing two fingers inside of her.

"I need you," she moaned, her hands sliding across my chest.

"And I need you, but I must prepare you first," I murmured, pressing her thigh wider with my other hand. "Need to make sure you can take all of me."

Oralia nodded, her hair flying around her face from the quick movement before she moaned again, nails scraping against my chest. A fluttering beat against my fingers as her pleasure rose. The wet sound of her desire filled my ears.

Slowly, I twisted my fingers, working them deeper. Her hips canted, a sigh ghosting across my forehead as she bowed forward. Her fingers tangled in my hair to either pull me closer or push me away.

I slowed my rhythm, and she whimpered in frustration. But then I gently eased another finger in. Her eyes grew wide with her gasp at the stretch. Yet she did not pull away, nor did she cry out in pain either. I groaned as my cock throbbed again, tracking the flush that crept across her chest as her nipples peaked into hard points. Leaning down, I flicked my tongue across one before drawing it into my mouth and sucking hard.

She came with a cry, her release spilling over my palm. I eased my fingers out, sliding her orgasm over my cock before I eased her nipple from between my teeth.

"Are you ready?" I asked, lowering my forearm beside her head so I could stroke my fingertips across her hair.

She nodded, panting against my mouth. "Yes, yes, yes."

Positioning myself at her entrance, I looked up at her. My thumb brushed across her cheekbone. "There will be pain, but it will not last long."

"I trust you," she answered immediately and with such sincerity, it was like a blow to the chest.

I kissed her softly, tenderly, before drawing back, wanting to watch her face to ensure I did not give her too much too soon. "I will take care of you. I promise."

Then, with aching slowness, I pushed into her. Images burst behind my lids, and emotions skittered across my skin—a wide yew tree, darkness rippling in the sky, contentment, and *peace* circled my chest.

In that moment, my heart cracked open, and her power flooded my senses.

CHAPTER
FIFTY

Renwick

There they were, suddenly, within me.

The fractured pieces of my soul I thought would be gone forever. There was the bitterness of pain balanced by the sweetness of joy. The weight of grief buoyed by the lightness of hope. The cold of despair warmed by the blazing fire of love.

Peace.

I finally felt peace here, in her arms.

Oralia gasped, nails scrambling against my shoulders as her eyes widened, a whimper slipping through her teeth.

"Shhh," I soothed, pressing kisses to her cheeks, working to calm the roaring inside my heart. "Breathe for me."

Stars, that she could bring about this...*change*.

She whimpered in pain, her walls clamping around me as I pushed a little further inside. Another gasp made me freeze for a moment, to allow her to get used to the stretch. My other hand slid to her thigh, drawing it up so she could open for me more easily. I gave a few shallow strokes, gritting my teeth at the exquisite feeling before stilling my hips.

"Can you take a little more?" I rasped.

She blinked at me, considering before she gave me a small nod.

"You are doing so well," I said with a smile, and through her pain, the slick slide of her arousal increased against my cock.

I knew that smile was different from any she had seen. My cheeks ached with it. The corners of my eyes pricked with heat. Joy. This was joy flooding my senses, and it took everything in me not to cry out with relief.

With wonder, her fingertips touched my cheek.

"Almost there, *eshara*," I whispered, pushing slightly farther inside.

Checking back in with her, I tried to read her face as I pressed in further. Her eyes were bright, tears clinging to her lashes as she panted roughly against my lips. I was close to fully seated, with only a few inches left, her breasts brushing my chest with each sip of air.

"What does it mean?" she asked breathlessly.

I smiled again, warmth curling through my chest and up my throat when she returned the expression, wonder dancing across her features. When I was completely sheathed, I drew my head back, watching the way her chest moved with her ragged breathing.

"My darling." I kissed her forehead. "My pulse." I kissed her cheek. "My life force." I kissed her mouth. I bit softly against her lower lip, reveling in the joy that sparked across my skin.

She moaned. Whether it was from the pleasure of my words or my cock, I was not sure.

"I'm going to move now."

Oralia nodded, hands sliding to my back, fingertips resting against the scars from my wings.

Carefully, I withdrew halfway before sliding back in. Her eyes widened, discomfort clear across her features. But she nodded in encouragement, so I did it again. She was wet, slick and hot, so I continued with shallow thrusts, dragging my hand between our bodies until I found her clit.

Her eyes, which had closed as I'd begun, fluttered open when I circled my fingers, pressing against her. She bit her lower lip as her hips tilted up tentatively to meet mine. The look of discomfort leached from her face with each movement of my fingers.

"More?" I asked.

Her face flushed. "It feels so good, Ren. *More*."

Hiking her leg up higher, I tried to brush against the spot inside that I knew would push her off the edge before returning my fingers to her clit. Our moans tangled together like our magic.

"You feel like a dream I do not deserve," I breathed, wondering at the feeling of peace in my chest. "As if you have been honed by the dark for me alone."

I pulled another moan from her as I thrust again, biting the inside of my cheek to hold off my release. A thin sheen of sweat coated her chest and forehead, and I leaned down to lap at her nipple, biting and sucking the rose tip.

"Oh, *Stars*, Ren," she gasped.

Possessive pride rippled through me, and I moved my attention to her other breast. Her fingers tightened through my hair, holding me to her. I licked at the skin above her nipple, circling the peak with the tip of my tongue and matching the pattern of my fingers between her legs.

I was close, so close, but I wanted—no, needed—her to come again.

"Come for me, *eshara*," I commanded.

Pressing my fingers hard against her clit, I tilted my hips up. She fell apart around me, my name falling from her lips like droplets of rain. Shadows and sunlight and starlight exploded around us. Her walls clamped down tightly, pulsing with her orgasm, drawing me over the edge.

I came with a roar, pushing to the hilt as I spilled myself inside of her, shallowly thrusting up until she clenched down on me again, pulling another, smaller orgasm from her. I kissed her once, twice, three times, as my thumb stroked her cheek. She was smiling, her hands brushing the stubble on my face, drawing my hair over my ear before running down my shoulder.

Gently easing out of her, I pressed my lips to the vee between her brows before I leaned back, watching my release spill from between her thighs and onto the sheets.

Mine.

Carefully, I drew her into the circle of my arms until she snuggled her head against my chest, sighing with what I hoped was contentment. We lay like that for a long time. My fingertips slid up and down her spine while she traced patterns on my skin. The broken pieces of my soul continued to swirl inside of me, searching for the places they now fit. Occasionally, I pressed a kiss into her hair, breathing in her scent.

"Is it always like this?" Oralia asked, her voice quiet like the dark falling around us.

I knew what she was asking. The way we fell together like a cataclysm, how our magic fit together. I could remember back to my previous lovers, and the tentative way they handled me as if I were a predator that might strike at any moment.

There was no comparison. Not with the ease that had settled between us—the great sparkling warmth that tingled within my soul that told me this was *right*.

"No, it is not," I answered, rising up to gaze down upon her. "I am yours if you will have me, for as long as you want me."

Her lips parted softly, dark green eyes flitting between my own. "And if I want you until the end of time?"

"Then it will still not be enough."

Oralia rose on her elbows to press her mouth to mine, dragging me down as we were lost again in the union of our lips. One breath melded into until she was soft in my arms, head nestled beneath my chin. After a while, I tugged one of the blankets at the foot of my bed up and tucked it around us. I could feel her smile on my skin, and it set my heart to aching again. I thought that, perhaps, I could stay this way forever with her, safe and happy, in my arms.

But even as the thought came, I knew the soldiers might be picking their way through the mist even now. I remembered the way Mecrucio had described Typhon looking around his inner circle to assess who meant the most to her. His golden sword was still pinned above our heads. I only hoped that when it came crashing down, I could shield her from the blow. The thought of it made my throat burn. The found pieces of my soul trembled in anticipation of revenge.

Even now, Thorne was training the soldiers who protected Infernis, tightening our defenses, and preparing for the time when we would come to blows.

"Can I ask you something?" she whispered.

I nodded, stroking her hair back from her face as she turned to look up at me. "Of course, anything."

She smiled, pressing a brief kiss to my palm. "How did your mother die?"

My hand froze in her hair with the question.

You have your mother's eyes, she had said. That felt like a human lifetime ago.

"She did not," I answered slowly. "At least...not in the way you are asking."

Oralia nodded as if this information did not surprise her.

"Time created more than the seasons, more than life and death. It created in my father a monster...a tyrant. He was hardened by the wars with the giants and then the humans who found their way through the rift." I sighed, sitting up and running a hand through my hair. "And as time passed, his fear grew until control was the only thing he knew. Until he believed it was he who must rule all others as if he alone were the creator."

She frowned, pushing herself up so we were sitting shoulder to shoulder with the thick blue blanket pooled at our waists.

"My father was not the only creator of this world, Oralia," I said carefully. "He was surrounded by the Great Mothers and many others who made the grass, the earth, the wind, the sky." I swallowed, grief circling my throat. "The stars."

"Your mother," she whispered, covering my hand with her own.

That small gesture of comfort broke me, but I took a deep breath, trying to control it. I had not felt these emotions in centuries.

"My mother questioned his actions, his right to rule. She was not alone. Other gods who had sprouted from the earth, wind, and seas did as well." I looked down at our hands, flipping her palm up and smoothing my fingertips across her scar. "Father saw her as a threat to his throne, a threat to the world he felt he alone had created—though nothing could be further from the truth." I scoffed. "He did not even create time."

She nodded, pressing a kiss to my shoulder.

"What did he do to her?"

I let my head fall back onto the headboard, staring unblinking up into the dark hangings above us, as dark as the night outside. I did not know how to tell his tale—how to properly put into words the monstrosity that had occurred.

"In the morning, I will show you," I replied, wrapping my arm around her shoulders and drawing us back down onto the mattress. "And then you will understand everything."

CHAPTER
FIFTY-ONE

Oralia

I woke slowly to the strange feeling of warmth wrapped around me.

It took me a moment to remember that it was Ren. His heavy arm was slung over my waist. My hips pressed tight to his, our legs tangled together. There was a danger here, I knew, that I could become addicted to this feeling. That without it I might waste away into nothing. The way his warm breath skittered across my neck, now and then swirling my hair. The way his arm tightened around me every so often. The steady beat of his heart. I knew if I allowed myself, it would become the anchor I relied upon within this world.

Shifting, I muffled my gasp when he pressed himself against my backside. His cock was hard between my thighs, and though I was sore from the night before, wet desire blossomed within my belly at the feel of him. Ren groaned, still asleep, I was sure, his hips sliding forward again lazily until I moaned, angling my hips back to meet him.

His arm around my waist tensed as he woke, his muttered curse sliding across my cheek before his hand reached up to cup my breast.

"Oralia," he moaned, thrusting again.

The feeling was exquisite, like I imagined it might be to stand on the edge of a cliff, knowing the ocean at the bottom would break my fall. It was the feeling of morning sunshine on my face or cool water on a hot summer day. Relief and need, hunger and satiation, tears and laughter all rolled into one.

Reaching back, I grabbed a fistful of his hair. The movement pushed my breast firmly into his wide hand while he squeezed and plucked at my nipple. His mouth brushed my cheek and jaw as he set a rhythm against my clit that had my cries bouncing off the hangings. I lifted my top leg, moaning as his hand curled around my thigh to hold me open. His fingers bit into the flesh of my leg, the sensation just enough pain to intensify the pleasure as he spread me wider.

"Just like that, *eshara*," he praised.

The endearment, now that I knew what it meant, sent me toppling over the edge.

"Say my name," he pleaded in my ear, and I was putty in his hands, crying out again and again.

Ren. Ren. Ren. Ren.

He followed, spilling his release between my thighs and onto the sheets, biting down on my shoulder as he did. His teeth sent shockwaves of pleasure through my core before our bodies quieted. Ren stroked my side soothingly, pressing kisses into my hair.

"So perfect," he whispered, sliding his hand down to where his release was smeared between my thighs.

I shivered as his fingertips brushed across my sex. But he did not press inside, seeming merely content to slide against my clit. I bucked my hips, over-sensitized and aching.

"Will you give me one more?" he asked, turning me onto my back.

He was glorious above me, hair mussed and wild. His eyes were dark with pleasure but somehow also infused with a new light. I bit my lip while he continued to circle my clit and a trembling pressure curled tight within my belly.

"Y-yes," I gasped.

In reward, he pressed more firmly to me before leaning down to capture one of my breasts in his mouth. *Stars*, the feeling of it. My body was already shaking, legs tensing under the onslaught of sensation. Last night had been...overwhelming. Overwhelming and incredible. Though I desperately wanted to try again, the soreness between my legs told me it would have to be a little while before we could.

Slowly, Ren built my pleasure. His mouth moved between my breasts, sucking, biting, and kissing until I was moaning so loudly from all the stimulation that a small part of my mind wondered if I should be embarrassed. I was right on the edge, dangling off the precipice, my brows pulled tightly together, hands gripping his shoulders.

"Come for me," he growled, before closing his mouth over mine.

I cried out, and he swallowed the sound. His tongue tangled with mine, sweeping across my mouth as if I were a delicacy. Firmly, he pressed his hand against my sex, and the pressure was comforting—grounding.

After a few long moments, he drew his hand back as he kissed my cheeks.

"We will bathe and then we can start our journey," he said, pain or anxiety coloring the end of his sentence, I was not sure which.

"How does it work?" I asked while we stood in my chambers after he'd helped me dress in a clean gown and cloak.

We were hand in hand, his thumb brushing against my own, as we prepared for the journey that would take us to a spot on the northeast edge of Infernis.

"Shadow walking?" he clarified.

I nodded. Ren had taken me through the shadows countless times now, and though it had been uncomfortable at first, it became easier each time. His gaze moved from mine, trailing over my bookshelf.

"It is a matter of intention, as any magic is really. Inside, as we are now, it is easier to gather the shadows because we are not in the direct path of the sun. But it costs more energy than, say, stepping beneath the shade of a tree or the castle."

He checked in with me, and I gave a small noise of understanding, encouraging him to continue.

"So I call the shadows." At his words, they slithered around us, curling over our intertwined hands and slinking through our ankles. "And then I focus on our destination. I cannot go where I have not been before. I must be able to see it clearly within my mind." I nodded again, and the shadows grew thicker. "Then, once I have the intention set, we step forward into *the in-between*."

We took a step, and the shadows engulfed us before dissipating. Now that I was used to it, the sensation was not as disorienting as it had once been. Or perhaps now my power paved the way easier. But after a heartbeat of darkness with strange swirling shapes, I found myself standing beneath the gnarled branches of a wide oak tree, its limbs so heavy some dipped down to brush against the surface of the rushing stream beside it.

Here, the mist was sparse, faint tendrils merely circling our shoulders and our intertwined hands. I squinted against the bright light of the sun, shielding my face with one hand. The land was beautiful, though. Fragrant grass was lush and green beside the river, slick onyx rocks and stones gathered at the water's edge. On the other side lay an enormous expanse of fields that sloped downward, the grasses gently swaying in the light breeze.

Ren stepped across the narrow stream first before holding his hands out to assist me across. He smiled at me, but it did not quite reach his eyes. There was something there within the set of his mouth and the tension of his shoulders that made me reach out and stroke my hand across his cheek.

"What is wrong?"

He shook his head, his hand covering mine. Gently, he pulled my hand from his face before pressing a kiss to my palm, then my scar. "You will see."

His ominous response had anxiety clawing its way deep into my chest, but he said no more. Ren only interlaced our fingers and guided me through the field. It was beautiful here.

"Is this Infernis?"

Ren shook his head. "It is just outside the boundary lines to the north, right before the sea... Unclaimed land. That is why the mist is so thin here."

When we reached the top of the hill, he turned me to him, free hand cupping my cheek.

"You asked me what happened to my mother... Well, it is important to understand that my father and Typhon were threatened by her. Asteria's power was beyond their understanding. The love she shared with the other gods who shaped the world was so deep it became a risk to the power he and Typhon craved. A threat to the right my father had to rule. And so, in the middle of the night, they took her from her bed and brought her here, to this place."

Pain dripped from each word. His shoulders rounded with the weight of the tale. I squeezed his hand gently, leaning one shoulder against his in comfort.

"Sometimes, I wonder if she did not allow it. If somehow, she understood some greater destiny. Regardless, she was too powerful for them to kill on their own, so instead, Father used his magic to entomb her in the trunk of a large kratus tree. Before that time, they had been like any other tree—dark brown bark, green leaves, and harmless to gods." He lifted his hand and gestured down the large hill we stood atop.

There, at the bottom of the hill, loomed a tall, wild tree within a ring of onyx stones. Its bark shimmered silver in the sun. Twisted branches spilled out in all directions while black leaves dripped from their tips like tar.

"Her anger, mixed with her powerful magic, forced the tree to transform. And each kratus tree, regardless of where it had taken root, was changed as well."

Carefully, we made our way down the hill. He moved his hand to my lower back, allowing me to lean on him as I held the skirts of my gown out of the way.

"At first, my father tried to destroy the trees, but he learned quickly that even pulling one from the root would not kill it," he continued, steadying me when I slipped on a small rock. "Kratus trees always come back stronger and mightier than before. Then, once they learned what the wood and resin could do to a god—even a timeless one—they set about harvesting and using all they could."

"That is horrible," I murmured, continuing to flick my eyes

between the ground and the large, shimmering tree we were moving toward.

He hummed a note of agreement, assisting me the last few steps before we were back on level ground. There was a rustling of grasses and the soft, muffled sound of footsteps before a tall figure emerged from behind the tree. Morana stood in her usual black finery, her sheet of silky black hair pushed over her shoulders as she gazed upon us with a soft expression. One of her thin, elegant hands was pressed against the root of the tree, thumb gently brushing the bark.

"*Myhn ardren,*" she greeted in her smooth voice, pressing her free hand over her heart.

"*Maelith,*" Ren replied, placing his hand upon his heart and bowing his head reverently.

My brows furrowed with the title. I did not recognize it from the smattering of the old language I'd heard. Morana's ice-blue eyes flicked to me, and like every interaction with her, it sent a shiver up my spine.

I bowed my head respectfully, placing my hand over my heart. "Morana."

She returned the gesture, the soft expression turning warmer. "*Myhn lathira.*"

A playful glint flickered in her eye as my back stiffened. But Ren made no comment on the title.

"I will give you three some privacy," she continued, turning to press a kiss to the bark and murmur softly in the old language.

Without another word, she disappeared in a swirl of shadow.

CHAPTER
FIFTY-TWO

Renwick

Familiar magic swirled around my senses, crawling beneath my skin and aching through my bones.

Oralia gazed upon the tree, her eyes sliding over the silver bark, the black leaves, the gnarled roots. The trunk was wide, big enough to fit a god with wings and then some, which, of course, was why it had been chosen.

"May I?" she asked, lifting a hand in question.

"Of course," I answered.

After she gave my hand another squeeze, she dropped it and moved forward. In what appeared to be a respectful gesture, she carefully lowered to her knees, folding the fabric of her skirt around her legs. Her shoulders moved with a sigh before she tangled her hands in her lap and leaned forward to press her forehead to the rough bark, lashes fluttering against the skin of her cheeks.

I took a deep breath, trying to steady the torrent rushing through my heart. Ever since her power had infiltrated my soul, I was struggling to control the emotions I had not felt in centuries—millennia even. All the broken pieces of my soul fused together again. It was a tide threatening to sweep me away, and I was unsure now if I could fight it. My throat burned. My vision blurred in the strangest way as I gazed down upon her with her forehead pressed to the prison behind which my mother lay.

"How did you know?" When she did not answer, only looked at me in question, I cleared my throat. "That I had my mother's eyes."

I needed her to say the words I thought might tear me in two. Oralia leaned back on her heels, running a hand over her face before turning fully to face me. "Because when I fell into my magic, it was Asteria who was there to catch me."

I froze. She hovered a reverent hand over the bark, not quite touching, but yet it appeared as if she was placing her hand on the shoulder of a friend.

"Your mother was there when I was bitten, though I did not know it," she continued, lowering her hand back to her lap. "I ran a dangerous fever for over a week. Maybe longer. I am not quite sure. However, in the middle of the night, a beautiful woman with large silver wings would come into my bedchamber and take me in her arms. She would sing a song to me that I never forgot, but after it was done, I always found it difficult to recall."

I stared at her, reeling. "That is how you found your magic..."

She nodded. "It came to me perhaps a year later when I was walking through the grounds with my guard. It was the first year the springtime flowers did not bloom, and it upset me. The melody merely...came. And every time it flows through me, it is as if I have always known the song, and yet the moment the magic has taken its course, I cannot seem to recall it."

With a nod, I lowered myself to the damp grass beside her, a hand reaching out to trace the texture of the bark. "I recognized it that day in Rathyra. It was the same song she would sing when she would make the stars in the sky and create the constellations."

Oralia smiled in a way that told me she already knew. She had learned so much from her time in the black pit of her magic—so much more than I could ever know. There was an assuredness within her now that radiated from her very being. She no longer needed the world to tell her what she should be.

For she had already decided.

But then her smile faded as she looked back at the tree. Her face crumpled in a mixture of agony and rage that I knew so well from my mirror.

"How could they do this and not suffer the consequences?" she grit through her teeth.

I sighed, passing a hand through my hair before letting it drop with a *slap* against my thigh.

"They suffered," I answered. "Just not enough."

"What did the rest of the gods do?"

My mind whirled back through the millennia, seeing with perfect clarity the look on the faces of the gods I'd known so well—gods I had considered family—when they found out what had taken place.

I saw the glittering throne room behind my lids and felt the ancient robes heavy around my shoulders and wings I had not yet lost. I'd been standing atop the dais behind my father. By that time, I had become disillusioned with the ways of my brother and father and had begged him to allow me to oversee Infernis in his stead. My mother had fought on my behalf, demanding he allow me to step in while he remained as regent. It was the last battle she'd won with him. My magic was working its way through the kingdom to do what it could for the souls, leaving me weaker than usual.

My mother was missing in the crowd when we gathered. Usually, the Great Mothers stood slightly off to the side in a small group, with my mother, Samarah, and Kahliya at the head. When my father announced that my mother was gone, grief struck me so hard my knees had buckled. Before I'd truly known what I was doing, I reached for my axe, ready to wield it against my mother's *murderer.*

Horace was the one to stop me. Father and Typhon, distracted as they were by the pandemonium in the room, had not noticed me behind them. Nor had they noticed Horace darting up the side of the dais to wrap his wide arms around me. He cupped a hand over my mouth to muffle the wail that burst from my chest.

But the court saw it. The timeless gods who had followed my father and the Mothers so mindlessly for so long saw my grief and stared with clear eyes at my father and brother. Finally seeing them for the monsters they had allowed them to become.

"They left," I said, turning to look at Oralia. "Only a handful of gods stayed behind, but the rest left that very moment, turning their backs on him and his crimes." Turning their backs on all of us. I tried to temper the bitterness in my voice. If only they had stayed, if only they had fought, then perhaps things would have been different. "They created the island of Iapetos and are rumored to be there to this very day."

She took my hand, squeezing it gently. "And your father?"

I bit the inside of my cheek.

"In his bid for power, he grew frenzied. In the end, he believed if he imbibed the blood of other gods, he would obtain their powers. He had this…" I paused, trying to search for the right word, "*obsession* with obtaining and wielding the power of the universe. He had heard of other realms in which gods might possess such a thing. Eventually, his pursuit of power through his experiments created the first daemoni, which then destroyed him."

His cries of terror had rung all the way to the shores of Infernis. When I finally understood what I was hearing, I'd stood at the lapping shore of the river shoulder to shoulder with Horace until the last of his screams died in the mist.

"That obsession, unfortunately, has extended to Typhon. Though as I understand it, he prefers to collect power through the gods he controls, rather than trying to take their magic himself."

Bright red spots stained her cheeks, and she turned from me, her eyes roving across the bark and limbs above her.

"He must be stopped," she whispered, more to herself than to me, it seemed. "By whatever means necessary."

Again, the image came back to me of us standing side by side with her fist clenched tightly around Typhon's golden crown, thrust high into the air. It was so clear, so real. If I had not already been kneeling, it might have brought me to my knees.

"Yes," I rasped. "He must."

CHAPTER
FIFTY-THREE

Oralia

"I have something for you," Ren murmured as we wandered through the thick forest that lay outside the kingdom to the west.

It had been a few days since we visited Asteria's tree, and though I knew we both thought of the agreement we had made, we did not discuss it. Instead, we talked of our powers, our lives—or existence, in his case—and the way they had shaped us into who we had become. It was so easy to forget that I used to see this god as my enemy when now he was...

Beloved. It was the only word that came to mind.

He continued to train me in the use of my power, slowly preparing me for the eventuality that I would face Typhon, as he perhaps had been all along. He spent long hours with his inner circle and Morana, trying to find the gap in our defenses. No matter how long they searched, the hole that the soldier had slipped through could not be found. This trip into the forest was not only to see a new part of his kingdom, but to explore my ability to defend myself.

I had to admit it was not much.

"What is it?" I asked as he stopped us with gentle pressure on my hand.

Ren's hair was pulled back with a thin cord. His heavy cloak hung around his shoulders, dragging through the bracken of the forest floor. He was smiling, an expression I'd seen him wear more in the last few days than my entire time here in Infernis. Some great change had taken place within him—something that had seemed to change the very essence of his soul.

He flipped his cloak over his shoulder, exposing the bottom of his baldric, and closed his hand over a silver-tipped weapon. With the soft sound of metal on leather, he pulled it from its holster, extending it out to me in the palm of his hand.

The dagger was perhaps the length of my hand from heel to fingertip, with a slight curve, the hilt carved from obsidian. The kratus resin of the blade had a strange dark sheen that made my magic shiver.

"It is one of my own," he breathed, extending it out to me in offering.

But I did not reach for it, merely floundered beneath the weight of such a gift.

"Does this mean you trust me not to stab you?" I asked instead of professing my gratitude. I glanced from the shimmering blade to him and back again.

Ren chuckled and gave a small shrug, flipping the dagger up into the air and catching it by the hilt.

"It means I trust that if you stab me, you will have not only excellent reason but excellent form," he answered, eyes glittering before he reached to tuck a stray strand of hair back into the crown braid atop my head.

Once more, he offered me the handle, and this time, I took it.

"A weapon is only as good as its wielder," Ren said softly, unhooking the fastening of his cloak and letting it fall to the ground. "For you, with your gifts, it will be a way to finish what others may have started if your shadows are not enough."

I nodded. My shadows might have been enough to destroy a human or a demigod, but they would be nothing to a true god. One needed a weapon like the one in my hand. Yet now that I knew where the resin came from, I could not help but stare at it as a monstrosity.

Ren stepped back, his arms wide open in invitation. "Attack, let me see what you can do."

Nerves fluttered in my stomach. He had to be almost a foot taller than me and rippled with muscle. Any attack on him would be futile. But I took a deep breath before rushing forward, my dagger aimed right at his throat.

Easily, he sidestepped me. One hand grabbed my waist while the other closed over my wrist. In an instant, my chest was pressed against a nearby trunk, his hips pushing against me. I thought I could just feel the outline of something hard on my backside.

"That is your first mistake," he rumbled. "You are smaller, so any attack you make will be overpowered easily. It is better to wait, allow your target to come to you, and then you can use their larger size to force them off balance."

I nodded, and he stepped away. Turning, I released my cloak from my shoulders and threw it over his before weighing the weapon in my hand.

"Patience is crucial," he continued. "Panic and fear can help focus the mind, but give them too much power and they can distract. When I come at you, step to the side and try to stay poised on the balls of your feet."

Then he sprang, and though I tried to follow his directions, he took me down easily. His face was only a breath away from my own. The rigid planes of his body pressed me deeper onto the damp earth beneath us. A ripple of desire shuddered between my thighs. A soft chuckle bubbled through his chest at the look of frustration on my face before he slid his nose against mine.

"It takes time, Oralia," he murmured, lips moving against my cheek. "Why would you expect yourself to be good at something you have never done before?"

"My magic came to me easily," I huffed. Though that was not quite true. Not *all* my magic had been easy.

"Your magic is instinctual. Fighting is not, which is why we started with the former," he answered simply before pressing a chaste kiss to my mouth and pushing himself to his feet.

He extended a hand toward me, drawing me up and brushing the bracken from my gown and hair. With a smile, he stepped away, flipping his dagger once in his hand before settling his gaze back on me.

"Ready to try again?"

We worked like that for over an hour until I could confidently maneuver him off his feet, not only using my body, but my shadows. I had to admit that though he'd said that fighting was not instinctual, using my shadows to debilitate an attacker definitely was. It had felt the same when I'd stopped Aelestor from rushing at me in Rathyra. I had needed him to keep his distance, and my magic responded.

As time passed in the forest, however, I became more distracted by Ren. At some point in the training session, he removed his shirt, and I could not look away as his muscles tensed and rippled with each movement. Though it had only been last night that I'd had him in my bed, the sight sent my core throbbing.

That was what made me stumble, allowing him to turn me at the last second until I found myself pressed up against the same tree, my dagger clattering to the forest floor. A small moan escaped my lips at the pressure of his body against mine. The scent of him was thick in the air. He stilled, his hands splayed wide against the bark, face pressed into my hair.

I pushed back against his hips, my heart thundering in my chest as his erection grew against me. A low rumble echoed through his chest, one hand moving off the bark to slide across my waist.

"Is there something you need?" he asked, lips brushing against my shoulder while his hand drew lazy circles against my hip.

"No," I rasped, my body contradicting my words, pushing into him again. I moaned softly when he thrust against me. The fabric of my gown was a frustrating barrier between us.

His chuckle was low and ominous. "No?" The hand at my waist grabbed the fabric of my skirt, drawing it up. "So if I was to slip my hand between your gorgeous thighs, right here where anyone wandering by could see, I would not find you wet and aching for me?"

Cool air slithered around my exposed calves as he drew the gown up high enough for the breeze to reach the bottoms of my thighs.

"N—no," I answered.

His other hand came down to bracket my throat, tilting my head back until it was resting against his shoulder and his face entered my peripheral vision. I was trembling, completely at his mercy as his warm fingers drew up between my thighs.

"*Eshara*," he groaned, his hand easily sliding through my need. "So wet for me."

I moaned. His fingers circled my clit once before pressing inside of me.

"More, Ren."

His laugh was low in my ear as he pressed a kiss to my cheek.

"I know," he soothed, nipping at the space below my ear.

I groaned softly in frustration as his fingers left me, but the sound died when I heard him opening up the placket of his trousers.

"Wider," he breathed, pulling again at the skirt of my gown to expose my backside to the chill winter air.

My pulse echoed in my ears, excitement tightening my core as I stepped my feet apart and his cock nudged my entrance. The hand on my throat tightened, holding me firmly in place. He circled me slowly, gathering up my wetness before slowly pushing inside with a groan.

Each time we came together, it felt more like magic than any physical union. As though some distant part of my soul that I did not know had been crying out for him was suddenly fulfilled.

He thrust up, setting a brutal rhythm that had me gasping with each slap of his skin against mine. The pressure on my throat was enough to hold me firmly in place. His free hand pulled down the neckline of my gown to expose my breasts to the air, plucking them between his fingers.

I bit my bottom lip, whimpering as he kissed along my jaw, sucking and biting my throat, rolling my nipple. The pleasure was building, especially with the angle he'd found with my back arched against him. He played my body like an instrument only he knew the melody of until I fell apart around him.

"*Oralia*," he rumbled, thrusting harder before his hand dropped to the fabric of my gown, once again rucking it up from the front until I grasped the fabric for him, pulling it up higher.

Two fingers slid across either side of my clit, keeping time with the brutality of his thrusts until I was gasping against him. Ren was moaning right alongside me. His hips stuttered every so often as if he were trying to hold off his release.

"One more for me, *please*," he begged. "Give me one more."

He changed the angle, his hips driving more forward than up, and I screamed as my orgasm crashed around me. I was barely aware of his cry as he spilled into me, his hips bucking wildly through my aftershocks until we both crumpled to the ground.

Ren pressed soft kisses to my temple, stroking my throat gently before gathering me into his arms.

I thought, perhaps, I could rest for a little right there in his arms. The first few tendrils of sleep began to take me under as his voice slithered through the dark.

"You are the only one I have ever wanted."

CHAPTER

FIFTY-FOUR

Oralia

I woke maybe a half hour later, snuggled in Ren's arms.

He had wrapped me in my cloak, somehow refastening his own around his shoulders, and we were now right at the edge of the castle. The turrets loomed overhead, casting us in shadow, and I shuddered, nuzzling farther into his chest. He chuckled, leaning down to press a kiss to my ear. It was nice, this intimacy. The way he was unable to stop himself from touching me, as starved for our connection as I was.

"Are you well?" he asked.

I nodded, pressing a kiss to his chest before tracing a finger across the silver buckle of his baldric beside my cheek.

"Ren!" a voice shouted far off. The panicked noise cut through the bliss of the moment. "*Ren!*"

"Put me down," I said, shifting when he tightened his hold around me. "Ren, put me on my feet."

He complied, though he wrapped his hand firmly around mine,

linking our fingers together as he drew the shadows around us. We stepped forward, and I blinked away the darkness quickly to find my bearings. One of the large trees that overlooked the wide, lapping river suddenly loomed over us.

Dimitri and Mecrucio stood in the shallow depths, arms wrapped around a limp body clad in golden steel. Far off in the distance, Vakarys in her boat was winding her way back to the opposite shore. They were struggling with the body—whoever it was could not hold themselves up on their own and flailed within their grasp as if they were trying to fight. A weight dropped inside my chest, stealing my breath and chasing my voice.

I knew that armor.

Before he could stop me, I dropped Ren's hand and darted from beneath the tree, falling over myself to get to the shore. He cried out my name, but I did not stop, not even as icy water bit the skin of my ankles and calves and chilled me straight down to my bones. Or perhaps the chill came from the sight of the golden-haired god in their arms.

"Caston!" I cried, grabbing for his chest plate.

But it was all wrong, rust smeared across the golden metal. His rose-gold skin was pale, lacking its usual shimmer. I wanted to hug him, throw my arms around him, and rejoice at being reunited. Yet as my hands fluttered uselessly around him, he gave a great groan of pain.

"Stay back, my lady," Dimitri instructed softly.

Caston's eyelids fluttered once before opening, his voice nearly an incomprehensible rasp. "Oralia? *Oralia!*"

Panic ripped through me, nausea pulsing deep within my gut. I reached for his hands but hesitated. I could not touch him, not without my gloves.

"I am here. Right here."

My stomach lurched with his next cry of agony. It was not rust on his armor, but blood. Blood that was splattered across his neck and face, speckles of it mixing with the freckles on his cheeks. It was everywhere, even dripping into the dark water beneath him.

"Kratus arrow to the back," Mecrucio answered my silent question, his hard gaze flicking to Ren and away again. "Pierced through to the front here." He tapped two fingers gently to a spot right at Caston's solar plexus where a small hole lay, a golden tip pushing through the metal of his chest plate.

If he was still alive, then it had missed his heart. I thanked the stars for the mercy and settled for gripping the top curve of his chest plate, leaning down until I was in his eyesight.

"You will be okay," I whispered, tears thick in my throat as I tried to blink them away, repeating the words again and again.

He groaned, lids falling shut once more.

"We need to remove the arrow before it causes any more damage," Mecrucio said, his voice so tense it was almost a rasp.

Ren moved to Mecrucio's side at once. He and Dimitri each grabbed onto one of Caston's shoulders so Mecrucio could grasp the arrow at my brother's back. Bile crept up my throat, horror slinking through my chest.

"I am sorry, Your Highness," Mecrucio said to Caston before he gripped the arrow and pulled.

Screams rent the air, rippling the surrounding water. I squeezed my eyes shut against the sound, childishly wishing I could press my hands to my ears and pretend this was not real. Caston's body dropped limply into our arms. The silence that followed was deafening.

Stars, please let him live. He had to live.

"Let us move him, my lady," Dimitri said. "We must get him to Thorne."

I nodded, keeping hold of one of the plates of armor. Ren's face was pale across from me as he looked over my brother, mouth tensed in rage.

"Can we shadow-walk him to the palace?" I asked, a tremor wavering through my voice, hot tears scalding my cheeks.

Ren nodded. "You will need to help me. I cannot walk the four of you alone."

Mecrucio moved to Caston's feet, lifting them carefully. He'd tucked the bloodied arrow into his baldric, hands stained red and crusted with dried blood. With Ren's help, they drew Caston out of the water and over the dry grass until we were beneath the shadow of the gnarled tree.

The world trembled around me, my very bones shaking. He had to live. This could not destroy him. If he died, there was so much hope that would die with him. Caston's eyelids fluttered, drooped, then opened again. His breathing came in quick gasps, followed by terrible silences.

"Oralia, look at me," Ren commanded. "You must focus. Do you hear me?"

I nodded, closing my hands more firmly around Caston's armor.

"We will call the shadows together. We will intend to move *together* into the center of the antechamber to the palace."

I nodded, my lips trembling, fearful of what might happen if I could not do it. But I pushed that thought away, tried to push away the panic and fear and rage bubbling beneath the surface. Caston needed me. I could not let him down.

"Tell me you understand," he commanded, his sharp tone pulling the world into greater focus.

"I understand."

His shadows swirled around us. "Call them."

I took a deep breath as my magic slithered across my bones, singing deep under my skin. The power responded to my call, and I knew then I did not need to plead. Ren's words from our first meeting beneath the mountains floated back to me: *It will come when you call. Soothe when you are hurt. Fight when you are in danger.* I sighed in relief. My shadows, a shade or so darker than Ren's, slid around us and circled over Caston's bloodied chest.

"On the count of three," Ren instructed.

One.

Two.

Three.

The darkness disappeared and was replaced by the light of the shimmering blue torches at the entrance of the castle. My knees buckled.

Sidero was there, their arm wrapping around my waist to steady me.

"I have you," they murmured, pulling me upright.

The three men did not hesitate. They moved as a unit down a hall I'd never walked before. It was not as narrow as the others, nor as winding. We trailed behind, Sidero steadying me with an arm around my back as I tried to explain in a halting whisper what was happening.

Ren's power pushed open large double doors at the end of the hall, and they moved into the room, hauling Caston up onto a large stone table. It was done in practiced movements that told me they'd done this many times before. Thorne stood at one of the large windows at the back of the room, his red beard glinting in the torchlight.

Caston woke then, his eyes wide and bloodshot, hands closing over Dimitri's wrists, pushing him away. Though he made no recognizable words, it was clear from his groans he was afraid. Some dim part of his mind or magic recognized where he was. After only a few moments, however, his body grew limp as he gave over once more to his wounds.

"Did the arrow splinter?" Thorne asked as his wide hands closed over Caston's shoulders, rolling him carefully onto his side.

"No," Mecrucio answered, drawing the bloodied arrow from his baldric.

The arrow in his hands was narrow and ornate, tipped in gold at both ends. It glittered faintly in the light. The kratus wood was gilded with gold to make it look as if it were made purely of sunlight.

Acid tore through me, eating away everything inside my chest until I was a hollow shell. I knew that arrow, had seen it nocked within a bow thousands of times. I had touched the golden tips—weighed them in my hands. I had seen them stuck through the bodies of Aethera's enemies as the mark of his triumph.

The arrows of the Golden King.

The arrows of Typhon.

FIFTY-FIVE

Renwick

I was not sure if the young god on the table would make it through the night.

Though Thorne preferred to spend his time welcoming new souls into the kingdom and training our army, he was also the most gifted healer we had. Born to Petra, one of my mother's closest friends and sometimes lover, only a few months after the creation of time, he was one of the oldest gods within the kingdom who was not time-less. Thorne's father had been one of the many gods killed in the first battles with the giants. Having felt the loss keenly, in its wake, he had thrown himself into learning how to use his magic to heal others.

"1 found him at the edge of the mist less than an hour ago," Mecrucio explained quickly.

I held the young god's shoulder to keep him on his side while Mecrucio pinned his legs. Dimitri held his arms above his head, keeping him steady as Thorne closed his hands over the gaping wound on his back.

Oralia was beside me now. Silent from the moment Mecrucio had shown us the arrow. I knew she recognized it. Her face had gone deathly pale, eyes hardening into flecks of emeralds as she had watched Mecrucio place it on the table.

Now was not the time to hold her in my arms, though I desperately wanted to. I was all too familiar with the rage that was burning inside of her. But I would need to help her quench the flame before it tore her apart and left behind someone unrecognizable.

Typhon would pay, but she would not be the cost.

"Tell me about him," I said softly, looking at her from the corner of my eye.

She took a breath, her chest barely rising with the movement. Slowly, her eyes closed and she licked her lips.

"Caston is...*good.*" Her voice was rough, as though she had been screaming. "A brilliant leader, a skilled warrior, but good. So unlike his father." A small flinch, her hand jerking at her side with the desire to touch him before it fell back to the table. "He asked after the story of your wings countless times when he was small. He could not wrap his mind around what could have been the cause for such cruelty."

Her eyes flicked to me, then back to him.

"It is his kindness, I think, that sets him apart. His men revere him for his ability to listen, to take advice, but also because he knows the limits of his goodness. He knows when kindness has run its course and violence must take its place."

I nodded, humming to show her I was listening. Flecks of blood littered her face.

"When he was little, he was afraid of the dark," she whispered, her voice cracking, knuckles straining from her grip on the table edge. "He would practically break down my door at night trying to get in.

Eventually, I slept in his room, much to the chagrin of his nursemaid and Typhon—though I always kept my distance."

"Did he never question why you could not be touched?"

She bit her lip, tears sparkling in her lashes. "I do not think so."

"I did…" a voice rasped from below, and we froze as a pair of dazed bright blue eyes half-opened. His face was hollow, scrunching in pain. "For years, I asked until I was sent awa—" His jaw slackened, and his eyes fell shut, a soft sigh scratching through his throat.

"Apologies, my lady," Thorne murmured in his gruff voice. "Sometimes, this part can knock them unconscious. I tried to hold off as long as I could."

She nodded, working a fragile smile across her lips. "There is no need to apologize. You are doing brilliantly. Thank you."

After another moment, she leaned against me, unable to keep herself up any longer. I lifted one of my arms, directing her underneath it before grabbing hold of Caston's shoulder again. She clutched my baldric, the side of her face pressed against my chest as she looked down at the soft, peaceful expression on the young god's face.

It took hours for Thorne to clean the wound and then heal the organs the arrow pierced. Caston did not wake. For her not to witness his agony was a small mercy.

By the time Thorne was smoothing a bandage over his torso, dawn was creeping slowly through the windows behind him. Only an hour ago, the prince's breathing had evened, his heartbeat picking up a steady, hopeful rhythm.

"He will need time to heal, Your Grace, but he will survive," Thorne said, though he was looking at Oralia when he spoke.

She nodded, reaching to place a hand on Thorne's shoulder over the thick leather armor he wore. "I am in your debt."

He shook his head, placing a hand over his heart. "There is no need for debts."

"Then at the very least, you have my thanks," she replied before dropping her hand and turning to me. "Can we move him to my chambers?"

Thorne gave his assent. I stepped forward, sliding my arms beneath the prince's shoulders and legs.

"I will take him up," I said, drawing the shadows to me.

A heartbeat later, I stood in her room, and she appeared beside me, her shadows lingering to offer her a moment of comfort before they disappeared. We arranged him in the bed, drawing the covers over him, though I could tell she was careful not to touch his skin.

"You could ask your magic to only allow that power to come forward when needed."

She turned to me, shocked. "Do you think that would work?"

I thought about it. About the way she seemed to commune with her power, rather than commanding it. "Perhaps, though you should discuss it with Morana. I am sure she could tell you more definitively."

We sat quietly on the couch nearby while the muted light of dawn spilled across the sky. When it became too bright, she stood, closing the hangings around her bed so the prince could sleep undisturbed. But instead of folding herself back in my arms, she sat beside me, her feet tucked underneath her.

Her gown was destroyed. Splatters of Caston's blood littered her chest and arms from when Thorne had cleaned the wound. But she had refused to step away at any point during the night.

"Why would he do this?" Rage tinted the edges of her words, firming her lips and tensing her shoulders.

I sighed, running a hand through my hair. Caston was Typhon's heir, though I knew he treated him more as a general for his armies. An heir for a god like Typhon—like me—was unnecessary.

Typhon had weighed each member of his court's importance. Though I had wondered many times who might be next, never once did I dream it would be the young god, barely settled into his prime, now feverish behind us.

But how did it play in Typhon's favor? Other than infuriating Oralia? It broke my heart that though she knew the reason, she needed to hear it said aloud for it to be made real.

I stared at her for a long time as though I could see past flesh and bone down into her very soul. She held inside of her the power of life and death, sunshine and shadows—a great expanse of power so deep I could not fathom it. I wondered, perhaps, if there was even more than life and death within her. Could she call upon the wind? Heal a ghastly wound? Turn day into night? We already knew she had the power to raze Infernis to the ground, to twist its magic into her bidding. It was why I had saved her in the first place.

But perhaps, there was more. In the beginning, before time, there were gods in other realms similar to ours who possessed all the power of the universe inside them. That had been what spurred my father forward in his mad experiments. It was said that one who held the potential for such power would receive it from the world itself. Born with one power, infected with the other. Hence why my father had drunk the blood of other gods, trying to *infect* himself with their power.

She had been born with the light and infected with the darkness.

"Ren?" she asked, covering my hand with hers.

I cleared my throat before squeezing her hand gently.

"It is you," I said, an apology in my voice. "He is doing this to get to you."

CHAPTER
FIFTY-SIX

Oralia

I slept on and off for the next few hours.

Ren, I learned, did not need sleep, though he did sometimes crave it. A trait of most timeless gods apparently, though he held me when I asked. Eventually, he tucked a blanket around me where I lay on the couch after he had convinced me I'd be more use to Caston rested than drained.

Typhon had done this to get to me. The idea circled my mind like Caston's blood down a drain, though I could not understand why. I had known that Typhon would not stop pursuing me, but never once had I thought he would risk his own son. Which meant that Typhon valued my power more than he valued his heir.

Around mid-morning I woke with my head in Ren's lap, his fingertips brushing soothingly through my hair. Pushing myself up to a seat, I ran a hand over my face.

"Here," he whispered, reaching for a steaming mug of tea on the table in front of us.

"Thank you." I wrapped my hands around the warm mug as if I could transfer the heat into my soul.

"Oralia?" a voice rasped through the curtains of the bed hangings.

I jumped to my feet, and Ren took the mug from me before I could spill the contents over the both of us. I was at the bed in an instant, drawing back the hangings. "I am here."

He looked better than the day before with a little more color in his rose-gold cheeks. There was a small bloodstain on his bandage, but it was not as gruesome as I had been expecting. Caston smiled softly, and I bunched my hands into the fabric of my gown to stop myself from touching him, though I perched on the edge of the bed by his knees.

"How are you?"

He took a deep breath, one of his hands coming up to press against the wound, before sighing. "I am...alive... Whoever healed me has a true gift."

I smiled. *Stars*, I had missed him perhaps more in these last months than in any other time apart. Those long spans of time in which he had been off leading his men through uncharted territories or else defending the kingdom had always come with correspondence. His letters arrived worn and tattered from the miles between us, speaking of the far-off lands beyond the palace grounds I would never see. He had always signed each letter with the words that brought me some semblance of peace: *Your Brother.*

We were not blood, but that had never mattered to him.

"Thorne will be happy to hear that," Ren said softly.

Though he stood close enough that Caston did not need to move his head to see him, he left ample space between himself and the bed. Even so, Caston jerked away, grabbing my arm and pulling as if he could get in front of me.

I tried to soothe him with crooning sounds, but nothing cut through the tension now vibrating through my arm. "All is well."

"You are not in any danger," Ren added calmly, raising both hands in front of his chest. "I will not harm you or Oralia."

Caston did not react to his words, merely gripped me tighter. "Not in any *more* danger, you mean."

"Listen to what he is saying." I took a deep breath, wishing I could cover his hand with mine, but I settled for trying a small smile. Caston's control of his power was only a recent thing. He was only a year or so out from prime, and his emotions sometimes still bested him. "I trust Ren with my life."

But his grip only tightened to the point of pain, pulling again until I was kneeling on the bed. Some primal fear bled into his eyes; all reason was wiped clean from his mind. There was danger here in this room, and I feared it was not Ren who was the threat. I winced, a hiss sliding through my teeth as he tried to draw me back further.

"Let her go," Ren commanded, his eyes flashing. "Your Highness, I understand you are afraid, but you are hurting her."

Caston's grip faltered on my arm. He was trembling, his chest stuttering with the rapidity of his breath.

"You are safe here," I murmured, placing a hand on his blanket-covered knee.

He did not look as if he believed me, as his eyes searched mine. His grip loosened until I could move back to my perch beside the bed. Ren stepped closer, respect for Caston's space forgotten while he looked me over.

"I am fine."

But Ren took my arm in his hands, running his fingers over the spot Caston had gripped to soothe the pain. Caston watched warily, looking as though he was ready to throw himself between us at any moment. Ren gave me a pained smile and nodded.

"I apologize for my rudeness, Your Grace," Caston said in a stilted voice.

Ren shifted, and the mask of indifference fell into place over his features—some deep part of him recoiling at the mistrust in Caston's expression.

"There is no need to apologize, Your Highness. Of all the reactions to me, yours was the most peaceable of the last few hundred years. I will leave you two to catch up." Ren gestured toward the fireplace. "There is food when you are ready."

He turned to me, his hand twitching at his side before he smiled.

"Thank you," I said, wanting to take his hand, to kiss him, but uncertainty held me in place.

This god should be my enemy according to Caston. His reaction had been a reminder of that. But I knew the truth deep within my soul: my enemy was not here in this room. No, my enemy was the man who had strung that bow, who had let that arrow fly.

"Of course," Ren replied softly, bowing his head once before sweeping from the room.

I watched him go, sighing quietly to myself and wishing things were clearer.

"You should eat," I said, turning back to Caston. "It will help build your strength back, and we must discuss what happened."

He was eyeing me with uncertainty, but he nodded, awkwardly pushing himself to sit upright. I took my time going to gather the tray from the table, adding my forgotten tea to it so I could hold something to curb my temptation to comfort him. A few months away from the gilded walls of Aethera and I'd become so accustomed to touch. It was difficult now to repress that instinct.

Carefully, I set the tray across his lap, removing the covering to a large bowl of broth. He looked at the bowl with distrust, and I sighed, picking it up and taking a sip from it.

"It is not poisoned," I snapped.

Caston gave me an apologetic smile before taking the bowl from my hands.

"Slowly," I cautioned as he brought it to his lips, remembering how ravenous I'd been once I had woken from injury.

For barely a moment, his crooked smile appeared before he began drinking the broth. I sipped my tea. It was odd having him here, to be somewhere with him other than the golden palace.

"What happened?" I asked gently.

His eyebrows furrowed, and he stared into the bowl. "Michalis is dead."

Shame lanced through my heart and the image of his guard, no, his *mate*, swam in front of my eyes—face down and lifeless on the dining room table, blood trickling from his ears. My mouth opened and closed a few times, a small squeak sliding out of my throat.

"These last months have been..." Caston trailed off, slowly lowering the bowl.

"I am so sorry," I breathed. "I did not..."

He nodded, fingertips sliding across the smooth ceramic edge.

"I know you did not mean for it to happen," he said just as softly. "But... *Burning Suns*, Oralia. You exploded into shadow and when the darkness faded you were gone and Michalis... Michalis..."

I slid closer until our knees touched and placed my hand across his covered shin.

"That night is one of my greatest regrets. I ran because I was frightened, not only of what I had done but of how I would be punished. I never meant to abandon you, Caston, nor did I mean to take away someone you loved."

"I lost two whom I loved that night."

Tears welled, then overflowed. I took a deep, shuddering breath, trying to calm the torrent of guilt and shame. "Will you ever forgive me?"

He turned to me, tears tracking down his rose-gold cheeks. But his smile was achingly tender as he placed a hand over my silk-covered forearm.

"I am already on the road to forgiveness, Oralia," he answered. "But have you forgiven yourself?"

My smile was watery as I brushed away my tears with the back of my free hand. "I am on that road as well."

Caston nodded, releasing my arm and trying to settle back onto the pillows. A little of the flush from when he had woken was faded now. His fingers trembled as he pulled at the covers. "Has...has *he* been kind to you?"

The blossoming tension in his mouth told me well enough he meant Ren.

I weighed each word. "It has not always been easy, and I have not always allowed it. But yes, he has always been kind. It took us time to wade through the murky waters of distrust that existed between us."

Folding his hands over his stomach, he winced and let them drop to his side. "You two are..." His voice trailed off while he looked for the word. "Friends?"

I bit my lip. This discussion seemed important to him, but I was much more concerned with how he found himself on the shores of Infernis with an arrow through his chest.

"You seem like friends," he continued. "You appear comfortable with him—more comfortable than I have ever seen you with anyone."

I nodded, taking a long sip of my tea. "He is unlike anyone I have ever met. He is as kind as he is fearsome, patient as he is ruthless, nurturing as he is deadly. When Ren looks at me, he sees more than what my power can do for him. I am not a prisoner here."

Caston made a small derisive noise in his throat, his eyes moving around the room. I knew what he was thinking. He considered me a prisoner here, though I had not felt that way for so long, not since Ren first placed my father's journal in my hands.

My muscles tightened, preparing for a fight.

"You were not—"

"Come now, I know you are not so foolish," I cut across him. "You know as well as I what I was."

Caston pursed his lips, his chest rising with a deep breath before he screwed his face up in discomfort. I knew that his power was slithering through him, whispering the truth of my words. The tension remained in his face. His shoulders were stiff with the words I knew he wished to say.

"I am sorry...for not doing more."

I sighed, my chin dropping. "You did everything you could."

With careful deliberation, he placed his hand on my silk-covered elbow. "And yet, it was not enough."

FIFTY-SEVEN

Renwick

M y feet dragged heavily across the floor as I pushed open the doors to the dining room.

There was a scraping of chairs as those seated around the table jumped to their feet. Murmurs of *myhn ardren* hummed in the air, but I only waved a hand in their direction before running it down my face. My clothes were bloodstained, clinging sickeningly to my skin. The blood was an itching reminder of the horrors that had passed and of the horrors yet to come.

"He is awake," I said, gripping the back of the nearest chair to rest my weight upon it. I looked at my healer. "He looks well."

Thorne's face broke with relief, his sigh heavy as he thanked the Great Mothers. Beside him, Mecrucio clapped him on the shoulder, shaking him with quiet words of praise. After a moment, I withdrew the chair, falling heavily into the seat.

"And Oralia?" Dimitri asked, rising from his place to set a goblet of wine in front of me.

Her name was a prayer within my mind, a balm to soothe the ache within my soul even as fear prickled down my spine. I nodded at him in thanks but did not drink.

"She wears her anger like a heavy cloak she thinks no one can see," I replied, twisting the stem of the goblet between two fingers. "She is no stranger to the fear that grips us all. She knows there is much that must be done."

All three gods hummed their agreement, but it was Mecrucio who dabbed his lips with his napkin, placing it slowly beside his plate, and said, "I cannot understand Typhon's actions."

Pursing my lips, I nodded. In those hours I held Oralia, I thought I now better understood the actions of this man whose greatest dreams were just out of reach. What would such a man be willing to sacrifice to grasp them?

Everything. He would sacrifice everything and anything.

"We know better than most how difficult it is to understand the actions of a madman," Thorne offered before taking a deep drink of wine.

How true that was. Thorne and Horace had been in the room when he announced what had befallen my mother. We had lost so much that day. The war with Typhon arrived mere centuries later, the mist a relic of that ancient battle.

"Where did you find the prince, Mecrucio?" My voice was as heavy as the weight upon my shoulders.

He dropped his hand to the table, a wet finger drawing a serpentine line across its black surface. "Where the river curves to the west upon the edge of the largest human settlement only a few paces from the mist."

The same path the prince often took to visit those within that village when he was home from his travels. A place he often traveled alone and unprotected.

"And did you see who loosed the arrow?" I asked, searching the god's face.

His brows fell as his lips tightened into a thin line. "I did not. I stumbled upon him perhaps minutes later following the scent of blood. I was afraid one of my own men might have been discovered."

Mecrucio had a small handful of spies placed within the kingdom where my soldiers could not travel. I nodded, already certain I knew who the culprit was. The hinges of the large doors creaked, footsteps echoing across the dark marble. I pushed to my feet and moved toward them.

Oralia was the first to enter. Her face was drawn, hair flowing over her shoulders. She had changed from her blood-streaked clothes and had haphazardly swiped at the specks upon her face and neck. But there was that same heaviness in her I felt in myself. Her expression only softened when her eyes met mine. Behind her, Caston limped into the room, waving off Sidero's helpful arm as he crossed the threshold.

"*Myhn ardren*," she greeted, placing a hand upon her heart and bowing her head as she dipped into a small curtsey.

Shadows prickled across my skin, heat snaking through my chest. The old language slid across her tongue, and when her lips formed the words, it felt as if I was reliving a dream. And there was the answer to a question I had not thought to ask: Oralia was making her loyalty clear with this simple action.

I bowed my head, hand pressing over my heart, and though I longed to use a different title, to dress her in obsidian jewels and place her upon an ivory throne, I knew we were not there yet, so I replied, "My lady."

Caston's face tightened, mistrust bleeding across his cheeks, and then his eyes widened, mouth popping open.

"Mecrucio..." The name was practically a breath as if a hand was wrapped around his throat.

Mecrucio stepped forward to place a hand over his heart. "Hello, Your Grace, I am happy to see you are well."

The prince shook his head, hands balling into tight fists. "You are working with the Under King."

I sighed, running a hand through my hair while Mecrucio nodded solemnly. "Mecrucio has been one of my inner circle for over a thousand years."

The glare Caston sent both of us was as sharp as a dagger, his chest rising and falling with heavy breaths. "You are my father's most favored adviser."

Mecrucio nodded, a look of regret passing over his face as his hand dropped from his heart. "I have climbed the ranks within your father's court to better serve my king and his people."

Caston opened his mouth to argue, but Oralia cut across him, gesturing to a chair. "Sit."

Thorne patted the one beside him, his loud voice booming through the chamber. "By me, lad."

With wooden steps, halted by pain, the prince found his seat, lowering into it with a soft hiss. The scent of ash and asphodel flowers swirled around me as Oralia's small hand slid into mine.

"Are you well?" she asked, squeezing once.

I sighed, drawing her hand up to press a kiss to the scar on her wrist, my back to the group settling into their meals. "I should be asking you that."

She only shrugged, the dark green gown catching in the light of the blue flames and dancing like a waterfall down her waist. Her attention settled on Caston behind my shoulder. "He would not tell the story of what happened."

"I am sure we will hear it before this night is done," I answered, positive it would be even sooner than that.

A small frown pulled at the corners of her mouth, but I let her go, guiding her with a hand on the small of her back toward the table and the plate Sidero had already filled for her. Thorne and the rest of my inner circle rose as she approached, their hands placed over their hearts and heads bowed in respect. Her cheeks heated at the gesture, lips quirking when they did not sit until she was comfortable within her chair.

All the while, Prince Caston gazed upon me as if I were a rat who had snuck into his bedchamber.

"Yes, Your Highness?" I asked, fighting back a frown at the ice dripping through my veins.

His face twisted in disgust as his rose-gold skin flushed. "You mock me with such a title, Under King."

With measured steps, I approached. My hand curled around the back of a chair. "I assure you, I do not."

Caston scoffed, shifting uncomfortably in his seat. His hand wrapped around the dinner knife beside the plate laden with food. "You do. You mock us all with your civility, with your pleasant smiles and bows. I know you are a wolf within the flock even if my sister counts you as a sheep."

Oralia pressed one finger to the tip of his knife, forcing it toward the table. "That is enough."

The laugh that burst from him was bitter, a true mockery. "You sit at his table as if you do not wear his chains. You spoke of kindness, but it is merely manipulation, Oralia. How can you not see—"

"No, it is you who cannot see," she snapped, shadows flicking out for a mere instant before recoiling. "Blinded by a god you call father and spewing acid at the king who has saved you—who accepted you into his kingdom at great risk to his people. Ren could have let your magic return to the earth to start anew, and yet here you sit."

He blinked at her as if she were a stranger, fear stark across his face from the small display of her power. "What has he done to you?"

Oralia smoothed the napkin on the table, a slow breath flaring her nostrils before her eyes met mine. "It is not what he did to me."

My heart thundered through my skull; knuckles bleached white against the dark wood chair that groaned beneath my punishing grip. A small, victorious smile curled her lips, answering his question before he could ask. Her sharp gaze flicked back to pierce his. Shadows curled around her shoulders, winding down her arms to thread between her fingers before vanishing into smoke.

"I threw off the shackles of Aethera and freed *myself*."

Caston's face paled at her words—at the fire in her eyes. Something within the god appeared to crack.

"Tell us what happened," Thorne rumbled softly. "How you came to find yourself here."

"And what do you know of the attack?" Caston turned on me, ignoring Thorne, and though the fire of his anger was no longer raging as bright, the words were sharp as a knife's edge.

I nodded once at Sidero, who rose and quietly left the room.

"Only what I have learned in the last few minutes: that you were found on the western edge of the forest close to the human settlement."

A shiver traced down my spine as Caston surveyed me, searching for the lie within my words. I wondered if truth was part of his magic—if it gave him that innate ability to lead, to choose his men. Sidero slipped back into the room, a bloody package balanced in their hands.

"Perhaps this will help to clarify things," I murmured as they placed it in front of the prince, and I took my seat.

Slowly, as if it might bite him, Caston unwound the fabric to reveal the gold-tipped arrow, stained with his own blood. "No...this is a trick."

Oralia shook her head, leaning closer to him, all anger leaching from her face. "It is no trick, Caston. I saw them pull this arrow from your wound."

His eyes closed with his teeth gritting tight. "He is a murderer, this king we sit before. A monster, a tyrant."

Her shoulders tensed. The prince's words were an echo of the very same words she had spoken on her first night here in this castle.

"I am afraid that you are describing the wrong king." Her voice was a warning and an apology as she gently touched the arrow in his grasp. "It is you who must open your eyes and see the truth. Control your emotions, Caston. Use your power."

His hand flexed around the golden wood, his blinks slow, measured as he gazed up at me. There it was again—that shiver of magic sliding down my spine. His lashes grew wet, his eyes glassy, before he wiped his cheek on his shoulder. I thought I could understand the despair warring within his breast. The betrayal of a father. The reminder that to a god such as Typhon, such as my father, we were all expendable in the end.

"We were ambushed in the forest," he whispered. "It was as if night had fallen. A storm was upon us, lightning streaking through the sky. We were blind in the dark, unable to tell if the bodies around us were friend or foe."

I could see it perfectly as if I was standing beside him. Stillness crept across the table as he took a deep breath, steadying the fear rising through his veins.

"They were screaming your name, calling out formations in a language I could not understand. Your soldiers speak the old tongue. They were your men."

With a shake of my head, I smiled sadly at him. "My soldiers cannot cross the river, Caston. I have no assassins within Aethera, only spies."

His shoulders slumped as that crack within his spirit widened. His gaze fell to the arrow in his hands. "When I was hit, I acted upon instinct. I dragged myself through the bracken to hide from the attackers. I lost consciousness, and when I woke, I was alone and the forest was silent. I forced myself to my feet, to start walking, to get myself home."

"And that is where I found you, Your Highness," Mecrucio added, his voice careful and kind.

Caston nodded, his lips parting to speak but shutting as the doors flew open. Horace and Aelestor strode into the room, the former looking as calm as always, while the latter was distinctly disheveled. Aelestor's flaming hair was wild and tangled, his cloak was askew, and his boots were muddy.

"Your Grace," Aelestor said, his face reddened with exertion as if he'd run a great distance. "I can explain."

Oralia

The moment Aelestor walked into the room, Caston shot to his feet. "You."

Before he could go any further than a few steps, Thorne had his arms pinned behind his back, careful to avoid the still-healing wound.

"I should have known you would be working with the Under King," Caston gritted through his teeth.

Aelestor's eyes flashed, but he was calm beneath Caston's rage. There was a softness in him that I had not seen before that might have been growing since that day within Rathyra.

"You should sit before you injure yourself further, Your Highness," he said before turning to me and placing a hand over his heart. "My lady."

I nodded in reply, though Caston tried to wrestle out of Thorne's grasp once more. His eyes blazed with fire but his cheeks were already paling. *"You shall not speak to her!"*

"Lady Oralia has given me a great gift," Aelestor said slowly as if trying to reason with a child. "I am no longer her enemy. I am her ally."

Caston went limp at the sincerity in his words. That was the curse of Caston's magic—the reason for his success as a leader in the Aetheran army. He could sense dishonesty. His magic whispered to him with every word from another. Often, he joked that he could catch the scent of a lie. It smelled metallic and rotten in his nose. And now, he breathed deep, his walls crumbling with each inhale he took. I clenched my fists, wanting to do something, anything, to comfort him.

"I was there in the forest when you were attacked, Your Highness," Aelestor continued. "Typhon asked me to position myself on the edge of the mist with a small group of his men. I was to wait until your band came into view before I brought down a large storm."

Regret splashed across Aelestor's face, and he shook his head, trying to jostle the memory from his mind. His next inhale rattled in his chest, hands clenching and releasing into fists.

"He did not tell me why, I assure you. But the men rushed into the storm, banging their swords on their shields and yelling nonsensical words. It was choreographed chaos. And then, as the men retreated to the castle, Typhon himself carefully aimed through the storm and shot his arrow into your back."

Caston shook his head, leaning against Thorne. The large god had a comforting hand on his shoulder and was murmuring quietly to him. It broke my heart to see him in such a way, like a child looking for comfort. His eyes were wide, pleading as he looked from Aelestor to Ren and back again as if one of them might wake him from this nightmare.

Aelestor took another step forward until he was kneeling before

Caston, raising his first three fingers to his brow.

"I am sorry, Your Highness, for my part in your pain. Yes, I serve King Renwick, but that choice was not made by me but by your father's actions. Centuries ago, my love was taken from me." Aelestor looked up at my brother imploringly. "Think of what you know of your father. Think of his schemes, his lies, his temper. Think of the treatment of the god you call sister."

Caston's gaze fixed on his boots for a long moment before drawing to me—a magnet for his shame. I wanted to absolve him of it, take his hand, and tell him I did not blame him for the treatment I had endured or for his long absences that allowed him to be ignorant of such things. But I could not find the words. All I could do was stare back at him and fight the burning tightness in my throat.

"He is obsessed with Oralia's return," Caston said softly, looking me over as if he was seeing me for the very first time. Slowly, Thorne let Caston go, though he kept his hand on his shoulder to steady him. "But I do not understand... Why hurt me?"

In my peripheral vision, Ren shifted, his hand sliding through his hair in a gesture that spoke of his discomfort.

"Because by hurting you and making it look like my people did it, it pits her against me. Or...perhaps this was his plan all along. For us to find you and bring you here." He looked at me for a long moment, and the pain was clear on his face, the ice of our first meeting only a distant memory.

Caston swayed. Thorne guided him back to his seat with a, "There's a good lad," muttered under his breath.

"But why does he want her so badly? Especially after the way he has treated her... The way we all have treated her." Caston's voice broke. His fingertips pressed against his temples.

Ren sighed, looking at his hands, flexing them slowly.

"There are many reasons," he replied before tucking his hands into the pockets of his trousers. "Typhon, in his way, continues the work of our father toward total power. He collects gods the way boys collect sticks and breaks them just as easily. This is also not the first time Typhon has pressed our borders. Though it is the first time in millennia that he has an opportunity to get through. He wants Infernis—has *always* wanted Infernis."

"For what purpose could he possibly want the land of souls?" Caston's rose-gold eyebrows raised in distrust.

"For an immortal army," Dimitri answered before Ren could. "I was there the last time he attacked these shores, wearing gilded armor." Shock echoed through Caston and myself at that pronouncement. Dimitri's expression darkened. "He wanted—*wants*—Infernis to craft an army so he may conquer other realms and lands beyond Aethera. Two millennia ago, he was overeager, pigheaded in his assessment of Ren's strength and forces. He was pushed back easily."

Ren nodded. Respect and gratitude were clear on his face for his second in command. I wondered what had happened to have Ren place one of Typhon's own soldiers at his right hand.

"I created the mists to keep him out, and until now, it has held," Ren said, fingertips tracing the sharp edge of his dinner knife.

"But why does he want Oralia?" Caston pressed.

No one spoke for a moment, and I was surprised when Horace— who had been silent since he entered the room—spoke up in his measured, even tone.

"Because she possesses the power of the universe, Your Highness. And, in doing so, could replace Ren as ruler of this land to maintain the magic required here."

I froze. Horace was wrong. Yes, I possessed a depth of power unusual for most gods, but that was because of being bitten by a daemoni. I had no power to call storms, or travel beyond the shadows, or heal wounds.

But even as I thought it, my power rumbled inside of me, urging me not to be so quick to judge.

Caston was looking at me, disbelief written across his features slowly melting into uncertainty.

"I possess both life and death," I whispered, holding my hands palm up before me, the dark scars glittering in the lamps. "I can call light and shadows."

"And within her, she holds the power of us all," Horace said reverently. "I saw it the first time I met you."

There was a softness in his demeanor, kind and gentle. And though I knew this was the timeless god who punished souls, who sent them to the torture pits and the caves of retribution, I could also see the god who cared deeply. I'd heard from Sidero how, through his power, he could see all the unique pieces that made up each individual soul, but I'd always assumed this power was limited to those who were deceased.

"What happens if I do not return?" I asked the room at large.

Aelestor shifted, pushing to his feet. There was fear clinging to the corners of his eyes. His jaw feathered with the effort to restrain the agony caged inside him like a wild bird. His shoulders stiffened, hands clenched at his sides, and he took a deep breath to control his rising emotions.

"War, my lady," he answered, some of the rage sliding out with the words. "War upon Infernis. As we speak, Typhon is preparing, and this time, there is no doubt he will find a way—not after one of his own already made their way through. I say we have a week, at most, before they are on our shores."

We stared at him, and pain twisted through my stomach, slicing up my heart. But Ren did not look surprised. No, he looked as if millennia of suffering had settled upon his shoulders. I could see the true weight of the crown he wore as the king of Infernis, as the God of Death.

"Is there no repairing the place in which he slipped through?" I asked, turning to Ren.

Ren sighed, running a hand through his hair. He wore a tiredness so ancient it made him look like stone.

"If we can find it. The mist has evolved through the years into something complicated—sentient. It is an extension of me, and yet it is also ever-changing. Morana and I have been working to find where the defense has weakened, but it takes time. Time we unfortunately do not have."

I thought of the souls wandering Pyralis, grieving their lives; the souls isolated in Isthil; and the souls journeying through the caves. But it was the ascended souls in Rathyra I thought of most, and then of Sidero, Josette, and Lana. I tried not to think of Ren, of his wings tacked to the wall of Aethera's library and the broken way he'd whispered as I'd fallen asleep:

You are the only one I have ever wanted.

"Then I must go back to Aethera."

Ren stepped closer to me, his eyes blazing.

"No," he said. "It is too soon. I cannot allow you to do this."

"And I cannot allow our people to be put at risk for the whims of a tyrant to forestall a war that is coming whether we wish it or not. This way, we bring the fight to him."

CHAPTER
FIFTY-NINE

Renwick

Our people.

Not my people, but ours.

In a flash, I crossed the room and cupped her face in my hands, my palms heating with the warmth of her blush. "If you do this, it will be to the end we discussed."

Oralia's fingers gripped my wrists, thumbs brushing the exposed skin of my forearms. If she left, it would be to end Typhon. It would be to put a stop to his tyranny and cruelty.

"I understand," she replied, resolution hardening her eyes.

I pressed my forehead to hers, ignoring the murmured confusion of the prince and the replies from Thorne. That she would do this. That she would risk herself in order to protect Infernis and to protect me... It solidified all the wayward thoughts and wonderings in my mind. Standing before me was not merely a powerful god, not merely my lover, but my *queen*.

Myhn lathira.

"Then much must be done to prepare." My hands slid to her shoulders before I found Dimitri in the room. "We will meet you on the grounds in an hour to begin training."

My second in command nodded, placing a hand over his heart before leaving the room in a swirl of dark cloak and shining armor.

I turned my attention to Mecrucio. "You and Aelestor must return to Aethera, spin whatever tale you must to ensure that Oralia and the prince will be able to reenter the kingdom."

"Yes, my king," the two gods replied together before vanishing through the door.

I settled on Sidero. They were a few paces behind Oralia, where they had hovered protectively throughout the entire conflict. More than once, I had seen their hands twitch and their lips part before shutting in consternation.

"Start the preparations, Sid. I know you have already had one made."

They smiled at me, nodding before quickly exiting the rooms as silently as they had entered. Oralia raised a brow, but before she could question my commands, I brushed my lips softly against hers.

"I cannot ask you to do this."

"You are not asking. I am offering. It is the only way."

My head shook, not truly in disagreement but in regret as I slid my hands up her neck. My fingertips traced the line of her jaw. There was an ache in my heart—no, in my *soul*—at the knowledge of what was to come and the sacrifice she must make. I burned her features into my mind, the deep green of her eyes, the slope of her brows, the planes of her cheekbones, the curve of her lips.

"I do not deserve you."

Her smile was heartbreaking as she touched my cheek, pressing our foreheads together. "Yes, you do, Ren."

There was the sound of a chair scraping. The voices of Thorne and Caston intruded upon our quiet moment.

"What is this?" Caston's voice broke, a strangled hollow anger taking root.

Thorne tugged gently at his arm. "Come on, lad."

But the Prince of Aethera shook his head, leveling me with a stony gaze. The rose of his cheeks flushed a deep burgundy, eyes hardened into chips of ice. There was an echo of my brother in his face, but it was wiped away as Oralia threaded her fingers with mine.

"Fate," she answered simply. "This is fate."

I thought those newly formed shards of my heart might have trembled in that moment. No one had claimed me in such a way— not in all of my damned existence. Her chin did not dip, not even as Caston's eyes pierced hers. A thread of his magic tremored through the room before he gave one short nod. With that nod, her shoulders lowered a fraction, and a soft relieved exhale slipped through her lips.

Thorne nodded, gently grabbing hold of Caston's arm and steering him toward the doors. "Come, I need to take another look at that bandage."

When it clicked behind them and the sound of their footsteps died from the room, I turned, grabbing her by the waist and drawing her close.

"What did you mean—"

I cut her off by slotting my mouth over hers, taking advantage of her surprise to slip my tongue between her lips. She moaned, hands closing over my shoulders as I gripped her hips. Lifting her to sit on a clear space on the table, I pushed aside the plates and goblets in my haste.

"Ren," she gasped as my mouth moved to her throat.

"Not now, *after*," I growled, rucking up her skirts and tearing off the lace that hid her until she was exposed to me. Not now. I could not speak another word even if she held a kratus knife to my throat. I thought I very well might truly die if I did not touch her.

Stepping back, I drank in the sight of her panting and exposed on the table. Lingering on the glistening of her need against her thighs. The silence deepened between us. Her breasts strained against the lace of her gown with each heavy inhale. And then one of her hands snaked down her belly to slide two fingers over her dripping sex.

I groaned, fists balling, unable to look away as she spread her legs wider, one shoe dangling from her foot as she bent her leg. My cock strained against the fabric of my trousers, aching for the siren perched upon my dining room table, fucking herself on her fingers.

My resolve snapped as I grabbed a nearby chair and dragged it between her legs. Shadows curled around her wrist to pry them off her cunt and pin them to the table.

"What are you doing?" she asked, her chest heaving.

A feral grin pulled at my cheeks before I leaned forward, blowing a stream of cool air against her center. "Finishing my meal."

With the flat of my tongue, I gave her one, long lick. She leaned back against her hands, moaning as I circled her clit before delving into her entrance. The taste of her, *Stars...* It was almost as good as the feel of her. My moan vibrated against her core as her hips tilted up to meet my mouth, giving over to my ministrations.

"I am absolutely starving," I growled, before sucking her swollen clit into my mouth.

Her moan was more akin to a gasp and her legs trembled around me. I released one of her thighs before sliding two fingers inside of her. She was tight, always so tight, greedy, and needy for pleasure. My cock throbbed in my trousers, aching for her.

"Ren..." she whimpered when I curled my fingers. Pressing there always turned her into that shaking, whimpering mess that I loved so much.

But I slowed my movements on her clit as her walls fluttered, drawing her back down from her impending release. She moaned in frustration and continued to tilt her hips up. I did it again, finding that perfect rhythm. Her cunt pulsed around my fingers. The sound of the slick slide of her need filled the room.

"Ren!" she cried. One of her hands threaded through my hair, trying with all her strength to hold me to her.

I did not respond, merely raised a brow at her in challenge.

Her high cheekbones were dotted with red, and her lips parted with her ragged panting. A flush blossomed across her chest, over her gorgeous breasts and collarbones. Those pitiful doe eyes were almost enough to make me give her what she wanted—but only just.

"Make me come," she commanded, the flush on her cheeks deepening.

Yes, my queen, I almost answered before sucking her clit firmly into my mouth.

She shattered, her body shaking as she fell back to the table with the force of it. *Stars*, she was exquisite. The throb in my cock grew deeper until it was painful, straining and dripping against my thigh. Once the tremors of her body slowed, I drew my hand away, pushing the chair back to stand between her thighs. She pushed herself up onto her elbows, her hair mussed and eyes bright. Brushing a stray lock from her cheek, I pressed a lingering kiss to her lips.

Her hands reached for the placket of my trousers, ripping it open and drawing out my cock. I moved even closer, letting her trembling hands position me at her entrance.

"Hold on to me, love."

She obeyed, grabbing hold of my shoulders as I thrust inside of her. We groaned in unison, my hands finding her thighs, wrapping them around my waist. I set a brutal rhythm that had her head falling back. Her moans came out as gasps. I freed one of my hands and pulled down the neckline of her gown so I could roll her nipple between my fingers before sucking it into my mouth, lapping the starlight and sweat from her skin. Her walls fluttered around me, so hot and wet and tempting. But I pulled back, gripping her hair and tilting her head back so I could lick up the column of her neck.

"I want you like this forever," I rasped, snapping my hips forward. "Need you like this forever."

With desperation, I tried to sear this moment into my soul—to memorize the curve of her lips as she cried out in pleasure, the blush on her cheekbones, her wild hair.

"Yes," she groaned, tears springing into the corner of her eyes. *"Forever."*

I swallowed her moan, tilting my hips and forcing my hand between our bodies to circle her clit. She shuddered, her walls clamping down on me until my hips lost their rhythm, and I was rutting into her with the table squeaking against the marble with each thrust.

"Oh, *Stars*," she cried. "I... Ren— I..."

"Come, *eshara*. Come for me."

With my name on her lips, her release found her again. She threw back her head, one of her arms flying from my shoulders to hold herself up against the table. I barreled through her aftershocks, pressing a hand to her chest to lay her back on the table as I pounded into her, chasing my release with a strangled cry and her name falling from my lips.

In the silence that followed, we stared at one another, breathing in each other's air. She was beautifully disheveled with her pink cheeks, swollen lips, and messy hair. Carefully, I slid out, replacing my cock with two fingers against her sex and gathering our combined release. With slow, gentle movements, I pressed it back inside. Some wild part of me was unsatisfied until she held something of me inside her.

The way I carried her within my very soul.

Oralia rested her forehead against mine, her fingertips threading through my hair. Reality crashed down upon us. A heavy weight pinned against my chest. She would leave soon, and there were so many unknowns. Would she return? Would she even survive?

"I love you," I whispered.

The moment the words escaped from my lips, fear circled my heart. Never had I uttered those words to anyone, not even my mother or father. Love was dangerous. An invisible predator that could destroy if one was not careful. But I did not care, not anymore.

If I would be destroyed, let it be by her.

And like the coward I was, I closed my eyes, unable to face the pity or fear that might mar her features. But then soft fingertips stroked my cheek, and a watery chuckle that was more a sparkle of joy than a laugh ghosted across my lips.

"And I love you," she answered, kissing me again.

CHAPTER
SIXTY

Oralia

I stood facing the large, dark wood door of the throne room, my knees trembling beneath my skirts. The last time I had been in this room, I had been shaking in fear, helpless and alone. This entire kingdom had appeared monstrous, unnatural, and deadly. But now?

Now, it was home.

"Are you sure about this?" Caston asked quietly.

I nodded, giving him a small smile. "Of course."

"Do you love him?" he pressed in an even smaller voice.

This time, my smile grew so wide it hurt my cheeks, and my heart fluttered painfully against my chest.

"More than anyone has ever loved another, even from before time was made."

It had been a few days since we had discussed the reality of what happened to him in the forest. A few days had been plenty of time for him to recover, and now he stood before me, tall and leonine with his shimmering rose-gold skin and sunlight hair. His white tunic was crisp beneath the dark green cloak he wore, embellished with golden leaves around the edges of the fabric.

In those few days, he had grown to trust Ren more. There was no denying the magic that spoke to him of truths. And when I had asked him how he could not have seen the lies Typhon spun like golden silk that threaded through the kingdom, he had only shaken his head sadly.

My power has no sway over him.

He had become fast friends with Thorne, whose raucous laughter could infect even the most somber of gods. Mecrucio, he had always known and trusted, but now, with the shackles of Aethera removed from the God of Thieves and Travelers alike, a deeper friendship was taking root.

Dimitri and Horace were not as present with Caston, but I'd seen him in discussion with both many a time when I'd come in from training or planning with Aelestor, Ren, or Morana.

"My lady?" Sidero murmured, adjusting the neckline of my gown.

It was so different from any of the ones I'd worn before. It was sleeveless. The lining was black as night and clung to my curves before flaring out at my thighs and pooling down to the floor. Over it, I wore a layer of sparkling diamonds linked by tiny silver chains that reminded me of armor. The metal was cool against my skin. It fell off my back in a glittering cape to the floor, the rest clinging to the bodice and skirt of the gown.

We had left my hair long—the singular request of Ren—and it waved down my back, a wild juxtaposition to the ornate structure of the gown.

"I am ready."

Sidero nodded, their eyes twinkling with excitement before I knocked three times upon the obsidian door.

I squared my shoulders as Caston and Sidero took a few steps back. Though I knew what would happen next, nerves jangled through my body, collecting in the pit of my stomach.

"Breathe, Oralia," Sidero instructed.

Nodding, I took a breath and lifted my chin high right before the double doors swung open with a hiss of shadow.

The large onyx throne room was packed with souls, gods, and demigods from the realm. A veritable sea of grays, blacks, whites, and gold, cloaks, robes, and gowns. Even the windows were open to allow some souls to lean in from outside the castle for a better look. Though the murmurings of the crowd through the door had been loud, silence fell upon the room as they swung open. As one, all turned to me, joyful expressions on their faces.

But I could not give them another glance.

There on the dais, at the end of the walkway created by the throng of bodies, stood Ren. He was resplendent in his black doublet. Its silver buttons shimmered in the blue flames that lit the room. A jagged obsidian crown lay atop his head, barely visible in his raven hair that was free and curling around his shoulders. His smile was blinding as he gazed upon me with hungry eyes, his hands clasped behind his back.

Behind him stood his throne, black as night and imposing as death, but beside it was its twin, wrought in gleaming ivory. Carvings were etched into the bleached curves, the moon, the stars, trees, and flowers—the cycle of life and decay, the passing of time. In short, all the creations of the Great Mothers were represented upon the throne.

I took a deep breath, taking my first steps into the room, and as one, the crowd around us fell to their knees with their hands pressed to their hearts. Power skittered across my skin, winding around my wrists, my waist, and my shoulders in comfort. It felt as if I was being guided down the aisle by someone beloved but long since passed. My heartbeat thundered in my ears, but I did not look away—could not look away from the god upon the raised dais.

"Who stands before their king?" Ren announced, loud enough to carry to all in the room.

"Oralia Peregrine Anemos," I replied.

I had grown up with the last name of *Solis*, Typhon's family name, but when I learned the family name of my true father, Zephyrus, I knew I could use no other.

Ren's eyes glittered at my pronouncement, and he cleared his throat before extending a hand toward me.

"Welcome, Oralia Anemos, to the kingdom of Infernis," he replied, his grip firm in mine as I made my way up the short staircase.

His thumb brushed the back of my hand once before letting it drop and turning to Dimitri. With solemnity, he took from him a large, round red fruit.

A pomegranate.

He held it reverently between us before pressing his thumbs deep into the center and ripping it apart, exposing the jeweled seeds inside. The tangy, sweet scent of the fruit swept across the air before he plucked a few of the bright red seeds.

Slowly, I slid to my knees. He followed until we were once again face to face. His joy was radiant on his face as he offered me one half. I pulled a few of the seeds free, holding them gingerly between my fingers before Sidero stepped forward to take the remaining parts of the fruits from our hands.

Ren and I spoke together slowly, rhythmically in the old language. It was a tongue I was committed to learning, but for the time being, he'd taught me the meaning.

> *Blood of my blood*
> *Soul of my soul*
> *As day turns to night,*
> *And winter to spring,*
> *All that is vital must wither*
> *All that begins must end*
> *I lay my heart in the palms of your hands*

It was old magic, binding magic, a variation of vows that had been used before time began. As we finished the last line, we placed our hands over each other's hearts, and the pomegranate seeds upon each other's tongues, before sealing the vow with a kiss.

Not marriage, no, it was deeper than that—stronger. Marriage was a game gods played to achieve power or status. This was something else entirely.

Something as old as magic itself: bonding our souls together.

CHAPTER
SIXTY-ONE

Renwick

Magic danced across my skin.

Mine and hers, intertwining until I could no longer tell the difference between the two. Beneath my own heartbeat, I found the rhythm of hers—steady and vital in my chest.

When she had first entered the throne room, I could not help but think of the difference between the god who stood before me and the scared, lonely woman I'd first dragged through those doors. She had been the personification of my failure

Oralia was nothing of the sort now.

Her gown clung to each of the curves I'd come to memorize, to crave. When she entered with her head held high, her shadows danced around her body like flickering black flames before extinguishing when she reached the edge of the dais. I tried to push the thoughts of the future away as best I could, knowing that for now, we had this moment. For now, we were together. For now, she was mine.

My hand cupped her face as I deepened the kiss, tasting the sweet and tangy fruit on her tongue. Our shadows tangled around us, magic mingling in the air as starlight danced around our heads. We broke apart. Her smile was as blinding as my own before I kissed her once, twice, three times. Her fingertips brushed my cheek, capturing the wetness I had not known was there. I was sure her power was once again working within me. My chest cracked wide open, and my tears fell freely. I had never known such peace.

But there was more to be done and further vows to be made.

Pressing a kiss to the space between her brows, I rose, turning to Dimitri, who now stood with a silver pillow in his hand, a circlet of obsidian resting upon it. It had been my mother's crown and had waited deep within my vaults beneath the palace for millennia, never again to see the light of day.

Until now.

With reverence, I took the intricate web of stars surrounding the waxing cycle of the moon in my hands. Though it felt delicate, the magic within it made it indestructible. My throat tightened at the sight—at the feel of the weight of it against my fingertips.

Oralia's head was bowed, her chest heaving. But her hands were still at her sides, the black scars against her skin thrumming with the beating of her pulse.

I took a deep breath and drew the circlet toward her. "Do you, Oralia, daughter of Zephyrus Anemos, heir of Peregrine Solis, swear to protect this realm with your magic, your strength, and your will?"

She looked up at me, her eyes fierce with her devotion. "I do."

I raised the crown higher.

"Do you promise to rule with the strength of the stars, the forgiveness of night, and the resilience of the seasons?"

A small, warm smile graced her lips. "I do."

"And do you swear loyalty to its people, past, present, and future, forsaking all other lands, peoples, and titles?"

The smile turned radiant, taking my breath away as her voice rang loud and clear throughout the throne room.

"I do."

Slowly, reverently, I placed the crown upon her head. My fingertips brushed her cheeks when I pulled away. Never had I thought I would be here. I had given no thought to a queen, to a partner, to a mate. But now that the crown rested atop her head, I could not imagine a reality where she was not by my side. The knowledge that soon I would be without her threatened to disrupt my joy until I shoved it away roughly, forcing my mind back to the kneeling god in front of me.

"Then rise, Oralia, Queen of Infernis, *Lathira na Thurath.*"

Queen of the Dead.

The power of the land shimmered in the air, reacting to the vows we recited, as if it, too, was celebrating its new queen.

With effortless grace, she rose to her feet, turning as the crowd gave a great cry, jumping to their feet to clap their hands and stomp against the floor. Their chanting was deafening in my ears.

Myhn lathira.

Myhn lathira.

Myhn lathira.

There, close to the edge of the dais, was Caston. Thorne shouted in his ear as they clapped. And though I knew he had his reservations, in this moment, he appeared to have given over to the happiness pouring out from those around him.

My mind flicked back to two nights before when I had taken him aside after we had dined together. It was important to me that I speak to him, that I try to impart the small bit of wisdom I had that perhaps would serve him.

A king who rules through violence may find power, but it is fleeting, I had said, my hand on his shoulder. *A king who rules through compassion, through understanding, may reign forever. For he serves his people, not his pride.*

He had listened solemnly, nodding once before clasping my arm. It had been all the confirmation I had needed.

On the other side of Caston, Mecrucio was jumping up and down, grabbing Horace and shaking him to force some excitement into the always-calm god. Dimitri was much more dignified, though I could see through his helmet a wide smile took over half his face. Sidero stood close by, wiping their eyes. Further back in the crowd, I spied Aelestor with his arms around Josette, kissing her roughly. Across the way, Lana and the other souls stomped their feet.

In all of my existence, I had never seen such joy within the kingdom. With this joy, I knew, would eventually come sorrow. That this new chapter must someday find its end, as Typhon must soon find his reckoning.

But not now.

Now was the time for triumph, for joy, to wrap my arms around my queen and kiss her until she gasped for air. She laughed against my lips, clutching my biceps to steady herself.

"I love you," she whispered against my lips.

"I love you *unendingly.*"

CHAPTER

SIXTY-TWO

Oralia

The bow of Vakarys' boat was barely visible through the thick mist, the blue flame lantern pulsing in the gray depths.

The water churned, lapping over the bodies that hugged the sides and carried us through the river. There was a powerful hand in mine, thumb brushing against my palm in a steady, familiar pattern. But it was his heartbeat I felt the strongest, beating out the same panicked rhythm as my own.

Ren's hand in mine was strange. I wore the gloves I had first cast off in the throne room to destroy him. Though once they had felt like a second skin, they now felt alien, stifling—a representation of the prison I was willingly walking back into.

"I will be close, *eshara*, I promise," he whispered, leaning close so that his lips touched my ear.

The mist curled around us, hugging us close and trying to stop our journey forward. Yet, all too soon, Vakarys turned the boat, sliding against the rocky shore.

"*Myhn ardren, myhn lathira,*" she murmured, and I could just see her outline as she placed her hand upon her tattered chest.

"Thank you, Vakarys," Ren replied with a nod, before assisting me off the boat.

Caston followed silently. He'd made his opinion that I should stay behind in Infernis clear enough. It had been a fight that had ended with both of us in tears and with Caston vowing to ensure no harm would come to me.

But I knew that was a promise he could not keep.

The mist lightened as we crossed over the bank and onto the damp earth—the magic resigning itself to our choice, giving Ren and me one last moment to see each other. He wrapped an arm around my waist, tugging me close to him. But we said nothing. Our good-byes had already been said a thousand times before in every kiss, every touch, every look.

As we stepped through the forest into the no-man's-land between Aethera and Infernis, Ren drew me tighter. Panic skittered through my chest, but I resolved not to show it. I had made this choice, and though my heart was breaking and I wanted to extend our time in this forest into eternity to never leave his side, I would not change my mind.

A faint light bled through the trees like rivers of gold. We were perhaps a mile or so from the boundary of the kingdom. Two figures stepped between the trees, Mecrucio and Aelestor, and as one, they dropped to a knee, pressing their hands against their hearts.

"My king, my queen."

We stopped, but I did not give them a second glance. Instead, I turned to face Ren. His face was pale. The midnight blue of his eyes was glassy in the light spilling through the forest. Slowly, he cupped my cheeks with his hands before one slid into the back of my hair, leaning down to press our foreheads together.

"I do not like this," he breathed, a wild panic creeping into the corners of his eyes.

Aelestor hummed his agreement, copper curls bouncing as he surveyed the forest around us. "I agree. Typhon was much too easily swayed."

But Mecrucio let out a heavy sigh, running a hand down his tunic. "We have been over this time and time again. He believed she was a prisoner and our story of breaking her free. There will be no danger for the queen."

And though my insides twisted like snakes, I wrapped my hands around Ren's wrists, forcing a smile onto my face. "You are my heart."

His eyes closed, face falling with defeat before he breathed deeply, drawing me into the circle of his arms.

"All that begins must end," he murmured against my hair, his voice breaking with the words of our bonding.

Drawing back, I pressed a soft kiss to his mouth, murmuring against his lips, "I lay my heart in your hands."

His kiss was soft, reverent, and I tried to memorize the feeling of his lips against mine. The way the calluses on his hands were rough against my skin, and the way I had to rise to the tips of my toes to deepen the kiss. Our magic intertwined, like starlight and autumn and peace. A feeling I hoped I would experience again.

"I love you."

"I love you," he replied.

We broke apart, his thumbs brushing my wet cheeks while I did the same for him. As he stepped away, he was not merely taking a small piece of my heart with him but my soul.

Caston came forward to place a hand on my shoulder.

Ren brought his fingertips to his lips, blowing me a kiss before he transformed into the familiar raven I'd grown up knowing and loving.

"Come, Your Grace," Mecrucio said softly to me.

I nodded, taking a deep breath and wiping my face. We began our silent journey through the forest until we approached the line where we knew Typhon's spies lingered. I allowed Caston to wrap his arm more firmly around my waist, letting him pull me the rest of the way through the forest as if I was tired—as if we had been running through the mist for days.

When we broke the boundary of the trees, stepping into the wide grassy fields of Aethera, the light was so bright it hurt my eyes. I had to cover my face against the glare. The heat was so intense against my skin, and for a moment, I wondered if I was roasting alive.

Then, through the light, a familiar voice cooled the heat, and dread circled my heart.

"Welcome home, Lia."

THE
LANGUAGE OF
INFERNIS

Myhn ardren (m-IN ard-REN) | *My king*

Myhn lathira (m-IN la-THEER-ah) | *My queen*

Eshara (eh-SHAH-rah) | *Love, life force*

Maelith (MAY-lith) | *Mother*

Thurath (THUH-rath) | *Dead, death*

Lathira na Thurath (la-THEER-ah n-AH THUH-rath) | *Queen of the Dead*

Eht natum myselna (e-HCT nAH-tium MY-cell-nah) | *You honor us.*

LANDMARKS WITHIN INFERNIS:

Pyralis (pier-alice) | *The fields of grief*

Mirvath (meer-vath) | *The lake nestled within Pyralis*

Athal (ah-THAL) | *The river of forgetting that snakes between Tylith and Isthil*

Thelaran (thuh-LAH-ran) | *Tunnels where souls receive punishment*

Isthil (IH-stil) | *A blackened field of isolation*

Vaelorin River (vay-LOR-in) | *The river souls must travel across to reach Infernis*

Rathyra (rah-THEER-uh) | *The city of souls*

Tylith (TIE-lith) | *Mountains nestled against the western sea where souls face their fears*

Cyvon Sea (CY-vonne)

Acknowledgements

I would be remiss if I didn't start these acknowledgements without first thanking the Dramione fandom. Without y'all I would 100% not be where I am now. Thank you for your unending support and constant supply of your therapy bills. I love y'all with all my heart.

Thank you to my husband, Dan. There is so much I could say here. I met you at a time in my life where I didn't know who I was anymore and instead of changing me, you gave me the space to figure it out while cheering me on every step of the way. You are the reason I started writing in the first place, all because I was complaining about wanting to find a particular kind story and you asked me: *"Why don't you write it yourself?"* Your unending confidence in my abilities and constant suggestion that I put ice cream or a banana peel fall into a story makes me fall in love with you more and more every day (as well as your constant supply of treats). I love you so much.

To Farrah Abernathy, who was the first one I told about this idea through a series of multiple Instagram messages I think were in all caps and was my very first alpha reader. Thank you for putting up with my love of ellipses and EM dashes, for always listening to my six-minute voice notes where I answer my own questions and pushing me to write even when I second guess myself (and for telling me to take breaks even if I ignore it). This story would not have happened without your support, love, and confidence in my ability to pull it off. Love you!

To Angie Cox — I wish I could better put into words the gratitude and love I have for you. From the four-hour long facetime while you were in Hawaii, encouraging me to make this story the very best it could be and not settle, to the three-hour long facetime while I wrote my blurb. You were there, scraping me off the floor and pushing me towards being the strongest storyteller I can be. Thank you doesn't feel like enough, but I guess I'll start there.

To my beta readers: Brooke, Dani, Allie, Rachael, Jessi, and Brit, thank you for your honesty and support. I am so incredibly grateful to have had such an amazing team on my side willing to tell me the hard stuff and celebrate the good. Ren and Oralia would not be who they are now without all of you.

Thank you to my brother, Chris, who was my first example of a storyteller growing up. When I began my writing journey you taught me a valuable lesson of asking "why" each step of the way that I still cherish. The last few years have been tough on us and our family, but I wouldn't want to navigate this path with anyone else. I love you!

Thank you to Amanda Richardson for your endless patience and help navigating the path of indie publishing, you made this journey exponentially less overwhelming.

A huge thank you to my developmental editor, Kate Angellena.

You were the first human to ever read my writing and see something in it.

Thank you to my sensitivity reader, Audris, my line editor, Lydia Shamah (sorry that I kept in all the stuff about them having a heightened sense of smell!), and my copy editor Jen Bowles for making this story the absolute best it could possibly be.

Thank you to my cover artist Kelly Guthauser/StoryWrappers and my map maker/interior designer Travis Hasenour for bringing this book to life in such a beautiful way.

Thank you to IRael Baldares. I wish you knew how to read but hopefully someday an audiobook will be released so you can finally know what I've been working on (*happy birthday, Courtney!*).

Thank you to Joey, Kate, Kaytee, and Justin for always asking me how the book is going even when that means I'll talk for the next thirty minutes without pause and you only have a basic grasp of what I'm talking about. The countless dinners, support, and interest in my work means the world.

Thank you to my dad and step-mom, who only has a slight understanding of what I'm doing and who I really hope didn't read this book (please don't tell me if you did).

Thank you to my mother who put up with my love of Anne Rice and fantasy novels when I was definitely too young to be reading them and would sneak them into the house.

Thank you to Mary Beth, Chris, Jen, and Bud for your unwavering support from my first book concept, I hope y'all didn't actually make shirts.

And finally, thank you to you, the reader who is holding this book in your hands. Thank you for spending a little bit of time with me in this world I love so much.

About the Author

Gillian Eliza West lives in Austin, Texas. With a passion for mythology that has taken her around the world (despite her fear of flying), she strives to infuse her own stories with a similar kind of wonder and magic. Her first foray into writing for an audience came through fan fiction, allowing her to hone her skills as a storyteller. When she isn't working on her debut duology, you can find Gillian snuggled up with her dog, Walter, and a book or her favorite fanfic.

To learn more about Gillian and her upcoming projects, visit her website to join her mailing list: gillianelizawest.com

ALL THAT BEGINS

MUST END.

BOOK TWO IN THE
INFERNIS DUOLOGY

RECKONING

COMING APRIL 29, 2025

For updates, first looks, and more, join my
mailing list at gillianelizawest.com

Made in the USA
Coppell, TX
02 May 2025

48964638R00229